D0422096

9781111491567

DINA CASHMAN

BY

KATHLEEN NORRIS

PALO ALTO EDITION

New York
P. F. COLLIER & SON CORPORATION

BY SPECIAL ARRANGEMENT WITH
DOUBLEDAY, DORAN & COMPANY, INC.

GARDEN CITY, NEW YORK

TO
THE LILLIPUTIANS

Your small hands batter down our walls; you throng
Like little Greeks who storm a parapet,
Wearing the names that we have loved so long:
Kate, Cigi, David, Helen, Margaret;
And bearing with new loves new titles too,
Lo, what a brighter, happier cycle starts
When Dick and Dan and Denny, Cam and Hugh
With Julie Page and Judy share our hearts.
And as a small Teresa joins the host,
One name comes back that has too long been lost.

Dina Cashman

Chapter 1

"Dina, will you help me with my composition?"

"Well." Dina glanced over her shoulder, turned back to her dishpan. "What's it about?"

"She give us three subjecks," said the overgrown boy at the kitchen table. "'My Christmas Holidays,' 'What the New Year Means to Me,' and 'The Effect of the Crusades upon the Universities of Medieval Europe.'"

Dina laughed quietly.

"I certainly wouldn't take that last one," she said. To herself she added, "I laughed then. I'll bet everything's going to come out all right."

"I don't think anyone'll take that one," said Arthur. "Unless maybe some of the girls do."

"Take 'What the New Year Means to Me,' Art, and make it full of manly spirit and everything. Ambition, you know, and steadfast endeavor."

"Oh *garsh!*" Arthur objected, appalled at this generous order. Shabby, dirty, disheveled, he sprawled over the end of the kitchen table, a stubby pencil in the large fingers whose nails were black and split; his sweater, worn into holes, curled its heavy, hot collar about his neck; his jaws moved rhythmically upon a wad of gum. "Tell me how to start it, Dina," he begged.

"Well, lessee," Dina mused. "How about 'The New Year offers to us all a chance'—no, make that an opportunity, Artie—but you're

the one that's been to high," the girl broke off to remind him.
"You ought to know twice as much as I do about school."

"Well, I don't," said Arthur, miserable with boredom and sleepiness and the effect of a dinner of underdone pork chops, fried
potatoes, fresh bread, strong tea, and doughnuts. "And I wish I
didn't have to go!"

"Pop wants you to amount to something," Dina said automatically. In her heart, to some power undefined, she said, "Oh,
make it not true, make it not true! Oh, I'll always be good—I'll
be different—I'll get a job and work and make something of myself
if only you'll make it not true!"

"Dina," said a dirty-faced little girl of twelve who was sucking
away at a pencil and looking in puzzlement at the numbers she
occasionally wrote upon the pages of a battered exercise book.
"Don't Pop want you to amount to something too?"

"I guess he'd like all of us to amount to something, Dooley,"
Dina answered. "But I had a kind of queer time getting my schooling, and I wasn't ready for second-year high when we got here
three years ago, and I'm not ready yet! Pop was sick then, and I
worked in Muzzy's, and I had only had a quarter term's high
when we left Arkansas, and then we were a whole year down near
Tombstone when I couldn't get in to school, and then in Bakersfield. Then Donny was born and Mama needed me."

The children—there were four of them in the kitchen—had lost
interest. Arthur, who was, at seventeen, next to nineteen-year-old
Dina in age, had crossed the fuzzy, dirty arms of his sweater on the
table, laid his tousled head upon them, and apparently dropped
off into a light sleep; Dooley was carrying on an altercation with
a younger child as to the possession of a small, hairless doll dressed
in a smart but filthy little red velvet coat and hat; and Myrna, fourteen, a slender, proud girl whose worn school dress was embellished
with a neat little collar and whose cuffs were well turned back,
continued silently to dry dishes and carry them to their usual
places on the shelves of the shallow closet.

The kitchen was not a large room, but it was the only one of
the four in the establishment that was available for daily waking

life. The others were bedrooms. In one there was a three-quarter bed for the accommodation of the father, John Cashman, and his wife Ethel, and a crib for Donny Cashman, aged three. In another Arthur had a cot, and his two smallest sisters, El'ner and Lou, shared a sofa bed. Dooley, Dina, and Myrna had as their chamber the third room, purportedly the parlor. The women and girls of the family were sensitive upon the point that there was no bathroom in the house and that the men were obliged to wash and shave at the dark, small zinc sink in the kitchen.

The Cashmans had settled in this rather grimy strip of the wide, fruit-filled Santa Clara Valley less from choice than from necessity. They had not prospered on their wanderings westward, through New Mexico and Arizona and into California. Now, some fifty miles south of San Francisco, with seasonal jobs in lumber mills, canneries, orchards all about them, with seas of fruit blooms and wild flowers in spring, cooling fogs and winds all summer long, winters free of snow, they were as well satisfied as they were likely to be anywhere. Their home was a cheaply built, dilapidated shanty. But they were as well housed as many of the families in the neighborhood and better housed than some, and they were migrants; migrant in plans, wishes, ideas, and often, as well, physically in continual transference. Any inconveniences were dismissed from consideration with the philosophical thought that the family would not be long in any place anyway. Pop would get a better chance somewhere and they would all be off again.

As the most used apartment—for the bedrooms were dark, cluttered, and small—the kitchen wore a battered air that no cleaning and no attempt at introducing order ever dissipated. It had been hopelessly cheap from the beginning; it was seventeen years old now, and every day of those seventeen years had taken its toll. The plastered walls had been kalsomined green and then blue; both colors showed in streaks between the long mud-colored marks that rain had left and the gaps where laths showed through. Light was supplied by a solitary electric bulb dangling from the center of the ceiling. The stove was a four-burner gas range whose three remaining legs were supplemented by a brickbat; its plates were blackened and broken; its dripping pan was burned into rusty holes; its oven door was dribbled from a thousand spillings of fat, milk, cereals, gravies, everything that could cake and smoke and smell and leave a permanent mark.

The floor was greasy and splintered; at the window dangled two dark gray shreds of filmy curtaining; dead flies and odds and ends littered the sills.

Through the muddy bath of the lukewarm dishwater went the plates, mismatched and chipped, and odd glasses, cups with handles and cups without. The blistered blue glass saucer that said "San Diego Exposition" was never washed, for it was the butter saucer; the sugar bowl was crusted with accumulations of months of use, brown and dried on its rim. The lost knobs of saucepan covers were replaced by corks and string; adhesive tape held the handle of the bread knife firm.

Dina was paying small attention to these details tonight. For one thing she was used to them; they seemed unimportant. What was important—or rather what had always been important until this last anxious week—was her own beauty, of which she took great care, and the interests of her own little group of friends. Frances Tack, who worked with her in the grocery, the Mulligan boys and the Beatty boys, Ward Binn and his sister Melda, and Tom O'Connor, the nicest boy in the neighborhood, who was in love with Dina but who had gone up to the lumber mills in West-wood for a time—these were her associates. Her life, rather than being compared with any other standards, was to her successful or a failure only as it seemed good or seemed unfortunate to them. What some faraway girl aristocrat in some world capital did with her hair was not important to Dina Cashman, but if Melda or Frances or Betty displayed a new hair-do, Dina was on pins and needles until she had tried it on her own thick, silky mop and dis-carded it as unsuitable or boldly adopted it.

Dina had been earning money since her seventeenth year; she always had handed most of her pay envelope over to her mother and often saw her father take it in his turn, but for some time now she had demanded of her parents tacitly—for it had never been put into words between them—that she be given certain liberties in return. There was not to be as much questioning and criticizing as there had been, nor insulting threats of whippings or locking doors. Dina loved to dance, and there were plenty of night clubs and highway restaurants in the neighborhood where chop suey or chow mein and music and lights were available. Home was a pigpen, acceptable and even comfortable, but still a pigpen, and work was dull and underpaid. But the nights belonged to youth and freedom, and Dina Cashman was the last girl alive to surrender them. Hers was a courageous nature; she had always been a leader, in mischief when she was a child, in plans, in the forming of clubs and arranging entertainments in grammar school. Now in this underprivileged group, with its shoddy amusements, its dependence upon radio and comic papers and cheap magazines and the cosmetics of the "dime" store, its gum and gossip, its eagerness for life and thrills and change and adventure on any terms, she was a leader still. They all waited for her, listened to her, laughed at her and with her. For until lately Dina had been always laughing.

Tonight she helped Myrna finish the dishes and turned about to look at the clock. Quarter to eight. In half an hour she could tumble the younger girls into bed, warn the older ones to be on their good behavior until Mama and Pop came home at half-past nine, and be on her way to lights and excitement and companionship.

Meanwhile, with the dishes done and the kitchen in its nearest approach to order, she must get dressed. Dina went into her bedroom, lifted her small brother Donny, three years old and heavily and moistly asleep, to carry him to his crib in his own room, and lighted the one light in the room by which to beautify herself to the best of her power.

There were two beds in here: one full-sized and the other a cot. Dooley usually slept on the cot and Dina and Myrna in the bed. But if any girl had a fever or a cold or was coughing distressfully, she took the cot and the others the bed. There was no space for a bureau even had the girls possessed one. A small chest held three shallow drawers, always stuffed to bursting, and there was, in lieu of a closet, a triangular enclosure behind a dangling curtain in a corner and in it a line of hooks.

The beds had not been made today nor the room aired. Dina slapped the covers back into place, jerking them straight and turning them down to a semblance of respectability. She sat down on the foot of the bed, reaching down under it for a cardboard shoe box. In this box were an old hairbrush with the bristles pretty well worn away, a tangle of fine safety pins, several lipsticks in various stages of use, powder boxes, flat mud-colored powder puffs, wisps of tissue paper stained with nail polish and rouge, nets, manicure files, curling wires, and a dozen other beautifiers. Beside the box on the floor rested a round tin can marked "Theatrical Crème," with the price mark of twenty-nine cents still clear upon it in black penciling.

Dina pushed her thick hair back from her face, smeared cheeks and chin and brow with the cream. A sodden towel was a part of her equipment; its limp touch and its reek of cheap perfume were essential to her dressing routine. When she had finished with it she took a broken angle of mirror from the top of the chest of drawers and stood up under the light, carefully training her thick dark brows with a small comb, marking her lips into luscious redness, powdering thoroughly with sharp little blows of the soggy puff, coaxing the vital youth and springiness of her hair into delicate spirals and curls about her forehead.

After this she unwound the cheap cotton kimono that had been wrapped tightly about her for these operations and took a striped silk dress from a hook. In her hand it looked what it was—a garment cheap and badly made to begin with and worn into shapelessness and discoloration.

But once on the firm curves and lines of the young body it looked better, and when Dina had snapped a clasp of imitation brilliants upon it, had placed a dashing little hat upon her mop of tawny hair, had slipped her arms into a brown coat whose collar still showed some signs of having once been creamy fur, she looked like a thousand—like a million other American girls who were that night sallying forth from homes almost if not quite so humble; pretty, smart, happy.

She won a few moments of forgetfulness as she made her way between the dark shanties of the neighborhood, past the odorous dump and over the railway tracks, and so to a paved and lighted street dismal enough in itself but by contrast a glittering thoroughfare of delights. Here were restaurants and dance halls and saloons and movies and the high school and the hospital. It was heaven to escape from the odors and the crowding, the noises and the disorders of home into this atmosphere of excitement and light. The candy store and the drugstore gushed brilliance, and many of the other stores, though closed, were lighted, and sports clothes and hats and purses and underwear were displayed in garish splendor. The opaque windows of the big downstairs swimming pool of the "Y" glowed whitely.

Dina looked at the "Y" and thought of the nice woman who had asked her to join the "Y" club in San José, and her heart failed her as anxiety and fear came rushing back. She had always wanted to join such a club somewhere; she never had had the freedom, the car to carry her the intervening miles, the clothes. But she had thought that she would be a great favorite if fortune had permitted her to be one of the busy, chattering, planning girls of that successful organization. She would be the girl at the head of the table, the girl who made announcements, at whose words everyone laughed in approval and affection and amusement. If she had only joined the "Y"!

Oh well, perhaps everything would even yet be all right, perhaps she would go on in a few weeks, a sadder and wiser but no longer a terrified girl. Oh, how grateful she would be! Grateful to what, grateful to whom, she did not know; but her heart was swelling even now, in the darkest hour of her apprehension, in anticipation of that rush of weakening, overwhelming relief.

"Hello, Dina!" said a friendly voice as a squarely built boy emerged from a shadowy doorway. Dina jumped, laughed, caught his outstretched hand, and smiled radiantly.

"Tom O'Connor! When'd you get home?"

"Tonight. I was coming down to your house and then I thought your father mightn't like it, so I waited here."

"Mama and Pop went to the seven o'clock show. How long have you been waiting?" For she knew he had been waiting, whatever the time had been, and that now his heart was beating thunderously in his breast, that he couldn't answer her because he couldn't call his swimming senses to order.

"Two months," he managed to say with a laugh.

"Oh, two months, yes," she said, stabbed again. Tom had gone away to the mills in Westwood before—before——

But she wouldn't think about it! It wouldn't happen! Everything would be all right!

They walked along the sidewalk linked together by his arm under her elbow. Tom was a big fellow but not tall, and Dina stood almost shoulder to shoulder with him.

"Do you like Westwood, Tom?"

"Sure, I like it. It's kind of like—oh, I don't know, being in the army—being in a camp or something. But I like it. I'm going back Sunday night."

"Girls up there, Tom?"

"Sure. What d'you think it is—a seminary? But I missed home at first, and lordy, I missed Ma!"

"She missed you."

"She said so. She said she kept lighting candles to Saint Joseph."

"I should think she'd light 'em to Saint Thomas," Dina said idly, thinking of the boy's name. She was pleased when he laughed.

"They don't often have Saint Thomas in church," he told her. "But they always have Saint Joseph. He was the guardian of Our Lord."

"Oh?" But her thoughts were not of his words. "Isn't Tom O'Connor good," she mused. "Isn't a good fellow a safe sort of thing! Well, I guess Vere Holland must be good too. Only he seems younger than Tom—sillier, not so responsible. Oh, I wish I liked Tom—I wish I'd fallen in love with Tom!"

They went into the lighted, hot drugstore that blended a thousand odors into a general one predominantly of vanilla, carbolic acid, and coffee. Melda Binn was there with Charlie Lomax; they said the others were at the seven o'clock show and were going over to Cotta's afterward. Dina sat on a high revolving stool at the counter and sipped a sweet drink flavored with wintergreen and looked at herself between the bright manifold signs that framed the mirror.

"Want to go to the show, Dina?"

"Oh no; it's nearly nine o'clock already. Let's have sandwiches or dogs or something at Cotta's and talk."

"Suits me," Tom said. They were joined in their discussion by the clerk, Len Hargess, who said he would come over to Cotta's too, after closing.

"We won't be that late. You stay open until nearly eleven, don't you?" Tom asked. Len said maybe Gus would take over about ten. Most folks went right home after the nine; they didn't want to be out much later than that.

"Find things changed, Tom?" Len asked, swabbing the counter.

"Only Dina. She's prettier than ever," Tom said.

Dina, who had been studying her own reflection in the mirror, pushing up a curled lock, touching a tiny powder pad to her nose, smiled absently. Her appearance was not her immediate concern! Nothing of this familiar scene seemed the same tonight. An anxious trickle of thought underran it like a tiny stream of filth and shame, breaking it slowly but surely away from its regular course, undermining everything, changing everything. Tom's flattery and her own comeliness and the homage of her little crowd meant nothing now. Only one fact, one fearful suspicion, was significant, and until that fact was denied or confirmed she would live in a world apart from everyone.

Chapter 2

COTTA'S was an old assembly hall that had been abandoned for years until the present proprietor had rented it. He had swept its wide bleak floors, hung some limp bunting in loops under its windows, pushed a mechanical piano into one of its empty corners, arranged a group of small tables in another. Men paid twenty-five cents admittance; girls came in free. Beer and soft drinks were sold, and sandwiches wrapped in oiled paper might be had for a nickel apiece. If Cotta had a good crowd, he pushed out a few more tables, wiped them with a damp, colorless dish towel, shoved up more of the "Vienna" chairs he had bought on speculation. A stout, kindly man and a grandfather, he did not like disorder or rioting in his great barn of a dance hall, although he winked at certain irregularities in the dancing sometimes and never criticized the character of his guests until they gave him some definite ground for complaint.

All sorts of persons came to Cotta's. It was cheap, for one thing. Men brought queer-looking women there on Saturday and Sunday nights, and they sat laughing and murmuring over their drinks until the next morning's early hours. Sometimes absorbed groups gathered about the battered old billiard table that occupied one corner of the great space; often men played nickel poker or rummy or pinochle at teetering, scarred round tables.

Even with this furnishing there was plenty of room left. That was the great attraction at Cotta's. In the center of the hall was a dance floor large enough to accommodate a hundred couples. No crowding here. Forlorn and bare as the place was, when the piano duly began its pounding and the young feet moved on the smooth old board floor it afforded only sheer delight to the dancers from Railway Flats.

In the corner where the tables stood and where drinks and sandwiches were served some small effort at decoration had been made. Eighteen wooden columns, about seven feet high, had been set up to form a sort of arbor, twined with cotton grapevines and threaded with colored electric bulbs. These last shed a softened light upon Dina and her intimates as they took possession of a special table and prepared themselves for an hour or two of pleasure.

Young Tony came forward in shirt sleeves and vest to take their order. He wore no collar; his pleasant young face was beaded with perspiration.

"Big dinner tonight, Tony?" Dina surmised.

"Beeg? My God they say seventy and Poppa feed one hundred twanta-seex," Tony answered without punctuation. "Then we swipa da floor," he went on, "and Mama and Maria do-a da dish. The keetch," Tony finished with appreciation, "looka like we feeda da army!"

Dina always drank pop or coke or some other soft drink. Her mother had impressed her early in life with the dangers of intoxicants, and her father had contributed an unconscious yet far more forceful lesson. Tonight, sipping her dark, sweet-flavored beverage, she reflected somewhat sadly upon the irony of their warnings. It had not been drink that had brought her to her present predicament. She had not been carried away. She had loved, deeply, truly, and she loved now.

"Dance again, Dina?"

"Sure, Dunk." This time it was with the older Beatty boy. Dina went around and around the hall in a dream. In five minutes she was glad to be landed back again at her place at table.

Frances Tack and Betty Lomax were the other girls with her, and there were five boys—Tom O'Connor, Ward Binn, Dunk

Beatty, Willie Mulligan, and Charlie Lomax. Frances Tack worked with Dina in Meyer's grocery. Frances, at twenty-four, had had an unhappy marriage, a divorce behind her, and now a two-year-old daughter to support. Frances was hard, brief of speech, skeptical, disillusioned. She was hopelessly in love with Tom, who was indeed the most attractive, the most ambitious, steady, and best-looking of the boys. Tom's mother would rather have seen him laid in his grave than married to Frances, but as Tom was not in the least interested in the grass widow the alternative was not likely to be mentioned.

Betty and Charlie Lomax were nice but, in the parlance of the group, dumb. Charlie could bore any girl almost into a coma in five minutes, and Betty was a simple little fool who told everybody everything she knew or imagined she knew, babbled that her mother had an old friend who gave her a squirrel coat because she got him a new customer and that Papa was so mad he made her send it back, that every time Mama stayed with her friend Mabel in San Francisco Papa raised the roof and once when he telephoned Mama wasn't there but a man's voice answered——

Everyone knew that flighty, artificially blonde little Mrs. Lomax was as free as she was mysterious in her friendships, her engagements, her affairs of the heart, but everyone blamed foolish little Betty for prattling so innocently about it. Betty also was in love; she was crazy about Ward Binn. Ward liked a girl he had met in Stockton and wrote her every week. Tom O'Connor had always been in love with Dina Cashman; their affair and the pairing of their names were established facts.

But Dina knew tonight that all that was over. She had never loved Tom, had never thought seriously of marrying him. The possibility assumed a new charm as it faded forever. It would have been restful at least to marry Tom, go up to the lumber mills in Westwood, and take possession of a little cottage, be one of the young wives of that world. There would be a small Tom, a Mary for his mother, a John for her father. Tom would always be kind and good and provide for them all, love them always.

She put the thought away with an unexpected touch of heartache. She wasn't going to be sentimental, surely, over Tom O'Connor!

"Ever see What's-his-name, you know, that Holland boy—Vere Holland, any more?" Frances was asking idly.

"Who's he?" Tom wanted to know.

"Kid that came in here one night with a lot of Burlingame stiffs," Frances answered, her mouth full. "Awful nice kid."

"When this happen?" Tom demanded, instinctively jealous. Dina kept her eyes lowered, moved the straw lazily back and forth in her drink, but she was trembling; she was hot and cold with fear.

"Oh, some time in October, wasn't it, Dina?"

"About then." She managed a yawn. "He came in here with two girls and another man—a guy named Freddy Lippincott, you know, whose sister was stolen from a sorority house somewhere in the East," Dina said, rousing herself. She must meet this situation; she told herself there was nothing to be afraid of. "Remember, about three months ago?"

"This kid came in with them," Frances took up the story. "He came over to where Dina and I were sitting with the Beatty boys—you were there, weren't you, Dunk?"

"Looking for a pickup?" Tom asked grimly.

"No; he told the boys it was his birthday and wanted us to drink his health," Frances explained, "and he introduced himself to them and asked to be introduced to us. And then he sat down——"

"And fell for Dina like a ton of Coos Bay coal," Duncan Beatty said in his deep voice. Everyone laughed.

"I'll bet he did," Tom said. "Ever see him again?"

"Oh yes!" Frances said in apparent innocence. Dina knew that Frances would be glad to say anything that might upset Tom's devotion to herself. "He came into the store lots of times, didn't he, Di'? And he's been here evenings."

"Awfully nice," Dina said with an air of dispassionate concession. "Vere Holland. His mother's Mrs. Cutler Holland. Father's married again, somewhere back East."

Tom turned to her his kindly, big-brotherly smile.

"You know quite a lot about him, don't you, kid?"

"Oh, he's one to tell you everything!" Frances said. "He'd sit here and talk away by the hour. I liked him—plenty."

"Did you like him too, Dina?" Tom asked.

"We—we all did," she said, angry because her voice was suddenly so faint.

"Well, say, I'll have to find out more about this feller," Tom said with an air of good-natured disapproval. "Where is he now?"

"At home in—Hillsborough it is, I guess," Dina answered.

"What's he do?"

"Studying law. It's a long course, you know." Someone had put a nickel into the piano; a waltz thundered forth; couples began to move out upon the floor.

"Come on," Willie Mulligan said. Willie had a blue, hard-shaven chin; he was thin, black-headed, nervous, and wiry. "Tom don't know that you were nuts about that feller!" Willie said as they danced.

"What Tom doesn't know won't hurt him, and it's none of *your* business, Willie!" Dina said. She started the sentence with something of her characteristic spirit, but her secret knowledge, her secret fears weakened her anger halfway, and she ended it on a little girl's note of misery and appeal.

Willie had her in his arms; her tawny soft mass of hair, her firm, straight, tall body, her blue eyes were close to him. Her knees touched his as they danced; her warm hand was on his shoulder. He spoke thickly:

"I've always—you don't know how much I've always liked you, Dina," he said huskily.

"You've always been kind to me—ever since that day the boys took away the ladder and I was stuck on the chicken-house roof," she answered gratefully.

"Well, don't you double-cross Tom! There isn't a girl alive good enough for Tom."

"I know that!" she said quickly.

"He isn't our kind, Holland isn't," the big boy went on. "He was an awful nice feller, I'll agree to that. But chances are we won't ever see him again."

"Oh, but we will, we must—*I* must, *I* must!" she screamed in her heart. Aloud she said nothing, and they finished their dance in silence.

Back at the table she found Tom next to her again, and for a while they murmured, Dina with her elbows on the crumpled checked cloth, her chin in her hands. She had not known Tom was coming home from the mills for a week end; he had taken her by surprise, and although she knew that all his hopes of winning her had gone down in the wreckage of her own happiness, he didn't know it, and, being Dina, she still could not help turning upon him the full battery of the charm against which he was helpless. Her eyes were full of sympathy; her voice was low; her body leaned toward him so that her shoulder almost touched his. Poor Tom, he would drive all the way back to Westwood tomorrow with his head in a whirl of happiness, happiness that would only make disappointment deeper someday. But she could not help it.

"And is your foreman—this Bill Williams—nice, Tom?"

"Well, he's always swell to me." Tom drew her a little diagram of the plant on a card from his pocket.

Here was the river, the sawmill, the veneering plant where they made ply board, old Hudson's house, the general offices, the recreation hall, the rows of bunkhouses.

"Food pretty good, Tom?"

"Oh, sure. Lots of it, anyway. Breakfast is the best. You can have oranges and cereal and eggs and waffles—all of 'em, if you want 'em!"

"But you pay for all that, Tom?"

"Sure. You can feed at the store, if you like, but boarding's cheaper, and Mrs. Frankenstern sets a generous table. She's all right." He was in heaven. He linked his arm over hers, covered her hand with his own. "I had to bring Bill Williams down," he said. "It was too good a chance to see you and Ma. Bill paid all expenses, gas and everything."

"I should think he might!" She widened her eyes with pretended indignation—blue eyes under the blue hat. Tom laughed adoringly, jerked his big body a trifle nearer. "Who makes your beds and keeps your room straight, Tom?" the girl asked. She listened attentively without hearing a word of what he said; sudden depression had taken possession of her, and her thoughts wandered.

Oh, how pleasant this security, this dancing and flirting and gossiping would be if time might go back and everything be as it had been only a few months earlier! How simple, how uncomplicated life was when its only worries were poverty and hard work and the disorder at home and the aching ambition to do things and go places and be somebody! She could manage all those disadvantages, she could solve all those problems so easily now; they would be nothing, nothing, if she might only go back to them!

She, Geraldine Cashman, to be thinking these thoughts, to be obliged to think them! She, who did not drink, who never had allowed any boy to take the usual liberties with her, who hated necking and wooing and all the other forms of license which some of the girls she despised permitted so easily! Girls like Betty and Melda actually enjoyed going as far as they dared, stopping short of actual surrender, boasting that they did. Frances—well, Frances had been married and had more than once expressed herself to Dina as having had enough of men in her late husband to last her for life. But at the same time Frances occasionally made overnight visits of a mysterious nature to San José, the nearest city of any size, and twice had asked Dina to invent and support an alibi for her in case Cass came snooping around asking questions. He wasn't going to get Joan away from her nor get out of paying his monthly alimony either!

"You're tired," Tom said, watching her. Dina came back to the present with a start.

"I must be a little tired," she admitted, wishing her eyes were not so ready to fill with tears. The others were tired and sleepy too; they gathered up wraps, paid their check, stumbled out into the cold, sharp dark. Dina drew the mangy fur of her collar about her throat, tightened her hand inside of Tom's arm.

The few business streets were ringed with factories; their silhouette tonight was raised up in a forest of chimneys against the cold, high stars. The shanty settlement that had been given the name of "Railway Flats" lay to the southwest, across the space occupied by the dump where pigs flourished and the great harsh angles of the tracks. Faint odors of ashes and pigs and marsh were moving in the night breeze; pools of water that the late rains had left at the hardly distinguishable corners mirrored back the stars and the slim young moon. A train went roaring past, its windows flashing squares of light.

Tom and Dina picked their way cautiously along the stretch of plank sidewalk, followed the railway ties for a space, veered off to lumps of cement sidewalk that long neglect had buckled and broken into an irregular stony pathway. Shanties and cottages were set at all angles here; fences ran in every direction, and sheds and corrugated iron garages were interspersed with dreary attempts at gardening or impinged upon vegetable patches protected by twists of wire and rope.

"Can I come in?" Tom asked when they reached the Cashman kitchen door.

"And wake Pop?" the girl countered in a whisper.

"I'll be quiet!" There was a hint of laughter in Tom's answering murmur. Stertorous snoring that seemed to shake the kitchen indicated that it would not be too easy to wake Pop.

They fumbled their way in; Dina found the switch, and the grimy interior of the kitchen was revealed. Penciled papers had drifted from the table to the floor; twists of silver wrappings that had once protected chocolate bars, cores of apples, schoolbooks, rubbers and the heavy clods of earth that had fallen from rubbers, glasses, pencils, the ink bottle were adding to the confusion of chairs dragged about into every possible position except the orderly one, dangling sweaters, discarded shoes, and all the other indications of an evening that had found the young Cashmans at home.

Tom lighted a cigarette, and Dina rapidly reduced the room to something a trifle less chaotic; she flung armfuls of garments into the dark bedrooms, banished rubbers to the porch, piled schoolbooks into a small wooden box that had long been the recipient of odds and ends, jerked chairs into place. Then she sat down smiling at the other side of the table and faced Tom somewhat breathlessly but still with triumph.

"My brother and sisters are all pigs," she stated disgustedly.

"All kids are," said Tom.

"You'd think Myrna or Dooley would clear up," Dina complained. "But I guess Mama and Pop came in and sent them to bed," she decided on second thought, "and *Mama*——"

"Never cleans up anything?" Tom finished on a laugh as the girl stopped with a shrug of her shoulders.

"She hasn't the faintest idea of what to do. I wish she had to be in Meyer's grocery for a few days," Dina said. "Whoo! Do we have to keep things in order there!"

"Don't you ever get mad at your family, Dina?" Tom asked, his infatuated eyes never leaving her.

"Mad at them? I'm always boiling at them," Dina answered. "No, I don't blame Mama," she added after a moment. "She's had an awfully hard break. My father's never had regular work. That's why we left Arkansas. Mama's had ten children in twenty years— I had a sister named Grace, you know, next to Art, and then there was little Johnny who died just after we got here. There was a Dorothy too, in between El'ner and Donny. Dorothy was drowned."

"Swimming?"

"No; but we had a sort of farm and there was a slope to the back yard where the water made a sort of—a sort of pool. And she wandered out there—Thanksgiving Day it was. I'd gone to the store for Mama, with Dooley and Lou—Dorothy was asleep when I left. She must have waked up and gone out by herself; she was only about a year and a half."

"Lord, what things mothers have to go through!"

"Don't they?" Her face paled a trifle; a stab of realization brought all the misery and fear back again. She had forgotten for a moment of peace; now peace was gone.

"Are you going to marry, Dina?" Tom asked suddenly, oddly.

"Am I——? You mean—am I ever?"

"No." He laughed gruffly, cleared his throat. "I mean are you going to marry me?"

"Oh, Tom, I don't know!" She stretched out her hand and his fingers closed on it eagerly. "Even if everything goes all right—even if I'm worrying myself to death for nothing," she thought, "I can't marry Tom; I never can marry Tom!" But his devotion, his sympathy were so precious she could not refuse them tonight; she clung to his hand, and the blue eyes that smiled into his were wet with tears.

"Look!" he said. "Why shouldn't we get married? I've been sending Mom twenty-five a month, but she doesn't need that any more, now that Nellie's going to be married and Frank's got a job. She's got all her rooms rented too. I could send that to your mother.

"We could have one of those little cottages up at the mills," he went on, encouraged by her silence and the thoughtful, troubled expression on her face, "and we could fix it up little by little. It only costs fifteen a month! We can get green and white things at the store—kitchen stuff and checked curtains—things like that. We can get secondhand furniture too, and the company'll lend you money for a stove and a· refrigerator. They're glad to help. You'd like your own home, wouldn't you, Di', and be there just for me, planning a dinner now and then, an' having Nichols and Bill Williams over? And then there's Saturdays and Sundays. We never work those days, and somebody's always motoring over to Reno for the week end or going skiing or hunting or fishing——"

"You know I'd love it," she answered very low and in a hesitant manner. "After this it'd be heaven to have a place all fresh and clean and nobody tracking in mud or. mussing things up."

"I've been thinking about asking you to marry me ever since you first came here; you know that, don't you, Dina?"

"I don't know why! If we weren't the original emigrant train!" the girl said nervously, forcing a little reminiscent laugh, determined to carry the conversation to safer ground. "The old green jalopy with mattresses and bedsprings roped on top, and the truck we borrowed, with the stove and Donny's pen and Mama's rocker sticking out all over it, and Pop smoking, with Lou and El'ner and Myrna jammed on the front seat with him. I'll never forget the rain, and the coldness of this house, and your mother sending us over a pot of hot coffee and a tin of cookies."

"I saw you that night. 'Member that it stopped raining about five, and the sun was breaking through the clouds, and you came out to the gate to call the kids in for supper, and I came over?"

"I remember thinking that I was about as filthy as a person could get and not be arrested."

"You were beautiful. But you weren't as beautiful as you are now," Tom said.

"Ah-h-h-h!" Dina laughed a little sadly. This talk in the garishly lit kitchen, whose crudely illuminated corners showed scratches and stains, breakages and makeshifts innumerable, had all the uncomfortable quality of a dream. Tom did not know what she was thinking; he did not know what she was fearing; he could not have said one word of all this if he had known. He had not even met Vere Holland; Vere, whose simplicity and charm and niceness won everyone's friendship instantly.

"Oh, Vere," she said in her soul, "where are you? Why aren't you here? You could make it all right. He may walk in tomorrow," she thought; "everything may be all right this time tomorrow. I may be laughing about all this tomorrow. But no, I'll never laugh about it——"

"You *are* tired! You're not listening!" Tom said good-naturedly. Dina came to herself with a little start.

They were standing. She wavered a little, swaying toward him, and he put his arm about her and looked down at her with infinite affection and sympathy.

"You do too much, Dina. At the grocery all day, cooking and cleaning here for the whole crowd of them, and then dancing at night!"

"The dancing at night is the only thing I *could* cut out, Tom, and it's my only fun. Unless it's the pictures, and they give me a sort of headache if I've been indoors all day."

"Well, will you think about it, Dina? After all, I can't do any more than *ask* you."

"And I love you for asking me," she said wearily and unsmiling. "I'm not good enough for you, Tom—and I'm tired—and Pop tried to borrow some money today and couldn't get it——"

"How much money?" His wallet was out instantly. But Dina shook her head.

"Don't begin *that*," she said, her eyes suddenly beginning to swim. "You know my father. Or rather you don't know my father!"

"It's just one of the bad times in your life, Dina," Tom said hearteningly. "You're bogged down with the family and no money and rain and dishes, and it's damned unfair! But Art ought to get a job pretty soon, and things'll straighten out, and you'll come up to a nice little four-room cottage up at Westwood, and we'll paddle our own canoe. Oh, listen"—he interrupted himself to reassure her as she suddenly drew back with widened eyes—"I don't mean that we won't carry on! We'll have Myrna and Dooley with us, or we'll take El'ner for a term. It isn't that. But I mean you'll be out of the main mess."

"It sounds good!" the girl whispered, as if to herself.

"Well, you think about it, won't you?"

"As if I could help thinking about it!" But she knew herself to be deceiving him; she accepted his good-night kiss apathetically, resting her head for a minute against his cheek, angry at herself because tears were coming again.

"Get as much sleep as you can."

"I will!" She locked the door when he was gone, considered ablutions. But the boiler was cold; the kettle was cold; the house was draughty and dark. Dina undressed by such gleams of the corner street lamp as crossed the bedroom obliquely and crawled in beside Dooley to pull the covers over her thinly clad shoulders, to lie with her head cradled upon her crooked arm and stare wide-eyed into the dark.

Chapter 3

VERE HOLLAND had come into Cotta's on a warm October evening, now ten weeks in the past. A tall boy with fair hair and the consciously audacious manners of a favorite to whom everything will be forgiven, he had obviously been the court jester for his group of four long before Dina and her special friends noticed him. They had been at an adjoining table; two girls from San Francisco's debutante group, whose attitude toward Cotta's had been one of amused superiority, and another man somewhat of Vere Holland's type. The four had been not so much entertained as in the mood for entertainment; they had danced, had sat smoking and drinking for an hour, and then Vere quite suddenly had come over to Dina's table, had introduced himself and been introduced with great easiness and laughter. Ward Binn had gone back with him to his table, and presently they had all been talking and sharing drinks and sandwiches at the two tables pushed together. There were nine in the party now, and everyone had danced with everyone else, and Dina Cashman had experienced the most bewildering, the most breath-taking sensations of her life.

For it had become instantly noticeable that Vere Holland had had eyes for no one else, and Dina had never known anyone like Vere. His sleek golden hair, his round friendly face, his fine clean hands that had never done any hard labor, though they were well browned and looked athletic, these all would have marked him as different from all the boys Dina had known, even if every word he said, his clothes and the way he wore his tie, the gesture with which he had jiggled a cigarette out of his silver cigarette case and offered it had not done so.

He was good-natured, amusing, and affectionate. He made them all laugh, he paid for everything, and when one of the other boys said somewhat gruffly that the check ought to be split two ways he looked genuinely surprised and said, with a pleasant readiness to grasp names and personalities that was characteristic of him, "Oh, shut up, Dunk! Or I'll come around to the machine shop tomorrow and poke you into the furnace."

While the others danced he sat with his chair pulled about, so his back was turned to the room, and murmured to Dina. He could not seem to hear enough about her. A migratory worker's daughter? Oh, she was *not!* And Myrna, hey?—and Dooley? What the dickens was the real name of a girl called Dooley? Julia? Then for heaven's sake why not call her Julia?

"It sounds rough to have you say you room with Dooley," he had told Dina. "Your name's Geraldine, is it? All right, I'm going to call you that. And when are you coming in to town to have dinner and go to a show with me? What's your telephone?"

"We haven't one. And if you came and saw where we live, you'd know why. Nobody has a telephone there. The nearest one's the drugstore, over on Thirteenth. We live in Railway Flats."

To this he had listened respectfully, evidently impressed. But he was too kind, he was too much of a gentleman, she had perceived, to show any pity. He had written down the name of Meyer's grocery carefully and had asked her seriously if she wouldn't go to dinner with him, and Dina's heart had sung paeans of joy. Then the others had come back, and she and Vere had danced again; danced, as far as the girl was concerned at all events, into a world of sheer ecstasy.

"Looky," he had said in a businesslike way, when the moment of parting had come, "this is Friday, see? I'm going duck shooting tomorrow; be back Monday. Looky, I'll see you Tuesday, hey?"

But he had not come in on Tuesday nor Wednesday either, and Dina had been in a fair way to recover from the dizzying sensations the opening of their friendship had caused her, sensations that had washed over her like smothering waves, when on Thursday, glancing over her cashier's desk in the grocery, she had seen him studying the soup shelves with absorption.

Her heart had given a suffocating spring. There was the brown coat, the fair head, the pocket with his yellow gloves carelessly thrust inside. There had been rains, but now the last rays of the sun were flooding the place brightly; dripping umbrellas were stacked in a rack at the door; women in mackintoshes were milling about through the aisles. The smell of fresh vegetables and wet clothing had been strong in the place, a wet-day smell forever to be associated in Dina's mind with the irrational wild delight of seeing him again.

"Excuse me, miss! Miss!" he had said loudly, half turning his head over his shoulder. "Have you any onion soup with the cheese already in?"

"I—don't—know—that we have," Dina had answered thoughtfully. Frances could take the register for a moment; Dina had walked across to stand beside him and look at the shelves. "How do you do?" she had said under her breath.

"Hello, my dear!" Vere had returned almost inaudibly. "I hate so to mess with grating cheese!" he had added aloud. "Now here's turtle; that's *nice*."

"We have the cheese ready grated," old Meyer, hovering about, had suggested.

"We have the cheese already grated in bottles," Dina had repeated seriously.

"Then suppose I take two onion soups, two mushrooms, and two bottles of cheese and sort of slumgullion them all together," Vere had decided brilliantly.

"That ought to be good," Dina had agreed. With him beside her she had returned to her desk, had rung up his money.

"How soon are you free?" he had asked.

She had glanced at the clock.

"Ten—seven minutes."

"I'll wait. I'll wait in my car. Right across the street."

That had been all. Dina had concluded her share of the day's business in a daze. The store would stay open for another hour, but young Ben Meyer always took over at five-thirty, checking up accounts, straightening out the books, consulting with his father about the morrow's procedure.

None of that responsibility was hers. She merely operated the cash register, handed change from the drawer, reached under the counter for bags, and tossed the empty market baskets back into the pen. If there happened to be a line of waiting customers with their filled baskets when half-past five arrived, Dina always stayed to serve them; on this particular afternoon there had been such a line and she could make no exception. So that it had been fifteen minutes after the promised time when she had stepped out into the swiftly descending dusk, half hoping and all fearing, and had looked across the road to see if Vere's patience had not been exhausted.

The lemon bars of dazzling light that had crossed the west at the end of the wild wet day had disappeared now. Twilight and winter had held the shabby street. Shops had all been closed, except the drugstore and the candy store and Mullins and Dave's, up at the corner. But the dark-blue rakish roadster with the canvas top and the white-and-red wheels had been waiting, and Vere had sprung out to escort Dina around to the seat beside him before returning to his own. They had sat close together, laughing at first and then not laughing. Six o'clock had rung from Saint Augustine's—half-past six, and Dina had said dreamily that she must go home. Her mother might, or might not, have started dinner preparations; her father would certainly be angry if she were much later.

Then Vere would drive her home. But the girl had objected that it was only two long blocks across the track and beyond the dumps, and the street outside the house was a mud bath. Then good night.

He had framed her face in his young, hard, big hands and kissed her. Not her first kiss from a man—boys had kissed her now and then—but the first one that had been important, the one never to be forgotten.

After that Vere had come to the store every two or three days. She had gone to dinner with him at a pleasant French restaurant, a family place far too respectable and quiet to be of interest to Dina's usual group but that was infinitely thrilling when she was in Vere's company.

Vere had told her his history in odd erratic bursts and snatches. He was the only son of divorced parents; his father was in New York with a second wife; his mother was Mrs. Cutler Holland of Burlingame. His mother had remarried since the divorce but after another marital failure had resumed the name by which she had long been known. Vere had had two years at the State University and then had gone on to Yale to prepare for the law school; he had taken a leave of absence for the fall quarter and was now being coached to re-enter after Christmas. He had wanted to be an aviator, but his eyes hadn't been quite up to the mark.

Quite evidently her talk had fascinated him; she had known it. She had been quite aware that his dancing eyes never left her face when she was talking, that any details she could give him of Dooley or Donny or the crazy finances of the Cashman family were deliciously entertaining to him in themselves and were all the more entertaining when retailed in her own way, with her eyes and color and laughter to give them point.

But whatever he derived from her was as nothing to what his talk meant to her. It was talk of a world whose existence she knew only from the movies but with which she had never dreamed of making contact. Doors opened into Bagdad itself when Vere casually mentioned polo, mentioned trips to Europe, mentioned what the butler said, or spoke of his mother's chauffeur. Vere went to dances and danced with the debutantes; Dina could find his name in the paper among the lists the next day. He did not care much for the prospect of these dances; he explained that they never really got under way until midnight, and he got terribly sleepy, but after you once got there it was kind of fun.

They had known each other about three weeks when Vere had asked her to come up to Paradise Valley on a skiing trip. Dina had naturally objected that she couldn't ski. Oh, that was easy, nobody else could either; all she had to do was fall around in the snow. But she hadn't any of the right clothes!

Easy too. All she needed was a sweater and a skirt; she had a coat, of course. Yes, she had this coat—the coat with the mangy fur collar. Well, that would do fine. He'd manage the sweater. He'd borrow one of his sister's; Mimi was away in Honolulu, and her room must be full of stuff.

And he had actually brought to the store for her inspection a day or two later a suitcase containing two pleated plaid skirts and two woolen sweaters. The clothing had decided Dina, but she had hesitated for a few more questions.

"Someone—someone married goes along?"

"Oh, sure. Half of them are married! We all have dinner together at the inn and break up early. Some of the mothers play bridge, but I don't. Our crowd gets up early to climb up Bald Hill; we get a two good hours in before breakfast. Breakfast about nine, waffles and thick bacon and biscuits—lord, it's good! And then we all go out until about three, and come in for·lunch, and loaf and bathe and start for home."

"It sounds such fun!"

"It's the greatest fun in the world."

"But who would I be with, Vere? I mean—my father'd skin me if anything was queer about it. I mean—suppose I was one of the other girls—who'd I be with?"

"You mean what woman?"

"Not—not to·be up there with a lot of boys," the girl had submitted doubtfully.

"Well, you see, here's how it is. Mrs. Thomas is going and Mrs. Waite, and I don't know who else. Freddy Lippincott says—for instance, 'Mrs. Waite, this is Miss Watson from Baltimore, who's staying with Mother; which room will she have?' Mrs. Waite says, 'Howdy-do, Barbara, you are in with Margot.' Still, if any funny business goes on at night," Vere had added, "those married girls don't interfere."

"Don't?" Her laugh had held a scandalized note.

"No. It's none of their business. They're playing bridge all night, anyway, and asleep all morning. But they're *there*," Vere had finished with an illuminating grin that had made Dina laugh again. "That's all the mothers want to know!"

"And does it?" she had asked seriously. "I mean—they don't do anything wrong?"

"Well, I guess some of the fellers and girls sort of have that in mind when they go," the boy had answered after a moment's thought. "But the thing is, if—anyway, here's what my mother's always said about Mimi," he interrupted himself to explain, as one suddenly enlightened, "if you can trust a girl, she's safe. And if you can't, she isn't. And where she goes, or what you let her do or don't let her do, doesn't much matter."

"And when would we go?"

"This week I can't get off until Saturday afternoon. But that's all right; we get up there for dinner."

"I'll ask about it at home." But she had already made up her mind that there would be no asking about it; she would tell them instead. She was nineteen, after all; she was no longer a child.

Rolled in luxurious rugs, she had sat beside Vere on the long drive, and to them it had been far too short. Then had come the bewilderingly joyful experience of taking possession, with one Martha Wilson, of a room in a beautiful little brown cabin—the most luxurious room and the most comfortable cabin Dina had ever seen, even if they were high up in the snowy Sierras. Soft lights, soft Indian rugs, a fireplace in which logs were burning, a bathroom whose towels were downy and warm and the size of small sheets, perfumed soaps, fat white pillows, hot water; nothing imaginable was lacking. It was ecstasy, after the long, cold, cramping drive, to stretch and relax, to waste a lazy, sleepy half-hour about the fire before separating for baths, to rejoin each other in time for the eight o'clock dinner, fresh and rested and completely in love with the adventure.

Vere was of course next to her at dinner; they were late in finding their places at a great round table at which several of the pretty young women, Dina was relieved to discover, were indeed married and so might well be counted as chaperons. She was casually introduced, no questions were asked, and although an evident state of intimacy existed between most of the other members of the party, no special attempt was made to draw her into it or evince the slightest responsibility for her.

But as the atmosphere was one of great freedom Dina was not made uneasy, and when the long meal, interspersed by dances accompanied by the radio, was over she was quite willing to end the day at quarter to ten.

"Where are you?" asked a handsome woman of perhaps thirty, who had been mentioned as "Lollie Reynolds."

"We're in the cottage at the end of the row," Martha Wilson answered as she lighted a cigarette. Everything seemed quite regular to Dina; she had never been here before and she did not know many of the persons about her, but everyone seemed to be taking the situation comfortably and for granted.

She had on a blue lace dress borrowed from Frances Tack. It was not new but, being lace, it fell into soft lines and was conspicuous neither for smartness nor shabbiness. And with it she wore a white woolly coat which Vere had brought along today; the coat was not new either; it was comfortably inconspicuous among a score of woolly coats, and Dina felt it deliciously warm and protective.

"Your sister Mimi had a coat almost identically like that, Vere," a girl said at dinner.

"Seems to me she did," Vere agreed, undisturbed.

"Only hers hadn't any pockets," the girl added after a scrutiny.

"Don't remember," Vere said.

Dina knew that she should not yawn, and she patted a yawn back with her hand. She saw Mrs. Reynolds look at her sharply, and as Martha Wilson had disappeared a few minutes previously with the clear statement that she was dead on her feet and making for bed, Dina smiled at Vere and, to cover a sudden uncomfortable rush of embarrassment, proposed she follow Martha. She had done something wrong, she knew, something that made Mrs. Reynolds look at her with that sudden keenness and that insufferable hint of a smile, and she wanted to get away before any further cloud could mar this thrilling evening.

She and Vere walked out under the cold clear November sky, and Vere looked up at the mountain peaks all about them and predicted that there would be swell skiing tomorrow.

"I wish I could ski!" Dina lamented.

"Well, you try it. And after you've tried it awhile we'll go up to the toboggans. That's swell. All you do is sit down and have me hang onto you."

They reached their own small cabin; Dina had gathered from the general conversation at dinner that in most of the cottages either girls or men had been quartered. In this one, which possessed four bedrooms, however, two quite young married couples had been placed, Vere, and Martha Wilson's young man, whose name was Travers Porter, Martha, and herself. The place was quite dark.

They went in, and Vere piled wood on the fire in the sitting room and it blazed up gloriously. He and Dina sat down before it, Vere pushing two low armchairs together, so that with his left hand he could hold Dina's right. It was an exquisite hour, so perfect she wished it might have gone on forever. Vere was serious now; she had seldom seen him so; he turned to smile at her now and then, stared into the fire.

Sleepiness was overcoming her; the warmth of the room, the comfort of her deep chair, the fatigue of the long trip in cold fresh mountain air were too much. When the honeymooning little Peatties came in, complaining over the luck that had given the Wendells a grand slam on that last rubber, Dina was ready to rise and to escape into her unbelievably comfortable bedroom. Bill and Laura Peattie dropped down to chat with Vere and have a last drink; Dina could hear the waiter's voice and the clink of glasses as she got into bed.

She was still awake, watching the angles of white moonlight on the floor, awed by the unearthly quiet of the great snowy mountains outside, when her door quietly opened. Her eyes went to it in quick panic; it did not sound like Martha, who always carried a great rush and noise and scent of cigarettes wherever she went.

It was Vere, in wrapper and slippers. He came quietly in and sat on the bed and covered her hand with his hand. Travers Porter had come in after Vere had gone to bed, he reported, to say that Martha Wilson was staying with the Hochheimer girls at the hotel.

"You won't be scared, Dina, staying here alone?"

"Oh no! Not with all these other people in the house!"

"I'm right next door here."

"I know." Her voice was almost inaudible.

He slid to his knees beside the bed and put his face against her neck.

"Gee, you smell sweet!" he said. "I've never loved anyone in my life the way I love you, Dina. My mother never loved me much, and I hardly knew my dad! It's changed my whole life, knowing you and loving you and our talking together. It seems to me you're the first thing in my life I ever found for myself. Not school nor teachers nor being told what to do—but myself. 'Member I told you that that first night at Cotta's? 'Member the red dress?"

"And Frances thinking you were Freddy Lippincott and Freddy was you."

"And that first time we went out and we were going to a movie and didn't ever get to it?"

"Because we sat and talked until nearly eleven!"

"I love you, Dina. Gosh, I love you!" He was browsing over her face with his hungry lips; she loved his bigness and the sureness of the arm that was about her, and she loved, too, the youngness of him, his little-boy eagerness to be loved, his affectionate anxiety to be reassured, to be told that he meant to her what she meant to him.

"You do love me, don't you?" he said.

"Ah, I do love you, with all my heart!" Dina whispered.

She was awake when the dawn came coldly over the mountains and began to fill the cold room with gray light. Dina lay thinking, wondering how she could face this day. What would she say, what would Vere say, when they met? She was not sure that she had been asleep at all, but when Martha, ready for bath and change, came yawning and complaining into the room at six o'clock Dina pretended to be asleep.

"Why we have to be routed out in the middle of the night!" Martha grumbled. "You'd better get up, Dina; everyone is!"

Someone was hammering on the door.

"Girls!" It was Vere shouting to them. "Get up!"

Dina caught her breath; the blood raced to her heart. That was Vere, and she loved him with every fiber of soul and body. Of course she could meet him; there was nobody else in the world for her now.

"How soon'll you be ready?" he was calling.

"Oh, for heaven's sake!" Martha called back. "Give us time. We'll be out in six seconds!"

Ready in that many minutes they actually were, Dina equipped head to foot in the warm, gay clothes that were a part of the fun of the trip. Vere had stopped on the way up the day before to buy her woolen stockings, cap, and scarf; she was wearing his sister's peasant sweater and thick plaid skirt, and she carried the great white coat to go over all. High up in the great snowy mountains, with the exhilarating freshness of the icy air stinging color into her cheeks and her eyes blazing like stars, she felt suddenly confident and gay. Her tawny hair, not gold, not brown, had fluffed up against the lemon, black, and blue stripes of her cap; her hands were lost in striped mittens that came well up on her wrists.

It was not hard to join the milling and hilarious crowd that was gathering in the breaking dawn, to catch at Vere's hands and feel herself lost in his big embrace. Her very soul was warmed by his kiss.

"Dina, you look marvelous! Did you have coffee?"

"No, did you?"

"No, but some of them did."

"I'd rather wait and be starving for breakfast."

"So'd I. Oh, darling, how sweet you look!" She had another kiss and a wild embrace under cover of the morning shadows; then they were racing along the snowy trail laughing and shouting with the rest. Her last fears disappeared; after all, she was nineteen and he was twenty-four; why shouldn't they be married? His family might not like it, but that had happened before. Families did not count. They loved each other, that was all that mattered!

And presently the winter sun burst out brilliantly, shining gloriously on the snow, and leaden clouds, spectacularly purple in the bright light, were massing on the southern mountains.

Nothing in Vere's manner in the slightest degree suggested that anything today was different from yesterday, and Dina quickly adapted her manner to his and entered into the business of the morning as wholeheartedly as he did. She immediately had her reward. He never left her side; there might have been no one else on the broad white hillside but themselves.

Vere's hand catching hers when she slipped in the snow; Vere steadying her body against his own, a big arm gripped tightly about her; Vere murmuring encouragements to her and laughing under his breath as she floundered and stumbled. Both of them becoming gloriously warm and breathless and ravenously hungry, so that the brightly lighted breakfast room of the hotel was heaven to reach at half-past nine, and the relays of hot coffee and bacon, waffles and fruit could not come fast enough or often enough. The big place was filled with feasting holidaymakers; everyone was in great spirits, and when snow began to filter down softly across the windows, and all the outdoor world grew dim and mystical, Dina felt that she had been transported to a land unknown, where nothing of the dark sordid past could follow her.

She knew she was lovely in her borrowed costume, and she knew Vere was proud of her. When they all scrambled out again after breakfast for a few more hours of excitement he stayed with her, hardly spoke to anyone else, and because of his complete absorption drew about himself and Dina all the other members of their own group, curious to see something of the girl who had so completely bewitched him.

They tobogganed down a long white hill with the powdered sugar flying down from the skies and up from the earth about them. They snowballed each other, and the scarlet, blue, and egg yellow of the girls' coats were plastered with white. They skated, first brushing off the snow with brooms from a small section of the mountain lake—Dina not so much at a disadvantage here, for her very small girlhood had been spent in Arkansas, and she was entirely at home on the ice.

Her easy prowess made Vere prouder than ever, and for a happy hour they circled about to the steady pounding of classical old waltzes from a loud-speaker hidden in the pines. Then, alarmingly, it was two o'clock and lunch time, and immediately after lunch bags had to be packed and the cars started down the long road through the snow.

"We've got to get out of the snow belt before dark," Vere reminded her. Dina did not care if they were caught in the snow; anything just to be with him, just to hear his voice.

And this long drive home was perhaps the happiest time of all. She rested against his shoulder, and sometimes he drove with his left hand and put his right arm about her. Big fur rugs were piled over her; she was snug and warm under them, and she might have fallen asleep but for the joy of being close to him—a joy that would end, for a while anyway, when he put her down at her father's door that night.

"It's so little to say that it's the happiest time I've ever had, Vere!"

His voice was very low.

"In spite of the fact that I love you too much, Dina?"

She pressed even closer against his arm.

"I didn't mean to," he said, "but you were so darned *sweet!* The sweetest—well, anyway, you forgive me and you love me! It's not as if we were kids. We've both liked other people, had crushes. But this is the real thing."

"Oh, this is the real thing!" she said fervently.

They talked tirelessly of their love. Of what he felt when first he had seen her, of what it meant for them to be together now, of how little the world outside mattered. He told her that he had been lonely all his life. He was always laughing, sure, and he made a lot of racket, sure; but he really never had had either a father or a mother. His mother was always at Palm Springs or in New York or in Europe. His father he hardly knew. He had an uncle, Rogers Holland, who was rich and kind of a nice old fellow, but he did not see him very often.

"He sends me a couple of hundred now and then," Vere said carelessly.

"A couple of hundred!"

"Well, his wife died and he has no kids. Cold, darling?"

"No. Terribly comfortable." The man glanced down sideways and saw her looking up, bright-eyed, out of her nest of furs and leaned down to kiss her temple.

They had a late dinner at the Palace Hotel; there was no one else in the dining room. They could talk, leaning on the table, and Dina could look deep into his eyes, with the new light of love welling in her own, and lay her hand over his and tell him that so long as he loved her she did not regret anything, she was not sorry for anything.

And then it was half-past ten and, tired and cramped and cold, she was getting out of the car at Railway Flats and lifting her face for a last kiss.

Then blankness.

Blankness. For though she saw him again she knew, as women have known from the beginning of time, that she had lost him. The fear came first with a chilling, sickening little tremble of her spine, an ache between her eyes. It grew; it strengthened. It was always with her. She had lost more than youth, she had lost more than girlhood, up there in the little cabin in Paradise Valley. She had lost peace.

More than once Vere came to the grocery and they talked, Dina fingering his coat lapel, raising her heavy lashes from heavy eyes to smile at him. But now there was so little to say!

They could not have another Saturday night in the Sierras because looky, he told her, Molly McGuire and Pen Stafford were being married on Saturday night and he had to "ush." And then, darn it, he had to go down to his mother at Palm Springs for

Christmas and the New Year's game in the Rose Bowl, and after that he was going East. Remember he had told her that he was going to take a postgraduate course there?

"But don't you care, darling," he said; "we'll write each other like anything! And before you know it I'll be back and get Mother to ask you up to Tahoe. Because"—the smooth firm cheek had been against hers as he spoke, and she had caught the clean odors of shaving soap, lotion, and the perfume of his thick blond hair—"because there'll never be anyone but you!"

She had had that to remember as she had turned back in December darkness to the ashes and rain pools, the shanties, noises, and smells of the Flats, to the garish light of the kitchen and supper plates plastered with the grease of lamb stew.

That had been before Christmas, before she had dreamed—before she had feared what she dreamed and feared now. She never should have let him go; it might have shocked him, it might have sobered or even disgusted him, but Vere was too affectionate, too much the loving, blundering puppy she had so often called him, to desert her now.

But how and where could she find him, and if she did find him what could he say to his father and his mother; what would his career be, going East to law school with a wife clinging to him and a baby on the way? Dina pondered it until she was heartsick with the hopelessness of it, and she could see no way out.

Chapter 4

DINA, DOOLEY, AND LOU and the two smaller children were out in the forlorn patch of earth they called the garden, ostensibly doing what they could to make it presentable after the deluging rains of mid-winter. But only Dooley really was helping. Dooley was a squarely built little girl of twelve who liked working with her big sister and was like Dina in that she was already assuming such responsibility as she could for the welfare of the family. Myrna, at fourteen, always had engagements on Sundays now; her pretty young face powdered, her pretty soft hair curled, her lips of the color and wetness of blood, she was off with her adored Nancy as soon as the breakfast dishes were done. Lou, ten, was a pale, undernourished-looking little creature who was hanging today like some small wood animal on the gate, letting the sunshine penetrate her very bones. El'ner and Donny, the babies of the family, were busy with an old wagon, ropes, bottles, and planks and paid no more attention to Dina's efforts than if she had been one of the gulls that were walking and complaining on the roofs of the old red boxcars that had been stalled on a siding for all the years that any inhabitant had known Railway Flats.

Dina had on an old cotton dress; she had tied a clean length of burlap firmly about her hips; her head was enveloped in a gypsy handkerchief; her slender legs were bare from where the dress stopped at her knees to where they disappeared into a pair of old tennis shoes. She was equipped for a mean job, and something in her rose to it and liked it.

"If the worst things in the world were only mean jobs!" she said to herself more than once. "If I were what everyone thinks I am, just Dina Cashman, cleaning up the place and talking to the kids; if I could go back to last October and get engaged to Tom and have a little wedding—we could have it at the O'Connor place—Miss Tipman would let us have the double parlors."

She was so sick and tired of fear and shame! Tired of thinking, thinking, thinking, with no end to the thinking! Days were going by and were weeks; time was bringing her inevitably to the moment when she must act, when something must be done. And she seemed helpless, like a frantic little mouse in a trap, running around and around desperately, sniffing at every outlet, and in the end only a few hours nearer destruction.

"Pretty hopeless, isn't?" Mrs. van Hooten, working away in her garden with three milk-blond babies for companions, called cheerfully.

"Hopeless!" Dina answered back, swallowing, managing a smile.

She had a rake; against the broken strip of side porch a broom worn down to the hard nubble of the strings was leaning. Dina had raked a snarl of cans, ropes, webbed papers, and straw into a heap and was pushing it onto a square of old sacking spread on the ground. The dumps were but a hundred feet away, and fires were smoldering there even on this Sunday morning.

"We don't have much trouble getting rid of it, that's one thing!" the little Dutch neighbor called.

"I was thinking that!" Dina set milk bottles, clotted with mud, in a row on the fence. Some ten feet of good strong wooden paling stood on one side of the Cashman lot. Just why it was there nobody ever seemed to know. On either end the unfenced lumpy ground was free again. But it did serve the purpose of a garage; the Cashman car, when not in use, was nosed into it on one side and the Brennan car on the other.

All around there were other bits of fencing, set at every angle, protecting nothing, keeping nothing out—or in. The Chiglias' fence was made of old bedsprings set up on end; it frequently was draped with the family wash, and Dina had often seen patterns of rust marks on the Chiglia sheets and towels and had reflected that there were simpler solutions with posts and ropes. The Brennans protected their rear property from the encroachment of friendly pigs with a row of scrapped motorcars, nose to tail. Often in summer the children played house, pirates, cops and robbers, in and out of the cars, slamming old doors, scrambling through empty window spaces, crawling under dented and dilapidated coaches. In among the fences, sheds, posts, clotheslines ran the crazily meandering streets and stood the heterogeneous homes—homes half finished, half painted; homes made entirely of windows and doors; homes patched with strips of corrugated iron or flattened kerosene cans nailed together; homes to which some woman once had had window boxes added; homes now abandoned, their windows boarded, their unhinged doors nailed securely shut. None of the buildings contained more than one low story; none boasted more than four rooms. In all the plumbing was of the simplest character, consisting in most cases merely of the faucet at the sink. All the sanitary arrangements were exterior, located in tipsy outhouses to which feet had worn tracks across ashes and mud.

But this morning the sun was shining, and somehow Dina could not be afraid as she raked and swept out in the sweet open air. The February day was hot and clear; the sun moved slowly across a flawless blue sky, and the leaves of the eucalyptus trees that wavered here and there among the buildings, and the grapevines raised on trellises behind the Chiglia and the De Luzoni houses, spread themselves visibly in the life-giving warmth.

Great pools of water still stood in the hollows between the tangles of track, but today they gave back the blueness above them and added their own note of beauty to a world reveling in yet another springtime. Grass had sprouted up everywhere, grass sown thickly with dandelions and buttercups. Along the rise of the railway embankment poppies were spattered like orange flame. Gulls swooped and cried, and the little crippled peach tree down by Mrs. Veerie's had burst into bloom like a great popcorn ball.

Dina panted in the heat, wiped her forehead with her forearm. She swept the soaked and rotting accumulations of rubbish from the steps, stooped to pull up a particularly tough bunch of grass, found it immovable, and straightened her aching back up to smile into the eyes of Tom O'Connor, unexpectedly beside her.

"Tom! Dunk Beatty said you might be coming down, but he said not until tonight. I was going to clean up and be all ready for you!"

"I like you the way you are," Tom said. They sat down on the steps together and stared at the threescore ragged children who were screaming and running in the sunshine, climbing rails, ducking in and out of freight cars, floating bits of plank on the pools. Now and then Dina turned to catch Tom's smile, and when she did she always found his eyes on her.

He had a new job, he told her. He had been offered better prospects with the Hamilton Pipe and Steel Company in south San Francisco. That was only a short half-hour's run from Bonita, and he could see Ma every week. How about it, now? Had Dina been thinking it over? How'd she like to go house hunting with him this afternoon in south San Francisco?

The dear usual progress; her heart ached at the thought of it! On Sunday afternoons the empty cottages were opened to young men and girls who prowled through looking at closets and kitchens and teasing each other about bedrooms and nurseries. What fun, what fun, what fun! And afterward to have dinner somewhere with Tom and perhaps have him produce the ring she could show to everyone tomorrow. "Dina and Tom, what do you know?" Frances Tack would say. And then, "Oh well, we all guessed that was coming!"

She needed him so now; she liked him so much and trusted him so completely! Nobody could look at the dark Irish face or touch Tom's big hard hand or hear his voice, with the rich hint of a burr discernible even in the third generation of Americans, without trusting him. Dina, sitting here in the heartening first hot sunshine of the year, drinking in the sweetness of the new green grass, was swept by a sudden feeling of utter weakness. If she could only take what Tom offered; if she could throw herself and her burdens once and for all upon him, how she would repay him! What a home his should be, what a wife, what comfort and sweetness and spoiling she would pour over him!

Would she have married Tom if the fearful predicament in which she found herself had passed her by? She did not know. She only knew that after these weeks of cold and dark, worrying and loneliness, he was the biggest, the safest thing that had come her way or could ever come her way. There was infinite rest in his mere nearness. Perhaps if he knew how desperately she needed him, perhaps if he knew how eternally grateful she would be to escape from the eyes and the tongues all about her, Tom might be big enough to help her, to offer her all the more eagerly the shelter and protection she must have.

"I'd like to be married this afternoon," she said suddenly and thickly. She half turned as she spoke, her face sober, and saw Tom's astonished eyes.

"What did you say?" he stammered.

"Oh, because I'm so tired—I'm so sick of everything." Dina's throat thickened; she looked away.

"Ah, sure you are!" Tom's husky voice said comfortingly. "You poor thing, you," he said; "you've had too much! It's not your father's fault and it's not your mother's, but you've had the whole load on you, and you not nineteen!"

"I am. I'm past nineteen; I'm nearly twenty."

"Well, you're no great age, whatever it is. If you'd let me take you out of it, Dina! We'd get along as well as most; I'm no drinker and I've money saved. And I'd take care of you to the last day of my life."

"I need taking care of," she said somberly, swallowing.

"That's all I want to do, dear," said Tom, his voice shaking.

"Pop's asleep," the girl warned him, jerking her head backward toward the house. "He's got a job this week and next, night work, and he's tired."

"Well, if he can sleep through the hell those kids are raising . . ." Tom offered reasonably. Dina smiled with still serious eyes.

"I wasn't thinking of that so much as thinking I didn't want Pop to hear us," she said.

"Everyone'll know soon!" Tom said in satisfaction. His deep-set small blue eyes danced in his dark, broad face.

"It's this." Dina had to swallow again. "I've been an awful fool, Tom," she said slowly, not looking at him. "I'm—I'm afraid I'm in trouble."

"Money?" he asked promptly, still with his fond and indulgent smile.

"No! But if I had money I'd go away." Dina had followed an irresistible impulse to confide in him, to confide in somebody, to find help—even if it were accompanied by blame and amazement— somewhere. But now she wished she could draw back. Put into words, her story had in it nothing that a thousand others did not have. It was a story of shame and weakness and stupidity. Of all persons Tom O'Connor was the last to understand it.

"What's the matter?" he asked, staring. She saw his face redden. She knew that he was angry at himself, not at her, as the first ugly touch of suspicion reached him. Nobody had any right even to think such things in connection with Dina Cashman. Tom was already blaming himself.

"Oh, I've been a fool," she said wearily. "I oughtn't to tell you, Tom, but you've always been so good to me, and I've got to tell someone! I—you see—I liked this boy, Vere Holland, so much, and we went up into the Sierras together—and we were—we are—in love."

"You mean you're going to marry him?" Tom demanded in the silence.

"Well, eventually, yes." Her throat was dry; she spoke with an effort.

"How d'you mean *eventually?*"

"He's at law school in the East," she explained; "he's taking a law course at Yale. At Christmastime he went South to be with his mother, and he went directly East from there. He wrote me. That—that part of it's all right. But you see—you see——"

She could not go on. She looked away and felt the hot color creeping up to her cheeks and her forehead and her ears.

"I don't know what you're trying to tell me," Tom said at last in a hard voice.

"That, I guess," Dina said very low. There was a moment of silence. She could not look at him.

"You don't know what you're talking about!" Tom broke out roughly after a stupefied pause. *"You!* Why, you've always been the touch-me-not, the girl none of the fellows could get near. You —you don't know what you're talking about!"

"We were up there in the mountains——" Dina stopped again. "I know how you feel," she said after a moment, "and you know how I do. I can't believe it even now. I can't sleep, Tom. It always seemed a thing that would happen to other girls—girls who felt differently about everything—not to me. I've always worried about Myrna, because she's so pretty; I never worried about myself. It's like a horrible dream. But oh my God, if it is a dream, I wish I could wake up!" Dina broke off to say under her breath. "I've no friends, Tom; we're not like other people; we haven't cousins and uncles and people to help us out. There's nowhere I can go, and I've got to go somewhere."

She stopped, and for a long time neither spoke.

"Mother know?" he asked briefly.

"Oh no! It'd kill her. She needs me and the girls need me. And Pop"—Dina went on, turning suddenly drenched eyes to her companion—"oh, I know what you think and everyone thinks about Pop! But his father was a country judge, and Pop had two years of high school, and if he hadn't fallen in love with my mother at a county fair—she was at the lunch counter—and if they hadn't eloped, and if there hadn't been so many of us, everything might have been different with him! He depends on me to keep the children straight and keep the house in kind of order, and now I've failed them all!"

"What does *he* say?" Tom slightly accented the pronoun.

"Pop? He hasn't any idea! He's never seen Vere."

"I mean him." The man's face, at the mention of the name, had darkened. Dina hesitated for an imperceptible second.

"He doesn't know. That is, I'm sure he doesn't."

The atmosphere had changed in the last five minutes. All the joy, the love, and tenderness had gone out of Tom's face, leaving it dark and hard. He looked older by years than the man who had seated himself on the steps beside her only fifteen minutes earlier; his manner was stern.

"Your friend Vere doesn't know, hey?" he asked.

"No. I'm only just sure, myself. He was South and then he went East. How could I write him that?"

"It's up to him, Di'," Tom said. "I don't know anything about the rat; I've never seen him. God knows I don't want to! But you can't rob him of a chance to square himself. I could kill him," Tom added, the four words falling with the weight of iron, though he said them as an afterthought and under his breath. "How often did you two go up to the mountains?" he asked heavily as Dina did not speak.

She brought her shadowed, tragic eyes slowly to his.

"Only the once."

"And you went, knowing what he wanted?"

"Oh no, no, Tom! There were lots of others—people he knew, married women, and girls and boys, all of them his friends. We—we neither of us dreamed of doing anything wrong! Truly, Tom," Dina pleaded as the man smiled sardonically, "he isn't like that. He's just—friendly, and we had danced and gone around and had such fun together!"

She stopped. Tom's lowering look had not lightened, and her own words seemed unreal to her. This couldn't be Dina Cashman talking, apologizing, defending herself!

"You tell me he doesn't know?"

"Well, I couldn't say it right out, I couldn't write the truth," she explained lamely. "He was with his mother, and she's—she's one of those tough women, I imagine. But I did write him—I sent him a handkerchief at Christmastime, the nicest I could buy in San José, and with the letter I said that he simply had to see me before he went away, that I was worried. He must have known from that. But he didn't say anything about it when he answered. That was just after New Year's, and I haven't had a letter since."

"Where is he now?"

"In New Haven, I guess. He was to take his first-year law there. I don't know the address."

She was silent and Tom silent too. He sat with his big fingers locked and dropped between his knees; his face, as he stared into space, was black.

"This is his affair," he began presently. "No one else can take it on. It's happened, and he's responsible. He's got to know."

Among all her other shamed and confused thoughts Dina was conscious of terror. Tom wasn't going to take it upon himself to notify him!

"It's mine; it's always the woman's," she said quickly and proudly.

Tom put his head down in his hands for a minute, rumpled his thick black locks. When he looked up his face was haggard.

"I don't get it," he said; "I don't get your falling for a guy like that. You didn't know anything about him, except the crowd he belongs to, and that isn't our crowd. I don't believe it yet! Has he money?" he demanded suddenly, looking up.

"Not of his own, I think. His mother gets alimony; I don't know how much. You see, she married again after she and his father were divorced——"

"I don't want to know what they did!" Tom interrupted with distaste.

"I mean that she forfeited what his father was paying her when she remarried. His father is rich—very rich, I believe, and I suppose Vere will come in for something when he dies. Now he sends him a hundred or so a month and of course pays for his tuition and board. He expects him to become a lawyer and go in with his firm in New York, but he says he won't give him anything more until he gets his degree."

"A nice guy!" Tom observed dryly.

"He's not a bit what you think. He's generous and affectionate and terribly—terribly nice," Dina mustered spirit enough to say appealingly. "It—it was my fault too. It wasn't anybody's fault—really!"

"Suppose not." Tom sighed. His was suddenly the weariness, the patience of the father-confessor. No use to blame her, to rage and scold now. The mischief was done, and the future must be faced; not the past. "You'll have to let him know," he said.

"How can I? A girl from Railway Flats, with perhaps—perhaps all—all this coming on me in midsummer! Think what it would do to him! I couldn't bear it. I couldn't bear his friends knowing how it all was; I couldn't go on! For me, *me,* to be begging them for things," Dina went on in a whisper, turning her head away, "for me to be pitied and helped by people I don't know——" She stopped, choking.

"If there should be a child, don't you see what you do to the kid?" Tom asked, his eyes sick with pity.

"But, Tom—but, Tom," she stammered, "it's not fair! It's not fair!"

"No," he said quietly, "of course it's not fair. Yet if I should say to you that you and I'd get married, that we'd go ahead just as if everything was—was all right, that wouldn't be fair either."

"To you," she said quickly, her face aflame.

"To any of us," he answered soberly. "I—how would I feel about the baby? How would you? We'd start wrong."

She had never seen him in this mood before. Tom was a grown man today, sorrowful, quiet, and wise. All his Irish nonsense had dropped from him. Both had put something of the past away forever in this hour, and lightly as she had valued it, Dina felt terror and heartache as it went.

"Tom," she asked him simply and pitifully, "what shall I do?"

"You'll have to join him, since he isn't here to join you," Tom told her.

"I can't do that!"

"Don't you see you *have* to, Dina? Don't you see that however hard it is on him—and you too—it's the only way? You've only

got a little while to straighten it out; you can't wait around for
him to graduate and come home and perhaps change his mind.
You don't want all the rest of your life to be sorry you've made a
mistake now!"

"I can't," she whispered, looking away.

"I'll give you the money. You find out where he is and simply
go East and tell him all about it."

"But what'll I say to Mama and Pop?"

"Anything. Tell 'em you're going with somebody—a lady is paying you to go as her companion—anything. I'll help you; I'll talk to
your father, say that I know the lady."

Dina sat silent. Her thoughts were one wild protest, but it was no
use to waste them on Tom. Unless Vere wrote her or wired her to
come she knew well that she would never have the courage to follow him. She could not turn their joyous young love idyl into the
burden, the wreckage that it would mean to a hopeful young
lawyer to have a sick, despairing woman suddenly appear with a
claim upon him.

And that claim, she thought now with a sort of frenzy, was daily
becoming more obvious, less concealable. Vere had been proud of
her—up in glorious Paradise Valley; he would have no cause to be
proud of her now! Misshapen, strange, sick, bringing into the
world too soon the baby that was the cause of all this agony, need-
ing a home, clothes, care, hospital—no phase of it could do anything except appall him! His young gaiety would go down into
somber reality as swiftly as hers.

"When you meet him tell him that as soon as you're married
you'll come back here," Tom was saying; "make it a secret. Tell
him that you'll never be a burden on him."

Hope flooded her heart.

"But what'll they think here?"

"You'll have to go away. San Francisco, perhaps, or Oakland. A
big place where you can get lost. Then you'll have to land a job."

"There'll be weeks—months, when I can't work."

"That part," he said, staring ahead of him with darkened eyes, "we'll manage somehow. You see him, tell him what's happened, be married! The rest you can work out from there."

"It's—it's something to do," she said. "It'll kill me, but I can do it! If it will make what we did less wrong, I can do it. And then I'll—I'll go on alone. Other girls have—they've worked it out!"

"Maybe," Tom suggested, still without smiling or glancing at her or altering his stern look, "maybe he'll want to keep you there. If he loves you—if he really loves you—perhaps he can talk his father into helping out."

"Oh, if it could be that way!" Dina gasped, her hands clasped as if she prayed. Tom gave her a look.

"You don't think it will be, hey?" he said. "You don't think he's the kind that will see it through?"

Her face was scarlet again.

"I know how affectionate he is," she explained eagerly. "I know that he—he always means to be kind. But—but he's always had so much fun, Tom; he's gone about so much and done whatever he wanted to do. So that if he did do this—I mean if we *were* married and had a house there in the East—it would mean that I was making him do something he didn't feel ready for—he didn't want to do—as a favor to me!"

"A favor to you, my eye!" Tom cried scornfully. "Good God, is this the time to talk of favors? He's wrecked your life, brought you trouble and disgrace, sneaked out on you, and you talk of favors!"

"Dina," said her mother, appearing in the doorway, "there isn't one single thing in this house for lunch. Hello, Tom; where'd you come from? Say, you two look like you'd been quarreling."

"Dina and I don't quarrel," Tom said, standing up. "Nothing in the house for lunch, hey? We'll go over to the dairy and get eggs or something."

"You've made the yard look real nice," said Mrs. Cashman. A thin, shapeless woman who would have been pretty but for the fact that most of her teeth were either missing or reduced to blackened prongs, she stood stretching and yawning in the sunshine. "I've not had my breakfast yet; ain't that awful, Tom?" she said. "But John is working nights now, over to Diehl's brewery, and I got up at seven and gave him something to eat and went right back to bed!"

"Glad to hear he's working," Tom said. Dina had walked toward the gate without facing her mother. Now she turned at a safe distance.

"Eggs and bread, Mama?"

"Get a pound of peanut brittle too; I feel like my sweet tooth was aching!" her mother called back. The younger children swarmed after their sister. If Donny, El'ner, and Lou knew anything of Tom O'Connor, they knew they were sure of lollipops or cones at the dairy. Dina's father came out to the shining warmth of day, stood blinking like an animal in the light.

He was twenty years older than the mother—past sixty. He had been a dreamy, impractical man when first he had met the pretty saucy waitress now his wife; he had had no job, no profession; his family had long regarded him as a settled bachelor, one of those mild superfluous members of a good family who, if they add nothing to its importance, at least do little to disgrace it.

But John Cashman's marriage had been felt a disgrace. In the first five years of it he had been a continual problem to his family. The girl was a cheap, common little creature with nothing but a certain undeniable yet flashy beauty to recommend her. She was uneducated, ungrammatical, illiterate, and, housed in a half-furnished cottage at the wrong end of town, she was proceeding with baffling speed to produce towheaded babies whose little noses continually whistled with colds and whose small paws were always chapped and black.

The family bought John a farm to which he moved his brood. News drifted back that he had exchanged it for another and more distant farm, and the family breathed in relief. After that it lost sight of him completely.

He was old now and looked older than he was. At sixty-one he wore a thin white beard, curled thin mustaches that gave the look of an old French cavalier to his lean face. His long aristocratic nose was always slightly reddened; his lips and hands trembled; sometimes his head shook gently for days. He had long ago succumbed to the life that was easiest for him: coffee drinking in the morning, patient listening to the crying and fretting of children, the clashing of dishes and smoking of burned food. In midmorning he began the slow processes of shaving and dressing, carrying water in to the basin, carrying it out again to pour on the struggling morning-glories or nasturtiums in the yard. Then came marketing errands and idle afternoons in some saloon, playing cards with thick, dirty old cards and thick, dirty old men.

Sometimes, when he had been a farmer, he had milked cows or weeded potatoes. But always with help, always after urging from his wife. The angry, nervous strength of her character might have saved her, but she had succumbed too, had learned to follow the line of least resistance. When a mortgage was foreclosed they moved, went into some strange bank in some strange small town, made arrangements to take possession of another farm. Home loans and federal loans, home relief and federal relief, clinics, free wards, free schooling, clothing from rummage sales or salvage shops, all were contributed to the Cashmans' migratory history. Only a few minutes' conversation convinced any executive of the innate fineness of John Cashman's character; this man had had some education, he was well-bred, he could talk. He was exactly the type relief always hoped to reach.

But relief never permanently relieved the Cashmans. It trickled through their irresponsible fingers just as life had trickled through their irresponsible souls. Warmhearted committees were eternally discovering them; women passionate with pity were telling each other that that unfortunate family over back of the race track were actually starving and one of the poor little children had recently been drowned in a back-yard pool. Help would be instantly forthcoming; encouragement, a job. But they never lasted, and when in due season Ethel Cashman told well-wishers that they were moving, Mr. Cashman thought that there were much better prospects in Arizona or Oregon, there was a general sense of thankfulness.

The disreputable household goods would be packed in the car, tied on top, stacked on a trailer behind; the children would scramble joyfully to the back seat; they would turn their faces to the glowing West, hope high in all their hearts.

Their residence in Railway Flats, perhaps because there was nothing further west now except the ocean, had been the longest fixed stay that Dina ever had known anywhere. To the little children it was home. Her father, mildly looking up at the welcome blue of the sky on this balmy morning, yawned and blinked in content.

"How about something to eat, Mama?" he said.

"I was thinking . . ." said Ethel.

Dina and the children returned to find their mother mixing quick biscuits. For twenty years these had pieced the meals Ethel Cashman whipped together for her children, and she made them expertly and well. She needed no measurements; she could use butter or lard or vegetable shortening or chicken or bacon fat equally well; if flour was short, she could do nicely with a mixture of cracker crumbs, oatmeal, cold rice or cold cereal. The children loved Mama's biscuits just the same, and if ever maple sugar or dates or raisins found their way into them, it was only one more cause for rejoicing.

"I opened two cans of hash," she said to Dina.

"Oh, that's fine," Dina said. "I know there are prunes." She had cooked the prunes herself; the whole house was scented with them. Other good cooking smells began to mingle in the air. Dina took the old granite coffeepot, soused into it with a small mop, poured away dark water and rolling grounds. "Pop'll want coffee," she said.

"I'll have a cup too," Ethel said. "I've got to dunk everything until I get my teeth fixed. Tom coming back?"

"He can't. He's starting for Westwood right away. But he's taken another job; he's going to be in south San Francisco," Dina said, her back to her mother.

"Fevvens sakes," Ethel murmured, not too deeply interested. She shoved the big black baking pan into the oven; the round pale circles of the biscuits were laid in even rows. "When's he come down?"

"Thursday." He had reminded her of this in parting. He had said that she must make her plans to leave at once for the East. If Vere positively was at Yale, then she must go to New Haven; Tom would find out all the necessary details about transportation and be ready to buy her ticket. Dina must meanwhile telephone Vere's family and find out his address.

Her soul was shrinking within her at the prospect. She might telephone his mother's home truly, to be told by some servant that Mrs. Holland was still in the South. What then?

Then a blank, unless she wanted to risk a telegram to him at college. "Worried. On my way to you. Please wire college address."

"Ha!" she gasped in her soul, on a bitter laugh. Could any procedure be more exactly calculated to infuriate and humiliate and handicap a boy than that? "Oh, why has all this happened—why has all this happened?" she thought, writhing. Why the horrible necessity for all this worrying and suffering? Why were girls so stupid? Why were women born to agonies like these? Why couldn't one ever go back and have this just one of the usual sloppy, disorderly Sunday mornings at home, with Art still asleep, Donny playing with the sweet potatoes all over the kitchen floor, and good little Lou clearing the table for lunch?

"If I had a hundred dollars," Dina thought, "I'd simply get on a bus and go somewhere. I'd disappear. I could always get work, even if it was cleaning the floors in a city and county hospital; they'd take care of me when I was ill. A hundred dollars.

"Suppose I took it from Tom? But he'd never give it to me. He'll buy my ticket and put me on the train and wire Vere that I'm coming. He's ready to kill Vere, and he'll never like me—he'll never respect me again. He said I was a 'touch-me-not'! That's what he *did* think.

"Other girls do worse than this. Lots of them. College girls and girls like Vere's sister too! That Mrs. Reynolds at Paradise Valley —Vere said she was promiscuous! Wait!"

A sudden gleam had shot across her thoughts. Something in the recollection of Vere's comments upon Lollie Reynolds and upon other members of the skiing party had reminded her of Vere's mention of an uncle. The uncle who was not married, who was going to leave his property to Vere, and who often gave his nephew a "couple" of hundred dollars.

Wouldn't such an uncle be interested enough, be generous enough, to tell her now what would be the wisest thing for her to do? What had Vere said the name was? Robert. Roger. Rogers. That was it! Rogers Holland. But now, how to find him!

Chapter 5

"Is MR. HOLLAND IN? Miss Cashman. By—by appointment."

Dina rather faltered the last words. For the butler was a dark and formidable creature, and the atmosphere of the house itself was enough to daunt the stoutest heart.

She had had great difficulty in finding it, for it was not among the accessible country homes of Burlingame. The winding beautiful roads and the great iron gates ended two miles below the old lane that wound up above the fashionable regions of Hillsborough and San Mateo. But for a friendly man driving a laundry wagon Dina felt that she never would have reached it at all, for the bus left her far down in the village, and the gas-station operators and workingmen of whom she inquired the way had never heard of the old Holland house.

When she did reach it, it was to discover an approach of a half-mile lane of dreary eucalyptus and poplar trees and a bare old garden presenting its wintriest aspect. By this time she was so tired and so discouraged, so utterly depressed by the nature of her mission, that it took great courage to mount peeling ornate entrance steps toward its bay windows, columns, turrets, and cupolas and present herself at all.

Inside it was exactly what the exterior promised. A heavy, old-fashioned house filled, if the hallways were any indication, with heavy, old-fashioned furniture. Fringed curtains, dark carpets

from baseboard to baseboard, cornices, tapestry papers in dark grays
and browns. From the north side of the entrance hall, which in itself was larger than the Cashmans' entire dwelling, an angled stairway some ten feet wide rose imposingly; stained-glass windows
rising with it contributed to the floor spots of crimson that looked
like pools of blood. Everything smelled of carpets, furniture polish,
staleness. Two clothy palms in pots as large as beer barrels did
little to suggest springtime and greenery.

Mr. Holland was in his library, seated at a large flat-top desk.
Dina, for no reason whatsoever, had expected to see a spare, schol-
arly old man. Instead she found herself in the presence of a person
not more than thirty-eight or forty years of age, a fat, eyeglassed,
smiling man with thinning fair hair, who gave the impression of
rolling in his chair. He had been working at a stamp collection;
stamps, pale pink, faint green, orange, were segregated in little
groups all about him; a plethoric album was open on a side wing of
the desk.

"A spider and an owl and a frog!" Dina thought.

He half rose from his chair as she appeared, sank back.

"You'd like to do secretarial work and you've had no experience
but you could learn?" he asked, and the girl felt that her suspicion
of something faintly mischievous, something perhaps actually
malicious, in the first impression she had had of his smile was confirmed.

"No. No," she said, sitting down opposite him. "I don't think,
when I telephoned, that I said anything like that."

"What *did* you say? Hinz—that's the old feller who let you in—
gave me the message. Who told you I wanted a secretary, anyway?
Ever see a stamp collection before? Anyone who wanted to help
me would have to know something about stamps. See that feller?
Two hundred in the world like him, no more. That little bit of
paper's worth ten thousand smacks.

"Not that I paid that for him," Rogers Holland went on as Dina,
bewildered, made no comment. "No; I bought this whole lot for
less than that from an English feller who had to part with them.
He could have gotten a better price, couldn't wait for it."

"I'd no idea that any one stamp was worth ten thousand dollars," Dina said, impressed in spite of herself.

"Man offered a million for a stamp once!" Rogers answered, narrowing his eyes triumphantly as he looked up from his magnifying glass. "Well, well, well," he said, sitting back, "let's have it. What's it all about?"

"It's about Vere," Dina said faintly.

"Vere?" He looked up sharply, taken unawares. "What's Vere been up to? You mean my nephew?"

"He and I were friends," she said, "and then before Christmas he went away, and I don't think he knows—I've had no answer to my letters for more than a month. And I *have* to find him!"

The inflection on the last phrase told the story. Rogers Holland looked steadily at his caller for a silent minute when Dina had finished speaking and then commented only with a brief "Ha!" But he laid aside his magnifying glass and settled back in his chair with an air of sudden attention.

He asked a few short questions. How long had they known each other? Where was the boy now? Back at Yale, hey?

"That's his father's doing," he commented. "Van can't wait to get the boy into his New York office, partly to get him away from Caroline. You know Caroline, my brother Van's wife?"

"No. I don't know who she is."

"Vere's mother; she's my sister-in-law, or was, when they were together. Proudest woman God ever made, just as his father is the proudest man. Caroline is cold as stone, moves over everybody and everything, but she will have her way! What does she think of all this?"

"She doesn't know," Dina said, beginning to feel cold and frightened.

"Oh, she doesn't know? I can't see Caroline feeling exactly pleased when she does," the man said with his sinister smile, speaking as if thinking aloud. "And you want—what? Is the proposition that you marry the boy? That will be a pretty stiff pill for Caroline to swallow. However," he ended dryly, "I can bear that."

"I've written Vere; I *had* to!" Dina said. "I feel—oh, *terribly* about it, but what can I do?"

"And he answered?"

"He hasn't answered at all! I don't even know that he had my letter. The last was from Palm Springs—he was there at Christmas-time with his mother—and he just talked about the hotel and the tennis and said he was going back to Yale."

"What makes you think that he will fall in with this arrangement?"

"What—what else can I think?"

"It's not going to help him much with his father, you know."

"I suppose not." She fell miserably silent. "I thought," she presently began again, "that I'd go away—go off somewhere—earn my own living—if I just had enough money to start with."

"I might loan you money enough to go on and join him," Rogers said with a twisted smile. "I'd like to be there when you meet Caroline. I suppose she's gone on with him?"

"He didn't say." Dina was beginning to be frightened again of this smiling fat man, lifting stamps in delicate scissorlike tongs, looking at them with squinted, bulging eyes behind strong glasses.

"Suppose," Rogers said, "you give him time to answer you. Then, if you don't hear in a week or two, come back here again. If your story is true, it would give me a certain satisfaction," he added, drawing out the words slowly, as if they gave him satisfaction too, "to have a hand in separating Caroline and her ewe lamb. She's spoiled him; she's given him his way ever since he was born. To have him faced with one of those little realities that life is continually handing us, Miss——" He looked down at her name scribbled on a pad of paper before him. "Miss Cashman," he went on, "would help to settle an old score. I have always despised her," he added on a hard note. "I don't envy you your mother-in-law! Yes, I'll help you. Oh, and by the way, in his letters from the South," Rogers said, an odd expression taking possession of his round face as he looked critically at a stamp, "did Vere happen to mention the bride and groom?"

"The—the bride and groom?" she stammered.

"The Andrew Havenses," the man said briefly.

"No. No; he said that his mother had lots of friends down there. But he didn't mention any names." Dina was completely bewildered.

"Mrs. Havens was Aline Pierpont; we were all kids here together," Rogers explained. "I was always crazy about her. Her first husband was a man named Pollock, and she has a couple of kids by him. I wasn't married until after she was, although I'm a few years older. I suppose I sort of hoped that she——" He paused, began again. "Well, anyway, after some years she divorced Pollock and married an awfully clever doctor in New York, Rosenstirn," he went on. "My wife, Anna, was an invalid then; I didn't see anything of Aline for some time. But after my wife's death she came back here to divorce Rosenstirn, and last summer we began to go around together. In November we told our friends we were going to be married—two weeks from today, as it happens."

"Ah!" Dina exclaimed involuntarily, her lips parted and her eyes wide.

"Just a month ago," Rogers said unemotionally, lifting a stamp in his tweezers to peer at it, putting it gently down again, "she changed her mind and married Andrew Havens, the artist. I'm entertaining them a week from tonight."

He leaned back in his chair, clasped his fingers on his chest, looked across at her amiably.

"I wouldn't do that!" Dina said indignantly.

"You wouldn't? Well, she asked me to," Rogers went on. "She made a point of it. I've invited quite a group of old friends to come here and share the delightful domestic picture of bliss she and Havens will present. She wants us all to like her new husband; she says he and I are to be great friends. She'll wear one of the costumes she bought in New York last autumn to wear as my wife. And I'll have to be very gracious when she shows us all the cute little wave in his hair and tells us what he likes for breakfast."

He stopped short, making a wry mouth, investigating a desk drawer. Dina breathed hard.

"I wouldn't do it!" she said again, red-cheeked.

"Well, I'm going to. I wish I knew some perfectly stunning woman, say around forty," Rogers added ruminatingly. "An actress —someone who could wear an evening gown—who wasn't too obviously ungrammatical—wait a minute!"

He was studying her now through narrowed eyes. A strange hint of a smile broadened his mouth.

"Take off your hat, will you?" he asked. "Thank you. Wait just a minute."

He leaned over and rang a bell three times. Dina watched him in bewilderment. Neither spoke again until a middle-aged, trim, stout woman entered the room.

"Did you ring, Mr. Holland?" the newcomer asked.

"I did. Will you look at Miss Cashman, Mrs. Bucket? I want to ask you something."

The woman obeyed with a friendly smile. The smile in its own lenience seemed to ask Dina's indulgence too.

"How would she look in an evening dress with her hair done correctly?"

The woman smiled again toward Dina, after a dubious look at her employer, and said in a faintly reproachful and faintly amused tone:

"She'd look very lovely, with that hair and her eyes being so blue. Is it your cousin Mary's daughter, Mr. Holland?"

"No; no relation," he answered briefly. And then, in a business-like tone: "Do you think you could take her into San Francisco tomorrow and buy her that sort of a dress?"

"Why, certainly," the woman said after a keen glance at him to see if he was joking.

"I'd like," he said, "to introduce her to Mrs. Pollock—to Mrs. Havens, rather, on Thursday night."

A great light came into Mrs. Bucket's eyes and a certain grim, satisfied tightening to her mouth.

"I see, sir," she said.

"You'd do that, wouldn't you?" Rogers said to Dina with his characteristic grin.

"Do what?" Dina asked, looking from one to the other.

"Come to my dinner party on Thursday night," he told her. "Be dressed, be quiet, be a mystery to them all. Steal her thunder. I'll introduce you—what did you say your first name is?"

"Dina. Geraldine," she said.

"Geraldine; ah, that's better! Miss Geraldine Cashman, a friend of mine. Look," Rogers said persuasively, in the pleasantest and most sympathetic manner she had yet seen him use, "I'm doing something for you. You'll do this for me?"

"But—but I couldn't talk to those people!" Dina protested.

"You wouldn't have to talk. None of them's ever seen you. None of them knows a thing about you. All you have to do when anyone speaks to you is either say 'yes' or 'no' or look over at me and smile. I'll do the talking. I'll send the car for you, and Mrs. Bucket here will go home with you, won't you, Mrs. Bucket, when the party is over?"

"I couldn't dress at my house," Dina further objected. "We haven't—we haven't even a bathroom."

"You can dress here."

"If you think I could do it," Dina said hesitatingly.

"There would be nothing to do. You would be simply one more guest at my dinner, and when Hall drives you home I hand you a check for—well, whatever we decide. Thanks, Mrs. Bucket," Rogers said with a careless nod. He picked up his magnifying glass, studied a stamp attentively. "There's only one thing I'd want you to do, Geraldine," he went on when they were alone, "and that's to get Mrs. Pollock—Mrs. Havens she is now—wondering about you. That's all. I want her to ask herself, 'Who's this girl Rogers seems to know so well?' Just be easy, just refer anything that stumps you to me. She's thirty-four, Aline is, and she's jealous as the devil. She's always wanted to know everything, wanted to be first. And by the way, you mustn't mention Vere. You're my friend that night."

"I'll not mention Vere," Dina agreed somberly.

"Meanwhile I'll write Caroline—Vere's mother. I'll stir her up a little, see what's going on. It won't accomplish anything, though."

"And you think," she said anxiously, "that I might go on to New Haven and see him? You think that's what I ought to do?"

He looked thoughtful for a moment, picked up a stamp with a delicate tweezer tip. His tone was unconcerned.

"That, of course, you'd have to decide."

"A month ago," Dina persisted, against a rising sensation of despair, "I'd have said he'd be glad to have me come on. I'd have known that he cared the way I do! But now it's all so queer. We did talk of getting married—always that was the way we talked; in the beginning it was sort of understood. And especially that Sunday driving down from Paradise Valley! But now—since Christmas it's all been so different. I've felt so sick all the time, as if I couldn't write him and laugh about things. And his letters"— Dina faltered, her eyes filling with tears—"his letters aren't the same! He wrote me about the hotel, about playing tennis, and having a good time, as if——"

A silence. The man glanced at her with the bulging eyes that the glasses made look enormous, busied himself again with his stamps.

"I can't help you out, I'm afraid," he said dryly.

Yawning gulfs of desolation seemed to be opening about Dina. She had a sudden realization that when she left this house, in a few minutes now, she would leave her one hope behind her. She would be all alone again, alone with her secret and her thoughts. Whatever she might have hoped of Vere, whatever she might have dreamed of his return, of his making everything all right, would fade into the cold winter dusk, and she would have no one in whom to confide, no one to whom to talk. Desperately she pushed on.

"Do you know his address at college, Mr. Holland?"

His surprised look seemed to disclaim all responsibility.

"I? No; haven't the faintest idea. I'm sorry Vere hasn't played a little bit handsomer part, but I've not ever been very close to him, although I've always liked the boy well enough. He's always seemed to me a decent young feller. Just how he'd act at a time like this I am sure I couldn't say. His mother," he added with his eyes again narrowed and his smile grim, "is a splendid example of the queen cobra. I was an usher at my brother's wedding twenty-five years ago; I was sixteen. I met her that day and I hated her at first sight. I knew then that she'd wreck Van's life, and she's done her best. She sees me now and then—knows the boy will come in for whatever I leave, in all probability—and that's why she did her best to break off my affair with Mrs. Havens. That doesn't interest you, of course."

"It *does*," Dina said politely.

"Aline and Caroline are great friends, and Caroline worked up this Havens match. She probably dictated the note Aline wrote me."

"But why should she break it off, since it was with her best friend?" Dina demanded, wide-eyed.

"Because of precious young Vere's coming in for my money," the man answered almost impatiently. "Because she hates me."

"Oh." Dina felt her spirits sinking. She did not belong in this group. She had no claim on them. The futility of traveling three thousand miles to see Vere came over her like a cold wave.

And yet, to see him again, to hear his laugh again, to feel his hand covering hers as they sat at some restaurant table talking things over—ah, that would be to live once more! There was no other way.

"What would you do," Rogers Holland asked, watching her, "if you didn't find Vere?"

"Oh, but he would be there!" she said, startled.

"Might not. His father goes to Mexico, goes to Canada now and then. He might take the boy along."

"Not if Vere knew I was coming."

"Maybe not." But he was smiling that secret, dreadful half-smile of his. Dina got to her feet. "You arrange with Mrs. Bucket about going into town," he said. "Saturday perhaps. Is Saturday a free day for you?"

"Our very worst day. At the grocery—I work in a grocery—Saturdays ten to ten. But tomorrow afternoon, Friday afternoon, I'm free. Or I could ask for any morning. Mornings are quiet."

"Fix it with Mrs. Bucket. And remember, if you get stuck, just smile as if you knew all about everything and look at me. Good-by, Geraldine."

"It's good of him." She was entranced, staring at a photograph of Vere that was on a table.

"You may have that if you like," the man said. "I've others."

"No; no, thank you," Dina said. "I'd rather he gave me one himself."

"You'd rather what?"

Her head was high. She faced the man, half turning, her cheeks blazing.

"He's never given me one," she said.

"All right, Geraldine," Rogers Holland said. "I think you and I are going to understand each other."

Ten minutes later she was out in the sharp winter cold, walking toward the bus.

"I am doing something," she said half aloud. "I am doing something. Perhaps if you do something it changes things. Perhaps there will be a letter from Vere at the store!"

"Letter there for you," Frances Tack said when Dina was back at the desk in the grocery. Dina's heart leaped. She took it with hands that trembled.

In a lull she could step unobserved behind the high racks that were filled with stacked cans of tomatoes and wrapped loaves of bread and tear open the envelope.

It was a short letter, scribbled in ink on one side of a thick square page. Dina read it twice. Then she put it back in the envelope and put the envelope in the breast pocket of her sweater. A moment later she was back at work.

"You look queer, Dina," said Frances, slamming cans and packages into a tall brown paper bag. "Headache?"

"No, I'm all right," Dina answered. She cleared her throat, for the first effort at speech was unintelligible. "I'm all right," she repeated.

Chapter 6

ROGERS' DRIVER, Hall, met Dina at the Bonita Station, or rather at the open weather-beaten shed that did duty as a station, just a week later. It was wiser, the girl thought, to keep the appointment as distant as possible from her home. She had had a shampoo early that morning before the family breakfast in the kitchen, but by no other sign did she show that there was anything unusual in the adventure upon which she was embarked. Under the some-what mangy coat she wore a plaid skirt that had seen almost equal service and a dark-blue sweater; even the hat was worn and wintry; she had had no heart for new millinery this spring.

The car rushed smoothly up the wide highway, turned at the bridge crossing, moved steadily westward on the rise of the hills, and took the road that climbed through Belmont, leaving the level reaches of the bay waters and the hundred real-estate develop-ments behind it. Homes were scattered and few now, most of them ancient mansions surrounded by gloomy trees, lifting their turrets, cupolas, and towers above long-vacated rooms.

The old Holland place stood in forty wooded acres and had a deep canyon to itself. It had been built in the days of the pioneers, gold-rush, railroad-fortune days; it had been somewhat modernized in the nineties. But it was still a pretentious, gloomy, clumsy old building, crouching with the square ferocity of a bulldog at the top of a long lane of pines and eucalyptus trees, with every window—

the famous plate-glass windows that had made a precarious trip around the Horn seventy-five years earlier—reflecting in its blackness one more vista of knotted branches and piny undergrowth.

Tonight it wore an aspect as cheerful as gushing lights and a wide-opened door could lend it. The Hollands had once been famous for hospitality, and although that day was long dead, something of its glory was on this occasion restored. In the wide hall a coal fire burned vigorously in an old-fashioned, steel-rodded grate; in every one of the downstairs rooms other fires were lighted; the house, even at half-past five in the afternoon, was warmed, brightened by great jars of spring blossoms and roses, the stiff outlines of door and walls broken by masses of magnolia leaves and huckleberry.

Music was playing when Dina arrived; the strains of a soft, faraway waltz were drifting through the house. In spite of herself it lifted her spirits, and she was conscious of a flutter of excitement and anticipation as she mounted the stairs.

Mrs. Bucket was waiting for her in a big bedroom that was also well warmed; in fact, the housekeeper assured Dina that a completely adequate furnace kept the place comfortable even in the keenest weather.

"But there's nothing like a log fire!" she said.

The dress, the slippers had arrived. Everything that she and Mrs. Bucket had bought, in a bewildering afternoon of shopping the previous Friday, was there. Her costume was complete, even to new stays. Dina was left alone to enjoy a bath, to get into her undergarments unobserved. The housekeeper returned to help her with the final touches.

The slippers were silver; there was a band of tiny silver roses for her hair. The dress was white, diaphanous white, falling and floating in clouds about her, but its scallops were edged with fine silver lines, and at her waist was a cluster of more silver roses from which hung delicate silver ribbons. Dina had never seen such a gown before; the saleswoman had indeed assured them that there was no other like it anywhere. The girl stood looking at herself in the mirror like one dazed.

Under the little crown of roses her soft burnished hair rippled and curved in waves. Her face was pale but alight with excitement; the line of her shoulders, the slender arms, and slim body were enveloped in a foam of silver and white. The gown was short-waisted; a quaint tightness forced up the young breasts so that a suggestion of a cleft showed between them; the narrowness of hips and waistline made the spreading skirts seem all the more flower-like.

Dina's eyes were blazing. Upon the advice of the saleswoman she had used only a pale lip red; her mouth looked soft and young, and when she smiled at her reflection the smile was sad rather than gay.

"My goodness, you look like another girl!" Mrs. Bucket said in honest admiration.

"Fine feathers," Dina said slowly.

At seven o'clock she descended the stairs; Rogers came out of the library to meet her. The fact that for one full minute he had not the slightest idea who she was was perhaps as honest a tribute to her appearance as could have been paid her. She saw admiration in his eyes before he spoke; she sensed, rather than actually observed, something courteous, formal, flattering in his manner that she knew he otherwise would not have shown to her.

"*Geraldine!*" he exclaimed.

He caught at her hand, holding her off the better to see her.

"Why, good *heavens,*" he said, "what on earth have they done to you? Good—good—my *God!*" Still holding her hand, he led her into the library, laughing triumphantly, his bulging eyes shining behind his glasses. "Well, Aline, perhaps we have something here!" he said.

She knew he was immensely pleased; responsive warmth stirred even in her own frozen heart.

"Isn't it beautiful?" she said, spreading her skirts.

"Yes." He spoke absently, thoughtfully. "Turn around," he said. "Who did your hair?"

"I did. But I can easily change it. I can put it down again. Sometimes I pin it up that way to make me look older."

"I don't want you to look a bit different," he said musingly, his eyes moving over her in intense satisfaction. "You look exactly right. You look—extraordinarily right. I'm delighted. I must congratulate Bucket and whoever sold you the gown. Now, you'll remember the general plan, won't you? No conversation."

"Dumb," the girl agreed briefly.

"No, not dumb. With those high cheekbones of yours and the way your eyes are set, you'll never look dumb. But be mysterious. You might smile, shrug. 'I'm not bothering with any of you!' That sort of thing. Now one thing more. Someone is going to ask you where you come from. What are you going to say?"

"Russia," Dina suggested promptly. The man widened his eyes, laughed approvingly.

"Russia. After the Revolution. Escaped through Vladivostok." Dina considered this.

"I think not," she said. "I wasn't alive at the time of the Revolution. I'd better say I've just escaped."

"Fine. But if you're just out of Russia, how did you get here?"

"Well"—Dina's look was anxiously helpful—"you said mystery," she offered, hesitating. Again he laughed.

" 'Mystery' it is," he agreed. " 'You're just from Russia, Miss Cashman? How very interesting! How'd you get out?' "

" 'Very complicated,' " Dina said slowly.

" 'You speak Russian, of course,' " Rogers Holland pursued.

" 'Very little.' " She answered the imaginary question seriously. " 'So many years I was with my English connections,' " she added.

"Excellent!" the man cried, rubbing his hands in satisfaction. "If you'll just remember to answer slowly. Or don't answer at all."

"They'll think I'm bored," the girl protested.

"Let them! Everybody worries about a bored person. Now sit there in that blue chair; lean your head against the back and put one foot up against the stool. That's right. Take that position whenever you can. This husband of Aline's is an artist, and it's highly possible that you'll do something to him when his eyes light on you."

"And is he rich, Mr. Holland?"

"Wait a minute! Are you to call me that?" he questioned, considering. "Yes, I think you should," he decided. "You're less than half my age; you haven't known me very long; I can call you Geraldine, but you aren't quite so familiar yet. You asked me if Aline's husband is rich," Rogers continued. "No, he hasn't a cent. And she has only what Pollock gave her in the way of stocks or bonds—whatever it was she lost most of it. And of course Rosenstirn's alimony stops like a shot now. That's what interested her in me, my dear," the man went on, comfortably settled opposite her now and smoking a cigarette. "Until now Aline has always had an eye to the main chance. This is her first venture in true love. They're to live in his studio, back of Los Altos somewhere, and he's to paint portraits—I don't know whose!—and keep her amused."

"I shouldn't think a person who's been rich and traveled a lot would be happy very long that way," Dina said thoughtfully.

Rogers did not answer. He sat watching her idly for a minute and then asked abruptly:

"Did you hear from Vere?"

"Yes." Her color fluctuated. "He wrote," she said. "I had the letter when I got home the day I came to see you."

"What'd he say? Why didn't you tell me?"

"That there is no use my going East," Dina said steadily.

"That's his mother," Rogers observed after a minute.

"His mother was there. I wrote him at Christmastime that I—that I was afraid. They went East, he and she, and he's written me now that I'm just—just imagining things—not to come."

"Did he say so?"

"Yes. He wrote that he was sorry I was bothered and that his mother was sure I was mistaken," Dina said in a level voice devoid of feeling.

"That sounds like Caroline," the man said almost with triumph. "That's Caroline. What else?"

"That his father might take him to South America and that I wasn't to worry." The girl finished the statement quietly and sat staring ahead of her like a person in a dream.

"As a matter of fact you're not mistaken?" Rogers asked.

"No."

"You seem to take this very quietly, my dear."

Her eyes moved to his, and he saw that they were no longer a child's eyes; they were infinitely grave.

"I have to," she said. "I think I've known from the beginning that it would be this way. Not—not that Sunday that we came down from Paradise Valley and we talked all the way. But since. Ever since. Watching for letters and not having them come; telling myself that he loved me, that he would make it all right, and knowing all the time that he didn't have to—that he could go away and forget it all, that I couldn't hold him.

"So now I know," she finished. "I know that it was just liking a girl—having a crush on her, to him, and that it's something that will stay with me all my life. A human being that I'm responsible for. And I'm going to be responsible for it," Dina went on in a firmer voice. "I don't know just how I'll start, but once I get started I'll be all right. I'll have to go away from home; I won't see my sisters and brothers any more. But that's what happens to girls like me."

Her lip shook at the mention of her brothers and sisters, and she sat still with her head held high.

"I guess I've had trouble all my life," she added as the man did not speak, "but it seems to me I've never had any trouble before."

"A boy, unfortunately," Rogers said slowly, "feels that he is very lucky if he can get out of a predicament like this. He's only too willing to forget it, to believe that it isn't serious. That's what girls don't know."

"Girls do know. They know," Dina said.

"I can only say that I think you're damn spirited and plucky," the man observed. Dina moved heavy eyes to his.

"I have to be," she answered. "I would like to get out of it too, if I could. I've always thought myself—I've always been—I've never been the sort——" Her voice thickened and she fell silent.

"I believe you," Rogers said. "And you're how old? Nineteen? Well, keep your chin up; here comes the vanguard!"

There was a stir of laughter and voices in the hall. Hinz began
to show in the guests; five of them, and then two, and two, and
three, and four. They came in cold and gay and noisy; two quite
elderly men, two elderly wives, a pretty girl Dina's age and the
rather uninteresting-looking young man she was going to marry,
a younger couple, a countess who spoke broken English, a man
who had evidently won some sort of tournament and who was
under a constant fire of congratulations.

Last of all, when everyone else had had cocktails and canapés
and had settled into groups, the Andrew Havenses came. The
man looked the artist, the hair on his handsome blond head just
a trifle long, his evening clothes just a trifle baggy. He was a tall
man with a pleasant laugh and a big firm jaw; his skin was
browned, his hands long, fine, and nervous. He seemed quite at
ease among all these strangers.

The woman, now for the third time receiving good wishes as a
bride, was perhaps three or four years older than her new mate.
At thirty-four she was at the peak of her beauty, and an exotic
beauty it was. Her hair was raven black, plastered tight to her
head; the skin of her arms and throat and her proud, lovely face
was all of a smooth creamy texture; her lips were crimson and her
eyes a strange dove blue, heavily lashed in black. The trailing
gown she wore carried out a general impression of oriental aristocracy; it was wrapped about her in a sheath of peacock-blue brocade patterned in darker blue, silver, and black, and clasped with
glittering shields of jewels. In her ears she wore heavy pendants
of pearls.

She came in with a royal effect of entrance, was instantly surrounded and kissed by the men and women alike, for to all of
them this was her first appearance since her runaway wedding.

"Is anyone speaking to me?" Dina heard her demand from the
center of the circle. "Billy—Olive—this is Andy Havens, and you're
all please to like him very much and have your portraits painted by
him next week!"

"Aline, you're more beautiful than ever!" a woman said.

"Happiness, darling, happiness! We're living on nothing, and my flushed little face will soon be bending over a dishpan, but I but I really do like the creature, and so I don't care!"

She was face to face with Rogers; she looked up boldly.

"Toppy, you've got to like my husband," she said.

"I've liked all your husbands, Aline," Rogers said in the silence, with a bow.

Dina saw the smooth alabaster of her face flush faintly; she came back at him promptly.

"Yes, and I thought for a while that I was going to like your second wife immensely! I mean me," Aline said.

There was a shocked little ripple of relished laughter from the circle that had more or less unconsciously grouped itself about the two.

"I never liked her, really," Rogers countered. And again there was a laugh.

"She wasn't very nice," Aline said with a dangerously quiet smile.

"I think everyone knew it but herself!" the man suggested sweetly. "You know how it is."

"*Indeed* I know how it is, Toppy." Aline finished the exchange on so significant a note that suddenly the laughter went out of it, and as she turned superbly away Dina knew that she had scored. Toppy! That had probably been her little pet name for him. Rogers might join in the laugh that greeted Aline's latest hit, but Dina saw the shadow that crossed his face.

A moment later in her triumphant progress Aline came abruptly upon the girl in the white-and-silver gown, stopped short. Rogers introduced them.

"Miss Cashman, Aline. Geraldine, this is Mrs. Havens."

Dina rose; her eyes were wide and dark, her face pale. She looked younger even than her years, startled, shy, naïve.

"Geraldine *what,* darling?" Aline demanded.

"Cashman."

"Oh?" Aline looked at him, looked at Dina for explanations. "Do I know her; do I know her people?" she asked.

"I don't think so. She's by way of being a ward of mine for the time being," Rogers said.

"A ward? Staying with you? But how very nice," Aline commented sweetly.

"Not staying with me. No; I'm under orders to send her home at half-past ten," Rogers answered amiably. "Was it half-past ten, Geraldine?" he asked.

"About then." The girl confirmed it simply.

"Although, since that perfumed little garbage barrel you call your mind jumped so quickly to conclusions, Aline," the man added, "I may say that I think Bucket would be equal to the situation even if Miss Cashman *were* my house guest."

"In school?" Aline asked Dina after an exchange of some low-toned pleasantries at Rogers' expense, upon the part of one or two of the onlookers, that she did not follow and at which everyone laughed maliciously.

"No."

"Just visiting California?"

It was cross-examination; he had warned her it would come. But surprisingly Dina found herself rather enjoying it.

"No. Not visiting," she answered thoughtfully and slowly.

"Try the red-hot pincers, Aline," Rogers said. "Try the iron maiden. You can make her talk!"

Dina turned dutiful eyes toward him.

"*Should* I talk?"

Rogers smiled; he came over to stand beside her. Aline had sunk gracefully into the chair Dina had vacated, and the girl was standing before her as if under inspection. But to have the man join her changed the situation and gave her the advantage again.

"You know very well you shouldn't talk," he told her.

"I seem to feel mystery and intrigue in the air," Aline said. "You're not Mata Hari, I suppose?" she said lazily to Dina.

Dina had seen Mata Hari in a movie. But she wasn't quite sure of the answer to this, and her startled eyes went to Rogers with an effect better than anything for which he might have hoped.

"No," he answered. "She's not Mata Hari."

"Come over here and talk to me, Miss Cashman," old Mrs. Prince said authoritatively at this point. She patted the sofa seat beside her with a puffy, ringed hand. "I like pretty people," she added. "Tell me all about yourself!"

This was a large order and infinitely alarming to Dina. But she had been bred in the hard school of having to please marketing women; she knew instantly what was Mrs. Prince's favorite topic of conversation and could find her way to it.

"They're beautiful," she said as she sat down.

The old lady's eyes followed Dina's to the onyx and pearl bracelet that encircled her soft, old, fat arm.

"They're old-fashioned," she said. "But I won't have 'em changed. They were my mother's."

"Oh, I wouldn't change them!" Dina protested. "Because what would you get for them?" she was going to add. Fortunately she stopped in time.

"Everybody's always for havin' everything reset," Mrs. Prince complained. "I think it's ridiculous. My mother was a Belknap of Virginia; she was raised like a princess. She had a young mammy when she was nothing but a baby, and that same mammy—Mammy Sula, they called her; I remember her well!—was with my mother when she closed her eyes. There wasn't a day of my mother's life ___"

After about ten minutes she paused for breath, and Dina said respectfully: "It sounds like a book."

"I could give you stories—wish I had time to write 'em—my cousin Missy-Lou Cromartie's just had a book published—calls it *Faithful to the Gray*," said Mrs. Prince. "My uncle, Senator Joe Belknap—handsomest man you ever laid eyes on—used to say it took him a day to ride over his own property—you can read about him in any book about the first families. . . ."

Again Dina listened. She could have gone on thankfully listening for hours. It was so safe, sitting here on the wide divan and letting the dinner party ebb and flow about her! She did not have to make any effort or take any chances with the dangers of conversation. A man or two joined them—one a very old man who listened attentively to everything old Mrs. Prince said and now and then commented with a reminiscent dry chuckle and an appreciative

"Remember it perfectly, Lily!" The other was the vapid-looking youth who was shortly to marry Miss Mary Louise Ledyard. He called Mrs. Prince "Granny," settled himself on a hassock beside her knee, and occasionally bit thoughtfully at one of her fat old hands.

Chapter 7

"GERALDINE, will you sit at the head?" Rogers said when they went out to dinner. Dina gave him a glance of wild appeal, but she had no choice. He sat at one end of the long table, and she found herself enthroned opposite to him, with the stretch of flowers and candles, silver and crystal glittering between. Fortunately for her, the man on her right assumed immediate control of the conversation. He was an impeccably handsome and well-groomed person of perhaps fifty whose life was spent on the polo field, at the bridge table, at formal dinners, on the golf course or tennis courts, at Palm Beach or at Easthampton as the season indicated.

He knew a great many famous persons in society, in New York's literary and dramatic circle, and in Hollywood, and he had a great many delightful anecdotes of them to relate—all of them flattering, kindly, and innocuous. Dina need feed him only the compliment of her bright-eyed interest and an occasional "Oh, tell me about her!" to keep him content and avoid any of the silences she so dreaded. He was rapturously describing the dove shooting at Pasa Robles when the woman on his other side suddenly engrossed him by the simple method of saying, "Reggie, stop talking to Miss Cashman and pay some attention to me. After all, you and I were compromised once, at Violet's, remember? Remember how awful that was? That ought to give me some rights!"

Reggie almost instantly obeying this command, Dina found

herself for a moment ignored; she leaned back in her enormous chair, surveyed the brilliant scene, and told herself that she would serve Rogers' purpose just as well in silence as in any other way. He had not asked her to make any of them like her.

"Are you trying to think of something to say? I am," said the man at her left. Dina turned with a quick smile and found him to be Andrew Havens, the bridegroom who was the quite unconscious cause of her being here at all.

"Well, I wasn't," she said; "but if you can't, I could try."

He laughed, and they brought their heads a little nearer.

"I'm really very shy," he confessed, "and I know the cure for it too."

"I wish I did!" Dina said.

"I never get up courage to use it," the man continued. "It's just to get on top of itself, if you know what I mean. Just to say, 'Oh heck, everyone's shy and someone has to talk!' Then you just rattle along saying everything that comes into your head, and that starts the others, and the first thing you know they think you're a social asset."

"And what's that?" Dina asked, liking him at once.

"A social asset? A person everybody likes and invites places. Just from what I heard I should think that man on your other side was one."

"Mr. Tegbury? He might well be."

"Then you don't know him?"

"I've never met any of these people until tonight. Except Mr. Holland, of course."

"You haven't! And I thought you knew them all and all the fathers and mothers knew yours."

"Oh no!" Dina was conscious of a little inward shiver as she reflected upon the impression that the Cashman family would make should it suddenly be introduced into this stately dining room.

"I knew my wife didn't know you, for she took me aside before dinner and cross-examined me," Andrew Havens said simply. "She told me to find out all about you."

"You wouldn't find it very interesting," Dina told him. "Isn't she beautiful?" she asked, glancing down the table to look at Aline, exquisitely posed in a high-backed chair beside Rogers.

"Yes," the husband said, his eyes filled with adoration. "She is the most beautiful woman I've ever seen. And the lovely part of it is," he went on, "that inside, in her nature, in her heart, she is just as beautiful. Sweetness—you never saw anything like it! Servants adore her; she'll stop in the street to speak to some poor little waif of a child. The other day it was an old Chinaman. It didn't make any difference to Aline! She's had very little happiness in her life," he went on, his eyes shining, "and—and we're very happy now," he finished shyly.

"I think Mr. Holland said you're staying at a place at Los Altos?"

"Back in the hills, yes; it's a friend's place. He's in the East. It's nearly up to the Skyline Boulevard. It was a farmhouse and barns when he took it; he's not done much to it. But now that the place has a mistress," Andrew said, his face glowing with anticipation, "we're going to do great things! Build a terrace and have a grill—so that we can have our friends there."

"It sounds lovely," Dina commented, anxious only to keep the conversation flowing smoothly and avoid pitfalls.

"It's pretty rough now, especially for anyone like Aline," he explained apologetically. "She's always had a maid, you know. I get breakfasts," went on Andrew, "and carry her in a tray, and we picnic. We've only been home four days, but we'll get it all licked into shape pretty soon."

"But she didn't dress—there—for this party?" Dina questioned. The man laughed.

"Oh no, no! We're staying with young Mrs. Prince tonight. We came in to her house this afternoon. You have Irish blood, haven't you?" he abruptly changed the subject by asking in his turn.

"Lots of it. My mother. Her father was a Mahon and her mother was Geraldine McManus."

"And you're Geraldine? Didn't Mr. Holland call you Geraldine?"

"Yes, I'm Geraldine."

"It fits you," he said. "I'd like to paint you in that chair and that dress and call it simply Geraldine."

"I used to wonder—why do artists call pictures such funny names?" Dina, interested in spite of herself, asked seriously.

"As what?"

"Oh well. Girl In White and Girl With A Canary."

He laughed heartily.

"You mean that we could see that for ourselves?"

"Well, yes. We had a hundred masterpieces at school, photographs of them, you know, and we used to have to pass them around and identify them; the names used to seem to me awfully silly."

"And which ones did you like?"

"I like Whistler," the girl said slowly. "And—the one with the maps—the Dutch one who does the rooms——"

"Vermeer."

"Vermeer. I like him."

"And you like Whistler's Mother."

"I like the little girl at the piano best."

"I do too. And how about the English school, Reynolds and Lawrence and Constable?"

"With their hats tied on with ribbons and the little squinchy dogs," Dina said thoughtfully. The man laughed again.

"You two are having much too nice a time," Aline said suddenly behind them and leaned over Andrew's shoulder to kiss the top of his head and lay her cheek against his temple for a second. "I had to come up here and ask you if you still loved me!"

"Aline, for heaven's sake, cut all this bridal-suite stuff!" a woman said.

"You're a complete idiot," Andrew said. He got up to escort her back to her place, and she looked about the company with her eloquent dove-blue eyes and said defiantly, "I don't care; he's the nicest person alive!"

When he came back to his seat Dina was talking with, or rather listening to, the agreeable and courteous Reggie, but when she was free again he said amusedly:

"There's one thing about my wife: she's completely unpredictable. She says herself she's like a little girl who's discovered happiness for the first time in her life. She hates to hurt anyone, and she hates anyone to be cross at her."

He reflected upon this with a half-smile and in obvious satisfaction while a salad was passed and presently said in a confidential undertone:

"That's why we're here tonight, you know. You *did* know, I suppose—everyone knew—it was announced——"

"About Mr. Holland liking her?" Dina filled in the pause.

"Yes. It's a very old friendship, and Aline had had two most disillusioning experiences—she's of a nature to trust anyone and believe anyone——"

"Yes, I know," Dina put in as he hesitated again.

"You do see it!" he said eagerly. "Well, how natural—feeling lonely and upset after that terrible experience with her second husband—how natural to think of Rogers Holland as a protector, as a person she could trust and turn to!—for rest, you know, and an end to all the newspaper talk! You can imagine what newspaper notoriety means to a woman like that! She tells me that it was always a sort of old-friends' arrangement, based mainly upon affection and good fellowship and all that.

"Well, then we met each other," he continued as Dina listened, absorbed. "I'd just arrived here in California; I didn't know any of these people, and I didn't know that Aline was engaged to Rogers or that there was an understanding or whatever you choose to call it. She didn't tell me! D'you see the consideration there, Miss Cashman? She didn't want to hurt Rogers Holland, humiliate him. It wasn't until after we were married that she told me that she had had to break it off with him, and then——"

He paused impressively, took a swallow of wine.

"Then she said," he resumed, "that the very first dinner engagement we made must be here; she wanted Mr. Holland to know me and me to know him; there mustn't be any hurt feelings or silences or anything unexplained! That, I think," Andrew finished with satisfaction, "gives you a pretty good idea of what she's really like. It's"—he spoke reverently—"it's angelic!" he said. And catching his wife's eye, down the length of the table, he lifted his glass to her. Aline raised hers, blew him a kiss, and afterward the entire company toasted the bride and groom.

Dina drank nothing. She had been feeling physically upset all day and dared risk only a little chicken and some salad accompanied by the dry, crisp crackers and toasted breads which all these eating and drinking folk seemed to feel were helpful to reducing. It was therefore in a state of chill and weakness favorable for the wildest apprehension that she found herself accompanying the other women upstairs after the meal.

An enormous bedroom filled with comfortable chairs and brightened by a wood fire had been placed at their disposal; they settled themselves comfortably in the old-fashioned luxury, preening themselves like so many birds of paradise, gossiping so fast and furiously that Dina could remain quite silent among them, ignored.

Mrs. Bucket was here, unobtrusively going to and fro; she straightened Dina's dress with the air of a friendly old housekeeper fussing over one of the young ladies of the family.

"That was fine at dinner," she said in an undertone; "he was pleased, I know. Now when you leave, my dear, I'll take you into my room downstairs, and you can slip out of one dress and into the other with no trouble at all. I'll be looking out for you."

Dina sat in a big chair, shrinking back into the protection of its depth, watching the other women, listening to them, managing never quite to catch anyone's eye. But Aline, powdering her nose, touching the shining, flawless helmet of her black hair with a ringed hand, had no notion of letting her escape.

"How long have you known Rogers, Miss Cashman?"

"Not—very long," Dina answered hesitantly.

"Your people's friend?"

She smiled demurely.

"I hope so."

Aline rose, strolled across the room, stood at the hearth looking down at Dina.

"Tell me something about yourself," she said winningly. "You see, I happen to know Rogers Holland extremely well, and I don't know that I ever heard him mention your name before tonight."

Dina's heart was beating fast; she looked the other woman in
e eye.

"He could have," she said. And she added innocently, "Couldn't
?"

At this one of the other women laughed a little, and Dina saw
little wave of color creep up under the smooth ivory of Aline
avens' cheeks.

"You know Caroline Holland, of course?" she said.

"No, I don't," Dina answered.

"She doesn't know Caroline!" Aline exclaimed to the company
large. "You mustn't think it is strange that I'm so surprised,"
e said to Dina, "but I know Rogers extremely well. In fact, I
as engaged to him."

"He told me," Dina said.

"So that it seemed odd to me to find you here tonight—his ward,
: said, didn't he?—when he never had mentioned you to me."

"Well, Aline," said a stout, handsome young woman who had
en complaining bitterly of her slippers and now had them off and
as studying one attentively, "I can imagine myself being engaged
a man, and even breaking the engagement, without expecting
know absolutely everyone he knew!"

"Certainly," Aline agreed sharply, resenting the reflection upon
r common sense; "but I'm surprised, that's all. What did he tell
u about me?" she demanded with an amused glance about the
cle.

"That you were engaged and that you married someone else,"
ina answered simply.

"I think you have the rottenest manners, Aline, I've ever seen
my entire life," the stout woman said dreamily, trying on a
pper and wincing.

"Thank you, Jean," Aline said, sitting down and resting her head
ainst the back of a chair. She closed her eyes, and Dina could see
w long and sooty black were the lashes against her cheek. "I
1 having a simply lousy time," she observed incidentally. "It
uld really interest me, Jean," she pursued carelessly, "to know
st why I have rotten manners."

"Rogers told me you asked him to give this party," anothe
woman said reproachfully. "I think it was wonderful of Rogers t
do it after the way you treated him."

"How did I treat him, Lucy?" Aline asked, not opening her eye

"Well," began Lucy uncertainly. Dina could tell from her ton
that she was a good-natured soul who disliked fomenting troubl
"I mean, you did throw him down pretty hard," she said; "th
wedding date all set and everything. And we all know, no matte
who you happen to be married to, that Rogers just blindly adore
you."

"Can't help that." Aline opened her eyes, looked into space wit
the hint of a self-conscious smile on her lips. "I met Andy," sh
said eloquently.

"I wonder if Rogers is going to let us have some bridge; Pa
will simply get up and go home if he doesn't," a woman said in
bored voice.

" 'I met Andy!' " Dina heard old Mrs. Prince mutter under he
breath.

"D'you like him?" Aline was now demanding. "Now, tell m
everybody, don't you think he's really—no, but I mean, isn't h
really divine?"

"Magnificent," someone said obligingly.

"I want every one of you to tell me honestly and truly what sh
thinks of him," said Aline. "We knew each other exactly tw
weeks when we were married, you know. We were both simp
bowled over. I saw him lounging in a doorway with Phil Banks, an
I went straight over and asked Phil to introduce him. In two se
onds we were dancing; he simply held out his arms and I wer
into them. That was a Thursday, and we were married two wee
from that day. He paints—but wait until you see some of the po
traits! Everyone comes to him! He could do twice as much wor
as he does, but he's lazy, poor dear! And of course we're goin
to be broke—I mean absolutely broke—until he gets started here

"But, darling, you *can't!*" the bridge-playing wife said in a pityin
tone that poorly concealed the pleasure she felt at the idea.

"Don't worry about *us*," Aline said haughtily. Immediately sh

elted. "But you *do* like him?" she asked. The women, powdering
their noses, fluffing their hair, pressing lipsticks firmly against
their mouths, said flattering things. He was simply a darling; he
was wonderfully tall; he was pleasant; he had a lovely manner.
And does he know how to make love!" Aline said complacently.

Dina was for the moment forgotten, and she was presently glad
drift downstairs with the other women and find Mrs. Bucket
bout to come up again, in search of her.

"Hall is here with the car whenever you're ready," said Mrs.
Bucket.

"Oh, but I thought he said half-past ten!" Dina exclaimed, her
heart rising on a wave of relief.

"It's nearer eleven," Mrs. Bucket told her, smiling. "You can
y good night to Mr. Holland now if you like," she suggested.
Dina, who had been all ready for departure, was reminded of
her manners and went at once into the big drawing room, where
several card games were already in progress. Rogers was playing;
he glanced up as she came near him and stood for a moment looking over his shoulder. He was apparently unconscious of her
presence, concentrating on his play, but after a moment he threw
down two or three cards, saying in satisfaction:

"Doubled and vulnerable—eight hundred. That'll learn 'em,
Lucy! Nice bidding. And are you going, my dear?" he added,
rising to face Dina. "Good night, and thanks for coming. Did you
like your first dinner party?"

"I loved it," said Dina.

"Have you far to go?" Aline asked with an air of casualness.

"Almost to San José," Rogers answered for Dina.

"Go on with your game," Andrew Havens said, rising and coming forward. "I'll take Miss Cashman to her car."

"Andy," Aline wailed, "we just went down three, double and
all!"

"Too bad, darling," he said. "But you know I haven't the faintest idea what it means!"

"I'll take you out, Geraldine," Rogers said. "Your deal, Paul.
I not be a minute!"

Dina walked beside him to the hall. Mrs. Bucket was waiting.

"You'll go home with her, Bucket?"

"I will indeed, sir."

"You were perfect, my dear," Rogers said to Dina, "and yo carried off the honors of war splendidly. This"—he put an envelop into her hand—"is for you. Thank you very much, and my be wishes." He bowed.

"Nobody need go home with me," Dina said, suddenly tired an depressed.

"Bucket will go, of course. And I mean," he said, "to see Vere mother when she comes back from the East and have a talk wit her. I'm only sorry that I can't promise you much from it."

"Thank you." She felt desolate, alone, and outside again. Silent she went with Mrs. Bucket to the housekeeper's room and bega to discard her Cinderella finery for the street clothes that no looked cheap and tawdry.

"He was pleased, you could tell that," Mrs. Bucket said, shakin and folding the silver-and-white creation. "And you did look love at the head of the table, my dear. I was peeking in from the pantr and I thought you looked an innocent child among all those other Half of them are divorced, with children scattered about de knows where, or living with each other's husbands and wives. Yo looked the way a girl ought to look, innocent and young and in white, listening to them and turning your face one way an another—what's the matter?"

For Dina had taken a chair, spread her arms on the table, an put her head down upon them and was crying bitterly.

"You're tired, dearie!" the housekeeper said, a comforting han on her shoulder.

Dina looked up, trying to smile. She thought of the house which she must go, the dark, odorous bedroom in which Myr and Dooley would be asleep in a tangle of worn blankets an thick, dirty comforters; she thought of waking tomorrow to h own approaching and deepening problem. To leave this luxury a safety, warmth and space and plenty behind her, to go out alo into the dark seemed more than she could bear. But it had to faced; it had to be borne; it had to be solved somehow; she wouldn't die—no such luck! No, she would live, but not as those perfumed, exquisitely dressed women in the drawing room lived— not one of them—never to enter their charmed circle again. She would be alone, an outcast, with the responsibility of her child——

"I probably am tired," she said. "I'm sorry. I'm all right now."

Chapter 8

DINA AND MRS. BUCKET slipped quietly out of a side door, to find Hall and the car waiting. The looming, lighted bulk of the old Holland mansion faded away into the night; they coasted down the long avenue of trees.

"I wonder if I will ever see it again," Dina said half aloud.

"I had a feeling about you," Mrs. Bucket said unexpectedly. "That day a week ago when you first came to see Mr. Holland. I had it then. I thought that you had come to the house for a purpose and that you belonged there. Seeing you in the library with him gave me a terrible turn. It was as if she—his wife—had come back. She wasn't anything like you, but I had a feeling just the same. And tonight, seeing you so lovely at the head of the table—you had a good time, didn't you?" she interrupted herself to ask, as Dina did not speak.

"Oh yes—lovely." The girl's voice was lifeless. "Mrs. Havens is beautiful, isn't she?" she asked in turn.

"She's a beautiful devil," the other woman said. "I've never liked her, not from the first minute I saw her, and that would be fifteen or sixteen years ago. She was having parties with the other debutantes; I couldn't stand her. From the beginning she's been cold and hard and spoiled. She's got two children! What does she care! The girl's with old Mrs. Pollock; the boy goes to military school and summer camps. His father takes him around sometimes."

"The father's living, then?"

"Both her husbands are living. I don't know," Mrs. Bucket said in a dissatisfied tone, "what makes a man want to marry a woman like that, but they all do.

"Look at Mr. Holland now," she went on, as Dina did not speak. "You'd think he'd have better sense than to break his heart for her! Oh, I know, you think he's a little queer, being so fat, with his stamps and his glasses. But that's just the outside. There never was a finer boy than he was, twenty years ago. But life twisted him and hurt him, and he tries to get back at it. He was married, you know, to a quiet, cold sort of woman—very small and delicate always, and dying—you might say—from her wedding day. One poor little baby she had after another, four of them, and they all died. Two days—three days—and the little things wilted like flowers. This was a dreadful house in those years, for he wanted a son and she did too, and they came to see that there'd never be a healthy child. She lived eight or nine years after the last one, but she never was well. He watched her and cared for her; that was his life——"

"He loved her?" Dina put in.

"Yes, I think he did," the housekeeper said judicially; "but her being so ill ended his life, in a way. He got so that he was always here at home, and when she died five years ago he didn't change his ways at all. Not"—the woman ended with sudden bitterness— "until *she* came along!"

"Mrs. Havens?"

"Well, she was Mrs. Rosenstirn then. But she took the name of Pollock back. Everyone knew her by that. He'd known her all his life. I can tell you my heart stopped when I saw the way things were going."

"Mrs. Bucket," the girl said suddenly, "you know Vere Holland, don't you?"

"I do indeed. He comes here now and then. But Mr. Holland and his mother—she's taken the name Holland back again—don't get along. She's another of the Aline sort," said Mrs. Bucket.

"And do you think he—Vere"—Dina asked, trembling—"do you think he is *good*?"

"Vere? I don't know that I'd trust Vere too far," the woman answered thoughtfully. "There isn't a mean bone in his body, I'll say that for him, but his mother's spoiled him, and she's talked a lot of worldly nonsense at him too. It isn't right that any woman should talk of a man as she talks to him of his father. I've met Mr. Van Holland, and you wouldn't want to meet a nicer man. What's the matter with you?"

The question came suddenly, for Dina had leaned forward in the car and by the flashing of passing lights the other woman could see the tragedy in her face.

"Will you help me, Mrs. Bucket?" Dina asked breathlessly. "I'm in trouble. It was that that first made me go see Mr. Holland. I've no one else to ask; I don't dare tell my father or mother; I don't know what to do!"

"What's the matter?" The housekeeper asked again. The change in her tone made Dina's heart sink. It was withdrawn, cautious. But Dina could not stop now.

"You see"—she stammered eagerly—"I know Vere Holland! I was trying to find him; I *have* to find him. But now, now I don't know what to do, whether to follow him—whether to go to New Haven if he's at Yale—or whether it would do any good. He doesn't want me to come; I know that. But what else can I do?"

"Vere?" Mrs. Bucket demanded in a heavy, incredulous voice.

"Yes! We went about together all through November. We went up to the mountains for the winter sports. And now he's gone away, and I have to see him; I have to talk to him! But I can't— I can't wreck his life."

Her voice sank. There was a silence, terrible to Dina.

"You that looked like a little girl," Mrs. Bucket presently murmured, as if she spoke to herself.

"I know, I know!" Dina said in a sick voice.

"Does Mr. Holland know?"

"I told him."

"And he said?"

"He said that Vere's mother was a hard woman and that she would try to make him think it wasn't true."

"Yes, and she will too," Mrs. Bucket said. "And you want to go find him, wherever he is, and tell him he's got to marry you, is that it?" she asked.

"What else can I do?"

"He'll deny it," the housekeeper said, thinking aloud. Dina's whole body jerked as if it had been struck.

"He couldn't do that!"

"They do," said the other woman dryly. "All you have to do, my dear," she went on, on a long sigh, "is give in. That's all the girl in the case can do. Then they'll tell her what a brave modern girl she is, not afraid of all the Victorian prudes. Then they'll say that they'll always love her, always respect her all the more for it. And then they'll go their ways, and she can begin to cry."

"I've cried," Dina said in a silence. "Oh, you can't say anything to me that I haven't said a thousand times to myself, lying awake in the night," she rushed on. "I know what a fool—what a *fool* I was! Almost from the beginning I knew that he hadn't anything to lose, that I was the one who would pay! Only for a few days I fooled myself; I thought he'd come to me, that he'd talk of a quiet wedding, of a secret wedding maybe.

"But he never came. And then he sent me a note from Palm Springs that he and his mother were going East. By that time I knew."

"Well, God help us all," the older woman said, sighing again. There was a moment of silence.

"You wrote him what you thought?"

"Not—not in words, exactly. But he couldn't mistake it."

"And he didn't answer that?"

"Yes, just a week ago. He said not to worry and that his mother was sure everything was all right and that he might be going to South America with his father."

"Well, he's not going to South America with his father, or I'd have heard of it," said Mrs. Bucket definitely. "But if he wrote you that, it amounts to the same thing. She's told him—his mother's told him—to put the whole thing out of his head and not worry about it. She gets home tomorrow. I think you ought to see her."

"Oh, I couldn't!" Dina said, shuddering.

"You have to take every chance of straightening it out for the sake of your child, my dear," the other woman said soberly. "You've got the child to think of now. He gave you a ring? He wrote you something about getting married?"

"No, nothing like that," Dina said, frightened. It was a fearful thought that one had to produce this sort of thing, show it—to whom? In a lawyer's office? In court?

"You're how old?"

"Nineteen."

"Nineteen, God help us! And you've a mother?"

"A father and mother and six brothers and sisters. The littlest one is only three, and there was another baby who died last year."

"And what's your father do?"

"Well, nothing mostly. We get state help and milk, and I work in a grocery, and over Christmas my brother got ten dollars a week delivering bundles."

"H'm!" commented Mrs. Bucket. "How long were you and Vere going together?"

"Only a few weeks. Then he asked me to go up to the Sierras, skiing. It was so wonderful—all of us up there in the snow, fires in the cabins, and such marvelous meals!"

"And you went every week end?"

"No, only once. We were planning to go again, we were planning so many things—talking of being together always——"

They were reaching the unsavory neighborhood of Bonita now. Mrs. Bucket looked out of the window into darkness and disorder with here and there a dim street light dangling, accentuating rather than breaking the blackness.

"I asked Hall to leave me at the station," said Dina, "because we live across the track and beyond the dump, and I don't believe a big heavy car like this could get in there."

"We'll have to do something about all this," the housekeeper said hurriedly as they parted. "I don't know what it will be, but there is some way out. Perhaps I could get you a housemaid's job with me, and you'd be hidden away in that big house——"

"Oh, if you would, if you would!" Dina said, clinging to her hand. "If this time was only over, if it was this time next year, I'd make it up to you! Just not to have my mother and father know, and my little sisters—they've always thought I was sort of an example——"

"Don't cry. I'll see what I can do. You know that he talked this over with his mother?"

"Vere? Oh yes. He wrote me that he had. But nothing serious. Just sort of joking. He didn't send me his address in the East. I didn't know where to send a letter. The one I did send went to Palm Springs, but I didn't know whether they'd know where to forward another after he left. I was so frightened and sick all the time and so afraid that time would go by—and go by——"

She stopped, swallowing, her mouth dry.

"I said in my letter," she went on, as the other woman made no comment, "that I'd have to come East, I'd have to get out—go away somewhere. But he didn't say anything about that! 'My mother says that it's silly to worry; nothing's going to happen.' That was what he said."

"That's what she would say," commented Mrs. Bucket grimly.

"Thank you a thousand times for being so good to me!" Dina had to climb past her companion to leave the car, and suddenly Mrs. Bucket drew her down and kissed her wet face.

"Mr. Holland has your address?" she asked. "Yes, I know he has. You'll hear from me. Good night!"

It was midnight. Dina picked her way carefully through wide, shallow puddles and heaps of refuse. The sharp, acrid dry smell of pigs floated on the cold night air; the moon shone down upon the shanties of Railway Flats, humble roofs set at all angles, tangled sheds and fences and gates. The road, a muddy track that meandered aimlessly, was unpaved. The only sidewalks were occasional planks, propped on rocks and tipping in the mire. There was no light in the Cashman house.

Long familiar with its limitations, Dina noiselessly entered the kitchen and in the warm atmosphere of grease and pipe smoke and coffee began rapidly to undress. She was clad only in her undermost garment and carrying the others over her bare arm when she went into the bedroom. A little groping under the curtain that hung at an angle across one corner of the room secured her night-gown, a limp soft string, and she pulled it on, reached under the bed for her precious shoe box and jar of cold cream, in the dark cleaned her face of cosmetics and brushed her mop of curled and tight-pinned hair. A dim shaft of light from the adjoining room and a step beside her made her start.

"Mama? Goodness, you scared me!"

Mrs. Cashman was carrying a candle; she shaded its light with a lean, ungroomed hand.

"Dina, have a good time?" she whispered.

"Oh, fine." It all seemed like a dream now and almost as hard to recall as a dream. Fires and carpets; servants moving about; women bare of arms and breasts in exquisite robes of lace and brocade and velvet; jewels, real jewels; silver candlesticks and flowers.

"Where were you?"

"Up Burlingame way." Mama thought, of course, that it had been just one more dining and dancing party with the neighborhood group. Dina hoped she never would think differently.

"What I got up to tell you was that Lou was real sick," her mother said. "I moved her in here because nothing would do but that she had to sleep in Dina's bed."

"Sick!" Dina stood still in dismay. Lou was her favorite among the sisters; the pale, anemic, undernourished small girl of ten had always seemed to draw actual strength and vitality from Dina. Myrna was getting very independent; Dooley was a bold, hand-some child who needed little encouragement in her vigorous fight for good times, popularity, movies, gum, and ice-cream cones; El'ner was still a baby at seven. But little Lou really needed mother-ing, warming, spoiling, and Dina had made an especial pet of her. In return Lou blindly adored her big sister.

"What was the matter?"

"Oh, her cold is worse and she felt real hot and her dinner came up. We had some pork sausage and hot cakes, but she didn't eat much. Dooley said they'd had some cake over to Bridges'."

"Ah, the poor little thing!" Dina, by candlelight, sank on her knees beside the bed, her practiced hand inside the collar of Lou's flannel pajamas. "She's good and damp; she hasn't any fever," she whispered.

"No, I think she's all right. But my gracious, what crying and carrying-on when she came in for supper and found you'd gone! She didn't want anyone but Dina; I think she cried for a good hour. Pop was in here and everybody, trying to comfort her. She certainly thinks the world and all of you."

"Lou, my little old sweet," Dina murmured, her cheeks against the damp, cool little face. The drowsy child stirred and mumbled contentedly. "Has she been coughing, Mama?" Dina asked.

"Not like she was last night. Well, I'll go back," Mrs. Cashman said, yawning. "I'm glad you had a good time."

"You came back, Dina," Lou muttered, clinging tight.

"Of course I came back, you silly! What were you crying about?"

"Becuz I missed you so." The thick, hoarse little voice dwindled away. "Don't go 'way again, Dina," Lou whispered. "I cry when you're not here."

"I'll be right here." Dina was kneeling beside the bed; now she drew an old blanket about her shoulders and settled on her knees, holding Lou's little relaxed hand against her cheek.

Beyond the window that was just above the bed winter moonlight was flooding the Flats. It lent beauty even to their griminess and disorder; it silvered the line of empty freight cars on the tracks and lay kindly on the jumbled humble roofs and sheds; the shadows of the fences were like lace. There were few stars; the moon had the great pale-gray vault of the sky to itself. Far off to the east the long line of the massive shoulders of the Sierras swam in misty vagueness, sky and mountains mingling in the wash of unearthly whiteness.

Dina, holding her little sister's hand, knelt motionless for a long while. She thought, with an ache as keen as physical pain in her heart, of this child's love for her and that she had betrayed her. Lou needed her; her mother needed her; Dooley and Myrna, just beginning to grow up in the disorder and danger of the Flats, needed her.

With all its poverty, crampedness, and ugliness, still this was home. These were the rooms she knew, the chairs and beds and plates and towels; these were her own people. They turned to her. Dina could do it; Dina could fix it; Dina could make them laugh, could find the right touch to make any meal satisfying, could solve their school ploblems.

She had known her moods of irritation, of bitter discontent. But they had been passing moods. Under them and around them all had been the satisfaction of being Dina Cashman, pretty and strong, capable and popular, and free to plan any future, no matter how glorified, and hope for any change, no matter how improbable.

And now the curse of womankind lay heavy upon her. Now she must carry within her for long, slow months the very proof of weakness, of unforgivable stupidity. Life would not forgive her and time would not forgive her. For that one hour of forgetting the law she would pay all her life long, through all the days to come, and an innocent human being would pay too; be shamed, be marked, be set apart.

A child! Her spirit writhed away from the thought of it. A little boy like Donny or a tiny, delicate girl like Lou, the Lou whose small, sweating body was lying against her arm. Small shoes to be tied; small mouth into which cereal must be spooned; little questions coming along, harder and harder to answer. Her child!

She had thought of having a baby, as all girls do. She had talked with the other girls, walking home from school in the early teens, deciding eagerly what qualities a husband must have, what his profession must be, what the first boy and the first girl should be named. But she had never thought of motherhood as coming to her this way.

No boy, in all the years that lay between those little-girl days and today, had ever been allowed any familiarities with Dina Cashman. She was the untouchable; there need be no overtures wasted on her, because the boys knew, Tom and Stew and Joe and Willie and Ward knew, that such advances would avail them nothing. She had thought it out herself; determined upon her course; they might as well understand it.

But there had been no thinking, no reasoning, no plan when Vere had come along. Kneeling in the dark, looking with wide, tragic eyes at the panorama of the Flats in the white moonlight, Dina told herself tonight that from the moment of their meeting she had never put Vere in the category of the other boys. His remoteness from her, his membership in a class to which no other person she had ever known could lay claim, his sureness when lunch and dinner checks were presented and waiters tipped, the very coat he wore and the big gloves stuffed so carelessly into the coat pocket—these things had marked him apart, had lent to his personality a glamour and a fascination. But then why analyze the details, why think out the road, when details signified so little and she had taken the road so blindly?

Geraldine Cashman, whose mother and father were proud of her, hoping for her courage and wit and capability a better fortune than theirs had been. Geraldine Cashman, telling Art and Myrna of the days ahead, promising them better times, a big house with a bathroom and a garden, a new car, a sitting room with no beds in it!

"Oh, there must be a God!" she whispered. "There must be, or people wouldn't go on praying to Him! O God, help me out just this once! Don't make me go away from home; give me a break! Don't let them all be ashamed of me, asking Mama what Dina did and why she had to go away! Help me, help me, help me!"

Chapter 9

TEN DAYS LATER Dina sat in Mrs. Bucket's pleasant downstairs room, finishing a long talk with the housekeeper. Outside, upon the dark old gardens of the Holland house, the warmth and light of a glorious hot spring day were doing their best to make an impression. Heavy old acacia trees had burst into pompons of gold against the foliage of the eucalyptus trees and pines; the new leaves of the lilacs were pale green about the scented plumes of the blossoms.

With two well-shuffled packs of playing cards and some unfinished knitting Mrs. Bucket had a little bouquet of wild flowers on her desk. Buttercups, satiny poppies, grasses tipped with tiny starry bloom, a branch of flowering peach in full blossom.

"I picked those on a walk yesterday; I love the first flowers every year," she told Dina.

Dina sat sober and quiet, facing her. The talk had been a serious one; they had differed at its beginning but they were in agreement now. Dina had steadily maintained her point; she could not come as a chambermaid, as assistant housekeeper to the Holland mansion.

"If you knew how I'd love it, Mrs. Bucket, and what it would mean to me to get away from everything and to be here with you!" Dina had said more than once. "But—don't you see?—I can't. It's too near my mother and father and all the people I know.

And there might be a chance—there'd always be a chance that he might come in—Vere. It's his uncle's house. And I couldn't bear—I couldn't bear ever to see him, to have him know where I was or what I was doing."

"But then where will you go, Dina?" the woman asked.

"I have a hundred dollars. I'll go—oh, not too far. Los Angeles, maybe, or maybe San Francisco. Some place where I can get lost, where I can work, where there's a big hospital that has free wards. It seems a pretty poor start for anybody," the girl finished, with a smile that her suddenly watering eyes belied, "but it's the best I can do."

"You'll get a job?"

"Yes. I'll stay here until—oh, April maybe. I'll stay home as long as I can. And then I'll go away. You see, I get eighteen a week at the grocery. That's all Mama has except what Art gives her when he gets after-school jobs and Pop's relief check the first of the month. That only pays the rent and maybe gas for the car. Anyway, it's always gone in the first week. So they need me. And someday," the girl said, with her pale face and tear-rimmed eyes suddenly filled with a look of determination, "I'll come back, and I'll really help them all—Myrna and Dooley and Lou. I don't know how, but I can live this down—I can live it down somehow and begin all over again."

"Being sorry, Dina, *is* living it down. Being sorry gives you something you never would have had if you didn't make the mistakes," Mrs. Bucket said.

"I wish I could believe that! I wish I didn't feel as if all our lives were going to be hurt." She seemed to Mrs. Bucket years older than the girl who had first come there less than three weeks ago. There was a quiet acceptance, a quiet resoluteness about her today that to the older woman, although she could not have defined them, were infinitely touching.

"What I'm wondering about," the housekeeper said, "is how you can get a job, the way you'll be, by April or May. I had a long talk with Mr. Holland about it," she went on, "and I think he's going to ask you to let him help you out, for a while anyway. You should take it, my dear," she went on, knitting busily now, "for though I know it's hard to be under obligations to anyone, you have to remember that his family owes you a—a—an apology. His family has done you a wrong."

"No, no, no," Dina said in a weary voice, her eyes staring out of the window. "I did it myself."

"Vere's twenty-four," Mrs. Bucket went on. "What he ought to be is horsewhipped and stood up before a priest and married to you. What he ought to be is taught his responsibility to his child. My God, when I think what a child is, the way my husband and I felt about our first one, that we lost!"

"I don't think either one of us thought much of the responsibility," Dina put in faintly as Mrs. Bucket, knitting furiously, stopped short.

"It doesn't matter what you did, you were both in it, and to have you driven out of your home, away from your mother and father when they need you and when you need them, and to have her—his mother—writing that she refuses to have anything to do with the matter, I tell you it's all unfair!" the older woman said vigorously.

"Did she write that?"

"That's what she wrote. And that the boy had some—I don't know whether she said 'chivalrous' or 'noble' or what she said— some notion that he was responsible. Some notion, indeed!" the housekeeper repeated.

Dina sat silent, her very soul racked.

"But then why doesn't he come back?" she presently asked. "He knows, he must know, how I feel! I wouldn't want to do anything that would hurt him—that would change his life. But just to have him to talk to——" Her voice suddenly thickened.

"I don't understand it and I don't understand *them,*" Mrs. Bucket said. "I know Mr. Holland wrote her, and I know he feels that she and Vere should make it right by you. I don't know what he felt when *he* wrote, but I can tell you *her* letter made him mad. I've never seen him so mad!"

Again Dina found nothing to say. The shame of being discussed, pitied, casually abandoned by the man she had so loved kept her silent.

"I'll not die," she thought, "and time will go by, years will go by, and there will be other things to think about and talk about."

"I want you to promise to write me, to keep in touch with me," said Mrs. Bucket. "I loved Vere when he was a little boy. Once when Mr. Holland was away"—she hesitated, went on in a somewhat hurried tone—"once when he was away Vere came here to stay; he was a lovely little boy then. Your child will be his child."

"You love him, don't you?" Dina said and then, without waiting for her companion to speak, asked, with her forehead faintly furrowed and her narrowed eyes fixed on space: "You think we ought to marry?"

"Well, of course you ought to marry!" the older woman answered promptly.

"Even doing—what that would do, to him?" Dina hesitated.

"It would do nothing to him that wouldn't be for his good!" Mrs. Bucket exclaimed. "It would do nothing to him that wouldn't bring him to his senses! The nonsense they talk about his position and what his friends would think, when a child's rights ought to be the one and only consideration! But he'll get his come uppance, Dina," she went on seriously, with that hint of the occult in her manner that she had once before displayed. "He'll live to know what he's doing, and then God help him!"

"I don't know how to thank you, Mrs. Bucket," Dina said, getting to her feet. "I don't know what I would have done if you hadn't been so kind to me."

"He wants to see you," the housekeeper said with a jerk of her head toward the front of the house.

"Mr. Holland?"

"Yes, he said he wanted to see you before you left."

"Shall I go into the library?"

"And tell him to send for me if he wants me."

Dina crossed a narrow hall, crossed the shadowy wider hall,

knocked on the library door. When she opened it she saw Rogers Holland just as she had first seen him, busy with his stamps, a magnifying glass assisting his strong eyeglasses.

"Come in, come in, Geraldine," he said. "Sit down. Did you talk to Mrs. Bucket?"

"I've just been talking to her."

Rogers sat back, squared himself about a little in his chair, fixed his eyes on the pipe he began to pack with tobacco from a limp old leather pouch.

"And what's the plan?" he said.

"I am going to stay at home and keep my job until April anyway," Dina told him. "And then I'll leave with some excuse and go to some city—San Francisco, maybe, and—and do the best I can."

"And what will you live on?"

"Well . . ." She began gallantly enough, but her voice wavered as she spoke and grew faint. "I have the money you gave me," she said; "it was much too much, but it will carry me for two months or more. I can live on a dollar a day. I can get some job somewhere, to make beds or wash dishes. And in July I'll go to the hospital."

"And leave the baby there to be adopted?"

"No," she said. "I've been thinking about that, and I won't do that."

"Won't?"

"No. I was thinking of Mama," Dina said with some difficulty, "and of how little she was ever able to do for us and yet how she's always loved us——" She stopped, her head held high, her mouth resolutely steadied.

"People love adopted children," Rogers said, watching her.

"I've done enough to hurt him," the girl said very low. "I'll not let anyone have him."

"But that's a heavy handicap, my dear. For a girl to make herself responsible for a child, take it about. You'll find yourself bitterly criticized for that."

"I wouldn't do that. I'd find some kind woman who liked babies and board him with her. It wouldn't cost much, and I could see him, and he would be mine."

"And come back to the family?"

"If I could. I'd live at home again, and get a job, and see that my little sisters had a break."

"Never telling your people?"

"Not if I could help it, no. I'll say, in April, that I've had a job offered me somewhere—somewhere far away. If it was just San Francisco, Pop would want to take me up and find out all about it. Then I'd write. I'd manage somehow to have the letters postmarked Chicago or Minneapolis—places Pop couldn't follow. And then, afterward, I'd come back."

"And nobody'd talk about you, suspect what was going on?"

"Not down our way," Dina said with a sad little smile. "Everyone's working and everyone's thinking about money or fun. Oh, they gossip a lot," she admitted, "but not about anyone coming or going. We're all moving round down there anyway, going after jobs or changing jobs. Only one person there knows."

"And that's——?"

"That's a boy named Tom O'Connor. He's wanted to marry me for some time," the girl said unemotionally. "I told him because I had to tell someone; I was frantic. I didn't know what to do. But I feel differently now."

She looked composed, pale, and resolute, and yet strangely young and helpless, sitting in her big chair. The shabby suit she wore with such an air, the plain hat, and worn gloves were well in accord with her colorless, serious face and her clasped, quiet hands.

"What did Tom say?" Rogers asked.

"He was sorry for me. I could tell he was terribly sorry for me. He thought Vere ought to be made to——" She paused. "But I told him that there was no use talking that way," she finished with a wearied sigh.

"I thought the same," Rogers said briefly.

"I think now that Vere never thought of it the way I did. I know he feels badly," Dina offered after a moment. "But I don't think marrying ever came into his head, really, any more than it would have with a little boy. I was the one who talked about that, and then he would agree with me—oh, sure, we'd be married when we were older and he had graduated from the law school at Yale."

"Even so, I suppose a boy might change his line of thought," Rogers suggested.

"I suppose so," Dina said, as he seemed to expect a reply.

"You lost your friend Tom? Were you engaged to him?"

"Oh no. I never would have married him, I think. But now he seems to be the person that's kindest, that understands." Her eyes watered although she tried to smile. "I've just," Dina said in a stronger tone, straightening her back and making herself look directly at him, "I've just made a mess of everything and hurt everyone! But I'm not going to let it go on this way. I told Mrs. Bucket I'd keep in touch with her, and I will; I'm not going away for a while, anyway. And I want to thank you for the money, because that's what I'm going to start on. That's *all* I have to start on."

He was silent for a full minute, watching her. It was a hard minute for Dina, for she felt rather deflated after her burst of determined bravery and anxious only to get away, to be alone, to have them stop talking about her and let her decide herself what she must do and face what she must face.

"And you're nineteen, Geraldine," the man said thoughtfully.

"Twenty in August."

"I suppose that if I offered you money, enough to keep you going without work and without worry, you'd not accept it?"

Her surprised eyes met his.

"But I would!" she said. "I would because of—because of the baby. I have to think of him." She added the last phrases hesitatingly, after thought.

"Then we'll talk of that later. What I'm trying to say to you, I suppose," Rogers said, "is that you have had a very unfair deal. Oh, I know, I know," he interrupted himself hastily, "that girls know everything nowadays, that you were old enough to know better, and that women even today have to pay the bill for this sort of thing. But when I got all this in the mail"—he turned aside to pick up a slim sheaf of papers—"it made me pretty—damn—mad. I've heard from Caroline," he said.

"Vere's mother?"

"Vere's mother. She sent me a wire first and then a letter. Now she's here."

"She's come to California!"

"Yes. She's here. Come over here to this chair, Geraldine." He indicated the seat opposite his own at the desk. "That's the wire," he said, pushing the yellow sheet toward her.

Dina read it slowly, twice.

"Story preposterous," it read. "Advise you to have nothing to do with party you mention. Caroline."

The girl swallowed with a dry throat. She looked at her companion expectantly, seeming to find nothing to say.

"Meanwhile I had written," Rogers said. "I wrote that I had met you, that I thought you were a nice girl, that you were very young. I said that I had seen the boy's letters to you and that there was no question in my mind that—well, that things were as you had stated them to be. I advised her to come home and bring Vere with her. Her answer was to walk in here day before yesterday. I'd not seen Caroline, except now and then in other people's houses, for months.

"She sat there where you're sitting now and we went into the whole thing. I told her my honest opinion, that the only salvation for Vere was to stand by the girl he had said he loved. The very idea drove her frantic. His career, his whole life, his invitations to Palm Beach, to Oyster Bay next summer, everything lost! Her idea was that there must be someone who would gladly marry you for a little money, and she proposed to send me a check. The check came this morning, made out to me, with this letter."

He picked up a thick, large piece of paper scrawled upon in a bold, spreading hand.

" 'My dear Rogers,' " he read. " 'I have always been interested in your charity cases and would be glad to have you use this money wherever you see fit.' You see," Rogers said, laying down the letter, "she runs no risk of being identified with Vere's affair. And she encloses a check for two hundred and fifty dollars."

Dina's face was blazing; her throat was closed; she could not speak.

"Caroline was always largehearted," Rogers observed dryly. "But remember, Geraldine," he went on in another tone, "ninety-nine mothers out of a hundred would act in exactly the same way, no matter what their positon. She happens to be a particularly cold-blooded woman, ambitious for her son. But the general maternal idea, I believe, is to ignore the woman who has led an innocent boy astray and forget the whole matter!"

"I understand." Dina had to clear her throat to make herself audible. "I understand, of course," she added, "that it *would* spoil all her plans for him. But I'm surprised—I'm surprised at Vere," she finished in a low tone, as if she spoke to her own thoughts.

"They've talked Vere into this, or rather they've blustered him into thinking as they do," the man said. "They've told him that what you fear very probably isn't true and that all boys get into scrapes like this, and the simplest way out of a bad business is to let Dad pay the bills and next time be a little more careful about taking strange girls on parties."

A red-hot wind seemed to be touching Dina's naked skin. She was breathing a little hard, her eyes fixed, her mouth firmly shut.

"Now Caroline," said Rogers, "is right to this extent. There *is* a man ready to marry you. It's for you to say how you feel about that."

"You mean Tom," she said. "Tom O'Connor? No. Not if I have to scrub floors! Not if I had to beg! Not after Vere Holland won't have me, to go to anyone as fine and good and straight as Tom!"

Rogers fitted his short, square finger tips together and looked at them thoughtfully as he spoke.

"I wasn't thinking of Tom," he said. "I was thinking of somebody entirely different. You were here the other night and played the part of hostess," the man went on, his eyes narrowed, his gaze fixed on her face. "I put you at the head of my table, and I liked your looks there. Thinking it over afterward, I said to Mrs. Bucket, who, by the way, is one of my best friends, that I saw no reason why you shouldn't stay here. There's plenty of room—we aren't using half the rooms in this house—and I said, 'She can wait for her child and make her plans for what she wants to do afterward.'

"Mrs. Bucket agreed that it would be perfectly possible, but on one condition——"

"But I've just been talking to her," Dina broke in impulsively, "and while I'm more grateful than I can say to you for thinking of it, don't you see—since it was Vere——"

"But wait a minute," he interrupted in his turn. "You haven't heard Mrs. Bucket's condition. 'Mr. Holland,' she said, 'ask her to marry you.' I thought she was joking, of course. I'm more than twice your age; I've been a widower for five years. To you I seem a fat old man."

Dina had shrunk back in her chair; her face was scarlet.

"I thought about it," the man said. "I thought what a young figure would mean in this house—someone at table with me, someone reporting on the garden or the news or the trouble in the kitchen. It was a completely new idea to me, but it grew on me. It grew on me until I came to see that I would like the arrangement very much."

"Oh, you are very kind," Dina said breathlessly, "but I couldn't let you! You know all about me—your friends would know—they'd never like me and never forget! I couldn't—I'm not smart enough to talk the way you talk or even to—to ask proper questions. I—I—I *couldn't.*"

"You seem to feel," he observed, unruffled, "very much as I felt. I was flabbergasted for a whole day! Two days! I've been in love for twenty years with one woman. You met her the other night— Aline. I'll be in love with her—or in hate with her"—the man interrupted himself to change the phrase bitterly—"as long as I live. I've got her under my skin. What she says, what she does, is supremely, maddeningly important to me; I can't help it. I despise her, and she is the only person in the world that matters.

"If you were here, Geraldine, I'd think of her less. You'd be company for me. You'd never be my wife; you'd be more like a daughter; you'd be voices and footsteps and opening doors and closing them in the house. But just your being here would"—his voice sank to a metallic, revengeful undertone. He was not thinking of Dina now, perhaps hardly conscious of her presence—"begin to repay what I owe her," he said ominously. "She hates you already. And he—that handsome artist nonentity she married—helped it along the other night. I could have blessed him for it! After you left he began it. Who were you? Did we all realize how unusual the molding of your face—or some other half-baked artist's phrase—was? He was anxious to paint you.

"I'd have him paint you!" Rogers added with a chuckle. His face, flushed with bitterness, reminded Dina of her first impression of him—a great spider in a web. But as suddenly as he had gone into the mood he escaped from it. "What do you think?" he asked.

"That—that I couldn't let you do it! It's not your fault! It's not your responsibility!" Dina said slowly.

"Don't imagine," Rogers began again, "that your life here would be particularly pleasant. I'm not a pleasant person. I'm twenty-one years older than you are. This is a gloomy house, with a tragedy in it—the tragedy of a sick woman's life, of lost children. The rain falls here and the trees creak, and there'd be nobody in the house of your age or your interests. You could read Dickens and Trollope and Scott if you liked, putter in the garden with McPherson and the Mexican boys. But you'd be lonely. You'd be cheated. You'd be condemned to life with a cranky, unhappy, frustrated old man."

"I'd have my child," Dina said steadily.

"Yes, that's another point. That's the point I'm counting on to persuade you. The child will be a Holland after all. He'll have his rightful name and his chance. For a good many years we hoped there'd be Holland children in this house." Rogers went on, his eyes absent. "My wife was a delicate pale girl when I married her, and I think that in eleven years she never had one single day of real health. Our poor little babies breathed for a few minutes, went their way.

"This child of yours would be born in wedlock, legally mine. Let

Caroline Holland say what she would, she couldn't deny him that right."

"She'd—she'd tell everyone!" Dina stammered, the room dizzily going around her.

"Tell everyone that Vere wouldn't play the man, that the Holland money—the money I'm to leave someday—is going *not* to him but to his son, *my* son whom he'll never have the right to claim?" Rogers countered.

"No," the girl slowly admitted. "She'd never do that; she couldn't do that." And then, in sudden tears: "Mr. Holland, then you don't think Vere will come back—Vere will never know how much I need him!"

He made no answer. But as her brimming eyes were raised to his she saw in the half-smile, half-frown on his face no hope for her.

There was time for no more. The library door was quietly opened by Mrs. Bucket, who came to her employer's side.

"Mrs. Holland," she said.

"Oh. Ask her to come in," Rogers replied quietly.

Dina had not time for more than a sensation of terror, a wild impulse to escape somehow, to get away at all costs, when a woman came into the library, gave her one careless, scornful glance in passing, and took possession of a chair between her own chair and that of Rogers Holland.

"Come in, come in, Caroline," Rogers, rising, said lazily, amiably. "That's it. Sit down."

"I had your letter this morning," the woman said abruptly.

"I thought we could talk things over. Caroline, Miss Cashman," Rogers said. "Geraldine, this is Mrs. Holland."

"Orkman said it was a threatening letter."

"Oh, you saw Orkman?"

"I telephoned him and read it to him." Except for the slightest inclination of her head and a cold stare, she had paid no attention whatsoever to Dina.

"And he thought it was threatening," Rogers murmured.

"He said I was under no obligation at all in the matter, that it was entirely optional with me, coming here at all."

"Surely you knew that, Caroline?"

"Certainly I knew it!" said Caroline Holland impatiently.

"Still, I don't quite see where the threats come in," Rogers mused.

"He said, 'He isn't threatening you, is he?' He used that expression."

"Oh, I see. But you came anyway."

They hated each other—these two. Dina lost consciousness of the chill of terror that had shaken her in a sort of terrible fascination.

"I came," said Mrs. Holland, "because I want to be done with this business once and for all. It is a brazen attempt to involve my son in something of which he is entirely innocent. He hardly knows this girl. You must excuse me," said the hard voice as its owner turned to Dina, "but you know yourself that that is the truth!"

A hard voice and a hard woman. Beautifully groomed, seeming, as far as the copper-dyed hair and the enameled face were concerned, to be sculptured rather than human—a woman in whose ears pearls were snugly placed, on whose beautiful manicured hands were displayed two large rings, whose furs wrapped her slender shoulders and touched her proud chin, whose tailored suit was of the correct length and style, and whose aristocratic narrow feet were lifted on high-heeled slippers.

Beautiful, yes, she was really beautiful, Dina thought, with the very essence of haughty, confident, and insolent beauty. The girl could not find the words for it, but she knew what it was and what she might expect from Vere's mother.

"My son," Caroline Holland said, "was simply stupefied with amazement when he understood what all this was about. He is—you know how young he is, Rogers; you know how completely unfitted he is to deal with a situation like this!"

"Yet the situation has to be dealt with, doesn't it, Caroline?" Rogers said blandly.

"A boy that age," she said, "faced with a thing like this! He aged. He aged overnight. I never saw anything like it. 'I don't know what to do!' he kept saying."

"He didn't come West, did he?"

"He couldn't." She hesitated, spoke irresolutely. "We've had trouble enough," she continued, "keeping him from being dropped from college, without running any risk of his asking for a leave. Not to come home to this sort of outrageous accusation and scandal!"

"I think we ought to think of Geraldine as well as of Vere, Caroline," the man said. His pudgy hand moved to the papers on his desk.

"Of whom? Oh, of—of *her!*" Her contemptuous look moved to Dina, moved away. "Certainly we should," she agreed sharply, "but not at a cost of his career, his whole life! During the Christmas holidays, while we were at Palm Springs, we met the Worthingtons—you know the Philadelphia Hosworth Worthingtons; she was Miriam Hosworth. Kathryn, the daughter, goes to Selwyn's in Virginia—well, that's neither here nor there. But she's simply devoted to him, has asked him down for the Easter holidays—all that. It would have been simply *ridiculous* for him to come West with me now. What was he supposed to have done if he had?"

"He might have married the mother of his child," Rogers answered simply.

"Oh well!" Caroline Holland said with a sniff. The sniff said plainly, "I don't believe one word of it!" Aloud she said, "Oh, I know you have some letters of his, and hers which I've kept. But Orkman says there's not one whit of evidence there. I'm sorry; I'm wretched over the whole thing. But that isn't the way out. We'll have," Vere's mother went on in a lowered, reasonable tone, "to make some provision, and you'll have"—she glanced at Dina again—"you'll naturally make whatever arrangements seem good to you. But mind you, Rogers, I don't for one moment assume any responsibility. Neither does Vere's father. 'I'll ship the boy to South America first,' Van said."

"And what did Vere say to that?"

"My heart ached for him. He kept saying, 'I can't believe it. I can't believe it!' And when I was leaving, poor boy—bothered with his studies and worrying about whether he can keep up or not—he said over and over: 'Whatever you say is right I'll do, Mother. I'll do whatever you say.'"

"So that if you said he had better come West and be married, you think he would?"

Mrs. Holland held her head high, looked into space.

"Which of course I wouldn't!" she said firmly.

"You don't think that's his duty?"

"I don't think that would be for the happiness of anyone concerned. Not for yours or his," she said to Dina; "your lives have been completely different; your backgrounds are different. It's too bad, but it can't be helped. It would be a false thing to do and it would ruin both of you! It's a tragedy—it's a *tragedy,*" she finished with feeling, "to have a thing like this come into a boy's life and get to be known—follow him—mark him for the rest of time."

"So that you think the situation had best be left as it is," Rogers said. Mrs. Holland bridled, spoke in an affronted tone.

"Not at all. Although I can understand you want to make me out absolutely hardhearted about it!" she added with a resentful glance. "I think that it has happened before—it is always happening—and the only thing to do is keep it quiet and—and help out, of course. But even if I were convinced that it is actually true," she went on, "which I am not, I would feel that to wreck two lives is worse than—than wrecking one! Besides, things aren't the same today as they used to be! It isn't ruin for anyone, any more. Why, everyone knows about Hilda Fletcher's daughter—all that money and Junior League and Europe and Palm Beach and all the rest of it—and yet last year she married one of the Boones!"

Dina had sat absolutely still during this conversation, her face very pale, her eyes moving from Rogers' face to that of Mrs. Holland, moving solemnly back again. Now suddenly she spoke.

"I—I would try to make Vere a good wife, Mrs. Holland," she said. "If—if I could see him, if I could talk to him——" Her voice faltered to silence.

"I'm afraid that's impossible," Vere's mother said decisively. "He's borne enough about it all! And this—I had this telegram this morning, Rogers," she added, taking a folded yellow paper from her bag. "I wasn't going to mention it, but now I think it's only fair to let you know. This was Van's idea, and while what I just said about keeping Vere in school was quite true, he isn't there now at all. They've left, he and young Worthington and a tutor; they sailed this morning."

Rogers took the telegram and read it aloud.

"'Boys off at nine. Worthington family all present at dock to say good-by. Confident this is best plan. Love to Mimi. Van.'"

"So you see that's *that*," Caroline said nervously with a nod.

"Yes, I see that's that," Rogers agreed.

"And I trust that as far as Vere and I are concerned the matter is settled," she added, rising.

"It would seem so. But wait a minute; don't be in any hurry to go, Caroline," Rogers said. "I'm sure you'd be interested in hearing about our plans—mine and Geraldine's."

Caroline, after a moment's sharp scrutiny, dropped back into her chair.

"I can't see that they concern me!" she said. But her voice and manner were uneasy.

"But they might interest you," Rogers said politely. "Geraldine and I," he went on with a smile for the girl who looked worn and white, shrinking back in her big chair, "are going to be married."

Caroline glanced quickly at him again and smiled.

"My dear Rogers," she began deprecatingly. She gathered up her furs, her gloves, and purse. *"Really!"* she murmured, rising.

"You don't believe me?" Rogers said, unruffled.

"I think it a rather—transparent——" She emphasized and dragged out the last words with an accent between amusement and scorn. *"Really!"* she said again.

"No, wait a minute!" Rogers pursued it, his own smile quite matching her own. "I have suggested the arrangement to Geraldine, and she has done me the honor to say 'yes'—haven't you, Geraldine?"

"Yes," Dina said, as unexpectedly to herself as to the other woman.

"Well, I am sure I wish you both every happiness," Mrs. Holland said civilly, turning to go. But by the complete silence of the other two her attitude was shaken. "That isn't going to alter my position. Or Vere's either," she added. She looked from one to the other for a break, breathing fast.

"On the contrary, it confirms it," the man said.

There was another silence. Dina looked at no one, but the eyes of Caroline and Rogers were fixed on each other.

"What are you talking about!" Caroline presently exclaimed. "I never heard such nonsense!"

"I felt you ought to know," Rogers assured her. She sat down again.

"I don't in the least understand what your object can be in making such a remark, Rogers." Her tone was steel. But there was still a hint of uneasiness in it. Dina heard it, and she knew Rogers did, for his manner became even more deliberate and urbane.

"I mean that there is to be another Mrs. Holland here very soon," the man said.

"You're joking!" Caroline said breathlessly. But *she* was not joking.

"Not at all. I've been lonely here long enough. We need young blood in the family. It might have been Aline, of course. Well, that evidently wasn't to be. I've been engaged twice to Aline, Caroline, and somehow it didn't take, did it, either time? Last month, just as soon as some bills were cleared off, she married someone else. Now *I'm* going to marry someone else."

"Rogers," his sister-in-law said in a low tone, a tone changed suddenly from the angry and scornful one she had at first used to one of nervous appeal, "you can't do this! Think of the family. Think of the talk. Oh," she broke off to say apologetically, "you know how I blaze up—I'm that way! But for Van's sake—and everyone's sake—and dear old Mother Holland's sake, if she were here to know it—don't—*don't* do something you'll regret all your life!"

"And Vere's sake," Rogers supplemented it mildly, looking down at his linked fingers on the desk.

"Do anything you like—we'll all do anything you like," she began, "but not anything as—as ridiculous as this!"

"Well, Geraldine, I like that, don't you?" Rogers asked.

Dina was incapable of speech. She managed a frightened smile.

"Our marriage ridiculous?" Rogers echoed. "Why is it? What's ridiculous about it?"

"I'm not going to say anything more because I know you're not serious," Caroline said, breathing quickly and trying for an effect of calm.

"I'm quite serious."

"You'll make yourself a laughingstock, Rogers!"

"Not any more than Aline, assisted by some dear women friends, has made me for twenty years. To be jilted twice by the same woman, I think that's a record for making an ass of oneself," Rogers said.

"Aline discovered that she had made a mistake, that her feelings had changed; that's a natural thing for anyone to do," Caroline said hotly. "It has nothing whatever to do with your taking a step like this! Sacrificing your life to a ridiculous idea of gallantry or chivalry or I don't know what!"

"I'm forty-one, Caroline; quite a large slice of my life has been sacrificed already, with no particular purpose gained," Rogers reminded her mildly. "It seems to me it is Geraldine who is doing the sacrificing. A girl of nineteen—that's all she is, Caroline—coming in here to brighten up my old house. I assure you I feel quite rejuvenated at the thought of it."

"You'll not feel so rejuvenated when everyone begins to talk about you—and about her," Caroline countered angrily.

"Why should they talk?" the man inquired blandly.

"Why shouldn't they! You don't think I'm going to keep quiet about what I know just because you do?"

"It seems to me," the man mused, "that might hurt a boy of Vere's age more than a man of mine. After all, my property will go to my wife."

"Well, we'll see," Caroline muttered. But she was worsted; she was losing face and she knew it. "What will be said about Miss Cashman won't especially help her or you either," she added in a little spurt of viciousness.

"Then it will be said of my wife," Rogers said, his own anger rising to meet hers. "It will be said about my wife—and my child. That child will be a Holland after all, won't he? Go as far as you like, Caroline; say what you please. It won't reach Geraldine and me half as fast as it will you!"

For a full minute there was a strained interval in the library. Dina thought she could hear her own heart beat; she could hear a bird busy in the ivy outside the open window, but these sounds seemed to underscore rather than break the stillness. Caroline Holland sat erect; a little stain of real color had crept up under the artificial color that was so delicately added to her cheeks.

"I don't see any particular object in prolonging this," she presently said. "I appreciate your attempt to bully me into doing what you wanted about this, Rogers, but it has failed. Good afternoon. If you really—if you really cheat Vere out of—but you won't! Let me know when you come to your senses!"

Neither Dina nor Rogers moved or spoke after she had gone until they heard the crunch of her car wheels on the drive outside. Then Rogers put his head down on his crossed arms and began to laugh deeply and noiselessly. When he raised his head Dina saw that his eyes were full of actual tears of mirth.

Chapter 10

THE CAR WENT ON AND ON through an uncertainty of rain and of spring sunshine, over long Dumbarton Bridge, on between the flat bay meadows that were rich with deep green grass, through the little towns whose corners were occupied by gas stations and marked by roadside signs. The swift, smooth motion and the sharp turns made Dina feel ill; she shut her eyes and leaned back against the cushions.

Rogers had brought a handful of mail, some magazine articles, and a government pamphlet or two to read; he was completely occupied in his corner of the limousine and paid no attention to her except for a rather abstracted greeting when they had picked her up at Bonita Station.

But when they had been more than two hours on their way, and Livermore and Stockton were behind them, he suddenly folded all his papers together, put them carefully into a leather attaché case, put away his glasses, and said with an easy friendliness that indicated that they had just joined each other: "Well, how goes it with you?"

"Finely," Dina, who was feeling ill, said faintly.

"We're coming into Sacramento," Rogers said. "Ever been here before?"

"No. I'm going to be sick," said Dina, whose mouth was marked by lines of green.

He picked up the speaking tube; the car drew up beside the road.

"Get out and walk about a bit. You'll be all right."

Dina staggered to a fence, clung to it. The day was very warm and the spot happened to be completely unprotected; the sun beat down upon her bare head.

"I'm so sorry about this," she whispered, getting back into the car after a wretched interval, wiping her colorless lips and her wet eyes.

"I'll tell you," he said, "suppose we go to a hotel in Sacramento and you lie down for an hour or two?"

"Oh, now I'll be all right!" she said gratefully.

"I practically didn't eat any breakfast—was late getting away. A bite won't do us any harm, but you can walk up and down in the shade if you like."

It was February, but awnings were already in sight at the capitol, and women were wearing summer clothes. Dina walked to and fro for a few moments, felt herself restored, and joined Rogers at a table in the hotel's coffeeroom. If she could have some very thin hot green tea, she said, and some very thin toast . . .

"Bother you, my eating ham and eggs?" Rogers asked, looking across the table.

"No, unless you ask me to eat them. I've been like this every morning for a month now." She smiled. "So it wasn't the drive."

"You're not being let off anything, are you?"

"Not much."

"That place where you live, Geraldine," Rogers presently said with his mouth full of eggs and toast, "that's a funny place for a man to move his family into."

"Pop never liked it," Dina hastened to say, "but you see when we came up from southern California we simply had to move into whatever we could get."

"And that was the only place?"

"The cheapest."

"Oh, of course. You were short of funds."

"Short! We had none." Dina showed her white teeth in a sudden laugh. "Donny was the baby then," she said, "and there were six more of us and Mama and Pop, all in the one car and a trailer. We had three mattresses tied on top of the car and chairs and Donny's crib roped on in back, and the trailer was jammed and packed with saucepans and a washtub, the girls' dolls and Art's bicycle. Packing up every time we moved was the most awful thing I ever did!"

"And where'd you stay the first night?"

"We stayed in the house."

"Moved right in?"

"Oh yes. We had canned herrings and fresh bread and coffee and some cookies Mrs. O'Connor sent over to us. And it was cold!" She shuddered. "The wind was simply rattling the whole place, and the kitchen stovepipe smoked in billows." She fell silent, a half-smile on her face.

"Great God, nine of you," Rogers said under his breath.

"We didn't mind. Yanking things out of boxes and getting something to eat. I remember the water wasn't turned on and Donny was yelling. Art and I went and got a man who was eating his dinner to come over and turn on the water. He was eating bread and sausage, and his kitchen was so nice and warm and smelly!"

"Good lord!" Rogers said. "And your father had no job?"

"No, but he got one almost at once. With a man named Hansen. Mattresses—making over mattresses."

"Making over mattresses, eh? Bring me another cup of coffee," the man said to the waitress.

"And bring me some more hot water, please," Dina added.

"So your father got a job remaking mattresses. In—that—particular—neighborhood," Rogers said in his musing way, "that must have been quite a job. Twenty-seven meals a day on that pay, was it?"

"We had relief then. Off and on we've always had it. And milk; the Woman's Civic Club sent us milk."

"I can see you are going to be a source of unlimited delight to me, Scheherazade," said Rogers. "I don't have to walk the streets

of Bagdad nights. You will tell me about—what is it? Railway
Flats?"

"Bonita is the town; the station is where you picked me up this
morning. I don't know whether it was something the matter with
me," said Dina, "but I never liked the *Arabian Nights*. They sort
of bored me."

"You lived in Railway Flats and the *Arabian Nights* bored you?"
Rogers asked politely. The girl laughed.

"I like true books best," she said.

"Like . . . ?"

"About real people."

"The books at my house are mostly old-fashioned, I'm afraid."

"I love them old-fashioned."

"Well, now, let's get down to business," he said. "How much
have you told your own people?"

"Nothing."

"They don't know we're getting married today?"

"They never heard your name."

"And what do you propose to do, go back tonight?"

"I hadn't thought. But wouldn't it be better for me to go back
tonight and go on just the same until I get a good chance to let
them know?" Dina began timidly. "My brother Art wants to stop
school at Easter and get a job."

"Mattress making?"

"No. He went out with the surveying gang last vacation, and
he thinks that as soon as the rains are over he could go again. He
gets two dollars a day. I think Pop'll let him."

"You still all obey your father?"

"Oh yes. Pop's never mean to us, unless he's been drinking.
And even then," Dina said leniently, "Mama usually gets him right
to bed. My father's father was a judge," she added.

"I thought there might be something of that sort in the background," Rogers observed.

"He had a horse and surrey; they lived in a small country town
and they had a colored servant named Nabby, and Pop says every-

one respected him." It was obviously a quotation; she relished the phrases.

"You're probably like your grandfather," Rogers said thoughtfully.

"Pop says I'm like his mother."

"I daresay."

"Our names, unfortunately, won't help us much to keep this quiet," Rogers said thoughtfully after a silence. "William Rogers Holland and—what is it? Geraldine Cashman?"

"Margaret Geraldine Cashman. But they've never called me anything but Dina."

"My mother's name was Margaret. I like that name. Well, I suppose," Rogers mused, "we'll have to let the thing come to light by itself. No announcement."

"Oh, no announcement!" she protested, alarmed. "Can't we keep it a secret for a while?"

"I've been thinking about that, and I think not. I think the thing for me to do is stop in at your house tonight, meet your people, explain that we've been married, and then take you home."

"You wouldn't tell them—about me, I mean?"

"Oh no, no; I won't tell them anything, ever, that you don't want me to. You don't want to do that?" he asked, impressed by her visible distress. "Why not? It's the only dignified way, Geraldine, for both of us."

"But it's not fair to you!" she burst out suddenly, red-cheeked. "You—you're doing this for me; I can't do anything for you! My father—and my sisters, maybe—they might come to the house and —I don't know what they'd want or what I'd do, and I couldn't stand them bothering you and apologizing for them! Because"— Dina struggled on against a rising tide of wild tears now—"I love them, I can't help it——"

"Calm *down*," he said firmly, interrupting her by closing a heavy, gloved hand over hers. "I'll take care of that if it comes along. I'm asking you to do what I want you to do. I like the idea of having a sweet woman at the head of my table, someone to talk to, someone to listen to me. I've not wanted to marry since Anne died until Aline came along and all the old feeling came back. Perhaps I've never wanted to marry at all. But I like company. I'll like very much showing you stamps, taking you on a walk now and then, having you round. You needn't worry about me."

Dina considered it. She was tired now, her face pale and strained; when they went out to the car she subsided into a corner like an exhausted child.

"I'll do what you want me to do," she said simply.

"Then we'll stop for a few minutes at your house and go our way. We'll tell your people, and for everyone else it can filter out by degrees. I haven't much hope that we can keep it a secret very long," Rogers went on, "and we don't want newspaper people prowling around your father's place—or mine."

"I should hope not!" Dina agreed fervently.

"I'll go in for a moment tonight, meet them all, and then we'll go off on a supposed honeymoon. Don't worry," he added unsmilingly as the color rushed into Dina's face; "what I feel for you isn't that sort of thing at all. I know where your affections are. Instead of Del Monte we'll go home; Mrs. Bucket will have dinner ready at half-past seven or bring you up a tray. And that's another thing," he added, "about Mrs. Bucket. She spoke of you this morning as 'Mrs. Holland.' She asked if Mrs. Holland would like her breakfast in bed, said she knew you had been feeling ill in the mornings."

"But she calls me Dina!" the girl said quickly.

"I know she did. But she's changed of her own accord, and very properly too. It puts you in a false position and it puts her in one to have her call you anything else. So you'll have to put up with that. And now about breakfast. Have it either way, but I think it's easier for them downstairs to bring it up to you. You'd be all alone in the dining room; that house was built fifty years before breakfast rooms came in. But she'll ask you, and you can arrange that yourself. I've suggested she sleep upstairs in the room across the hall from yours for a while, until you get used to the place."

Dina looked down at the ring on her finger. They had laughed— it was one of the few laughs the long day had brought her—over the ring. Rogers had entirely forgotten to provide one; he had had to go to a jeweler's in Reno to buy it.

Looking down at it now, her face wore an odd expression.

"Mrs. Holland," she said musingly. "I don't think I ever thought of it—this part of it—before. I hope someday," Dina went on, speaking a little thickly now and with her eyes still fixed on the ring, "I hope someday I can make it up to you. I hope it will really be pleasant for you to have me in the house."

"I'm sure it will," the man answered on the same note. He took out his papers again; Dina leaned back and closed her eyes and presently drifted off to sleep.

Two hours later, a little after six o'clock, they reached Railway Flats. At Dina's somewhat timid suggestion Hall and the car were left waiting on the main street of Bonita, some three blocks away. She and Rogers picked their way through the unsavory lanes and along the plank sidewalks; the spring day had been long and langorous and sweet; its last light was just dying away from the unpainted shanties, the tin-patched roofs, the crazy quilt of vegetable patches and fences and clotheslines.

The Cashmans were at supper. Dina had known what sort of a picture must greet Rogers' eyes as she opened the door, but even her imagination and familiarity could hardly have painted the details more glaringly. Everything that was characteristic of suppertime flurry and disorder was there; her father, mustached and lean and suspicious, was in his shirt sleeves, his chair squared about from the table, a handleless cup in his fingers. Her mother, incredibly frowsy of hair, a saucepan in one hand and a spoon in the other, was standing by the stove.

The children were scattered about; little Donny and Myrna and Dooley on chairs, Art half standing, half leaning against the sink, Lou beside Myrna. El'ner had stopped at the bedroom door in what was evidently a tearful retreat from the room. The air was thick with smoke, grease, and steam; every surface of chair or table or sinkboard that could be used was crowded with odds and ends of food, dirty pans and knives, dishcloths, paper bags, sweaters, schoolbooks, rubbers, plates. The window shade hung in tatters, having long lost its lower rod. Some thick and gummy substance, spilled on the stove, bubbled and smoked as it fell slowly from point to point on the knobs and doors.

"Mama," said Dina without preamble, closing the door behind herself and Rogers and backing up against him, "this is Mr. Holland, and he and I were married today!"

An electrified silence followed this announcement, then John Cashman spoke heavily.

"What are you saying?"

The children set up an excited babble of questions, exclamations, and cries of surprise, through which Dina's mother said sharply:

"Why, Dina, what do you mean by going and doing a thing like that!"

The girl glanced up over her shoulder at Rogers. His appearance was not entirely reassuring. He had worn an old raincoat on this uncertain day; his fair, thin hair was mussed above his round, owlish face; his eyes bulged behind their strong glasses.

"We were married in Reno at two o'clock today," he said. "Witnesses and all. What were the witnesses' names, Geraldine?"

"I don't remember." In a sudden rush of love for them all, longing to be back in her old place with them all, she had gone to her mother and put her arms about the slatternly figure.

"Well, I have it here." Rogers took a folded paper from his pocket; afterward she thought how deliberately he had managed that her father should see this evidence of the marriage, but at the time it seemed strangely unimportant. "William B. Barker and Florence Willcox," he said; "she was the clergyman's housekeeper, and his name—see here?—'Harold Clark Kirkham, D.D.'—and a mighty nice fellow too."

"Married?" her father was demanding with hostility. He hesitated, weakened. "You've got money to provide for her properly, I suppose?"

"Why, you said Vere was a college boy, Dina!" her mother

wailed. "I don't know what possest you to do such a thing! Why on earth didn't you——"

"I'm not Vere," Rogers interpolated; "I'm his uncle."

"His uncle!" Mrs. Cashman gasped.

"I don't understand it and I don't like it," Dina's father said without any particular emphasis.

"It seems funny you marrying anybody's *uncle!*" Myrna put in.

"I guess Dina knows what she's doing," Art said in his raw boy's voice. He walked over to her and kissed her, said: "Congratulations, Sis."

Dina clung to him.

"I'm sorry if I've upset any of you," she stammered, turning to face the circle. "We just decided it lately."

"I assure you I'll take very good care of her," Rogers told them, looking at her father as he spoke.

"Well, I don't doubt that, don't doubt that," John Cashman muttered, mollified. "Here, sit down."

"And let us get you something to eat." The situation was reducing itself to elements Dina's mother understood. "Dooley," she said, "you run over to Meyer's—he'll be open——"

"No, no, no!" Dina protested.

"No, thanks just the same. We're going home for dinner." Rogers looked immense and alien as he stood there among them in his raincoat, peering through his glasses. "Geraldine'll be in to see you in a day or two."

"Oh, Dina, don't go away!" Lou wailed. Dina kissed her.

"I'll come back." She began to feel tired and weak; she had had eight hours of driving on a changeable spring day; the motion of the car still was with her. Now her head was weary; there was a nervous throbbing pain between her eyes, and she felt as if the kitchen were beginning to waver up and down in dizzying lines. The hot, greasy atmosphere rose about her in fumes.

She sat down suddenly and asked Art for some water, which he gave her in a cracked old jelly glass, and things went on being dreamlike and unreal. Her mother asked if they were going to have a "place" somewhere, and Myrna said sharply, with schoolgirl superiority, "Mama, for goodness' sakes, he's Vere Holland's uncle!" Dina promised Lou that she and El'ner and indeed all of them should see her soon and they would all have ice cream. Rogers explained that the long trip to Reno had upset Geraldine and that she was tired.

"Reno! You don't mean that you were just divorced!" her mother exclaimed.

"Oh no. My wife died five years ago. But in Reno you can arrange a marriage easier than in San Francisco."

Then they were out in the muddy lane again, the Cashmans gathering against the red light of the doorway to wish them bewildered good-bys. Rogers gave Dina his arm over the planks and puddles, and she got into the car and sank into her seat feeling that at any minute she might faint.

After that it was effort upon effort. An effort to get out of the car, to mount the steps to the Holland doorway, to climb the stairway within; an effort to show her ring to Mrs. Bucket and begin to take off her clothes; an effort to wash her face, to raise her arms for her pajama sleeves, to move about the big chamber awaiting her.

But the piled pillows of the old mahogany bed were deep and soft, and her icy feet struck a hot-water bottle between the smooth, thick sheets. There was a tray with soup and chicken on it, and a blazing coal fire, and softened lights. Dina lay deep in luxury as if she would never move again. She ate languidly, soon satisfied, smiled her acknowledgment when Mrs. Bucket put two books on her bedside table.

"I picked 'em for you because I used to like 'em, but they're real old-timy," the housekeeper said.

"Oh, thank you!"

"You're feeling better, aren't you?"

"Oh yes. It was just that I got so hot and tired, and I was nervous, I suppose, about telling my family."

"Did they make a fuss?"

"Well, they were terribly surprised of course. But I imagine that

they've just about now gotten round to saying what they think!"
Dina smiled again.

"Mr. Holland said to say good night to you and that if you felt
badly tomorrow we'd telephone Doctor Lilienthal."

"I won't. I really feel fine and am glad my people know!" Dina
stretched out her hand on the blankets. "Thank you for everything," she said, her tone saying much more than her words.

Mrs. Bucket impulsively covered Dina's hand with her own.

"I hope you're going to be happy, Mrs.—Mrs. Holland!" she said.

"I'm sure I will be," Dina told her soberly.

For a long time she lay still after the housekeeper had left her.
Her first need was rest—body, mind, and spirit. Just rest. Just to be
alone in the silence with the fire sunken to a bed of glowing embers
and the lamp at her bedside giving the only other light in the room.
Dina could not think; she did not want to think. Her thoughts
surged about aimlessly—now a feeling of wonder that Papa had
not made more of a scene, now a regret that Myrna had chanced
to wash her hair that afternoon and had had it bound up in a rag.

Again in the wide, grim, rubber-scented passages of the City
Hall where they had gone for the license; again in the clergyman's
stuffy parlor, and the two strange and interested witnesses. The
Reverend Kirkham had been unmarried, but his housekeeper—or
perhaps it had been his servant—had been glad to oblige; the other
witness—what had been his name? Barker?—a neighbor living next
door. And always, under and over all the other sensations, they
were in the car again, rolling on and on and on between the hot
greenness or sudden warm rain of the fields and around the sickening curves of the endless highway. Three times—or was it four
times?—she had had to get out because she was ill; she had been ill
in the hotel dressing room in Reno. Why had not Rogers been disgusted enough with her to abandon the whole plan? Why had he
not walked out when first his eyes had fallen upon the Cashman
kitchen and the head of the Cashman family seated in his shirt
sleeves at the cluttered table?

Wonderment, doubt, stinging little pinpricks of memory swept over her. She had gotten this far in her strange adventure. Tonight she felt incapable of getting any further. Tonight she felt only capable of lying here, forever and forever, spent and silent, with her eyes closed.

But gradually the tide came back. Dina looked about the room, studied it thoughtfully. This was her home now. The Dina who had crept in beside sleeping Dooley or Myrna, glowing over triumphant evenings at Cotta's, planning to pay one more weekly dollar on the new suit, wondering if there was butter enough in the house for breakfast, was no more. This was her home, and this was her room.

It was an immense room with curtained bay windows on the south and west. The doors were nine feet high and of dark carved wood. The bathroom was as large as the bedroom Dina shared with her sisters at home; it had a large dark window of salmon-colored glass, wooden walls painted chocolate brown, a deep built-in tub.

There was a whatnot in her room with shells and fans and vases set on its descending cascade of shelves. There were two immense wardrobes with mirrored doors that swung out heavily. There were great chairs, fringed, tasseled, braided, and there was a mahogany desk with a drop leaf covered in green felt. The floor was concealed completely by a thick carpet flowered in several shades of red and green, and the thick rep curtains at the windows were dull green, tied with heavy gilt cords and tassels. At the bedside and fireside there were rugs. Nothing had been changed in this room, Dina felt, for fifty years.

A clock somewhere in the hall struck a slow, sepulchral ten. Dina hoped Mrs. Bucket had come upstairs to bed; the bulk of the house seemed tremendous, mysterious, menacing about her. A spring breeze was wandering over the world; it whispered in her chimney, fingered at the old shutters that were closed at her windows. She got out of bed; she must see if there was a light in Mrs. Bucket's room, opposite her own.

Noiselessly she opened the door and peered out. The wide hallway was flanked by doors and opened on one side to the great vault of the stairway. It was unlighted, but from the floor below a faint light came up and was diffused in the gloom.

She got back into bed, settled herself on her pillows, opened one of the heavy, formidable-looking old volumes that Mrs. Bucket had brought upstairs for her.

"I'm not going to think any more tonight. I'm going to read until I'm sleepy," Dina said half aloud. She opened to the first page, brought her mind resolutely to the opening words.

Chapter 11

SHE MUST ACCEPT EVERYTHING SERENELY, she told herself, and keep herself busy, and make them all, Rogers and the servants, like her. That was all she must do; not asking for anything, not seeming to be surprised or bothered about anything.

Every morning her breakfast came upstairs on a tray at eight o'clock. At Mrs. Bucket's suggestion she stayed in bed for a while afterward, reading the newspaper or reading one of the old-fashioned novels of Trollope, Scott, Henry Kingsley, Dumas, Victor Hugo. Dickens she knew fairly well already; the Cashmans had possessed few books, but several volumes of Dickens were among them, and Dina had borrowed the rest from various sources and knew most of them.

At ten she dressed and went downstairs, wandering out into the garden if the day was fair, gathering flowers for vases, talking with the old Scotch gardener. At noon Rogers appeared; sometimes only to tell her that he was going to San Francisco and would be gone for both lunch and dinner, sometimes to lunch with her, completely absorbed in the newspapers and mail. Afterward he might tell her that he had to go on some errand; to see a stamp collector about a rare stamp he had heard he possessed, to see his broker, to interview banker or lawyer, and when he went he was perfectly willing to take her along. Dina roamed about San Francisco contentedly enough, picked up little presents for her mother and sisters, drifted into a movie. She and Rogers would be quite silent, driving home, the man usually asleep.

But for dinner she always changed her dress and made her hair look as well as she could. And in the new gowns that she and Mrs. Bucket had bought Rogers' eyes approved her, even though he rarely complimented her in words. They were simple gowns, for Dina's figure was already changing, and her whole instinct was for plainness. But there was a silver-gray chiffon velvet infinitely becoming in its long lines, there was a black taffeta with a tumble of white frills at the square neck, and there was a soft striped crepe in dull mingled blues and browns that were accented by coral earrings and a coral chain and that Dina liked best of all. Whatever chills or misgivings the day had brought were dissipated when she was dressed and fires were lighted and she and Rogers talked through the meal. He laughed at her, asked her questions, and in the evening they played cards.

At first they played with anxious eagerness on her part and nervous anxiety to amuse him as well. Dina had played cards all her life; sodden decks of cards had always seemed to be available somehow in the Cashman family, and she was quite Rogers' match at cribbage and rummy and quick to grasp the essentials of poker patience. There presently came to be a pleasant contest between them, and the card-playing hour every evening sometimes stretched itself to two. Dina fought hard for points, and her shouts of "Oh, you lucky!" or "Oh, come jack, come jack, come jack," were as spontaneous as if she were back at Railway Flats again.

"I'm all ready to go out and you get sixteen in the crib!" Rogers would complain.

"Oh, I needed it so! You've had the last two games!"

"Well, come on, let's have another."

"Let's!" And Dina would laugh youthfully in anticipation of another game. The library would be warm and bright on the chilly spring evenings; shades drawn, fire blazing, and odd as the situation had seemed to her at first, and still seemed to her, there were times when she felt herself protected and secure and happy enough.

There was a small car for her use, not a new car but far better

than the Cashmans' old jalopy. Dina could drive in the afternoons
to see her mother and sisters. She had hesitated to make the first
call, dreading questions and criticism, and had asked Rogers' advice.

"Just tell 'em yes and no," he had said. "And immediately ask
questions. Keep 'em talking about themselves."

So Dina had gone down to make the dreaded visit and had
found Rogers' counsel excellent. Her mother did indeed ply her
with all sorts of queries, but Dina answered them briefly and
amiably and brought the conversation promptly to matters domestic. Art's cold was better? How was Donny's? Myrna was going
out nights; Pop oughtn't to allow that.

The home kitchen struck her as strangely grimy and cramped
after the bigness of the Holland mansion. Had things always been
so cracked and stained, spotted and streaked? Her father was reported to be sleeping off a heavy cold; she suspected he might be
sleeping off a night's "binge" as well, but it was a relief to have
her mother and little Donny to herself; even El'ner was in school
now, and the house was quiet.

Mrs. Cashman was doing the week's washing. She always washed
on Mondays, distributing gray dirt over towels and underdrawers
and shirts, rather than removing it, and hanging the wet garments
on the line in the yard even if the rain was falling. Sometimes they
dangled and blew there for days.

Today she was sousing small articles up and down in the dishpan, sometimes holding one of Donny's socks up for inspection or
scrubbing a particularly ingrained spot on one of Art's shirts.

"What sort of a place are you living in, Dina?"

"The old Holland place. Near Burlingame, in the hills."

"Nice place?"

"Old-fashioned. But big and comfortable. You'll have to come up
and see it sometime, Mama."

"That's what Pop was saying. You've got help, haven't you?"

"Oh yes."

"Cook?"

"Chinese cook."

"Is he real well fixed, Dina?"

"Yes, I guess he is. I never asked."

"We all thought it was Vere you fancied; seems it was his uncle all the time," Ethel Cashman said innocently. "But what I can't get over is your falling in love with a man old enough to be your father. That gets me. Quite a few people, people round here, were asking about it. Tom O'Connor talked to Art."

"He did?" Dina's face crimsoned. "Here, I'll hang these out for you," she said. She went into the back yard with the familiar old basket of wet wash, stood at the line with the sweet, warm spring breeze blowing over her and lifting the hair on her forehead. Other women were hanging out wet Monday's clothes; all through the crazy quilt of yards and shanties that was the Flats the lines of faded blue and faint red and dubious white were stretched. Presently her mother followed her out and began to pin children's socks to the line in bunches of four and six.

"Don't you need more clothespins, Mama?"

"Well, I could do with a few more, Dina. I declare, I don't know where they go. Mrs. Morley said she caught one of the Gomez boys stealing 'em a while back."

"Those little Gomez fellows aren't more than four and six. That isn't stealing."

"Well, he said he was taking them to his mother."

"I see Meyer has got his awning out." Dina stood stretching her shoulders, smiling in the sun. On her way home, she thought, she would stop at Meyer's and send Mama home a grocery order including clothespins and dish towels. Meyer's carried flour-bag dish towels at five cents apiece; it was a long time since the Cashmans had indulged in any.

"What do his folks think of Mr. Holland's getting married, Dina?"

"He hasn't many folks. Vere's off on a sea trip, and his father—Vere's father—is a lawyer in New York with a second wife."

"Vere's mother dead?"

"No, she lives here with his sister, Mimi Holland. But I don't know that they know Rogers and I are married yet. The newspapers haven't printed it."

"What's the sense of keeping a thing like that a secret? It's got to come out. What do his friends think when they come to the house and find you living there?"

"They don't come, Mama. He lives almost alone, taking care of the place, fussing with his stamps—he's crazy about collecting stamps—and sometimes riding before breakfast. He has some horses there. Then there's a ranch down San Bernardino way, and he says in the summer he goes down there for about a month. But we've been married only two weeks tomorrow, and nobody has come in yet."

"Well, he's pretty well fixed!" her mother said, duly impressed. "He must have a lot, I should say, but seems to me that's an awful lonely way for you to live, Dina. But I suppose newly married folks don't mind that. Is he crazy about you?"

"Mama, is that Mrs. Schmultz? Don't tell me that she—why, how old is Irma?"

"Irma isn't quite a year," Ethel said, diverted. "They'll be thirteen months apart. She's awful mad about it. Seven of 'em, and I don't believe Rosamond's more than ten. She's in Lou's class, anyway."

"I'm going to wait until the girls get home from school. Seems to me it's months since I've seen them."

In the house again Dina went naturally about her old tasks. She cleared the sink of dishes, did what she could to put the kitchen in order. Her mother, complaining of an aching back and dizzy spells, sat at the kitchen table in great satisfaction, watching her and enjoying a midafternoon cup of tea.

When she got home at five o'clock Dina gave Rogers a spirited report. She found him in the garden, discussing a bed of tulips, primulas, and hyacinths with McPherson, and they stood there together in the late bland flood of the sunset, laughing at the old gardener's earnestness and glad to linger in the spring moistness and sweetness and greenness.

Dina had taken off her hat; her hair, damp from its pressure, was tight against her forehead in rings and spirals. Her face was a little pale from fatigue and from the unwonted warmth of the day, but the pallor seemed to make her blue eyes darker and her lips more red.

"So you got your mother clothespins?"

"And dish towels and everything else you could think of. The girls went with me, and we each took a basket and went the rounds at Meyer's. Peaches and soup and bacon and cake flour—everything! They all went home with lollipops, except Myrna of course; she was too grand. Meyer wants Myrna to come into the store this summer, and she says that if she can hold the job she's not going back to school. She's only second-year high, though, and I don't believe Pop will let her."

"She impressed me as precocious, but she's pretty. Hello!" Rogers broke off to say in a tone of annoyance. "Here are callers!"

The approaching car swung round the drive, stopped. A woman jumped out and then a man. Aline and Andrew Havens.

Aline came straight to Rogers, a newspaper in her hand.

"Is this true?" she demanded.

"Aline, hello!" Rogers greeted her amiably. "Hello, Havens. Nice people, to come see us!"

"Is this true?" Aline asked a second time, showing the newspaper. "I just saw it. We were driving down to Menlo and I happened to get a paper."

"Yes, of course," Rogers said pleasantly. "Geraldine, I'm afraid the news is out. We're in the evening paper. I should have supposed dear Caroline would have told you, Aline."

"Why, it's preposterous!" Aline said indignantly. "Caroline and Mimi are in Honolulu," she went on. "I had no idea of it! Nobody had any idea of it! When were you married?"

"You know my wife," Rogers said, indicating Dina with a movement of his head. "Geraldine, you remember Mr. and Mrs. Havens?"

Dina stood disheveled and young and lovely against the sunset, her tawny hair an aureole about her forehead, the pale-green leaves and white spheres of a snowball bush behind her.

"Your wife! Oh, excuse me; I didn't see you," Aline said frigidly; then with reproach to Rogers: "And you never told me!"

"You never told me your plans with Mr. Havens here until about a fortnight before you hopped off to Reno with him. That's a nice little city, by the way. Geraldine and I took a leaf out of your book and went there too. Perhaps the same obliging clergyman married you. Krikham? Something Kirkham," Rogers said, all in an unruffled, leisurely tone. "But come; let's go in. It's going to be cold out here in about a minute. Geraldine, what about scaring us up something to eat and drink?"

"I'll see Hinz." Dina nodded and smiled as she escaped. She raced to the pantry, raced upstairs. Her new flowery dress; a wet comb dashed through her hair; changed slippers.

"You're all right," Mrs. Bucket said, helping her. "You look all right."

Dina descended, slackening her pace. She must be composed, not breathless, when she entered the library.

Hinz was stooping to light the fire. A tray with glasses and bottles was on a table. Aline and Andrew and Rogers were still standing; all three turned as Dina came in.

She looked young and sweet in the flowery ruffles; the freshly combed damp hair had fallen into waves and curves about her face. She was still a little pale, and her eyes shone darkly sapphire in faint rings of shadow.

"Ah, Hinz has taken care of you, I see. And Chong is making us some canapés," she said composedly. She did not look at Rogers, but she felt his satisfaction with her behavior like a tangible wave that touched her.

"What are you drinking, Mrs. Holland?" Andrew Havens asked with his agreeable smile. He was mixing a highball for himself; Dina smiled in return.

"Nothing, thank you. Rogers tries to make me drink milk, but not at this time of day!" she said. And then as the three others settled themselves by the fireside she pushed a leather hassock to the side of Rogers' chair and sat down, her shoulder touching his knee.

She had never taken this position before; she had not planned it; but something in Aline's hostility, her intolerance, had nerved her, and she knew she was right when Rogers changed his glass to his other hand and allowed his fingers to touch her shoulder in return.

"You shouldn't have bothered about food, Mrs. Holland," Aline said with a polite inclination of her head.

"Oh, it was no trouble," Dina assured her easily. "Chong loves to have someone to fuss over, and we don't keep him half busy enough!"

"It seems to be my fate to want to paint you," Andrew Havens said. Dina widened her eyes and, remembering her instructions upon an earlier occasion, turned to smile mysteriously at Rogers. But this time her face was much nearer his than it ever had been before, and the expression of grateful appreciation she saw there somewhat upset her. He was suffering in this other woman's company as he always must. His smile was strained and unnatural, his upper lip beaded with fine perspiration.

Aline knew it too. No snake charmer ever exerted a more confident sway over her victims than that Aline was exerting now, relaxed and graceful in her big chair, her beautiful slender body outlined by the glassy satin gown, her exquisite oriental head all ivory and black and scarlet, her eyes agleam with satisfaction in her own sneering power.

"Why didn't you tell us that night, Rogers, that you and Miss— I've forgotten the previous name, Mrs. Holland; forgive me—were planning this?"

"Oh, I don't know! We just got into the car one day, followed your example, and went up to Reno and had it all over without any fuss." He tried to say it carelessly, but he did not wholly succeed.

"So the paper says. Well, you'll have fuss enough now."

"Maybe we'll run away from it. Hey, Geraldine?"

"Maybe we will," Dina said thoughtfully, not moving her gaze from the fire.

"Mrs. Caroline Holland was telling me all about you," Aline said suddenly, turning the battery of her silken, smiling manner toward the younger woman. "You were a friend of Vere Holland's, weren't you? Quite a *good* friend."

Dina brought her shadowed blue eyes from the fire to Aline's face. There was a moment of complete silence in the room. Andrew Havens looked from one to the other in mild, amused bewilderment.

"Yes, I knew Vere," Dina said.

"Very well, didn't you?" Aline pursued.

"Who told you anything about Geraldine and Vere Holland?" Rogers demanded. Dina, whose face had slowly crimsoned, sank back in her chair, a great wave of relief engulfing her. She fixed her expectant eyes on Rogers, looking like a frightened and abashed child.

"There was something to tell?" Aline countered.

"Apparently," Rogers said. "I don't know what Caroline's been talking about," he went on, "but I'm having Callaghan go down and find out what she's been saying," he drawled. "After all, Aline, libel's libel, and Geraldine's my wife. I don't know what you told Betsey Berry, but the sooner that sort of thing gets scotched the better. Just what was your source of information, anyway?"

Aline's ivory face lost a shade of color.

"Why, I don't know anything at all," she said, proudly indifferent. But there was a suggestion of stammering in her usually assured speech. "I have nothing to do with it! Caroline told me that Vere had known Miss—known your wife, that was all. I had said that she was here at a dinner party and that I was wondering about her."

"Well, if that's all you quoted to Betsey, that's all right then," Rogers said with an air of being mollified; "but from something she said—however, she evidently didn't get it from you! I'll have to find out where she *did* get it."

"I said nothing to Betsey Berry that Caroline didn't say to me," Aline said quickly.

"And nothing about Geraldine?"

"Nothing Caroline didn't say." She was uneasy now, on the defensive; there were two red spots in her cheeks.

"Well, Callaghan will run the whole thing down," Rogers said comfortably.

"Don't go consulting Frank Callaghan; don't be so silly!" Aline said lightly. "After all, I think all that I said was that Miss Cashman and Vere had been friends, and I'm sure that's true. Tell me, what do you two honeymooners do here all day long?" she added in the social tone of one keeping a conversation going but obviously anxious to get on firmer ground.

"We never seem to have any time to spare, do we, Geraldine?" Rogers said, stuffing his pipe.

"We play cribbage," Dina contributed. "And I beat him," she added with a smile for Rogers.

"We'll have to begin to play cribbage," Andrew said unexpectedly. He had taken no part and apparently no interest in the little exchange of hostilities, merely glancing once or twice at his wife with a whimsical expression of surprise on his humorous, long-featured face. "The long winter evenings down at the farm have been boring my wife to death," he continued. "As a matter of fact, we've been at a hotel in town for the last couple of weeks."

"Bored, were you, Aline?" Rogers asked mildly over his pipe.

"Not bored at all," she answered lazily, looking at the fire between half-shut lids but first having given her husband a level, expressionless glance. "It's part of Andy's profession to meet people, to have them know he's here. And since quite a good deal was going on—the Richie party and the Stanfield wedding—we moved in for a fortnight."

"As a matter of fact, I like the country best in winter," Rogers observed. "Geraldine does too."

"I love it here," Dina said simply.

"You're evidently quite an ideal couple!" Aline said with a little laugh. "You've not heard from Caroline about your marriage?" she asked Rogers in an undertone.

"I only wrote her a day or two ago, and if, as you say, they've been in Honolulu—— Anyway, I've not heard!"

Dina lost the rest of the conversation, for Andrew had gotten to his feet and stepped to a lamp. He beckoned to her.

"Come over here and see what you think of this," he said.

Dina joined him, looking down at the little sketch he had drawn on a small square pad of white paper.

"Why, it's lovely!" she exclaimed. "It's me—I—me—I," she added, laughing and looking at Rogers.

And she carried to him the sketch of a girl in a flowery dress, a girl seated on a hassock with an old-fashioned fireplace for a background. Displaying it to Rogers, Dina seated herself on the arm of his chair and leaned against him familiarly.

"Yes, yes, it's really like you," he approved. "Why don't you paint her, Andrew?" he asked. "I'd like to have her painted."

"You were going to have Anne painted. Was Anne ever painted?" Aline put in. Rogers showed no sign of annoyance.

"No; we talked of it. But of course we didn't have Andrew in the family then. How'd you like to do it, and when could you do it?" he asked the painter.

"But look here, I wasn't drumming up trade!" Andrew protested, with his hard, lean, sunburned face flushing deeper.

"I know you weren't. But we might as well get Geraldine at nineteen; she'll never be any younger."

"I suppose you've been painted lots of times?" Dina said somewhat timidly to Aline. Aline glanced at her thoughtfully, did not answer.

"Of course I've done her," Andrew said. "She's a wonderful subject, too, because she always looks just the same. Whether it's ten o'clock in the morning or late at night, Aline's the same porcelain empress."

"I can see that," Rogers mused, half-shut eyes on Aline. "Ah, modern cosmetics—modern cosmetics."

"But Dina here——" Andrew began. He stopped, changed to an apologetic tone. "I call you Dina," he explained, "because it isn't in the nature of things to call a girl who looks about twelve anything as formal as 'Mrs. Holland.' "

"Please do!" Dina, back on her hassock, said eagerly.

"I was going to say that you change all the time," Andrew resumed. "You were quite different that first night; you seemed older, somehow; didn't she, Aline? When we got here today you were one girl, and now you're quite another."

"Infinite variety," Rogers said idly. "Well, how would you like to paint her? In that thing?"

"In that dress and that dark-blue chair. Sit there, will you?" Andrew asked. Dina rose, shook her flowery skirt, and sat down in the blue brocaded chair. It's back rose high above her tawny head; she clamped her young, lean hands firmly on the high arms. "That's perfect," Andrew said. "And we've got a north light too. I could pull aside these curtains and run up the shades, I presume."

Rogers waved his hand.

"How soon could you begin?" he said once more himself, imperturbable and amused. "I'd like that old marble mantel in it," he said, "and a corner of my mother's portrait."

"I am having an exhibition in May; I am having some stuff sent out from the East," Andrew told them. "We'll give the Portrait of Mrs. Rogers Holland the place of honor."

"I can't get used to the idea of there being a Mrs. Rogers Holland at all," Aline said. She rose, stretched her hand to her husband. "We've got to be going," she added. But when Dina and Andrew had preceded them from the room she drew Rogers back, and they talked together while the others waited in the hall.

"When are you going back to Los Altos, Mr. Havens?"

"Oh, look here, if I call you Dina I don't think you ought to call me anything but Andy. When are we going back? Well, I don't know. Aline had never seen the place when we were married, and I imagine she finds it pretty crude. I described it to her and she talked as if she'd love it; said she was sick of society and only wanted to get away and rest, but—well, we had pretty heavy rains after Christmas, you know, and the road was washed out. I imagine we'll wait until spring now." Andrew's young, honest face was a mixture of perplexity and indulgent amusement.

"Fixed the date of sitting for your portrait?" Rogers said, joining them.

"I've been saying that I don't think you ought to do that yet," Aline said. She looked angry, almost as if she had been crying.

"Why not?" the painter demanded innocently. "How d'you mean 'yet'? I'd like to have it finished in time for my exhibition; I won't do it any better three months from now."

"Well, I say that I don't think you ought to do it," Aline persisted quietly but stubbornly. "I have my reasons and I'll give you my reasons later."

"You'll have to give me pretty good reasons for throwing over my first commission, darling!" Andrew said with a laugh. Dina and Rogers stood in the side doorway and watched them depart in the spring dusk.

"Spoiled. I suppose there was never a woman quite so spoiled in this world," Rogers said, when they were gone, in a tone as if he spoke to himself. "She is determined now that he shall not paint your portrait. Well, we'll see!"

"But why should she be determined?"

"Because he is so anxious to do it, Geraldine. Because it's more than a commission with him; he thinks you're extremely paintable. He said so. Aline didn't like it."

"Oh, but that's—that's nonsense," Dina protested, flushing. "When she's so beautiful. Like a—like a Chinese lamp."

"A Chinese lamp who hates the country, never has learned to cook, and doesn't know how to manage without a maid," Rogers said with a quiet chuckle.

"But—but you love her?" She couldn't help saying it. They were back by the dying fire now and standing facing each other.

"Yes," he answered in a low tone, turning to kick at the steel-rodded grate with his mudstained garden shoe. "But her life would have been quite different if she'd married me, and she would have been different. There'd have been dignity here, the background she knows," Rogers muttered. "They've nothing to live on; she doesn't know how they're going to manage! She's infuriated because I could give him a commission to paint your portrait, infuriated because he needs it and because your picture will be shown at his exhibition."

"But I should think he'd have half a dozen of her there!"

"He probably will. But the crowd will gather around yours. Portrait of Mrs. Rogers Holland is bound to attract attention, and she knows it! Down there on a ranch in Los Altos!" Rogers was back in his own thoughts again. "A woman who could walk into any doorway in the world! And he is getting his taste of it, poor fellow!" he added. "Did you see the look she gave him when he said he hated the country? She doesn't want any of that before me."

"He is nice," said Dina firmly.

"Yes, he's a decent sort of fellow. You looked nice yourself when you came downstairs," Rogers said. "When did you get that dress?"

"The day I went shopping in San Francisco while you were at your broker's," Dina answered. "Twenty-two fifty."

"Twenty-two fifty, eh? Well, it looks worth it. It's five o'clock; I think I'll go up for a shower and change."

"Will you be down for some music at six, Rogers?" She had not used the name often; she was schooling herself to do so. The man hesitated. She knew that Aline's call had upset him, torn between the fascination that this mysterious and beautiful woman had for him and the angry satisfaction he took in annoying her.

"You liked that music?" he asked, his back toward her as he moved toward the door.

"I loved it."

"Well . . ." The point was not conceded. But when Dina came downstairs at quarter past six she found him sunk deep in a great leather chair in the small room adjoining the library, where the great carved case of a victrola stood. The place was almost dark; it was buried, inundated by the glorious music of a Russian opera.

Dina slipped into a neighboring chair, raised her feet to a leather hassock, lost herself in the beauty and passion of the music. Until Hinz, awaiting an interval between records, came to announce dinner, neither she nor Rogers spoke.

Chapter 12

"WANT TO GO TO STOCKTON?" Rogers asked her at luncheon next day. "I have to drive up there and look over a piece of property this afternoon."

"Oh, I'd love to! Right now?"

"Well, as soon's luncheon is over. Any other plans?"

"None important. I thought I might go down and see Mama. There was nobody at home yesterday, but I can go tomorrow just as well."

"Oh, are you driving?" she asked with pleasure when a short fifteen minutes later she came out of the front door, coated and dressed for the trip, and found him waiting for her in his own open roadster.

"Like that better?"

"Well, I do. But I don't know why." She settled herself beside him in great satisfaction. "What a day to go anywhere!" she exulted. "How long will it take us?"

"About two hours."

"I'd like to drive anywhere—Mexico, New York—a day like this!"

"You may have an idea there. Tell me, Geraldine," he said as they drove along through the beauty and greenness of March, "exactly what does your family live on?"

Dina laughed, unembarrassed.

"Oh, I don't know," she said vaguely. "Mama sold a barrel of books that were my grandfather's before we came West. But I think she only got eleven dollars for them and for two pictures."

"What sort of pictures?"

"Engravings, I think. I don't remember. I've never been this way before," commented Dina, absorbed in the scenery.

"No, but tell me. Your father gets relief, does he?"

"Well, he had some trouble getting it, but now it's all fixed. It's always all gone by the end of the first week," Dina said. "Look, look, look at the white birds!"

"Herons. There are always herons here. All right. He gets his relief and it's gone. Then what?"

"Well, then there was my salary, you know."

"But that's stopped now."

"Yes, but I cashed the check you gave me for that dinner party and gave Mama that after we were married, and last week I had an extra ten in my purse, and I let her have that too. I hope you don't mind?"

"But how about before you were working?"

"I don't know," Dina said vaguely, and laughed at her own tone. "I really don't, Rogers," she said. "Lots and lots of the people we know live like that. You don't know how they do it!"

"That's an understatement," Rogers said, and she laughed again.

"What I mean is"—she elucidated it—"there are families and families who are just struggling along on nothing, and—well, say the father is the only person in the family earning any money, and then he gets sick."

"My God!" Rogers said under his breath. "Well, go on."

"You know, there might be little boys of seven and five and three," Dina pursued, "and a baby, or a baby coming. And there he is, coughing in bed, with blankets over him and his wife making him poultices."

"So what happens?"

"Oh, the neighbors, first," Dina explained. "Everyone hears Joe Schulz is home sick, and people take in things. And maybe Mama or someone takes the baby for a while. And then there's—oh, lodges and maybe employer's liability; I don't know," she finished lightly. "Everyone helps."

"But the poor fellow must worry so about getting well."

"Oh yes, poor people worry when something goes wrong," Dina conceded. "But they don't worry *unless* something goes wrong!" she added cheerfully. "They don't worry about anything."

"Well, that's a point," Rogers said.

"Then someone like Mrs. Sorenson or the Flints will have brothers or fathers who can help them out," Dina pursued. "Mrs. Sorenson opened a boardinghouse, and they say she's making more money than Ole ever did. She had four little girls and Jonny, but we think Jonny isn't quite all there. They all have white hair and are fat, but they are the *cleanest* children! They look as if they'd been boiled, and every Monday she has six or seven dresses for every one of them out on the line. Mama used to wonder how she did it. But afterward they bought a bathtub, when the Morris house burned down, and I think Ole set that up for her."

"Most of the houses haven't bathtubs?"

"None of them have. Has," added Dina under her breath, trying the sound of it.

"Your house had?"

"Oh no, it hadn't, Rogers!"

"I see." For some reason she could not understand he sighed and fell silent, and they drove along for some time without speaking. Dina let her eyes rove contentedly over the landscape that was flooded with sunshine and flowers and up to the eastern mountains, faint purple blue against a scarcely darker sky.

She was sorry when they reached Stockton and were in the pleasant streets of its outlying districts, between gardens and cottages and pepper and blooming hawthorn trees.

"My aunt Sarah Forrester lived up here," Rogers presently told her, "and since she died a year ago her place has stood empty. I've put some cleaners in there and had a little painting done, and I thought I'd see what it looks like."

The section in which they stopped had obviously once been the fashionable end of town, for neglected, forlorn, pretentious mansions still stood in bare garden spaces, their windows adorned with every sign that shabby gentility knows: "Modes," "Violin Studio," "Table Board," "Rooms," "Rooms," "Rooms."

Between these old dwellings factories, shops, and gas stations had established themselves and cheap apartment houses had risen; the house Rogers identified as the one they were seeking stood, however, well raised above a brick bulkhead on a corner and so had lost none of its air or light.

It was a yellow double-bay-windowed cottage with overgrown lilac and syringa bushes along the side street and two great shaggy palms flanking the front path. Rogers and Dina could walk in at the front door, for activities of all sorts were going on inside and all the doors and windows were open to the spring air and sunshine. A Japanese in his shirt sleeves was washing windows; a small Japanese woman was wiping down woodwork; paperers had their barrels and planks set up in the double parlors. Clean smells of ammonia, paint, and wet plaster were combated by other older smells of old wood, plumbing, and the still lingering taint of air that has been shut for months within walls.

"Aunt Sarah left a lot of furniture here," Rogers said, indicating with a jerk of his head a canvas-covered mound in the back parlor. "Beds and chairs and bureaus. Caroline came up after she died and took some of the rugs and all the silver and china. Pretty nearly finished?" he asked a paperer, with a glance about.

"Finish tonight, sir," the man said.

"Man come put down carpet tomorrow," contributed the small Japanese woman with an insucking of breath and a smiling bow.

"Carpets all cleaned, were they? Look here, Geraldine, this is the kitchen. Little room off it—they've got blankets stored in here. Now here are the bedrooms, three of 'em, and then back to the front room again. Built about eighteen eighty, I should say. My uncle built it, and my aunt lived here for fifty years. How about it?"

They were in the dining room again, and he leaned against a round oak table that had been pushed against a wall, took out his pipe and stuffed it without removing his eyes from Dina.

Dina sat upon one of a row of aligned chairs and stared at him.
"For what? Us?" she asked.

"Un-hun," Rogers answered briefly.

"But—but why are we moving, Rogers?"

"Oh," the man said with an enlightened look, "when you said 'us' you meant you and me?"

"Of course," she agreed simply.

"I meant your family. The family of Cashman."

Her face showed an electrical change.

"You didn't!" she gasped. And then in a low, convinced tone, "You *couldn't!*"

"Would they move?"

"My family," Dina said, "would move anywhere. But you don't mean—you can't mean—that you're going to let them live here?"

"Why not? It's been standing empty since my aunt died. I've a man who comes once a week to keep the grass cut; that's all it costs me. Why shouldn't it be occupied? It's a nice house." He indicated with a wave of his pipe the darkened room, whose window shades were drawn against the afternoon sun.

"Oh, but—but"—her eyes were pulsating wells of light—"but they'll go perfectly crazy. Myrna will go *crazy!*" she said. "A bathroom! And closets. Big closets! Oh, but I don't believe it!"

"I'll send a truck to move their things, and your father can drive the family up," Rogers planned. "It'll be a nicer place for them, and when it rains they won't be under water, at least. You might suggest they come up and look at it next Sunday, if you like."

"Rogers," said Dina, glowing, "this is awfully kind of you! This is *terribly* kind of you! I can't tell you—they've never lived in anything like this—I can't tell you what it'll mean to my mother! And all of them—Myrna and Dooley, growing up and wanting to have boys come to the house. Oh, the bureaus," Dina exulted, walking about now from room to room, "and all that furniture under that canvas—I *wish* we could see it!"

"Well, here, we can!" He nodded to the Japanese, and they flung back a part of the covering.

"Oh, Rogers, not a piano!" Dina gasped, actually turning pale.

"Un-hun, her old upright. They're getting to be curios, but I suppose it could be tuned."

"Tables," Dina said in a trance, "and books—and those are curtains! And a standing lamp! My mother has talked about a standing lamp she had, for years! And so many chairs! My sister Myrna took music lessons when she was only ten," Dina went on, striking a rusty chord from the keys; "we all did because a lady boarded with us who owned a piano, and Myrna was talented—she said so, and she said Myrna ought to go on. They're paying twelve dollars rent," she finished anxiously. "You'll let them go on paying that, won't you?"

"I don't know as I will," Rogers said, touched by her enthusiasm. "Why, good heavens, Geraldine," he added, "towns are full of empty old cottages like this that somebody might as well be using! I don't know that I could rent it if I wanted to. If you think they'll like it——"

"*Like* it!" she echoed reproachfully as he paused.

"Then you go down and see your mother tomorrow and ask her about it. By the way, what does your father do?" Rogers asked. "Beside mattresses, I mean."

"What Pop likes to do is to be a night watchman," Dina said. "Mama says that when he's a night watchman he never touches a drop. He used to read."

"That factory across there is a mattress factory; he might get something to do there. And that other—that big shed higher than the rest—is the plant my uncle owned—a bottle factory," Rogers said as they came out into the afternoon light again. "See there, 'Forrester Glass and Bottle Works.' I could always get him a berth there, I should think; I know young Sam pretty well. They probably keep a night watchman or two."

"You see, if he's working at night my father's asleep when the other men go to places like Murphy's and Mulligan's." Dina explained it simply, getting into the car. "Oh, look at it!" she exclaimed. "Isn't it darling! Isn't it a *home*! You're *awfully* kind. . . ."

Her voice died away and she sat silent, staring ahead with un-

seeing eyes. What she was seeing in a blinding wave of home
sickness was the Cashman family, wild with excitement, moving
into the new home. Herself alone in the gloomy Holland mansion
when Dooley and Lou went to the nearest grocery for that first
moving-day order that Dina knew so well: bread, butter, and eggs
of course, and coffee, oatmeal, lard, flour, and sugar, and canned
milk and bacon and potatoes—and then, slackening off as the
staples began to be exhausted, oranges and ten cents' worth of
onions—and yes, the chocolate cake that El'ner had brought to
the counter, and the cookies to which Donny had passionately
attached himself, and everything else to which the money in the
Cashmans' hands would stretch in one glorious orgy of marketing
because it was moving day!

Then the unpacking into real bureaus and real closets; the
laughter, running from room to room. "Is this our room, Mama?
Mama, is this our table? Dooley, come look and see out of our
window!" And the wild interest in the first baths—hot water run
ning plentiful and clean into a clean tub, soap and towels. There
had been piles of towels, not the finest, not the newest, but clean
towels, stacked with housewifely precision in the linen closet.
What fun for Mama and for them all! Pop backing the rickety car
into the yellow garage; Myrna trying the Venetian blinds at the
parlor windows; El'ner and Donny racing the folding doors to
and fro! To find the nearest schools, to explore the neighborhood
for movies, candy store, library! She would have been guide and
leader in all this once; she would have shared her family's bettered
fortunes as she had shared their darkest ones. The agony of home
sickness, its keen pang of feeling joy unnecessarily sacrificed, over
whelmed her.

"Myrna'll take that little room off the kitchen to have for her
own," she said. "It has a little washroom off it, and she'll rather
be there. She's always talking of a room all her own."

"I wondered what was keeping you quiet so long," Rogers said.
"You were moving them in, eh? They'll be further away from
you, Geraldine; you've thought of that? But we'll put a telephone
in, and you can call them every night if you want."

"A telephone! Myrna'll drop dead," Dina commented simply.

"They have no telephone now." Rogers made it a statement rather than a question, and for a time there was silence again. Presently the man broke it.

"There's something I've rather been wanting to say to you, Geraldine," he began, "and I haven't exactly known how to put it. Or perhaps I didn't realize it myself. But lately, lately—and this was what I wanted you to know—I've been feeling happier than I've felt in a good many years."

It was impossible to mistake his meaning that she had something to do with it; Dina's face as she turned to him was bright with pleasure.

"Falling in love is a sickness, I suppose," Rogers went on. "And sometimes one gets well. I'm not cured," he added as Dina did not speak, "but I'm convalescent. It's been for years—*years* that every time I thought of Aline Pierpont I've been almost suffocated. Whether she was near me or far away, or married to someone or divorcing someone, or whether I just heard her name mentioned, it was the same. For years I thought it was love; then I knew it was hate; and sometimes it was both at once."

"I can understand that," Dina said.

"I hope you can't! When she divorced Rosenstirn," Rogers said, driving steadily ahead, "she came to me in some financial trouble. I straightened it out, or rather Callaghan did. Callaghan's a simple fellow and he always spoke of her as 'the she-cobra.' He didn't like her. But she had the same effect on me she'd always had. She was —under my skin."

A silence. Dina did not speak, but when he glanced at her he saw her bright eyes fixed on his in complete attention.

"Well, what I wanted you to know," said Rogers, "is that the spell is breaking. It's partly her marriage to that nice big boob who is going to have a terrible waking up one of these days, and it's partly because she sees herself that she ought to have married me. She said as much yesterday. She'll divorce him, and this time she'll come to me, not I to her. Yes; after twenty years of it she'll come to me.

"By that time," he went on, "you'll want to be free. You'll still be a kid in years, with a little boy to bring up, and you'll want to make other plans. I'll have served my turn.

"But what I'm trying to say," he added, after a side glance that showed him only Dina's half profile and one curved ear tip, "is that you've done something for me. More than I ever could do for you or your family. Just having you in the house, young and pretty and interested in what I am saying and doing; just our music and our games and listening to me talk about my stamps and hearing you downstairs in the garden chatting with McPherson while I'm shaving—it's done something for me that all the years I was married to Anna didn't do.

"You see, when I married Anna I was in love with Aline. I was sick with love, as only a boy of twenty-one can be. She'd just married Pollock; she'd been presented at St. James's; she was everything, and I was—well, you can imagine me twenty years ago. Fat, weak eyes, blubbering because she didn't love me. My mother and Anna's arranged our marriage; Mother talked to me about it one day, Anna's mother kissed me, and it was in the papers. That was all I knew about it."

"You never asked her!"

"I never thought of asking her. She was a quiet, pale girl, nicely raised. She loved a chance to show off her French and German; quietly, you know, as if everyone who counted at all must of course have been educated in Europe. I think we both were dazed when we found ourselves on the train going to Banff for our honeymoon.

"She almost never spoke, Anna. We were married and living in the same house and that was that. I'd ask her at the table, 'How'd it go today?' 'Why, just as I expected it to,' she'd say, looking up surprised. Quietly surprised, of course. 'Did you go to the hospital and see Jean?' 'Certainly.' That would be all.

"She was great on making calls and seeing old people and going to hospital board meetings. But she never had anything to say about them. Anna hated the old place, and we moved into town. She felt she had to have a child or two for the Holland and Farjeon families. I wanted kids too, but she never had a healthy child. After about four years she became a chronic invalid. We went down to the old place for the summers, moved back to the city. She had nurses around her, and finally she fell in love with one of her nurses, Helen Johnson. Nobody could do anything for her but Helen; I couldn't go into the room without asking Helen's permission, and after Anna had dismissed me in the evenings, saying that her head ached, I'd hear her and Helen laughing and murmuring for hours. Helen waked her up as marriage couldn't and motherhood couldn't; I don't know now what the answer was. That went on for the last four years."

"Helen probably made her feel comfortable and saved her pain," Dina said thoughtfully.

"She did that. She understood Anna, too; joked with her and teased her in a way I never could do, somehow. Anna adored her. I was glad of it."

"And took up stamp collecting," Dina suggested shyly. There was surprise and pleasure in Rogers' brief laugh.

"And took up stamp collecting," he agreed. "Well, then Anna died," he went on, "and Aline came back here. She was Mrs. Rosenstirn then, married to a fine fellow, musical, cultured, and of course thinking she was the most beautiful woman alive. And indeed she was. He had a place in Honolulu, another in Philadelphia—he was a big nerve specialist.

"Mental cruelty was what she accused him of. She had two children by Pollock; she got hold of them for a visit and went to Reno, and I went up there to see her. Beautiful apartment of course, beautiful children, nice nurse in charge, and everyone making a fuss about Aline. This was—let's see—last year."

"Only last year!"

"Yep. She told me she'd been a little fool all her life, that she had come to appreciate my old friendship and that it would be heaven to get down to the old place in Burlingame and have her children with her. She wanted to be a country lady, she said. She said, 'We'll ride horses and garden and have a few friends in and keep dogs——'"

"My old dream," Rogers began again after a moment's pause. "The dream I'd dreamed since I was twenty years old. I said to her that she needn't bury herself; we'd go to New York and perhaps Europe; we'd take in the symphony concerts and the opera in San Francisco. Everything was all straightened out. Her estate was pretty well wrecked; we saved what we could. Some debts she had run up I wiped out. It was all wonderful!"

He stopped on a bitter note, and Dina, looking at him timidly, saw that his face was dark.

"I hate—I hate to have you look that way!" she said, her fingers on his arm.

He shook himself as if to shake off a tangible hurt.

"Well, as I tell you," he said in a milder tone, "I'm not feeling it as I did. Not always. Yesterday and today there've been breaks—rifts in the clouds I've been under for so many years. It's like coming out into the air after stifling, Geraldine. It's like finding water when you are dry—parched all the way down—mouth and eyes and stomach and throat!"

"And the next thing you knew, she married Mr. Havens?"

"Went down to visit my sister-in-law—dear Caroline!—at Palm Springs, wrote me from there that I must love her Andy, that she was packing off her two children to their father, and she and Andy were going to be married right away, and that she had known all along that she didn't feel about me the right way!"

"But—but yesterday," Dina said, bewildered, "you said she said something about *this* marriage being a mistake!"

"She did. But in a way that didn't blame him and didn't blame her," Rogers said. "You see, she's changed, and it's partly you who are responsible. From the moment she saw you in my house last January she said she felt changed. She knew then—d'ye see?—that she'd been fooling herself all this time. She"—he laughed indulgently—"she's jealous of you, Geraldine. She said so! She said she couldn't bear to see you in my house, mistress there, and if you had a child to have it *my* child. And then she—she came close to me and said 'Toppy'—that was her old name for me, you know—'Toppy,' she said, 'haven't we been the fools, you and I? All that

I ever needed was——' Well," Rogers broke off with a gruff little laugh, "anyway, she said the things I've been waiting twenty years to have her say. But at the same time she couldn't say kind enough things for Andy. 'He's a darling boy,' she said, 'and I know that I'm not harming him. I'll never hurt him. But someday when he sees someone else——'

"He's not apt to see anyone he likes as much as he does her," Rogers interrupted himself again to say. "But she let me see that it was all on his side. He had fallen hard for her, down there in the summer warmth and the palms and all that, tennis and swimming—amusing themselves all the time, and she just—she's got the tenderest heart. . . ."

He fell silent and Dina was silent, too, marveling.

"Wouldn't you and she—you were quarreling so yesterday——" She presently offered hesitatingly.

"Oh lord, we've always done that!" Rogers said comfortably. "Once she was my wife there'd be no more of that! Because you see," he added confidently, "I'd have the whip hand now. She's come to *me* this time. She wants peace and quiet and companionship and security for her children; she said so. And she—she put her hand on my shoulder yesterday," Rogers finished with another gruff, half-ashamed laugh, "and said, 'Mind you never let me go again, Toppy!'"

Dina could think of nothing to say, and as he now seemed to sink into his own happy thoughts the drive was finished without further words.

Chapter 13

IN THE DREAMY SPRING MORNINGS she walked through the scented, foggy world to the convent, where a small, wrinkled Spanish sister took her through the first miseries of Spanish verbs. Dina loved the atmosphere of the big school; while she struggled with grammar and drew pictures to supplement her scanty Spanish and Sister Mary Felippa's almost equally deficient English she could hear girls practicing piano scales furiously behind glass doors, hear their feet chipping in the halls and their shouts over basketball at recreation. Sometimes bells rang; sometimes a little nun came in to interrupt the lesson and murmur quietly to the Spanish teacher, who murmured as quietly in reply. Once they were all summoned to the chapel, girls and nuns, and Dina went with them and knelt, watching absorbedly the ceremonial of benediction. There were flowers on the altar, roses and freesias whose breath mingled with the sharp sweet smell of the incense; there were many candles burning bravely in a bar of sunlight.

Dina would get home, flushed and hot from walking, just as the sun was bursting through the mist. She would put on an old smock, a straw helmet she had bought in the five-and-ten-cent store, and descend to work in the garden, stopping only in time to wash her hands for lunch. At luncheon she would give Rogers a smiling, sleepy account of her adventures before going upstairs to lie down, perhaps to read and perhaps to nap.

Afterward they often had an engagement. Dina went with him to the city, half an hour's drive distant, to concerts, pictures, cocktail parties, or perhaps to see some visiting friend at one of the big hotels.

Sometimes Mrs. Bucket packed an evening dress for her and she and Rogers changed to dinnerwear in the rooms he kept in an apartment house on California Street. If they did, he always had some errand between six and half-past six, returning only when Dina was dressed. She was never conscious of any embarrassment about it; he was like a good-natured older brother, a brother whose admiring talk of another woman sometimes bored her and often made her feel a sense of pity for his simplicity.

She never got quite used to being introduced as his wife, but that was perhaps because so many of his friends were amazed at the situation too. The men would hold her hands, laughing, looking admiration at her youth, and teasing Rogers for being a cradle snatcher. The women were almost invariably nice to her; she grew less afraid of them and more sure of herself. Always she remembered his first advice, to be silent and smile, and although she knew that some of them thought Rogers' wife an absolute fool, she made few mistakes and often really enjoyed herself.

"That Mrs. Berry—that Betsey Berry—was she the one who talked about me, Rogers?"

"When'd she talk about you?"

"Don't you remember? Don't you remember Mrs. Havens—Aline—telling you that day—or no, you asked her what she'd said to Betsey Berry?"

"Oh, that was a shot in the dark, Geraldine. And you saw how it took! No, I don't think Betsey ever said anything unkind about anyone. I was trying to scare Aline, and it worked."

"I'm glad Mrs. Berry didn't say anything mean about me, for she was so nice to me at the club today."

"Have any fun at the club lunch?"

"Well, I liked watching the tennis. I'm beginning to understand tennis—how they score it."

"And how much do you like all this going around? Pebble Beach next Saturday and Minnie Carelton's dinner Tuesday night and people coming here Wednesday."

"But the people coming here Wednesday are going to play bridge, aren't they?" Dina asked, alarmed.

"They are, until about half-past one, probably! You don't mind all this gadding?"

Dina hesitated. They were playing backgammon, and now she slowly turned the big dice about, sometimes setting up one number, sometimes another. The spring evening was warm; they had no fire tonight. The light from a floor lamp fell upon her shining head.

"I like it better when we're just alone here, like tonight," she presently said.

"You really do?"

"I like the days with nothing in them but my Spanish lesson or maybe our going to town to a movie or walking or working with your stamps, and I like evenings like this one. If we have a date I'm thinking about it—I'm a little scared about it—all day."

"It's years," the man said, "since I've gone around this way. I think it's your doing. I get a great kick about arriving places with you and having you peel off your coat——"

"Always an effort when it's my new coat," Dina said. Rogers laughed.

"They all like you," he said, "and it makes me—it makes me important. Everyone's interested—all my mother's old friends, Van's friends."

"I make you important?" Dina echoed, faint emphasis on the pronouns.

"You do, my dear. And one reason is"—Rogers worked it out—"that you're happy. They can see it. The way you talk of this place, the way you let them see that you're not anxious to be asked to parties, not interested in dancing and night clubs——"

"Good heavens!" Dina said under her breath.

"Well, things will be quieter now," Rogers went on. "Everyone's going away. But this has been a queer sort of happy time for me, Geraldine, seeing people I haven't seen for years, getting into

things again. Having my bride steal Aline's thunder," he finished
with a smile.

"What'll they think—what'll they think in July, Rogers?" she
asked, shrinking, her troubled eyes meeting his for a second, moving away again.

"Nothing. They'll all be away, going off to Honolulu and the
Rogue River and Lake Tahoe and the East, and there'll be a baby
here when they all get back—a premature baby, and that'll be
that!"

"I thought—you remember we talked once?—of my going away,
not coming back until perhaps October. But now I would rather
not do that. I'm so—so sheltered here," Dina said, getting up to
go look out of the window into a moon-washed night. "That is,
unless you have some feeling about it."

"My feeling about it is that I'd rather have you here. Nobody
bothers us, and what goes on is nobody's business. We couldn't
be better hidden than here. We go only the places we want to go.
No one bothers us."

"I'm in a sort of dream, Rogers," Dina said, coming back to
her chair, beginning to set up the men for another game. "I've
been in a dream since that day we went to Reno. Before that,
maybe. I hope I won't wake up—I hope I'll never wake up!"

"Not a bad dream, Geraldine?" he asked, watching her intently.

"Oh no, not a bad dream." Her earnest, shadowed eyes, with
their look of young pain and puzzlement, went to his. "It's just
that nothing is quite real," she said. "It began when I first liked
Vere."

She had rarely mentioned him; the color came into her face as
she said his name.

"After—after Paradise Valley," she went on, "it was all like a
dream in which, you know, you sort of feel ahead, with a kind
of—of being frightened, of being terrified, what's going to happen.
But you can't stop it. You say, in your dream, 'Oh, here it comes,
here it comes'—and it's so horrible. But you can't stop it.

"You remember, Rogers, when we went down to the Community Playhouse to see *Six Characters in Search of An Author?*

Something like that. I think I knew from the very beginning
that I was one of those girls who had to play it out—had to watch
for the postman, and worry, and say to herself, 'No, it can't be
so! Vere does love me! There's some mistake. He'll come back
and make it all right!'"

"There are lots of them, Geraldine," Rogers commented mildly
as she stopped with a faraway look in her eyes.

"Oh, lots of them! But all through I had that dreamy feeling
that Vere *was* the kind that would go away, that after all I'd
heard and all I knew—and all I'd been, Rogers, in school and in
my job—it would happen to me!

"And then to come here, and see the ring on my hand, and go
around this house with the servants calling me 'Mrs. Holland.'
That was still the dream, and these lunches and dinners and cocktail parties—they're still the dream too. Reality," she said, "is Railway Flats and Dina Cashman getting breakfast and taking her
brown sweater off the line not quite dry and rushing over to
Meyer's."

"After a while it'll seem realer to you. Gradually you'll awake."

"I'll come alive," she said. "Instead of dreaming true like Peter
Ibbetson I'll begin to live true and stop dreaming. Well, see if
you can shake a five, Rogers, and we'll start on a double."

The Cashman family moved to Stockton on a hot May afternoon. Their heavier movables made the sixty-mile trip in the
battered little truck of a Chinese fruit farmer; Art and Myrna,
with the two younger girls, drove up in the family car among ropes
and bales, bags and boxes, brooms and bedding. Their father, with
his favorite, El'ner, had preceded them by bus, leaving his wife
and Donny to settle matters at Railway Flats and report the loss
of the key to the landlord.

The advance party was to spend the night at an auto camp near
their new home, a prospect which filled them with an excited
sense of being travelers. The girls had packed pajamas and brushes;
they fluttered about in a very glory of departure and adventure.

"But where'll we have dinner, Art?"

"Oh, some restaurant! Tomorrow we can cook lunch in the kitchen."

The thrill of it carried them over any twinges of farewell to the neighbors at Railway Flats. Envious schoolmates stood about; the Cashmans were going to live in Stockton!

Dina remained behind with her mother and Donny; two days later she and Hall returned with the big car, and the last members of the Cashman family were taken in state to the new home. By this time, she hoped, Art and her father and Myrna would have the yellow house in some sort of order; she was pleasantly surprised, upon arriving, to find that they had taken the business of settling in very seriously and that the place already presented a homelike and orderly aspect.

Rogers had seen to it that the rugs were laid and the old curtains, freshly starched, restored to place at the shining windows. To the Cashmans it was incredible that there should be so many big comfortable chairs, so many deep bureaus. When Dina and her mother arrived El'ner and Lou were shyly making friends with two pig-tailed small blondes from across the street, Dooley was putting scalloped oilcloth on kitchen shelves, and Myrna was trilling joyously at the piano.

Only superficial tasks were left: the distribution of a grocery order; directions to the nice young man who came to connect the telephone; arrangement of the family's shabby small addition of sheets and towels with the comfortable stacks of linen already in the linen closet.

"Me with a linen closet! Pa'll have a vallay next," Ethel Cashman observed.

Dina sat watching them all in the light of the warm spring afternoon. There was an apple tree outside the kitchen window; there were roses and flat lilies and marigolds in the garden. Everybody was busy; laughing, coming and going. She felt herself far away from them now; she was tired, and the prospect of being taken quietly home through the green countryside, presently to be resting on her wide bed in her own big room, presently to go downstairs in the taffeta dress and sit telling Rogers all about it,

was infinitely restful. She looked at the clothes her sisters were
hanging in closets, folding into drawers. The same old clothes that
she had seen them wearing only a few months ago, yet such aeons
away! Ma's mottled red-and-yellow comb; Donny's little reefer
with two buttons gone; Myrna's glassy, transparent yellow raincoat. She had no part in them now, no part in this swarming hive
of life and youth and eagerness. Something stronger than any
mere physical barrier, any physical distance between them, had
shut her away.

Chapter 14

IT WAS SOME THREE MONTHS LATER, on a chilly, windy July afternoon, that the evening papers had the news: there had been an
accident on the Bayshore Highway; Rogers Holland, who had
been driving the car, was only slightly bruised, but Mrs. Holland,
his only passenger, had been taken to the hospital in a serious
condition.

The morning papers confirmed the story and added that Mrs.
Holland's little daughter had been born some hours after the
accident.

"Save me everything the papers say about Margaret!" Dina said
when Rogers came into her room at midnight. "You've been crying," she reproached him. "And what a bruise! And your hand
tied up!"

"I was scared about you," he said. "You—you're wonderful! I
just wanted to say what a sport I think you are and they all say
you are!"

"She said you could stay three minutes. Did you see the baby?"

"I'm to see her now."

"She's perfectly whole, anyway," said Dina. "I made them show
her to me. I was afraid going over that bank might have been
bad for her. They said I was brave?"

"To have your leg set while you were having a baby."

"Rogers, don't be disappointed in her. Black hair and red spots.
She looks so like a baby rat I almost pushed her off the bed!"

"You better let go, dear. They'll throw me out."

She had been clinging to his hand.

"It was awful, Rogers."

He set his jaw, shut his eyes, shuddered.

"But it's over. I had chicken soup. Imagine, Rogers! Lunching with you at home, and now this!"

"I know. God, what an afternoon! And, Geraldine, have you thought of this? The accident takes care of the question of dates—there won't ever be any talk now."

"You mean her coming too soon?" Dina's eyes, in a pale face, were wise and content. Her wet hair was still clinging to her forehead; there were still about her the odors of anesthetic and antiseptics; she wore a high-collared hospital nightgown of coarse, unbleached, much-laundered linen, buttoned in back. But perhaps the man found her beautiful, for the look in his eyes had in it something of reverence.

"Nothing seems to matter now except that she's here and all right," she said. "My mother asked me to name her Margaret, for her mother. My name is Margaret Geraldine," Dina added. "Is that all right with you?"

"It was my mother's name too."

"I know. Is that all right? I'm still a little dopey, so don't be afraid of tiring me," Dina broke off to say. "I'm slap-happy."

"You won't be slap-happy tomorrow. Why wouldn't it be all right? Another Margaret Holland."

"I didn't know." She looked straight at him. A nurse came in from behind a screen at the door.

"Mr. Holland—I'm sorry—but this girl was smashed all to pieces at noon today and she's had a baby."

"I know! Good-by, dear. I'm going to see Margaret. What is it?" For she had beckoned him back.

"Only this, Rogers. I've known it all day long," Dina whispered. "I'm still stupid; I'm not quite sure where I am or what's happened. But just this last hour or two—when I waked up with my leg in plaster and Margaret here—I've known it. I'm awake!"

It was strange to be invalided. It was strange to lie day after day in her big comfortable room, with Mrs. Bucket coming in morning and afternoon to stop and gossip, Miss Rafferty, the nurse, bringing up trays, and Ida, the gentle, quiet colored woman, taking full charge of little Margaret.

The broken leg had knitted satisfactorily and in record time; the fracture had been slight and there had been no need of pulleys and weights, but a tedious complication had developed in the other leg long before Dina was allowed to walk, and the weeks stretched into months, and still there seemed to be no change in sight.

They had brought her home from the hospital in ten days, miraculously escaped from the accident that might have killed both her and her child. Dina was patient. She conceded a four- or five-week imprisonment in bed. A broken leg and a baby were a bad combination, and, after all, she wanted to get quite well while she was about it.

But the joking stopped for a few days when she realized that as one leg came steadily back to normal the other began to show signs of poisoning and that all the courage and patience she could command were going to be needed in the long weeks ahead. For a while it seemed to her that she could not face it, and Rogers came in more than once to find her unable to keep back the tears.

She had never been ill. She had looked forward to the care of her baby, to peaceful days in the old house when she and her child would be alone for hours.

Instead her room became the center of an unwonted activity. Friends who had not come to the Holland home for years appeared with good wishes and presents for the new Holland baby; messengers with flowers and with telegrams came and went, and the tiny Margaret was regularly displayed by her beaming attendant to afternoon callers.

But with the rapidity characteristic of the invalid who does not suffer, and with her own active mind and imagination to aid her, Dina presently settled to the inevitable and found her days surprisingly full. Miss Rafferty, whose affection and enthusiasm and sympathy were in themselves a cure, was busy with her for an hour or two after her leisurely breakfast. When the newspapers and the tray, the soaps and towels and basins had gone the baby came in, and her bassinet was placed where her mother, looking downward, could study the small placid face for quarter hours together. Before Margaret's two o'clock and six o'clock bottles Dina could hold her for a blissful interval, and now and then when Margaret roared in the night Ida brought her in to her mother while a warm meal and a dry crib were being prepared.

Every day the little Spanish nun came over for a lesson, and Dina worked hard at her written exercises. In midafternoon, when the baby slept, she dozed, and afterward she was helped into her prettiest nightgown and her Japanese jacket, and callers found her fresh and philosophical and there was much laughter in the room.

Sometimes Rogers came up to join the women, and Dina rejoiced to see that he grew more and more to enjoy these visits and these visitors, when Lily would bring up trays of tall glasses and the talk turn to old days. Rogers' mother had been a social leader and a friend to all these women as young girls or younger wives. There was much congratulation for the father of the small, sturdy, flourishing Holland baby, and he accepted it pleasantly and watched Margaret's progress with almost as much interest as Dina's own.

The big victrola had been moved upstairs, and after a few games of cards after dinner, when Dina grew tired of her somewhat cramped position, there was a concert. Rogers brought records upstairs, assorted them and arranged them in order, and himself went about lowering lights and placing chairs. Dina would settle on her pillows, Miss Rafferty come in quietly to slip into a chair, Rogers lie back in his own great leather chair, and the glorious strains of operas, *Rosenkavalier* and *Rheingold, Boris* and even *Iolanthe,* would drift through the quiet place. Dina came to know Tchaikovsky's symphonies, Beethoven's majestic sonatas, Vienna waltzes, and Russian ballets. Sometimes tears would be on her cheeks as she listened; she would open her eyes to smile across the room at her husband.

"Chopin," he would apologize. "Too sad for you!"

"No, I love it. I *love* it!" And she *did* love it, even though it seemed to have the power to wash away all the changes and pain of the past years and take her back again to the wild, gay, gypsy little Dina who had mothered her brothers and sisters at ten, and camped wherever her parents' fickle fancy stopped the shabby car, and dreamed of a future in which whatever happened she, Dina Cashman, would always be a leader and an idol.

She played patience if ever there was a dull hour; she had books of puzzles and became so absorbed in them that often the announcement of a visitor caused her a pang of regret. And she had books; an endless river of books poured through the room, Mrs. Bucket rarely entering without one or two that she had picked from the old library downstairs, Rogers instructing a San Francisco bookseller to keep her supplied with what was new.

Above all, there was the baby for an inexhaustible distraction, joy, pride, anxiety, and responsibility. All the women in the house circled about Margaret, and the slightest fluctuation in her little routine caused them wild excitement. Miss Rafferty, the tiny, dainty, always immaculately clad nurse, would go skimming downstairs for fresh bed linen or a malted milk from the refrigerator; Chong would come puffing upstairs with the baby's bottle; Ida, the colored girl, and Lily, the upstairs maid, debated daily as to just what corner of the sun porch should be honored by the crib; Mrs. Bucket was early convinced the baby knew her and repeatedly sent both maids off to an evening's movies for the express purpose of being left in charge of the sleeping infant. Eager advantage was taken of every excuse that anyone could find to pick Margaret up, change her clothes, bathe her, poke her limp little arms into sweaters, or wrap her up in her "bunting" on a foggy morning. Fortunately she was a serene, sweet lump of a baby, passing amiably from hand to hand and rewarding her attendants with smiles.

What Dina thought of her nobody could have said, least of all Dina. The familiar phrase "having a baby" and the cataclysmic, world-shaking experience of having brought Margaret into the world seemed to have nothing in common. It had taken her to new depths of terror and suffering and raised her to new heights of joy, new heights of that relief that is the blissful forerunner of joy. These were her secret; she could share them with no one. But she liked to lie still at night and bring them to memory like treasures to be turned over and hugged to her heart in the darkness or to waken before the summer dawn, when a pearly light was in the room and Margaret, fussing for her first meal, could be heard in the adjoining apartment, and remember it all again.

Of the accident she had no impression whatsoever. On that fatal morning Rogers had been driving her to the city. Andrew Havens had been at the house earlier in the day, adding some finishing touches to her portrait. The portrait had been completed weeks earlier, but Andrew's exhibition had been postponed until the fall and he had wanted to lighten the shadow on Dina's face and—so he said—give more life to her hair. Dina and Rogers had been talking casually as the car approached the underpass entering south San Francisco. She had not even glimpsed the small, tearing jalopy that had forced a great truck to swerve and to knock Rogers' car from the road. Her first impression, when she had been conscious of any at all, came when she was being picked up for the ambulance trip to the hospital.

The gravelly wet thing that had been laid on her eyes she had discovered to be her hand; a great many other hands were lifting her; voices were murmuring shocked monosyllables. Her head, there! Look out! Easy there!

She had been wheeled somewhere, a flat, broken thing with a blanket laid over all the blood and sweat, smashed bone and flesh. Pain had suddenly assailed her from half-a-dozen directions at once; her leg, her shoulder, her head aching heavily, and nausea shaking her whole racked being in spasmodic attacks. And then a new pain, creeping and all embracing—lessening and coming back, stabbing and rending again. Swooning off into blackness, swooning back into consciousness, she had heard a doctor's voice, close to her face, "I don't know!"

She and Rogers had started for town shortly before twelve.

Margaret Holland had been born to a bandaged mother with her leg in a cast at five. Hills and valleys of pain had lain between; Dina had been soaked with blood and sweat when first she had heard her child cry; her voice had come from a throat that was sore with screaming.

But strange mystery of pain and relief from pain! She loved the memory. She loved to think of resting, resting, pain over, and of the receding headache, the relaxed muscles. Then, so gently that she was not moved at all, had come the fresh nightgown, fresh sheets, warm blankets, lowered lights after the glare of the surgery, and someone saying: "She's a little darling; six pounds and a half, and quite perfect!" Then the taste of chicken soup—such good soup——

"One never goes back," she said to Rogers.

"Was it so awful?"

"I don't mean that. I just mean that—one never goes back."

"I suppose not."

"To start," Dina mused, "in that terrible little kitchen of ours in Railway Flats. I mean my first inkling that there might be a baby. Rainy and smelling of ashes and swill and pigs, and my feeling so sick, and everything dark and muddy with no money anywhere, and then to have her turn out to be a little fresh warm rose with everything clean and safe about her! And to have been so anxious—so frightened and anxious," she went on, "and now to feel so proud!"

"I think you may well feel proud," he told her.

Her head drooped. She spoke in a low tone.

"Never proud again," she said.

"Not proud, I suppose," Rogers said in a tone as thoughtful as her own, "not proud of doing—anything foolish, but proud, I should think, of the way we pull ourselves out of mistakes, make up for them. Mightn't one be proud of that?"

"Perhaps," she said, her shadowed eyes brightening.

"I remember thinking about Anne—about my first wife," the man presently resumed, "that I'd not played fair with her. I never loved her, and she knew it when we were married. The Farjeons were prominent people but they had no money; Anne knew, marrying me, that it would be a good thing for them. So that when she went into invalidism I felt there was something I could do to make it up to her. I could take care of her. It made me feel better afterward," he finished simply.

"Perhaps what you've done for me is going to make you feel better afterward too," Dina said.

"It was my proposition," he reminded her promptly. "I wanted to impress Aline, to call off a little of her joke—her practical joke on me! Instead of that I don't know exactly what has happened," he added with an innocent look of bewilderment that made Dina smile, "but I seem to be—as you might say—in the driver's seat. From the beginning she took your being here as a personal matter. Just as everything that touched her used to torture me, everything that happens to you seems to—to worry *her!* She always knows all about you. If I meet her, she's up on all the news; she knew that your mother and father came to see you, and she wanted to know all about them."

"I imagine they were safe with you," Dina said, unalarmed.

"And if Andy really exhibits your portrait in November, she'll be wild," Rogers said thoughtfully.

"I don't see why." Dina was talking lazily; Aline's opinions seemed much less important than they had once seemed; she somehow felt quite secure against Aline and Caroline in these quiet days of invalidism. The great awakening of motherhood, the lessons of helplessness and pain had changed her values.

"Well, it's excellent! The best thing he's ever done!" Rogers said.

"I suppose," Dina mused aloud, "that the reason people go on having their portraits painted is because they're always so flattering."

"And then nothing looks so important over the mantel as a painting of Great-aunt Louisa."

She laughed delightedly, said:

"I suppose not. Everyone agrees it's one of the best portraits Andy's ever painted, and if he wants to show it, I should think

Aline would realize that it's his business; it's important to him. Why didn't he have his exhibition in May, Rogers, as he was going to?"

"Too busy painting. He's had five commissions, I believe, and he thinks you brought him all his luck."

"You did, you mean. I never would have thought of such a thing."

"Well, if I did, it was to spite Aline," Rogers confessed, smiling. "Lord, lord," he said under his breath, "but she is the spoiled baby!"

"The day he came to change the hair in my portrait—the day of the accident—you and she had a talk, didn't you?"

"Yes, downstairs in the drawing room. He proposes to exhibit only two portraits of her, and another in which she is only part of a group, and this one she doesn't like. It's of some well-known musician, a cellist, I think—forget his name—and Aline is only a minor figure. I think that's part of the trouble."

"You say you think she's spoiled?" Dina smiled.

"Aline? Spoiled from her birth! Her mother and father spoiled her, Pollock let her do anything she pleased, and Rosenstirn spent money on her as if she were a princess—jade necklace and chinchilla coat!" Rogers' tone was fond, amused. "That quiet little mulish way of hers . . ." he mused. "But she is fascinating, Geraldine?" he roused himself to say interrogatively.

"Oh, she is!" If Dina's tone lacked heartiness he did not discern it.

"I have never," Rogers went on thoughtfully, "I have never seen her as charming as she was on Wednesday. She was down on the terrace in that blue outfit——"

"Beautiful clothes!" Dina put in as he paused. "That hat!" She went into a reminiscent ecstasy.

"But it wasn't only that she looked lovely," Rogers went on. "She was in such a sweet, gentle sort of mood. And she told me—well, things about herself that I never understood before. She's always been trying to help people, ever since she was a little girl, and—as she said herself, laughing—she's always made a mess of it. She married Pollock because he said he would kill himself if she didn't. 'Oh, I know,' she said, 'he mightn't have. But I loved his mother and she'd been good to me and I thought there was nothing else to do.'"

"They had children, didn't they?"

"Two. They're with his mother now."

"And is she still devoted to his mother?"

"The mother took his side in the divorce. No, I don't suppose she is. She was awfully funny telling me how she'd tried to be an influence for good and how she'd come out! You know, wherever she goes, men make it terribly hard for Aline," Rogers said simply.

"You mean they admire her so?"

"All of them. *All,*" the man answered. "In Europe, on trains, in theaters and hotels, men are noticing Aline, trying to get to know her. For instance, she says that at cocktail parties and dinners in New York the men would gather around her and Pollock would naturally be furious."

"And Doctor Rosenstirn, was he jealous too?"

"Worse!"

"A woman as beautiful as that doesn't have so much fun," Dina conceded after thought. "She can only marry one man—at a time, that is. And getting out of a marriage, arranging for a divorce, must be such a fuss!"

"She suffered horribly in this last divorce. She says that's what made her ready to jump into marriage so quickly with Andy. She was dizzy with freedom, down there at Palm Springs, having a glorious time, and she lost her head."

"Then she thinks marrying Andy was losing her head?"

"Think of what she gave up when she married him! Rosenstirn was paying her fifteen hundred a month!"

"Whew! She *did* lose her head," Dina exclaimed, impressed.

"That stopped at once, of course. I don't know exactly what she thought they *would* live on," Rogers added, "but it was characteristic of her that she didn't stop to worry about that! It seems that her father had a portrait done of her in England when she was a girl, in the dress she wore at the Drawing Room, and she had an idea that artists got ten and twelve thousand apiece for portraits. Some of 'em do, of course."

"Then her people had lots of money too, Rogers?"

"Her father was one of the richest men in the country until the crash came. Then he put it all into some oil scheme and lost most of it."

"So that she and Andy really haven't much now?"

"Nothing. She says he hasn't the slightest idea what becomes of his money. For one of these portraits he was paid in advance and that's gone, and one of the others hasn't paid yet and doesn't seem inclined to pay."

"Shaky," was Dina's thoughtful comment.

"Shaky! And she is beginning to feel that she wasn't fair to Andy in marrying him in the first place. She's extravagant, she knows it. The other night, she tells me, she called up a friend in Newport and talked for fifteen minutes. 'I ought to be shot. I never thought what it would cost,' she said."

"So that that marriage may not be a success either?"

"It's a success as far as their liking each other goes. She says she'll always respect him as one of the finest men she's ever known. But—no," Rogers admitted slowly, "I don't believe it will go on for very much longer. Their backgrounds are too different. Aline doesn't belong in a country studio with just one old Chinese doing everything and a bathroom that Andy's friend built in himself of old boards and secondhand plumbing. Things done in that slapdash bohemian fashion don't fit her somehow."

"But if she divorces him, Rogers, then she'll have to marry again."

"Yes, I suppose she will. No trouble there!" Rogers said with a short laugh. "She was telling me that when she's in New York she always has dinner or lunch with Frank—Frank Pollock, I mean. He'd be only too glad to have her come back to him."

"You'd think she might because of the children."

"The children have been her first consideration all through," the man observed. "'I could have had them two months a year,' she told me, 'but I wouldn't upset them by dragging them to and fro over the country. Far better to leave them quietly with their grandmother and their schools. They have the first right!'"

Dina was not so deeply edified by this instance of maternal devotion as she might have appeared. She regarded Rogers steadily, making no comment. She was as aware as he of the fascinations of Aline Havens, if less affected by them. She knew that Aline had seen fit to be gracious to him of late, affectionate, confiding, appealing. Rogers was basking at last in the favor for which he had hungered for years. Dina could tell, not only from what he reported to her but by his changed manner, that he felt happy with Aline at last.

Incurring no blame at all from the group in which she moved, Aline could divorce Andy. Beauty and position like Aline's were a law unto themselves; nobody would blame her.

"Suppose—suppose she wanted to divorce Andy and Andy objected?" Dina asked.

"She would never do anything to hurt Andy. She feels that possibly—oh, she wasn't talking of today or tomorrow—but she said that if ever she thought she was standing in Andy's way she would gladly free him."

"Andy mightn't see it that way." But Dina felt a half-angry, half-jealous conviction that he would. She had seen him twice since the beginning of her long imprisonment; once when he and Aline had called, and he had peeped into her room only for a half minute, and again when he had sat with her for half an hour.

"Rogers," she said now, out of profound thought, "I never was brought up in any religion. We went to Sunday school for a while, Art and I, but we didn't have any real religious training. But it seems to me queer to feel about marriage the way Aline does."

"Well, I was brought up to go to church, and I know what you mean," Rogers answered, his head tipped back against the cushion of his chair, his pipe in one relaxed hand, his narrowed eyes on space. "But Aline has been unfortunate. She never should have married Pollock, although they stuck it for eight years and had children. The Rosenstirn marriage was a little different. He's quite a big shot in his profession, and she adores power. I think Aline really was deeply in love with him for a while. When it ended she was miserable. She was saying the other day that she'd rather be a man's mistress if she loved him than live with a man she didn't love. She told Rosenstirn so, frankly. He saw it. He didn't try to stop her. That's her idea of honesty."

"But after all, she did say 'For better, for worse,' didn't she? I know it made me feel very serious when *we* said it. And yet ours wasn't the—the usual sort of marriage at all."

"I suppose she said those words. But perhaps later she found she didn't feel them. As for the Havens marriage," Rogers resumed, "that never seems to me like a marriage at all! Aline as fine and chiseled and rare as a Chinese porcelain, and this fellow like a big puppy rollicking around her! She's quite a bit older than he, for one thing. No, she'll not do anything hasty," he finished, "but one of these days I think they'll talk it all over and come to some agreement."

Dina made no comment. She wondered what her own position would be when that agreement was made. If Aline really was tired of love experiments, worn out with passion, then she might be glancing at the security of the position of Mrs. Rogers Holland with more than an impersonal interest. Between what she had guessed and what Caroline had told her, she must know that Dina's marriage was no real marriage; she must know that Rogers' generosity had served its turn and that Dina and the small child, who was now secure of her name, who had been protected and made presumably legitimate, might go their way.

Well, if that was the verdict, Dina could not protest. The understanding from the beginning had been that she should supply a counterattraction to Aline, make herself a foil, and she had apparently succeeded. Dina sighed, feeling suddenly tired.

They were talking in the bedroom she had not left for long weeks. Margaret had been born in July; it was October now. Dina was at last allowed to get up, in these beautiful autumn days, but only for a short time. She was carefully lifted to a wheel chair; she could propel herself to the window, station herself in the nursery doorway to see Margaret getting her bath. Even this much freedom was intoxicating. The sight of the woods and the hills, the treetops and the roofs of village houses was thrilling beyond belief. And yet there had been pain, too, in the convalescence that she had awaited so eagerly. The time of invalidism had been a happy time, contented and protected and safe, a time of learning and reading and thinking, a time of pride in her child and new dreams for herself and the baby.

She had come to feel that life in the somber, heavy old house might be complete and satisfying. Rogers was more than twice her age, but they were companionable. They loved to talk, to play games; he laughed at her; he was brighter and better for having her with him. With the baby for an added distraction and delight, with her health completely restored, with Mrs. Bucket to play grandmother as well as guide, philosopher, and friend, Dina's life was sheltered and remote; she need see few outsiders; she was not anxious to see anyone.

If she wanted to visit her mother, she had thought, it would not be hard to take the car and the baby and Ida and drive up to Stockton any day she chose. The Cashman family had moved in April; all the reports that Dina had had, and her two calls, had confirmed her impression that never in their lives had her own people even dreamed of felicity and pride like that they had felt upon taking possession of the yellow cottage. She had found in them a change that had made her more than a little thoughtful. She had wondered how many other forlorn, slatternly women like her mother would turn housewifely and brisk and ambitious under such a change of prospects and environment as her mother now had. How many self-declared failures like her father would have risen as he had to the responsibility of a steady job? How many pretty, frivolous little sisters like Myrna, transplanted to the dignity of a room to herself and a home with a real parlor in it, might grow up overnight to a sense of fineness and character?

At all events, the effect of the transplanting had been miraculous on the Cashmans. The kitchen now was only a kitchen, and the big back parlor a family sitting room, comfortable with lamps and rugs and old-fashioned chairs and table, where the younger children could gather for homework every night. Myrna's and Art's friends used the front parlor for their card games or radio entertainments. "And we go out in the kitchen and cook things," wrote Myrna in an enthusiastic letter to Dina, "and there aren't a lot of kids and dirty dishes there. Gee, we have fun!"

Now she found Rogers' words vaguely disturbing. If Aline once were free again and in this new mood of tenderness and confidence toward him, then what would her next plan be?

"She's worried about something and she wants to lunch with me and talk it over," Rogers was saying. "So I may go into town tomorrow and see what it's all about."

"I go downstairs tomorrow," Dina told him proudly. "I can sit for one hour on the terrace!"

"Walk downstairs?" He was pleased.

"Walk downstairs. I'll take my time. But today I walked into the nursery and out on the porch and wasn't a bit tired."

"You're well again," he said with satisfaction. "You know I may go off with Salter on his yacht over the Christmas holidays?" Rogers asked.

"I heard you and Mr. Salter talking about it the night he was here. Remember he came upstairs here and spoke about it?"

"You wouldn't mind that? Being left alone?"

"Oh no! I never have a minute to spare. And over Christmas, Rogers, I was going to ask you if I could take Margaret and go up and stay with Mama for a few days."

"Could they squeeze you in there, do you think?"

"You don't know the Cashmans! Margaret's little crib goes along with us, and Ida'd board in the neighborhood. And I'd take them all presents," Dina said, her eyes shining. "China for Mama—she was so excited over a teapot and cups she got for her tea coupons that I thought I'd give her plates, and for Myrna a sport suit with a hat. But Pop—he's hard. He really needs everything!"

"Tires for his car are always good," Rogers suggested, pulling on his pipe.

"I thought maybe an overcoat." She fell into a dream of the delight of it. To arrive with her nurse and baby a few days before

Christmas, to take her old place, to hear all the news—ah, it would be fun! Back in the kitchen on the cold frosty mornings, seeing the warmth of the stove dissipate the pearly traceries on the windows, getting the good smells of boiling coffee and sizzling bacon, kneeling to see that the toast or the biscuits were browning, that would indeed be heaven again.

Art would come out of his room ready for the day; Art was working in a gas station now and, to Dina's intense amusement, was shaving, and Art had a girl and was beginning to be rather fussy about the colors of shirts and ties. Gradually the rest of the household would awaken and come into the kitchen, and there would be wreaths and bundles to tie and plans to make.

By this time the light might be turned off, for the day would be shining in at the windows and the sun rising and flashing on the white frosted roofs and the streamers of smoke that arose from all the houses in the neighborhood. Men would be moving toward the factories, Pop among them, children running and screaming in the holiday streets, and women with coats buttoned over slacks hurrying to bakery and dairy.

Dina would be busy now with Margaret's meals; the ring of bottles sterilized, the formula warming, strainers and funnels waiting, and Margaret's wash moving through Ida's experienced black hands. Mama would sit in a kitchen chair, watching, with the thistledown head of her granddaughter bobbing in her arms. This was Dina's old world and she loved it. She had loved it in the days of poverty and anxiety and uncertainty; these days were over for the Cashmans now, and Dina loved it all the more. With her father's pay, Art's help, and Myrna's first earned money a new day was dawning for them. Bills could be met; new standards of comfort and respectability were being reached every day.

"How about my getting back some of my own, Dina?" Rogers said, glancing at the card table upon which a backgammon board was set. And as he moved it toward the bed he added, "I wonder if your father would wear an overcoat of mine? It could easily be fitted, and it would probably be a better coat than he could get in Stockton."

"How he would feel!" Dina echoed in light scorn.

"You mean he wouldn't mind? I have one or two that I'm not wearing. One's too small for me."

"My father," Dina said soberly, "would be extremely grateful, and so would I."

"I could fix up a box of things," Rogers said. "Two six; I don't like it; I double."

He threw a two and a six again, scowlingly considered his play. Dina looked about the big room, pleasant in soft evening light. She knew its every angle and contour now; she had lain through many a wakeful night studying the patterns shadows made on the walls, the old-fashioned wallpaper of trellises and roses, the gold-and-brown cornices from which the curtains hung. If Aline wanted her place here, Aline would get it; Dina would have to go away.

She played, leaned back against her pillows watching Rogers' face. It was as fat, as owllike, and froglike as it had been a year ago when first she had seen it. But one could come to like an owl's face, a frog's face with strong glasses, when that face and those prominent eyes had never expressed anything but kindliness and interest.

"I love him the way a daughter might love him, I suppose," Dina mused. "I never can pay him back for what he's done for me. But I have paid him back a little. He's happier; he's more human. He's taking the chairmanship for the Community Chest Drive; he never would have done that before. And Aline likes him better than she ever did, even the times when they were engaged. But she shan't have him! I'm not going to let her wreck his life!"

"Your play. What were you thinking about?" Rogers asked.

"Nothing," Dina answered with a smile.

Chapter 15

"You KNEW Aline had left me?" Andrew Havens asked.

Dina brought startled eyes to his face.

"Left you!"

"Last Sunday. Yep," the man said briefly.

Her own interest in this situation touched Dina with a first premonitory finger of fear. She turned and went to a great leather bench, and Andy sat down beside her.

The little gallery was flooded with November sunshine and deserted except for themselves. It was ten o'clock in the morning; other visitors would trickle in to see the Havens portraits before noon, and the afternoon would find a smart crowd there, talking, drinking tea, studying the canvases that lined the walls. But it was empty now.

There were seventeen portraits in all. Ten had been loaned and sent on from the East; four were of local patrons, and three were of the artist's wife. These last were a full-length presentation of Aline dressed in a sheath of white Chinese brocade with the famous jade-and-pearl string encircling her throat and caught in her ivory hands, a crayon portrait in white and scarlet and black, and a large canvas, not quite finished, of a man with a violoncello, a standing girl with a violin, and a woman glancing over her shoulder with her hands on the keys of a concert grand. The woman at the piano was Aline. The other musicians were the great Marinkoff and his daughter, who had been at Palm Springs when Aline and Andy had first met each other there. It had been Andy's idea to paint the famous man and his equally gifted daughter with their instruments; the absence of their accompanist had given Aline the additional inspiration of taking his place. Not that she played more than a few pieces on the piano, remembered from childhood. But it would be such fun!

Everything had been fun for Aline in this halcyon time. After several years of marriage to a man who had consistently expected her to be everything, as a wife, that she was completely unfitted and unwilling to be, after a long dearth of compliments and spoiling and flattery, after a dark Eastern winter of snows when she had been ill, and an unsatisfactory hot summer in which she had attempted to get hold of her children whenever their father made it difficult and felt them an embarrassment and a burden when she did, Aline had blossomed in the atmosphere of the southern California resort like a plant languishing from long abuse.

The bland sunshine, the gently waving palms, the pleasant people, so many of them famous, the enchanting cottages with their lush foliage and patios, the stimulation of rides and walks, tennis and golf, swims and bridge, laughter and friendship had transported her to a world free from unpleasantness and responsibility. In that world one was always lovely and admired; one felt young and free and giddy; one wore enchanting daytime frocks of white and scarlet, white and French blue, evening gowns of oriental beauty and splendor.

To be on terms of cordial friendship with Ivan Marinkoff and Olga, to have the handsome young painter following her about with undisguised adoration had set the world right again for Aline. And Caroline had been there, aiding and abetting! She had laughed at Andy for a week or two. Dear silly boy, didn't he know that she was ages older than he and had two unsuccessful marriages behind her and two children rapidly growing up!

Apparently he had not. Before the picture could be finished the Marinkoff's had gone, the group had shifted to another just as brilliant but not so familiar, and Aline had been more and more fascinated, teased, tortured with the idea that it would be quite

simple to drive to Reno one day with Andy and again be an
adored wife.

So perhaps Morning Trio never would be finished. Even as it
stood it was the finest work Andy had done; the old maestro, a
commanding figure with his wild gray hair and his poised bow,
was complete. Aline's portrait was complete; he had had leisure to
work on that on a dozen mornings since. The background of sun-
flooded room, the chintz curtains, and even the subdued figure of
a Chinese boy dusting the dim bookshelves were finished. But
Olga's hands, the important and beautiful hands of the artist, were
only vaguely sketched in, and Olga's mouth was a mere smear.
But the critics praised the work, and it was reproduced in the art
journals nevertheless.

Dina's portrait, however, was the one most admired and most
studied. It had behind it a story that all these audiences knew.
That was Rogers Holland's wife. The mysterious girl, ages younger
than Rogers, who had suddenly appeared in poor Anne Holland's
vacant place. They had a baby now too; she had been in a motor
smash, and the miracle was that both she and the child hadn't been
killed. She'd been laid up for months—the murmuring, milling
crowds in the afternoon told each other—but she was all right
again. She'd been in, opening day, with her husband—a very pretty
girl and apparently terribly fond of him.

Now Dina was in the gallery again with Andy. Her morning in
town was, as usual, filled with engagements; she was having a session with her dentist, she must get Margaret larger dresses, she
was to meet Rogers for luncheon, and there was a symphony afterward which they were to hear from Billy Salter's box. Billy had
been away from California for years; now he and his yacht had
anchored once more in San Francisco waters, and an old intimacy
with Rogers had been resumed with great enthusiasm on both
sides.

This circumstance, too, with all the others, had helped to rein-
state Rogers in his own and public estimation. Billy, with his
bachelor apartment, his social connections, and the yacht, whose
hospitalities were famous, was an important figure in this particu-

lar world. He and Rogers had been close friends as younger men, had drifted apart, were now intimates again.

And Billy liked Dina, had accepted her not with mere politeness but with great formality. He had given her a dinner in his apartment, given a second dinner. He had been a sort of auxiliary host when Rogers had returned the dinner. Other social leaders had taken the hint; Rogers and Dina could discuss their invitations at his late-breakfast table now and decline them all and yet feel the better for being asked. Rogers had long ago had his fill of dinners before coming-out parties, dinners with bridge to follow. Dina was afraid of them. Once again they agreed perfectly upon their policy.

Today Dina had had an interval between engagements that had given her an opportunity to slip into the gallery and see her own portrait again. Like everyone else, she thought it was beautiful: "The way I'd like to look, Andy," she said. It was flattering, of course, and yet the serious face, the shadowed eyes, the firmly clamped young hands on the chair arms were all Dina, too, and youth and youth's eternal questioning incarnate.

Coming into the gallery, she had found Andy in conversation with the proprietor of the art store of which the gallery was a part. When old La Motte had said what he thought of the Portrait of Mrs. Rogers Holland and had departed she and Andy had gone the rounds, discussing the various pictures. He had broken in upon a talk of art and art work in Paris, and his experiences there, with the flat statement of Aline's desertion.

"But, Andy, what *for?*" the girl said.

"I don't know." He sighed, crossed his arms, and leaned back, his lips pursed for whistling, his narrowed eyes on space.

"Quarreled?"

"Nope."

"She's just—tired?"

"Guess so. I don't understand her. She says I never have. We moved down to Bill Cutter's place at Los Altos in June, you know. I thought it was swell down there. Everything blooming and warm, and we had Bill's old Looey Koo to run things. We couldn't go on in town; it was costing us more per week than I make in a month. Orders had stopped, and after old Bowen died the estate refused to pay for his picture. I didn't have anything in writing, and the daughter said she understood I had asked her father to pose as a favor to me.

"Well, in August Aline said she wanted to go East to see her children. Your sister-in-law was going and she wanted to go with her."

"My sister-in-law? Oh, Caroline! Yes."

"She wanted money; she didn't know how much—a couple of thousand. Of course I didn't have it. That fussed her. Where could we get it? I said we couldn't get it anywhere. Afterward she told me she'd tried to borrow it from Rogers, but he said not while she was my wife. Then she said she was sick of the place and of me and she was going to stay with—oh, someone—Mrs. Clyde, I think. She went off to the Rogue and to Lake Tahoe, was gone about six weeks. When she came back she began to talk about divorce."

A silence. Then Dina said timidly:

"How do you feel about it?"

For answer he put his head down in his hands, his body doubled over his knees; he rumpled his hair and groaned.

"Oh, I'm so sorry!" Dina said. "I know how you love her!"

Suddenly the man sat erect and looked at her with bright, angry eyes under his tumbled hair.

"No, I don't love her; I suppose I never did," he said definitely in a hard voice. "I was carried away, as she was. She is one of the beautiful women of all time; I was flattered; it was all drinking and dancing, moonlight and cocktails—I don't know what happened. But it breaks me up to—I mean I'm all mixed—it doesn't make sense!"

"She wants to marry Rogers," Dina said calmly.

"She'd throw him over at the drop of a hat if she got a better chance. She has twice," Andy answered moodily.

"She may not get a better chance this time," Dina observed. The man looked at her curiously.

"Rogers is married," he said.

"You needn't tell me!" Dina answered with a mirthless little laugh. "But he's been in love with her all her life."

"Who said so? She told me that. But she says that of lots of men," Andy said skeptically.

"Oh, but this time it's true. He admits it."

"Rogers?"

"Yes, and if she'd look at him he'd jump right through rings," Dina said, too much in earnest to pick her words.

"But he's—he's married to you!" Andy stammered.

"Yes, but I'd never refuse Rogers anything he asked of me," Dina said, her voice dreamy and her eyes far away. "He's been too wonderful to me; he's done too much for my people——"

"But if you love him, my God, I'd not give him up to anyone like Aline!" Andy protested. "She's shown him twice what she thinks of him. She did love me," he went on. "We had some wonderful times together at first. But she's never loved him."

"You see, there are twenty years between Rogers and me, Andy, and it makes what he feels for me and what I feel for him, too, more like what a father and daughter might feel," Dina began with some difficulty.

"You've got a child!" the man countered, bewildered.

"Yes, yes, I know."

"You don't mean that you and Rogers might separate so that he and she could get married?"

"Well, there's no plan," Dina said hesitatingly, "but he has loved her all his life."

"Well, for lord sakes!" Andy ejaculated under his breath.

"What will you do, Andy, if she sues?" Dina asked a little timidly. "Will you contest it?"

"Certainly not. If she wants her freedom, she can have it!

"No," he went on after an interval, "I'll go back East. You see, Dina, I don't belong here; I belong there; I did all my studying there. I was working along at the League and eating about every third day when a fellow I knew asked me to donate a portrait to some charity bazaar; that's how it all happened," he went on. "I had a lot of spare time and he said he'd pay for the paint, so

I agreed. Well, the girl who won the raffle happened to be that Marion Sloat who was all over the place, remember? Debutante or Glamour Girl Number One or whatever she was. So I went down to their place at Huntington to paint her. A lot of her pals came in to see the work going on, and we all got friendly, and from that I did—oh, five or six more. So one thing led to another, and I took over the studio of an old French artist who was going back to Paris. Work kept coming in, and I thought I was made. I came West to Hollywood last year and went to Palm Springs for the Christmas holidays, and there I met Aline; Bill Cutter offered me his studio at Los Altos, I had lots of commissions, and the future looked rosy. But I've found out in the last few months I'm not anywhere nearly as soundly grounded in portraiture as I thought I was. I've a lot of hard work to do, and so I'm going back to study with a pal of mine—Emilio Bernasconi—in New York."

"Oh," she said, regret in her voice.

"If Aline and Rogers are really planning anything," he presently added, "I'd like you to know—— What is it?"

For Dina, suddenly pale, had gotten to her feet and turned so that her back was toward the entrance to the gallery.

A young man and a middle-aged woman had entered, the one a tall blond young fellow in well-tailored clothes, an overcoat over his arm, the other a fashion plate in furs, white gloves, trim small hat.

"That's—that's Caroline—that's Mrs. Holland," Dina said hurriedly. "I have to go—come with me."

The room was small; it was inevitable that the new arrivals should see them. They were all face to face. Andy was the first to speak.

"How do you do, Mrs. Holland? Aline told me you were back."

"How do you do?" Caroline Holland repeated. She faintly inclined her head. "Geraldine," she added briefly.

The skylights and the floor and the pictures in their gold frames began sickeningly, slowly to reel together. Dina blindly put out one hand and steadied herself by gripping the back of a leather seat.

"My son, Andy," Caroline said. "You remember each other at Palm Springs last year?"

"Oh, hello, Vere. Glad to see you again," Andy said.

"Hello, Dina," Vere said, clearing his throat, speaking in a low tone. She gave him her hand; it was as cold as ice.

"Vere—Vere." She had to say it twice to make herself heard. She stood looking at him while he held her hand.

"Andy's been doing some pretty swell painting, hasn't he?" Vere said.

Dina could not hear him. All that she heard was the remembered voice, the voice that had been the only one in the world to her once. Vere was with her again, tall and broad-shouldered, with that husky unforgotten note in his voice and those eager eyes on hers.

"I wanted to see your portrait," he told her. "Everyone's—everyone's talking about it."

Dina had turned from the others in an instinctive need to keep them from seeing her face. Now, still clinging to the back of the great leather davenport for support and fighting to the best of her power the vertigo and weakness that enveloped her, she blindly indicated the picture.

"It *is* good!" Vere said. "Did it—did it take him long to do it?"

They moved toward it, leaving Caroline and Andy conversing.

"To—to what?" she asked faintly, swallowing.

"I mean, have to sit to him a lot?"

As if that mattered, as if that was what they two had to say to each other!

"Oh no." Her voice, thank goodness, was audible at last! "He came to the house to paint it, six or seven times, I think."

"It's beautiful. That's the library, isn't it?"

"Yes. That's Rogers' mother's picture, that little bit there in the corner. He wanted that in."

"You live down there now, don't you?"

"We have, right along. We've always been at home, Rogers and I."

He musn't ask for Margaret, not her little Margaret!

"Home, huh?" he echoed. And then, awkwardly: "You were awfully sick, weren't you?"

"Never dangerously. We had a smash when Rogers was driving me in to town one day, and I broke my leg. And that same day Margaret was born. But it was never dangerous."

"Lord," he said.

"I don't think it looks very much like me, but it is a lovely picture." Dina was regaining her self-control. She was many, many years older in experience now than was this boy with whom she had danced at Cotta's a year ago. He could not reach her. She was safe in another world.

"Dina," Vere said in a low tone, "will you let me tell you something?"

"But this is the picture everyone thinks is so fine," Dina said hurriedly. She nodded her head toward Morning Trio. "That's Andy's wife at the piano," she added.

"I know. I was at Palm Springs when he was painting it," Vere reminded her. "That's Aline; all she can play is 'The Happy Farmer,'" he added scornfully.

"Andy thinks it is the best thing he has done."

Vere studied the rest of the canvas.

"He's smart, all right," he conceded.

"He's wonderful," Dina agreed.

"It sounds funny to me to have you call Uncle Rogers' place 'home.'"

She had steered him away once from dangerous ground. She fenced again.

"Have you the time, Vere? I'm supposed to be keeping a twelve o'clock appointment."

"Weren't you laid up most of the summer?"

"From July twenty-third until—well, about three weeks ago. I came downstairs then. But I'd been getting up for about two weeks."

"You've had a rotten time, haven't you?" Vere said.

Dina looked up at him squarely.

"I didn't mind it at all. I had puzzles and books and everything

I wanted. I have to go; I know I'm late. Andy," Dina said, breaking away deliberately from Vere and interrupting the painter's conversation with Caroline, "we have to go now."

Her hand, to all appearances, was laid lightly on his wrist. But he felt the fingers close like a vise.

"We're late," she told him, and there was warning and appeal in her glance. "Good-by, Caroline. Good-by, Vere. Andy," Dina murmured, taking his arm, propelling him toward the door, "we said quarter to twelve, and my dentist's at twelve—— Oh, get me out, stay with me!" she whispered when they were out in the gallery. "Come with me, Andy!"

"I'll go with you anywhere!" he said, bewildered, holding open the door, accompanying her as she went hurriedly into the street. "What's the matter?"

"Don't—don't ask me!" Dina breathed. "Just stay with me. Let's turn here—anywhere. Let's walk—fast."

"What the deuce . . . ?" His big hand was under her elbow; they were racing along together blindly, hardly noticing where they were going.

"Yes, let's go up to Chinatown," Dina said. She looked up at him and tried to smile. "I'm all right now," she went on, slackening her pace and beginning to breathe more normally. "But I—I was afraid I was going to faint or something. What a comfort you are to me!"

"I gather you don't like Caroline," Andy observed, "but he seems a nice boy. He was down at Palm Springs, you know."

"Yes, I know."

"You'd met him before today?"

"Oh yes."

"I feel that I am going to buy you something, Dina. Something as a souvenir of the day you came to my exhibition. What would you like?"

"How—how high would you go, Andy?"

"Say thirty-five cents."

"Oh well, then, one of those bowls. Come on, I'll show you where! Here in the window down the alley, see?"

"I see ducks that look as if they had been strangled and sausages apparently composed of grease, cockroaches, and black string," Andy observed.

"Yes, that's the place! See the bowls in the window? Those; one of those. They're twenty-five cents."

"But that leaves ten cents over."

"Well, then we can buy some honey-and-flaxseed candy."

"What horrible fancies you get, Dina. Which bowl? The red one? Squaw likee red bowl one chop," said Andy.

Dina laughed shakily; tears came into her eyes; she did not look at him.

"This one is a quarter," said the young Chinese.

"I think I'll send my mother some of these," Dina said, her voice still unsteady. "They were eating oatmeal out of the weirdest collection of saucers I ever saw, when I saw them in Stockton. You deliver?"

"In the city and in the bay counties, madam."

"Stockton?"

"There'll be a small extra charge for shipping."

"I don't like your belittling my present by sending your mother eight of it," Andy objected. "It's what's called making small of me. I'll send your mother this elephant."

"You will not!" But still she could not trust herself to look at him. "It must weigh fifty pounds! It's supposed to stand in a garden."

"It weighs about twenty-one pounds, madam," said the clerk.

"Why didn't you tell me they'd all been to Harvard?" Andy said in an embittered undertone.

"Because I love your Indian dialect!"

She put down her money, wrote the address in a long account book of folded soft pages. The clerk began to wrap one red bowl in tissue and newspaper.

"Yes, we take that one and you send the eight. Well, nothing else, I think, this morning," Dina said.

"Are these oysters?" Andrew asked respectfully.

"Dried oysters, yes."

"Dina," he said in the street, "what with those soft yellow cakes that looked like folded-up wool socks and those rotted oysters and the strangled ducks, how does it happen that all these Chinese aren't curled up in spasms of cramp from dawn until dark?"

"Perhaps—perhaps they *are* from dark until dawn, when we don't see them."

"Here's the church. Want to go in?"

"No. I'm afraid I might cry."

"I bought all my Christmas presents here last year. They made a hit, too," Andy said conversationally.

"Everyone in San Francisco does."

"Feeling better?"

"Every minute, thank you. I've missed my dentist appointment, haven't I?"

"Yep. It's twenty to one. I don't like things to upset you, Dina."

"Neither do I!"

"Caroline Holland has been catty to you."

"She doesn't like me, but I don't blame her."

"Are you lunching with me?"

"I can't. I'm meeting Rogers in twenty minutes."

"May I suggest a short session in the dressing room with powder and lip red or rouge or something? You look somewhat like a young weasel coming out of retirement after a long winter."

"I'll fix up. Andy," Dina said, clinging to his arm as they walked down the hill, "you are terribly good to me. You've been awfully kind. I—I needed you terribly then."

"I don't suppose you know," Andy said in a tone suddenly strained and low, "exactly what it means to me to be needed by you."

Dina stopped short on the narrow Chinatown sidewalk, drew away and faced him, her color changing suddenly. For there was no mistaking his tone. She tried to laugh.

"Andy!" she stammered.

"Yes, it's been that way since the very beginning," he said. "I never would have told you; perhaps I oughtn't to be telling you now. But what you say of Aline and Rogers, of their possibly planning to marry someday, makes me feel that sometime you might need me again and that—that I'd be glad to be there. It's a funny place to be telling you this, I suppose—Chinatown. But I'm glad you know. I'm off for Beverly Hills tonight—I won't have another chance."

"You mean——" Dina began, and was silent.

"I mean that you're the most wonderful woman in the world," Andy said. "I mean that I've been living for months now on just the glimpses I've had of you, the little I've heard people say. At the Carter wedding and at the Musgroves' dinner and the day I came and painted you, when you were still in bed, everywhere, every time, it's been you."

She had backed up against a window filled with kimonos and small wooden toys and red and black chinaware. Her slender figure was enveloped in a brown coat with a great brown fur collar; her blue eyes shone at him under a tipped little brown hat with a feather curled about it.

"Dina, I'm flying South this afternoon. I may not see you again for a couple of weeks, but if you ever are free, if Rogers is still in love with Aline, might I have a chance?" Andy, tall and lean and burned of skin, his hands plunged into the pockets of his big coat, stood facing her.

"I—I never thought of it," she said, April color in her face. "I never—I never thought anyone like you—as nice as you——"

A silence, while they stared at each other.

"I'm late," Dina said nervously then. "Rogers will be waiting. We'll have to hurry."

"It's only three blocks, but all steep." He glanced up at the most formidable of all the city's hills. "Here, we'll grab this taxi."

They did not speak again. But in the taxi she slipped her gloved hand into his and he held it tightly.

Chapter 16

FIVE MINUTES LATER Dina went into the dressing room of the hotel and busied herself with powder, lip red, pocket comb. She took off her hat and seated herself at a mirror, pushed her dampened hair into smooth rings and waves, working miracles about her eyes and lips with powder puff and lipstick. Then she stood up and covered her face with both hands and whispered, "Andy, Andy, Andy!" with her eyes closed and the light that never was on land or sea in her face.

When she went out into the great square foyer she bought herself a corsage of creamy gardenias and pinned them on the brown fur of her coat. She had just finished this operation when Rogers came in at the revolving door, and they walked toward each other, smiling.

"Nobody ought to look as fresh and sweet in November as you do, Dina!"

She caught at his hand; they went into the dining room and took a table by the high windows that command the whole stretch of the bay, command the cluttered lines of shipping and the mystical arches of the bridges, the blue far shoulders of the Berkeley hills and Tamalpais receding into the vague north.

"I bought myself some gardenias," she said, glowing.

"As a reward of virtue for letting Lane hurt you?"

"As a bucker-upper for having missed him completely. It was

only to be about ten minutes, Rogers," Dina pleaded in self-defense, "and I can go in before the symphony if you like. I telephoned his nurse and she said it would be all right."

"But what were you doing?" He was conscious of admiring glances for her beauty from the tables all about, but Dina was unaware of them.

"Well, I got Margaret's dresses. I only got four because she grows so fast. And then I sent flowers to Mrs. Pierce and telephoned Miss Hoey about Vera—remember the waitress who wanted a reference? And then I sneaked in to see my picture. I'm ashamed to say it sort of fascinates me."

"Many there?"

"Nobody at all except Andy, talking to Mr. La Motte. But he said there are crowds every afternoon." His name set bells ringing in her heart; she turned her attention to her salad.

"And how did it look?"

"Lovely. And then, before I left," Dina said after a pause, "Caroline came in—with Vere."

"With Vere!"

"Yes," Dina said with an anxious little frown. She did not meet his eyes.

"You've not seen him before?"

"Oh no. I knew he was here; the paper said so. But I thought he might be going South as he did last year."

"What possessed them to come into the gallery?"

"Caroline said he wanted to see the pictures."

"I see. Talk?"

"Just a minute. Andy spoke to Caroline, and Vere asked me how I was or said he heard I had been sick—or something—I don't remember."

"Isn't it just as well you met him?"

"I suppose so."

"Did he say anything about seeing you again?"

"No. But he mentioned that there was something he wanted to speak to me about."

"What'd you say?"

"I talked about one of the pictures—Morning Trio. He was down at Palm Springs when Andy was painting it."

"A-hah? How'd you feel?" Rogers asked the question after a moment during which he had proceeded vigorously with his lunch.

"Awful. As if I was going to faint. And then as if—as if it somehow didn't matter. I mean as if it had all happened to someone else long ago. I wanted to get away; I couldn't say anything and I couldn't think clearly. But not—not the way it was at first."

"This was in the gallery?"

"Yes. And it only lasted a minute. And then we went up to Chinatown."

"You and Vere?"

"Oh no. Andy." Again the wave of dizziness enveloped her, and for a second her senses swam. "Oh, and Rogers," she said, leaning toward him, her blue eyes very serious, "Aline has left him."

"Left *Andy!*"

"Sunday. He says she's been talking of it for some time."

"What's she framing up now?" Rogers said as if to himself. He was silent a moment, folding a lump of butter into a bun, disposing of half of it at one bite. He picked up his coffee cup, drained it, set it down again.

"He's serious, I suppose?" he asked quietly.

"He said *she* was."

"H'm!"

"You saw her only a few days ago. Didin't she say anything?"

"She talked vaguely about it. Nothing definite. Where d'you suppose she is now?"

"She went to Mrs. Rutherford, Mrs. Pierce's daughter. Andy says they're thinking of going to Honolulu."

The man was silent for a few moments. Then he said:

"She told me she was thinking of it as long ago as July. But she's always said she'd not do anything to hurt Andy. Well, I guess it had to come. Poor Aline! She'll be criticized for this. I don't know but what it's the honest way out. Did he seem broken up?"

"No." Another burst of skyrockets in her heart. "Perhaps he knew it was coming too," Dina offered.

He pulled out his watch.

"Symphony," he said briefly. "Come along! Andy may come in late to the box this afternoon, by the way. I met Meg Brown—she was hurrying along Post Street with Billy Salter and Bill happened to mention that Meg had asked permission to invite him. She and her mother are running that Christmas charity affair and they want him to donate one of his canvases. They've got a gall, if you ask me!"

Andy might be in the box this afternoon! Dina heard nothing else for fully five minutes, and when she found herself in the gracious great half circle of boxes in the opera house, with the lights dimmed and the rustle of frocks and murmur of voices silenced for the beginning of the music, her one thought was consciousness that at any minute he might slip into one of the empty chairs behind her. She would see him again today! She would hear his voice!

It was like discovering a sixth sense, this thought of him. It was an emotion so powerful that all other sensations and emotions were sublimated by it. She could think of nothing but Andy, and she had no desire to think of anything else. She knew now that for a long time he had played an all-important part in her life. There was nothing new in today's situation; what was new was her discovery of it, her realization of it. It seemed to lift her on wings. It was good to forget it for a moment, only to have the ecstasy come flooding back again. Dina sat motionless, her eyes fixed on the conductor and his baton, her ears drowned in the beauty of the rising and falling cadences of the symphony, and it seemed to her that she was floating in a halcyon sea.

Presently there was a whispered monosyllable to Rogers, in the back of the box, and a man took the chair directly behind her. Instantly there was complete silence and immobility again, but she had heard the "Sorry!" and she knew the voice. She need not turn her head. Nothing could rob her now of a few minutes' talk with him during the intermission.

But when the music had risen to a magnificent finale and the house was filled with the noise of enthusiastic clapping she turned to find the chair behind her empty. Everyone was drifting into the corridor behind the boxes now, and Andy was gone; Meg Brown and Billy Salter had gone too; only Rogers sat, still rapt, in his chair, his hands automatically clapping and his eyes blinking tears.

"God, that was beautiful!"

"Oh, wasn't it!"

But she felt blank, bewildered, and bitterly disappointed. As he rose she stooped to drop her purse and program on her chair and they went out together.

The wide corridor was filled with drifting couples and groups; the air was sweet with perfumes and the scent of violets and gardenias; women in furs were standing chatting; youngsters were elbowing their way through the press in a mad search for friends; the broad stairs were a river of figures ascending and descending. Dina's eyes found Andy at once.

He was leaning against the wall deep in conversation with a long-haired, stout, foreign-looking little man who, from his constant glances at the program he held and gestures of his hand, was evidently analyzing the interpretation of the symphony they had just heard. Andy's expression was one of indulgent amusement. He saw Dina and waved, but he did not interrupt his talk, and with a sinking heart she strolled beside Rogers among the shifting groups.

"You're coming up to us for cocktails; Vanucelli is going to be there!" said Mrs. Hunter Jackson.

"Not tonight, I'm afraid. Dina mustn't use up her strength too fast," Rogers answered. "We've got to get back to the country."

"And to that baby. I hear she's adorable," Mrs. Jackson said. "I've just been asking Vere what he thinks of his new aunty," she added, laughing.

"Is Vere here?" Rogers asked.

"Yes, he's with the Livermores. What's he going to do, Rogers? From something Aline said I guessed he failed to pass his bar exams again. Isn't that awful? I should think Van would be wild.

Listen, Rogers," she added, "I saw Ethel Rutherford at the club this morning, and she said——"

She drew him aside; Dina heard the warning bell, went swiftly back to the box. Andy might be there!

But he was not. She settled herself in her seat; Meg Brown and Billy Salter came hurrying in; the orchestra was already in place, awaiting the conductor's entrance. Andy did not return.

"Have you heard of any trouble between Aline and Andy, Dina?" murmured Meg Brown, her lips at Dina's ear.

Dina half turned. Their eyes met in the dark.

"I did hear she had left him."

"Everyone's buzzing about it," Meg Brown said. "If it's true, I think it's outrageous. I thought there was something queer when he came in; he looked—different, somehow. He said he couldn't stay except for that one number; he's catching a plane, I think. I don't blame *him!* I don't know what Aline thinks she is, playing fast and loose with men this way. Oh well," the young matron added, answering herself, "maybe it's a fight; maybe it won't last. I do think he's one of the nicest men I know; we all do. Just when his exhibition is on, too!"

The baton tapped. An instant hush fell over the house. Dina stared ahead blindly, sick at heart.

Chapter 17

THREE DAYS LATER Dina and the baby were in the library enjoying a late-afternoon scramble. Margaret was on a rug; Dina had been encouraging her to turn over, but Margaret made only halfhearted efforts and returned comfortably to a stomach position on all fours.

"You're lazy. You have no ambition," Dina told her. Hearing a step in the doorway, she turned from her sitting position to smile over her shoulder. "Rogers," she said, "she all *but* does it, and then she welshes on it——"

She stopped. The man who had come into the room was not Rogers but Vere.

Dina scrambled to her feet, catching up the baby.

"Lily," she said to the maid who had ushered Vere in, "take her up to Ida, will you?" She caught up the blanket rug, folded it, and put it over Lily's free arm. Her face was pale and her voice cold as she added: "Sit down, won't you, Vere? Rogers ought to be here any minute."

Vere had watched the baby out of sight. Now he turned, took the fireside chair she had indicated, and spoke hesitatingly:

"I wanted to see you."

Dina, seated opposite him, made no answer. She had known that they must see each other sooner or later; she had dreaded unspeakably what must be said. Now the moment had come unannounced and she must face it. She felt her breathing quicken.

"Don't blame the maid for letting me in," Vere began. "I told her you expected me. She's new, isn't she? She wasn't here last year."

Still Dina did not speak. She looked at him steadily, like a young judging priestess in her plain brown wool gown with the double chain of gold beads at her throat. Her eyes were curious, speculative, wary.

"Will you let me talk to you for a few minutes?" Vere began.

"Oh yes," Dina answered simply, clearing her throat.

"I've been saying this to you in my mind for almost a year, since I went away," he said. "I couldn't write it. I tried to write it and tore everything up. I suppose what I wanted to say—and what I'm trying to say now—is that I'm *terribly* sorry! I acted like a —oh well, a rotter! I didn't want to believe what they told me, and mother assured me it wasn't true. Father backed her up. They said you were trying to hang something on me; they said lots of fellows got into similar scrapes—you know what I mean——"

"Yes, I know what you mean," Dina said thoughtfully. Her mother's squalid kitchen in winter darkness and rain, her own young body sick and cold and weak, her nineteen-year-old heart burdened with the heaviest fears a woman ever knows—this was her share of the "scrape"!

"I'd be awfully glad if you could say you'd forgive me, seeing it's all turned out okay and that you married Uncle Rogers," Vere was saying. "I can't say more than that. I'd give anything *now* if I had stood by you, come back to see you, anyway. We could have done something. . . .

"Mother was wild when you married Uncle Rogers," he went on, trying to laugh, trying to get over the bad moment. "I was always a favorite with him—Mimi and I are the only kids in the family—and he always said that when I got married he'd see that I got started—and he used to hand me out a couple of hundred now and then——"

He floundered, explanatory, nervous, attempting to carry her along with him, stopping short.

"As far as forgiveness goes," Dina said, "there needn't be any question of that. When that sort of thing happens one person is just as much to blame as the other. I've always felt that," she ended in an undertone, as if she spoke to herself.

"Lord, you're generous!" Vere said. But something in his appreciation was lacking, something had gone flat. "It isn't as if," he went on uncomfortably, "it isn't as if that sort of thing wasn't happening all the time. I don't suppose my mother would want me to mention this, but you take my sister Mimi. She got in deep with a fellow from Columbia—awful nice fellow he was, too—and I want to tell you there was hell to pay! Mother rushed East to the school where Mimi was, and my grandmother took Mimi off to Paris. She and this chap had a little apartment and used to give cocktail parties when Mimi was only seventeen. Nothing wrong, you know, but was my mother mad! And I knew," Vere went on in a voice rising steadily with relief, "that things would work out. Of course I didn't see you becoming my aunt!" he finished, daring a little pleasantry.

"So much has happened there doesn't seem any use discussing it," Dina said. "It's as if it all had happened many years ago. Your uncle has been terribly good to me."

"Well, everyone says he's waked up, and lord, he certainly seems to like it!" Vere said. "And hardly anybody knows anything —I mean anything about you and me," he went on eagerly. "You see, my father and mother aren't especially anxious to talk about it. Mother—" he laughed—"still feels sore about Uncle Rogers marrying you," he said. "You can see that she feels the whole thing was a sort of frame-up. And now that you—that everyone likes you so much and Andy Havens has painted your picture and everything . . ."

A silence. Dina looked at the fire.

"You're certainly prettier than ever!" Vere said with an awkward attempt at lightness.

To this she did not even raise her eyes nor change the grave expression of her face.

"I'm glad you came to say this, Vere," she presently said. "It doesn't make it right, maybe, but I'm glad you said it, just the same."

"I didn't—I didn't know what I was doing," Vere stammered. "You don't know what it means to me to be friends again with you."

"Not that," Dina countered with a nervous look. "We needn't hate each other, but you and I—we mustn't see each other—I don't want that."

"Someday maybe you'll take that back," he said, trying for his old confident air.

Another silence. Vere cleared his throat to speak, said nothing.

"Say, could I have a drink?" he broke out suddenly, as if the solemn quiet of the shadowy big room was affecting his nerves.

"Not until your uncle comes." She was mistress here, this twenty-year-old girl in the brown woolen dress. There was a bell on the table close to her hand; she did not touch it. "She wouldn't like her husband coming in and finding us drinking together," he thought. He remembered that she had done very little drinking in those old days when they had gone up and down the peninsula, dining at various roadside restaurants and at chop suey places. But up in Paradise Valley she had had a cocktail before dinner, and he remembered how the cold pure air had made her eyes sparkle and her cheeks glow and how pretty she had looked sledding, skating, and skiing in Mimi's sport clothes.

She seemed more than a year older now; she seemed ten years older!

"You can bet I thought of you a lot on that trip we took," Vere presently began. "Here's what happened. Did my mother tell you what happened? Here's how it was: Chester Worthington—you know, whose sister is Kathryn Worthington—she's just about the most popular girl in that Philadelphia crowd; her uncle's Senator Hosworth. It was her grandfather Hosworth who left her a pot of money. When she's twenty-five she can write a check that would buy and sell her father ten times over! And it was her brother that was tubercular, they thought. Well, the doctor recommended a long rest and a sea trip for Chet, and they were going to send a nurse along with him, but Chet said, 'Um-umph; no soap! I don't go!' I happened to be down there that Sunday—they were playing court tennis at the club—and I said to Mrs. Worthington—she's a *peach,* by the way, Kit's mother!—that if she could talk my father into it *I'd* go and keep an eye on Chet, see that he rested and all that. I was just fooling, of course, but, by golly, if she didn't have Dad on the phone in ten minutes, and say! we had some fun getting ready to sail in two days!" He laughed briefly in recollection, recalled himself and grew sober again.

"Did you have a wonderful trip?" Dina asked levelly.

"Well, yes," he answered with an air of admitting it reluctantly. "Barbados, you know, and Pernambuco, and then Rio. It was quite a journey—on one of his uncle's freighters, you know."

"The senator?"

"Nope. His father's brother."

"And did he—Chester—get better?" As if she cared!

"His lungs today are as good as mine. And lord, what that family did for me! His father gave me the swellest gun I ever saw in my life!"

"Then you went to Maine with them in the summer, Rogers told me."

"I was up there six weeks. They've got a dandy speedboat."

"And what is the sister doing now?"

"Well." Vere's face flushed as he looked at her, and he laughed a little awkwardly. "That's—I guess that's partly up to me. She's the swellest girl I ever saw, and I guess they think that she and I—that is, I guess they sort of expect that we like each other!" Vere floundered on the confused phrases, but Dina could see he was proud and happy.

"So you're engaged?" She could say the words, but she could not put life into them. She must sit very still and let these things be said and try not to think that it was Vere Holland and herself talking. It was just a scene from a play!

"Well, not exactly. They want us to wait," Vere confided further. "But Kathryn's accustomed to having her own way," he added with a fond laugh, "and if she doesn't want to wait—that's *that!*

"Well," he went on leniently as Dina did not speak, "that's all right with me. I talked to my father, and he'll kind of see us through, and I told her Uncle Rogers was a regular prince about things like that. Say, he let your family have the old Forrester place, didn't he?" he asked, his thoughts going off at a tangent.

"In Stockton. Yes, they moved up there last spring. My father and Art both work in the factory now, and Myrna has a job too."

"So my mother said. Well, I thought if I told Uncle Rogers about Kathryn and me it would sort of please him to know about it first," Vere pursued artlessly.

"Will you live in the East?"

"Oh well, we don't know. Nothing's settled. If we can work it we'll go abroad for a while. You know, Dina," Vere went on, "I told them—Kathryn's father and mother—about us."

Dina winced as if she had been struck. A hot wind seemed to scorch her body, head to heels. She sat immovable, shrunken down against the deep cushions, but she felt the muscles of her fingers tense as they grasped the chair arm.

"No names, of course," continued Vere. "Lord, I should hope not! But I wanted to start square. I thought it over and thought maybe I ought to tell Kathryn's father, but then I was talking to them both one night while she was dressing for a party upstairs; I got into it and I thought I might as well go through with it. And was I glad I did?" he added with a little shiver and a reminiscent laugh. "They were simply swell about it. They asked me about you, where you were, you know, and I said you had married. Well, that made a hit!"

He stopped, lost in his own thoughts now and quite unconscious of Dina's silence.

"Kit's mother," he resumed, "said right away, 'Thank God for that!' and then the old man said, 'Mudsie, don't let this be too much of a shock for you. It's not unusual. What is unusual,' the old boy said, 'is Vere making a clean breast of it.' We all call Kit's mother Mudsie," Vere interrupted himself to explain.

Dina did not move a muscle. Her eyes were on the slumbering coal fire behind the polished steel rods.

"Then she said something about Kathryn always having been so well protected, never going to public schools or anything," the boy went on, still lost in his own pleasant thoughts. "And she said she would never want Kit to know anything about it. And I said—oh, you know, whatever you can say: about my respecting Kit and having too much respect for her to worry her if they thought it was all right, and they said sure it was all right, and Mudsie said that she had *more* respect for me for being honest about it. But she said if you *hadn't* gotten married then she'd like to feel that you and I *would* have been, and I said that we surely would, and then Kit came down and we went off to dance. So I thought I'd like to tell you that much and that it was all right."

"Well!" Dina said, rising with an air of terminating the interview. She was suffocating. Her legs were trembling under her, her throat dry.

"Say, wait!" Vere urged her. "I've got to see Uncle Rogers!"

"Mrs. Havens to see Mr. Holland," Hinz said from the doorway as Aline came in. She nodded to the two at the fire, dropped into the chair that completed the half circle.

"Hello, Dina. Hello, Vere. What time did you kids break up last night?"

"We had breakfast at Morgan's," Vere confessed with a grin. Oh, he was very handsome and young and sure of himself, smiling there in the firelight, his body bent comfortably forward in his low chair, his long brown hands loosely locked and dropped between his knees.

"Lovely party," Aline said absently.

"Andy there?" Vere asked.

She looked at him steadily but without embarrassment.

"I thought you knew that since a week ago Sunday Andy and I are not making engagements together," she observed.

"So? Mother said something about it, but I didn't know it was official."

"It's absolutely official," Aline assured him briefly and unsmilingly.

"I'm sorry. I kind of like him," Vere said.

"I like him extremely," Aline said with a superior air. "Where did you get the idea I didn't? We were getting on each other's nerves, that was all, and I decided the kind thing to do was to give him a clear field."

Vere chuckled.

"You certainly bust up their lives!" he murmured.

"I certainly do nothing of the kind, you rude boy." But she liked the rudeness. She leaned back in her chair, her furs loosened, her long-coated suit of black velvet fitting her slim body as a sheath fits a sword, her hair, as smooth and shining as black enamel, only partly hidden by an absurd cockaded hat. "For eight years," she said, "I put up with a man whose own intimate friends pronounced him crazy. Nobody knows what I went through. His own mother told me that he had been subject to fits of ungovernable rage since actual babyhood. Eight years of it! The doctor told me he didn't know another woman who would have put up with it for eight weeks! The first thing they did after the divorce was pop him into an institution, and high time. Frank Pollock was shut up for three months. Now he's married to a meek, poor little creature who can't call her soul her own, and that's the sort he should have married in the first place. His own brother told me—we were on the same ship cruise a few years ago—that in his heart Frank Pollock has never loved anyone but me. That's how mean I was to *him.*"

She brooded on the situation for a silent moment. She and Vere had completely forgotten Dina. They fell into talk of their own group, discussing recent parties, an approaching wedding.

"Somebody order me a gin cocktail!" Aline then said abruptly.

Dina rose, went to the table, rang the bell.

"Hinz," she said when the butler appeared, "Mrs. Havens would like a gin cocktail and Mr. Vere Holland will have one too. Mr. Holland didn't telephone, did he?"

"He's just arrived, madam."

"Oh! Tell him where we are."

"Dear me, we are very much the mistress of the manor, aren't we?" Aline smiled.

Dina merely looked at her. She turned to the door to meet Rogers, who came in cold and ruddy, pulling off his gloves.

"Hello, Geraldine; bridge party off for tonight—on for tomorrow," he said. "Three fellers."

"I'll have Chong save the partridges," Dina said.

"Hello, Vere." Rogers was at the hearth. "Hello, Aline!" he added, peering through his strong glasses at the other visitor. As he recognized her his voice at once grew warm.

"I had to see you," said Aline simply. Her eloquent eyes as she gave him her hand said the rest. The look of confidence, affection, and sweetness upset him for a moment, and he laughed nervously and stammered for sheer pleasure when he spoke.

"Well, of course, of course! Glad you did. Tremendously glad you did! What brings you here, Vere?"

"See you," Vere said with his endearing, impudent grin.

"See me, eh? You've—you ordered something, Dina?"

"Vere and I were waiting for you. But we had just asked Hinz for cocktails when you came in."

"Dina is quite the housekeeper," said Aline's ivory-and-silver voice. Rogers glanced at her.

"Indeed she is!" he agreed.

"So I see. How nice!" But Aline did not see it at all and she did not find it nice. Her voice was cold and bored. She looked at the toe of her shoe.

"I wanted to tell you that Kit Worthington and I are—well, we're practically engaged!" Vere began with an embarrassed laugh. "Nothing settled, but I wanted you to know before anybody else did."

Rogers looked at him from under his brows, sampled the drink that Hinz had just given him.

"Her uncle's Senator Hosworth, you know," Vere said.

"Going to live on her money, eh?" Rogers said. Dina glanced at him, startled. It was the tone she remembered from her first visit a year ago, sneering, cynical, challenging. She had not seen Rogers in so disagreeable a mood since. "Her father lost everything he had in Tabasco Oil," he muttered, looking into the fire, "but she'll get Granddad's money when she's twenty-five. What are you going to do for five years? She's about twenty now, isn't she? I was at Yale with Pierce Worthington. He always seemed to me a good deal of a fool!"

Vere was silent, abashed. There was an ugly pause.

"Nothing's settled," Vere said then, sulkily.

"I should hope not!" Rogers growled.

"I'll go tell Chong about dinner," Dina said, rising. "Just the two of us, Rogers?"

"Evidently we're not to be asked, Vere," Aline said lightly.

"You're always asked if you'll stay," Rogers told her.

"I can't, Toppy. But I don't know how Dina knew it."

Dina glanced at the other woman with a completely blank expression and, without speaking, left the room. But her senses were in an uproar. Automatically she talked to the cook, automatically put Margaret through her little night routine, found herself presently in her room, at her mirror, working away with brushes and creams. Anything rather than think!

Anger and shame and resentment swept over her in waves, washing her thoughts and emotions this way and that, making it hard for her to breathe, closing walls about her.

"Oh, I can't bear it!" she said half aloud.

On her feet, she went blindly to the window and stood there, hidden in the bay behind the great looped curtains, trembling, looking down into the blackness and the night. She saw Vere's roadster, the very car that had taken a boy and girl up to Paradise Valley a year ago, parked on the drive, its lights tunneling two yellow spearheads into the gloom. Near it was Aline's neat sedan—Aline, who so much needed Rogers' advice now that she had discovered she and Andy were incompatible!

While Dina watched Vere came out, climbed into his car, and drove away. The red taillight dwindled among the trees and was gone. She stood very still, breathing a little hard, looking after it.

So he had told "Mudsie" about their affair and had been praised and forgiven! Since the unfortunate girl in California, the girl who had led him astray, had married, then everything was all

ight! Kathryn, the protected Kathryn who mustn't be distressed
by the ugliness of life, was to be kept in ignorance, of course!

"Mudsie, don't let this be too much of a shock to you; it's not
unusual!" No, no, boys must have their fling, and older men,
decorum itself in happy family life, could make allowances! Vere,
penitent and complacent, had been the hero of the moment! They
thought more of the boy for his honest confession of human weak-
nesses! And the girl was safely married to someone else, thank
goodness!

Her face blazed. Her throat felt dry and her hands cold. All
those dreadful weeks of worry, of rising in the bitter winter
morning to the cold, disorder, and odors of the house in Railway
Flats, of dragging fear about with her through the dark winter
days, had cost Vere not one second's doubt or misery! Rogers'
half-amused, half-insulting, and admittedly spiteful proposition
of marriage, the long trip to Reno, her recurring spasms of weakness and nausea—all hers to bear and hers alone!

The end of dancing and flirting for her! Quiet long days in the
strange big dark house, hesitations, timidities, and loneliness, the
odd glances of Rogers' friends, their barely concealed curiosity, all
hers! And hers the long day that brought Margaret into the world,
the sweat-soaked exhaustion, and the first agonies of mother love
and mother protectiveness! The first tiger loyalty toward the
precious scrap of babyhood that must never know shame or doubt!

While she had lain, week after week, in the big old-fashioned
bedroom, unable to walk, dependent upon the others even for a
glance at her child, Vere had been off camping with the Worthingtons, taking the impeccable Kathryn to dance at the hotel,
idling through sunny mornings on the shore, coming up to her
flushed and triumphant on the tennis court, his white shirt and
white shorts only emphasizing the magnificent brownness of his
young athletic body! He had been winning the golden opinions
of her people—that nice boy from California whose uncle Daddy
knew, the boy of whom their ewe lamb Kathryn was unquestion-
ably growing fond, the boy who had finally clinched their respect
and confidence by his manly confession! Poor fellow, as if he were

the only handsome young man in the world to be trapped by a designing girl of the poorer classes!

They had looked on with a deepened complacency when the unsuspecting Kathryn—the girl whose young hand could "write a check that would buy and sell her father ten times over"—had descended, ready to start for the dance, in the smartest of summer dance frocks, of course, with just the right white silk wrap and white bag. Mrs. Somebody would be chaperoning, and Kathryn would be safely delivered back to her own people at some given hour, to sleep deep in dreams of partners and moonlight, laughter and fascinating Vere Holland!

Dina hated her! Hated Vere—Vere who could sit there so smugly reviewing the situation! He and she had perhaps been foolish last year, but what of it?—everything was "okay" now, and he was going to marry a fascinating young heiress and Dina was safely married to Uncle Rogers!

Sickness of resentment shook her. Dina felt that physically she could not bear it. She could not go on; she could not live with herself! She wanted to tear herself to pieces, to lie on the floor and hammer it with her fists!

The worst of the mood passed and she could be calm again.

Half an hour later, dressed in a reconstructed old brown frock whose plain organdy cuffs and collar always gave her a feeling of being trim and neat, and with her hair freshly brushed, she descended to the lower floor to wait for the announcement of dinner.

The big stairway and the square enormous entrance hall were dimly lighted; Dina always liked the quiet of the house at this hour, the sense of orderly rooms and generations of dignified living. She was not thinking now, not letting herself think. She was living each moment for itself, not going back, not going forward, just pleased that there would be a fire, a book, a good dinner, and presently a game with Rogers. On the score they kept going month after month he was some thirty games ahead, but of late she had been winning, and she determined to fight hard for victory tonight.

At the door of the library she paused, hearing voices within.

he could stand in the shadow and see them without notifying
hem by sound or presence of her movements: Aline and Rogers,
leep in talk.

There was only one light in the big room—one green-shaded
amp making a dim pool of illumination by the reading table. For
he rest, except for an occasional pink glow from the fire when a
og settled in the grate, everything was dusk and shadows.

But Dina could see their two figures plainly: Aline in one of the
arge fireside chairs, Rogers beside her on the hassock which
rought his face below the level of hers. Both her hands were in
is; their faces were not far apart.

They were murmuring, murmuring. Dina stood rooted to the
pot, listening.

At first much of what they said was indistinguishable; now and
hen laughter broke into it, Aline's quiet silvery note of mirth
nd Rogers' gruff and eager echo. But after a moment of silence
everal phrases came out clear and audible.

"I can't bear it, Rogers. After darling Aunt Mag and poor Anna,
o have her queening it here! She ringing a bell for Hinz——"

"You little idiot," Rogers broke in fondly, "you had it all right in
his hand of yours. *You* didn't want it!"

"I've always loved it; I've always loved this house as I've loved
o other place in the world!" Aline said. "It kills me to have that
irl—that factory hand—posing here as your wife!"

"As a matter of fact, she *is* my wife," Rogers said quietly.

"Oh, I know, I know! I shouldn't have said that, and I know, too,
ou're mad when you crinkle up your darling ugly mug like that!"
line said quickly. "But truly—the airs! She'll go tell Chong about
e dinner! What does she think she is?"

"What a jealous little devil you are!" Rogers reproached her
aildly, her fingers against his lips. "Geraldine is a fine girl and I
m extremely fond of her."

More of this, but Dina could not catch it. It was interrupted by
line's impatient, "I don't believe a word of it! Where'd she get
em? 'All the instincts of a gentlewoman,' indeed! I've never
oticed them. I didn't notice them a year ago when you asked

Andy and me to dinner and she never opened her mouth! I tell
you, Toppy, I can't bear having her here. For you to go off and
marry her in that hole-and-corner way was—well, you'll never
know what it meant to me!"

"*You'd* just done something of the kind."

"Oh, I was a fool, I'll admit; I'm the sort of woman who'll always make a fool of herself."

The man laughed at this and their voices sank again. Dina noiselessly moved away.

She went upstairs, into her room, and sat there, working away
desperately at her desk with her Spanish grammar, determined
once again not to let herself think. She was so working, penciling
busily, turning pages, when there was a knock at the door.

"Come in, Mrs. Bucket," she said. Sometimes the housekeeper
came upstairs to announce dinner if either Dina or Rogers ignored
the gong.

It was Rogers who entered.

"Geraldine," he said, "dinner's ready, but if you don't mind
I'm going off with Aline. She and I have been having a heart-to-
heart talk and she's all upset. Lord," he broke off to exclaim on
a deep breath, "we've had the most amazing talk I've ever had
with anyone in my life! For the first time—for the first time I feel
that she—she likes me and needs me! No fooling this time! You
don't mind my running off?"

"Certainly not!" But she had an odd sinking feeling just the
same and a fear of what he was going to say next.

"I don't know what the plans are or what they will. be," Rogers
was going on. "You understand the whole situation perfectly, and
you know what this means to me. I've always——" He was like
a boy in his new delight. "I've always thought——" he began again,
stumbling. He dropped his head, shaking it bashfully, looking
away. "My God, she's wonderful!" he finished. And then, suddenly remembering Dina's own problem, he added: "By the way,
don't take that engagement talk of Vere's too seriously. Pierce
Worthington wouldn't let that kid get within ten miles of his
daughter unless someone came through with about a hundred

housand a year. I know that outfit! He's trying to get his father
and mother and me to help out, send them abroad on a honeymoon. Let him babble along for a few months, and then we'll
see how his plans fit in with mine. If you were free again, there
might be another setup entirely. Good night, my dear! You don't
mind missing our game?"

He was gone. Dina stood for a long time motionless, one hand
resting against the doorjamb, the other on the knob. Her eyes
were half shut, her forehead wrinkled. Moments went by; everything about her was quiet, spacious, and dark—the dimly lighted
hall, the great vault of the stairway.

Hinz came up to announce dinner, and Dina thanked him in an
absent voice and went slowly downstairs.

Chapter 18

DINA was out on the terrace with the baby when Rogers came downstairs the next morning. It was not yet quite noon; warm sunshine was flooding the old red bricks and the painted wooden balustrades, and winter flowers, cosmos and chrysanthemums, battered by late rains, were being tied into bedraggled bunches along the paths by McPherson. In the fresh sweet air there was the odor of wet oaks and wet earth, the sharp sweet smell of a world drying and sunning itself.

Margaret was in her play pen, which was floored today with a warm folded plaid. Her small rotund body was snugly enveloped in a sweater suit, but her browned little arms and legs, her thistle-down head were bare. She lay making indeterminate gestures with a spoon in one hand and a silver cup in the other. Occasionally the spoon clinked against the cup, and the baby started in surprise.

Dina sat near her, determinedly reading a magazine article "The Vital Second Year." "Mashed prune, banana, or applesauce, three dessertspoonfuls," she read; "toast, four fingers, buttered. If the child grows weary of eating or shows distaste, remove the food immediately. Habits of dawdling, playing, expecting amusement at meals——"

"Oh, hello, Rogers!" Dina interrupted her reading to say with a gallant attempt at a smile. After last evening's succession of humiliations and shocks she had spent a long, sleepless night, her mind and senses churning with problems and responsibilities, re-

212

ntments and indignation with which the philosophy of her
venty years was completely unable to cope. She felt utterly
ashed out and exhausted this morning; she could never have
ced it, with its duties for Margaret, its occupation with the
aby's formula, wardrobe, bath, breakfast, if she had not come
 the conclusion, during hours of tossing restlessness, that she had
o choice. There was no other way.

Every instant of her talk with Vere had stung her with a thou-
and whips. His serene acceptance of the circumstances of her
arriage, the birth of her child, the long months of her invalidism
s all being part of a world that arranged everything nicely for
ere Holland and brought him out of every dilemma admired and
iumphant had been almost more than she could bear. She had
rithed remembering it, had gritted her teeth and knotted her
ands.

At the end of every furious thought she had emerged at the
me point. Vere's complacency was absolutely justified. He had
deed escaped the net of retribution and responsibility. Perhaps
ina was the one to blame; perhaps Dina was making a mountain
ut of a molehill, and there had been nothing so wrong in that
ttle Paradise Valley escapade after all.

No, there was Margaret, there was Margaret, there was always
fargaret, the innocent, floss-headed, radiant baby whose very life
as the fruit of that adventure, whose welfare and happiness must
 a ball and chain about Dina's heart forever! Dina, too, had
caped the worst dangers of her predicament; comfort and pro-
ction and security had been miraculously given her. But even
ese apparent compensations had not saved her from hours, from
eeks of shame and strangeness, loneliness and doubt; they had
ot saved her from the inevitable agonies and cares of young
otherhood.

They had not saved her from this night of wakeful anxiety when
ogers' parting words had occurred to her again and again and
hen their implications had made her face burn in the cover and
arkness of night and her whole body shake with chill.

"Let Vere babble along about marrying Kathryn Worthington

for a while," Rogers had said, with every intention of comforting her. "If you were free again, there might be another setup entirely!"

The thought had suffocated her. Vere asked by his uncle to marry her! Vere reminded that Dina's child was his child too, that honor and justice dictated this course! Rogers extricating himself from a marriage that had after all been no marriage, Rogers quite confident that this was the happiest solution for everyone. It wasn't thinkable, it wasn't bearable that after her spirit had settled into comparative serenity in the old Holland house the ground under her feet should be swept away again. For Rogers was planning now to marry Aline; that much he had made quite clear before his elated departure with her last night.

Aline would get a divorce too; no novelty for Aline. This would be her third, not by any means a record for Aline's group. That meant that Andy would be free too. But he would wonder at her divorce from Rogers only a year after their marriage; he would hear that there was talk of her marrying Vere. And perhaps he would think—Dina tried to work it out clearly for herself, but mind and senses were too weary for coherent thought—perhaps he would think that of course she *must* marry Vere, the circumstances being what they were. Perhaps the whole world would think so.

The sting that this thought brought was the keenest Dina had ever known. Andy, the strong, devoted friend whose belief in her, whose admiration for her had been like a tonic, Andy, at the mention of whose name her whole world turned right and safe and rose-colored, would have to know everything now.

She had finally gotten to sleep on the thought, "I'll run away!" Probably one couldn't run away these days, not with a yellow-headed baby and a numbered car. But perhaps—bribing someone to change the license number—taking a bus here and a train there——

So she had slept. But not long nor deeply, and with the morning all the nervous fears had returned in a body. The face she raised to Rogers as he came out upon the terrace wore its usual smile.

but it was a haggard, anxious face, and she knew that he saw it.

"Had your breakfast?" he asked.

"Had my breakfast! Hours ago."

"I was addressing Margaret."

"Oh, Margaret? Yes, she had breakfast at seven and orange juice after her bath, and now she's anticipating baked potato and spinach and custard, aren't you, Margaret?"

"She looked up when you said potato, darned if she didn't!" Rogers exclaimed.

"Oh, she knows any mention of food."

Rogers sat down in a basket chair, stretched his body appreciatively in the sunshine, rattled the pages of the paper. Dina opened her book.

"Would you like Hinz to bring you out a cup of coffee? It's more than an hour till lunch."

"No, no; this is very nice." He glanced at headlines, dropped the paper. "Mind eating by yourself last night?" he asked, his head back against a canvas cushion, his eyes shut.

"No. I was reading a book called *The Honorable Peter Stirling,* and it's good."

"That was a best seller years ago. Aline and I," Rogers said dreamily, not opening his eyes or changing his position, "had the most remarkable talk last night any man and woman ever had, I suppose. We sat at one table at the Saint Francis Hotel in the city from eight o'clock until ten minutes of one. I looked . . ." He paused. His voice was almost reverent. "I looked into that woman's very soul."

"I suppose you respected her all the more for what you found there," Dina thought bitterly, remembering Vere's words of the night before. Aloud she said nothing.

"She has been hungry for love all her life," Rogers continued simply. "Not travel and titled friends, jewelry and passion. She's had all those. She's sick of them. She wants to slip into the background somewhere, see a few friends occasionally, garden, walk, study Spanish—yes," he said, opening his eyes to smile in answer to Dina's half-smothered exclamation, "she knows you and I have

been going at Spanish, and she tells me that she began it year
ago and dropped it and that she's been anxious for years to tak
it up again. . . .

"Considering her beauty," he presently resumed in a dea
silence, "considering the court that has been paid to that woma
all her life, it's extraordinary to find her like a little girl wantin
to be loved and wanting to have everybody happy! The first thin
she said last night when we had ordered our dinner and coul
settle down to talk was that she wanted Andy to be happy an
me to be happy. 'What's the use of so many of us being squar
pegs in round holes?' she said. 'If we've been fools, if we've mad
mistakes, then for goodness' sakes let us admit it and get starte
with a clean slate!' She knows about you and Vere, Geraldine,'
Rogers broke off to say in a lowered tone, "and she spoke of that
She said Caroline had warned her she'd get herself into trouble i
she mentioned it, and she's never breathed it—even to Andy, so sh
says. But of course she knows, and she thinks that very probabl
if she and I straighten matters out—why, the natural thing will b
for you and Vere to patch it up too. I told her that I thought fron
the way you looked last night you still had a good deal of feelin
in the matter—well, it's too early to talk of that. But I'm goin
to fly to Reno in a day or two and see her lawyer."

"Does she keep a lawyer in Reno?" Dina wanted to ask in a
fresh rush of bitterness. But she did not answer at all; she sat mute
her serious eyes ready to meet Rogers' eyes whenever he glance
at her.

"So the upshot of the whole thing is this, I think," Rogers wa
presently saying in great satisfaction. "Our little scheme worked
Aline never paid much attention to me before, but having you her
worked the trick. She saw things going on very agreeably aroun
here, gardening and games and puzzles and good meals. I wasn'
any longer poor old Rogers moldering away in that mausoleun
of a house; I had a pretty girl with me; you and I were being see
at parties and dinners, and everything was going on very nicely
thank you. It sort of stumped her. She couldn't get used to seein
a girl your age mistress of the old Holland place. . . .

"I never dreamed," he added after a moment, in a musing tone, "that she would take it, hook, line, and sinker! But she has. I'm damned," Rogers finished with an indulgent chuckle, "if she isn't already changing the rooms. I don't know what it was all about, curtains and french windows and a breakfast room built on! I was laughing at her last night, and she got quite hot about it. 'You've got to understand that if I'm ever in charge there,' she said, 'you're going to have the prettiest home and be the most spoiled man in the world!'"

"Ha," was all that was audible of Dina's undertone.

"Now," Rogers went on, "the natural question is, where do you come in?"

"Or go out," Dina put in simply.

"Or go out!" he echoed with a laugh. "And there," he said, sobering suddenly, "you write your own ticket. I don't think you could live in any man's house, Geraldine, and not have him grow fond of you. I am fond of you—damn fond. I've often thought that I'd like to have a daughter with your kind of eyes and the way you laugh and your eternal questions and puzzles and rushing about. When you were lying upstairs in bed I used to like to sit in your room and hear the baby yap and feel that all this was going on in my house and that I was head of it."

This time her answering smile was misty with tears. She managed a nod; she could not speak.

"Damn it, I feel that way too!" Rogers said, his tone for a moment a little gruff. "Of course it's early days now; I don't know what we'll do or what we *can* do. But it begins to shape up this way: after Christmas you and I very quietly get a divorce. Either you can go to Reno with Ida and the baby or I'll go there for six weeks. It would be better to have you do it, because the woman is at a disadvantage otherwise. How does that strike you?"

"I can't imagine myself not falling in with any arrangement that seems good to you, Rogers," Dina said not quite steadily.

"Yes, but I want this to be the way you think it ought to be done."

"That seems to be the simplest way."

"That's what Aline thought. Of course the financial end isn't the problem. I give you the deed to the Stockton house and you can do as you like with it—give it to your mother or collect rent from them or whatever you like."

"I see myself collecting rent!" She swallowed a hard lump in her throat, managed a tone of ironic laughter.

"Your income will be all signed, sealed, and delivered, and, if you like, in a shape that won't make it too easy for your father to borrow it. That part we'll fix easily. Aline seemed to feel that since you may someday be married to Vere it ought to be handled by him as part of what he'll get of the Holland estate, but I'm dead agin that. As a matter of fact, unless that kid toes the mark there won't be any estate for him."

Dina looked at him steadily. Their eyes met.

"You mean toes the mark by marrying me?" she asked.

"I mean, my dear, that you're to be independent no matter what you do," Rogers said in his nicest tone, smiling at her as a father might have smiled. "The boy is talking big now about marrying Kathryn Worthington. Well, there's absolutely nothing in it. He did propose to her the day he left, and she wouldn't answer him. That young woman is going to have a good many offers from handsome young bucks before she gets through. I was telephoning Caroline half an hour ago about some taxes, and I mentioned Vere's prospects and she nearly went out of her skin. 'For heaven's sake, don't mention that!' she said. 'If the press got it, Pierce Worthington would go wild!' That's all there is to that. Tell me," the man said as Dina stared grimly into space, brow puckered and mouth set, "what do you feel about it? He didn't treat you squarely, but I know you liked him. How d'you feel about him now?"

The bulging figure, fat hands, the prominent eyes, and froglike face were too familiar to her to seem anything but trustworthy; she had never heard him use a kinder or more sympathetic voice

"I think not," she said quietly. "I think Margaret and I will go away. We'll go to Reno first and find some boardinghouse or modest hotel, stay the six weeks, and then for a while we'll go away. I don't care where, just so that people don't know me and I don't have to explain. And then I think I'll come back and either live with my mother in Stockton or near her and get a job!"

"You'll marry," he said. "You're too young and too sweet not to find happiness sooner or later. You'll have an income, and you've got this nice little kid."

"Yes, I've got Margaret."

"Vere show any interest in her?"

Her color was up like a flag.

"I—I didn't give him much chance. Rogers," she said, hurriedly changing the subject, "I hope this is the beginning of real happiness for you. I do hope that!"

"I have you to thank for it."

"Oh no, no, you haven't! To you our plot—our scheme, whatever you wish to call it—was just a sort of joke," Dina said, "but for me it was a very different thing. I don't know what I could have done! I never have been able to think what I could have done."

"What you did do," he said, "was carry your head high, take it all on the chin, make the best of it, and somehow win us all to loving and respecting you."

Tears came into her eyes although she was smiling.

"Sometimes," she said, "I feel as if I had—had done too much living for anyone not yet twenty-one! Sometimes I feel as if I ought to crawl in somewhere—crawl out of sight—and just rest and think and—and think it all out."

"Well, there's no need of our settling anything yet," Rogers reminded her comfortably. "I'll look into things, and we can talk again. So forget about it!"

The sun continued to shine with grateful winter warmth; the baby was carried away by Ida. Dina and Rogers sat on, basking and reading, but Dina's thoughts were not on her book. They were anywhere and everywhere else. She held the book as if it were a shield.

"Rogers?"

"Go ahead."

"If—if I ever did marry again someday, would I have to tell him —the man—all about—about the baby?"

"Not if it was Vere," he said, smiling.

"But if it wasn't?"

"Then I wouldn't," Rogers told her promptly. "You are a married woman with a child; he knows it isn't his child, and that's all he needs to know."

"Thanks."

She reopened her book, but Rogers sat watching her, a young slender thing in a dark-blue gown and loose blue coat. His expression was half amused, half pitying.

"You haven't got an eye on anyone, Geraldine?"

She merely looked at him, and although he laughed, he was ashamed too.

"I apologize." And after a moment's silence, "What are you wearing to the Cartwright jamboree, by the way?"

"Oh yes, that's next week. I have a dress I haven't worn. The one they sent East; it's just back. Remember, with the pearls on it?"

"Green."

"Green chiffon—but do we *have* to go?"

"Oh, sure we've got to go! Nelly Cartwright is going to revive the old Germans; she's got figures and favors and God knows what, all ready! She thinks I'll remember 'em, and I promised to help her."

"The old—Germans?"

"Cotillions—directed, you know—with figures."

"I never heard of them."

"Well, you ought to love it. And by the way, Geraldine, not a word of any changes here, you know. It may take us months to get this thing all straightened out; Aline wants me to get all her affairs into my hands, and we want to keep it quiet."

"I can see that, Rogers," she said submissively.

"Look here, my child," the man presently began, "this isn't taking it out of you too much, is it?"

"Oh n-no." But her voice was not steady.

"This is the way you'd want it to be, isn't it?"

"Yes, this is what we thought it might be from the beginning —to make her jealous, to make her envious!"

"Being only twenty, you know that something grand has plenty of time to come into your life, don't you?"

"Oh yes!" she said bravely.

"You'll always know that I'm your friend, only too anxious to do anything for you or get you out of any trouble, and that I'm always going to remember this year and our cribbage games and your illness and the baby and all the rest of it as one of the happiest times of my life, eh?"

"I'm awfully glad that you can say so," she said very low.

"You bet your life I can say so! Lunch, Hinz? Good work. Come along, Geraldine; let's eat!"

Chapter 19

"YOU ARE SIMPLY A VISION, Mrs. Holland," said Helene Cartwright when they were in the dressing room taking off their coats. "If I could ever look like that I'd swoon."

"You are divine," said Margot Illyan.

"I never thaw a dreth like that!" little Ann Talbot lisped.

Dina acknowledged the compliments with an excited laugh. She knew they were justified. Like Ann she had never seen a gown as beautiful as the filmy creation of green and paler green and white that foamed about her. She was twenty and she was lovely to look at and there was no past and no future; there was only tonight. The high, short waist of her frock was heavily embroidered with the pale, furry green leaves and pearl berries of mistletoe; a thin line of them bound the flying ruffles of her frail, full skirts.

She had not wanted to come to the dance; she had wanted only to be an onlooker if she must go at all. But upon reaching the Cartwright house all that had been forgotten in sheer joy of youth and music and dancing. Two young men standing at the door of the ballroom had turned to look at her as she came in; they had come up to remind her that she knew Billy Stern and Joe Cartwright, and the next instant she had been dancing, swept away on a wave of melody into a world of silver and green beauty.

The Cartwrights' house was a roomy old mansion remodeled from the clumsiness of an earlier day. Tonight it had been made even larger by the inclusion of the tennis court and swimming pool. These had been walled and windowed; the walls draped with pale green and hung with great Christmas wreaths, the windows recessed with deep seats and curtained in red velvet. The court had been floored and waxed; the pool was still itself, a great oval of emerald and silver shining under the night lights, but cushions and rugs and low chairs framed it, and small tables, scattered about, held cigarettes and glasses.

Parents and elders were in the house, busy at bridge and mahjong tables; this region was given over entirely to the younger generation. The season's debutantes were all here, fluttering to and fro, lingering in the flower-lined passage that led from the house to the court, sometimes stepping out for a moment or two into the cold blackness of the night to look up at the stars and the Christmas moon and listen to the words that have been said under every moon since the first moon of all.

And through it all the music wove its subtle magic, sometimes loud, sometimes faint and faraway, and through it all Dina Holland danced as she had never danced in her life before. For a long, strange year she had not known the intoxicating union of slippered feet and smooth floor, the rhythmic harmonies of jazz and swing, fox trot and tango, the firm hold of a man's arm about her. Her last dancing had been on a few disheartened, anxious evenings at Cotta's or one of the other roadhouses near Railway Flats, evenings when she had been half mad with doubts and fears. This evening, for a few hours, they were all gone, and she could not dance enough, surrendering herself and her sea-foam ruffles to one partner after another and raising to each man in turn the battery of her blue eyes and her friendly smile.

Suddenly, in one of the changes of the cotillion, it was Vere who held her: a grim, unsmiling Vere who whirled her away with the old swift mastery she remembered; not looking at her, not speaking, seemingly absorbed in the steps of which he was so easily master.

"I didn't know you were here," Dina said in a pause in the music.

"I've not been dancing."

"Are you—are you mad about something?" For she knew he was in an ugly mood.

"Yes, mad about you," he answered briefly, still unsmiling.

"Oh," Dina said, supplying the smile. She was equal to any situation tonight. She floated along beside him, smiling again now and then as her eyes met some friendly face.

"Come out here a minute," Vere said suddenly, catching her by the arm and pulling her toward one of the recesses which had been ingeniously contrived and concealed around the pool. There was a chair there made of silver pipes and striped cushions, and Dina sat down in it, still breathing a little hard from dancing, not sorry to rest for a moment. Vere pulled up a low stool, sat opposite her, and took instant possession of her hands.

"Look here," he said, "I'm sick of this! I'm sick of it! I've been— oh, crazy, since I saw you at Rogers' two weeks ago. I've been there twice. I had to see you."

"I knew you were there the day Rogers and I came in from a walk, that rainy day," Dina answered. Her breast was moving quickly, but her tone betrayed no agitation.

"Yes. But you went right upstairs." She had been rosy and spattered and laughing as she had come in, Rogers, grotesque in wet-weather attire, stamping and splashing beside her. Vere remembered the instant change in her face as she had seen him, the sudden pallor, the quiet nod with which she had disappeared into the afternoon gloom of the hall.

A most unsatisfactory interview with his uncle had followed. All his interviews with Rogers had been unsatisfactory of late; Rogers had shown no sympathy in his matrimonial prospects, and what had been even more shattering to Vere's self-esteem had been the fact that his Kathryn, in fewer and briefer letters, had also stressed them less and less and had dwelt with some enthusiasm upon the charms of a certain Comte Remi d'Aillcourt, a diplomatic visitor from overseas.

Vere had known Dina as the shabby, ambitious, spirited clerk in a grocery, as the bewildered, excited girl who had a first taste of the gay winter life of society on a trip to Paradise Valley. Recently he had come home from rather dazzling social triumphs of his own to find her in his uncle's house, a woman now, with her chief interest in life a small child—a woman who smiled at his uncle with an affectionate easiness that was partly that of a daughter, partly wife, partly mother—a quiet, composed, lovely woman who reserved her pleasantness for others and gave him to feel that she had small time for or interest in himself.

Tonight he saw still a third Dina, a Dina at her loveliest, a Dina young again, carefree again, accepted by the very cream of his own old group, admired and radiant. He knew—it was betrayed by her manner—that only the thrill, the rapture of this ball could have induced her to give him these few minutes, that she was, indeed, in no mood to analyze their significance or to regard them as she might have regarded them a few hours earlier.

"You're not dancing?" she said, her eyes on the changing and circling groups that were coming and going around the pool. "I've danced every dance."

"I was watching you," he said gloomily; then angrily, "Dina, why won't you forgive me?"

"Forgive you?" She widened her eyes; her tone was friendly and unruffled.

"Yes. I've said all I could say. I'm in hell! Why can't we be friends again?"

"Why, I suppose we can," Dina conceded thoughtfully, "whenever we happen to see each other."

"I want more than that," Vere said. "You know I want more than that; you know you are the only girl who has ever meant anything to me; you know that if Rogers and you break up that I'm going to marry you!"

Dina narrowed her eyes, conscious of a wild inner excitement. She was playing a part, of course; she might pay for this later, but it was a dangerous and fascinating part; payment could wait.

"What about Kathryn?"

"Oh, to hell with Kathryn!" he said impatiently. "She's forgotten me and I've forgotten her!"

"Vere, that wasn't what you said two weeks ago."

"Well, it's true." He looked away, sulkily, moodily. "The day I saw you in the gallery I knew, I knew it had all come back, that it was you or nobody! I tried to shake you out of my thoughts; I couldn't. Mother'd just told me that Aline and Andy were considering separating, and I'd thought that if you and Rogers were going to get a divorce, too, that was nothing to me—that was nothing to me. . . .

"But it's everything to me—*everything!*" he finished on a lower note and was still. Dina did not speak. A boy and girl stopped at the alcove, looked in, laughed, apologized, and went their way; the sounds of near-by trickling water and faraway music mingled with the constant rustle of voices and laughter and moving feet.

"Well, that's too bad," Dina said nervously. She stood up.

"That's all you're going to say?"

She looked up at him, clear-eyed.

"Isn't that about all there is to say?" Dina moved as if she would pass him, and he jerked her about suddenly, big hands on her bare arms.

"Look here," he said, "you loved me once, you know that! And that child is my child! Now listen to me, Dina——"

"You're hurting me!" Dina whispered, trying to wrench free.

"I don't care whether I'm hurting you or not! Listen to me. You belong to me, every inch of you, every hair on your head! I'm not good enough for you, I know that! But I'll spend my life, all the rest of my life, trying to show you how much I love you. We'll forget all that—all that happened; we'll begin over. But that's what's going to happen and that's what you're going to do!"

"I think you're crazy!" she breathed, escaping. He did not follow her. She went through the milling groups like a white-and-green shadow, found Rogers. He turned smiling from the card table.

"Little slam, doubled and vulnerable," he said in great satisfaction. "That helps to even things! Having a nice time, Geraldine?"

"Rogers, it's half-past three. I think if you don't mind I'll find Hall and go home."

"Half-past three, is it? Great Scott! Wait a minute until Jerry here pays me, and I'll go with you." He was in great spirits as they went away together. He had had a talk with Aline; oh yes, they had had supper together. Now she was playing bridge fast and furiously in a remote corner with three women as fierce over the game as she was herself. Dina and Rogers did not interrupt her as they went on their way.

Dina settled back in the big car luxuriously; when they passed road lights Rogers could see the glitter of her thoughtful eyes.

"Tired out?"

"No, not really. Just—thinking."

"Geraldine," said Rogers, "when we break up I'm going to miss you like hell."

"I'll miss you," she said simply.

"What d'you think you'll do?"

"Go back to Mama for a while. After all, there are six kids at home." Dina mused, her sea-green grandeur wrapped in a long coat now, her head resting back against the thick cushion behind her. "There must be something I could do for every one of them," she added. "Myrna's just the age when she ought to have a big sister somewhere in the picture; El'ner never gets through her examples without a little pushing, and Donny's a pretty steady pull on Mama. After all, he's only four."

"That's only four of you," Rogers said, checking.

"Well, there's Art, who's the finest really of the whole lot, and my Lou," Dina said. "Lou'll go mad about Margaret. Anything little and floppy drives her right out of her senses."

"I wish to goodness you didn't have to go away," Rogers grumbled.

"It's been a queer year," Dina said half to herself.

"It's been a good year," the man amended it.

"Oh, for me, yes." She was drowsy as she stumbled into the big warm house, but Rogers said he felt wakeful and was going to have a drink by the library fire. "But, Rogers—it's after four!" she protested.

"I know. I won't be long." Hinz, smothering yawns, took charge of his black coat and white scarf, his silk hat. Dina accompanied him into the library but she would not sit down.

"I'd never get up again," she said. "I'm dead!"

"Okay; scram." Rogers had sunk into a low leather chair, spreading his hands on the arms. Dina, halfway to the door, turned back, came swiftly and silently behind him, stooped to kiss the top of his head. She had never kissed him before; she had never thought of it and, amazed at herself, catching up her wrap, with her green draperies flying, she made her escape.

But at the door again she turned to give one glance back. The big room was dimly lighted, but the replenished fire was blazing up brightly, and Rogers' silhouette, deep in the chair, was outlined against it. He was half turned toward her; his eyes were closed; he had not moved.

She went upstairs, entered her own room, stood in the center of the floor looking at herself in the mirror. She was tired now, her hair a little disordered, her face pale. She looked at herself a long time.

Then suddenly she was whirling through the business of getting to bed. The green chiffon skirts went on a hanger, the pale green slip fell to the floor; thin stockings, slippers, the scraps of chiffon and lace she called underwear, all were rapidly shed, and Dina was in silk pajamas and wrapper, creeping in to the adjoining room to see that Margaret was safe. She had washed her face thoroughly with soap and hot water, scraped away her curls with a wet comb; she felt sensible and sane again. Thought came back; the woman who had danced with Vere felt young and anxious and doubtful again as she climbed into bed.

Chapter 20

VERE CAME TO SEE HER the next day; came every day. His time was always the before-dinner hour; he would sometimes play a game of Russian bank with his uncle. Dina detested this game and played it badly; she grew angry when Rogers called "Stop!" and laughed at her. Life, she protested, was altogether too short to waste studying a pattern of cards on the table and murmuring, "The five goes on the six; I get the space; I give you the queen."

If when Vere came she had the baby downstairs, Dina always carried her away immediately, not even waiting for Ida. If Rogers had not yet come in from some trip to his city club, she might sit with Vere, but they talked as if they were strangers, newly met. He was very much in earnest now, very humble; he sometimes brought her a book, once brought Margaret a pair of small white fur slippers with pink rabbit ears.

"Oh, thank you," Dina said on this occasion, box and tissue paper and slippers in her hands. "She needs them now that she's down on the floor so much."

"I'd like ever so much to see her sometimes," he once said wistfully. Dina made no answer.

One night Vere and Rogers were engaged in an especially tense game. Dina had been playing with Margaret on the rug, but when the old black marble clock on the mantel struck the half-hour after five she gathered up Margaret and her blankets and toys and carried her upstairs. Margaret was tired; her little head bobbed against her mother's shoulder. Dina sometimes thought that of all the hours of the baby's day these last minutes were the sweetest, the minutes of bathing and feeding, of changing into the angelic fresh apparel of the long-tailed nightgown, and of tucking up in bed. She tried never to miss them.

Tonight, descending again half an hour later, she was just in time to see Hinz admitting a late caller. A tall lean man whose voice sounded a little nervous and hoarse. She stood watching a moment and then went forward.

"Andy," she said.

He had flung aside an overcoat and gloves, set down a suitcase. He took both her hands.

"No, this is too much luck!" he whispered.

Hinz went away. They sat down on a dark carved bench and looked at each other, still holding hands.

"I thought you were in Hollywood, painting pictures."

"It was Beverly Hills, one picture. But it was of three children and it took me all this time. How—how are you?"

The banal question was so throbbing with excitement and his look as it feasted on her face was so eloquent that Dina felt life and joy and hope thrilling through her veins.

"Oh, fine," she answered him almost inaudibly.

"I'm leaving for New York at seven," Andy told her, "but I had to come up and just get a glimpse of you. It'll take me—what? Twenty minutes to get to the airport? I'm going to telephone for a taxi."

"Fifteen minutes. But Hall will take you." She spoke like a girl in a dream.

"Things are going all right with you?"

"Yes—I guess so." She was not very sure. "Why are you going to New York?"

"Have to. Time up and money running out. I've got a commission in Hartford and another promised. And I've got my little Connecticut place to clean up; I've not seen it. A pal of mine, Emilio Bernasconi, and his wife—she's a painter too—bought it for me, but we've never really gone over the place. Forty acres and creek and an old silvery-gray barn; that was enough for me!"

"Oh, I would love it!" Dina exclaimed.

"Under five feet of snow right now. But I've got to get hold of the deeds, that sort of thing. You like New England?"

"I don't know it. I was born in the Middle West and then we came here."

"I've an idea you'd like it. Dina, I said something to you the last time I saw you," Andy said hurriedly, "and I've not known since whether to be sorry or not. I'm glad, I think. I told you what I think of you. I was still married to Aline then, but she had left me, and you are still Rogers Holland's wife, but someday you mayn't be. I had to let you know how I felt, and that's all I want to say to you now. Just that if ever you want me I'll be here in fourteen hours."

"I will want you!" she whispered, clinging to his hands.

"My darling, you don't mean that?" Andy asked doubtfully.

"Oh, I do, I do! I've wanted you all this time. I want to be—first with somebody," Dina said breathlessly. "You seem to me the finest person I ever knew," she stammered on, "the most exciting and the kindest! The—the way you smile and the—the way your face is so brown and thin—and the way you wear your old brown coat!"

"Listen"—he interrupted her mildly, smiling and holding her cold hands tight in his big warm ones—"I ought to be saying all that to you! But I'm not—not making love to another man's wife. Only someday when the apple blossoms are all out on the Connecticut farm, and the creek's running again, and the snows are gone, you'll come out to tell me lunch is ready, and I'll be painting Margaret and some kittens, and then, if you like, I'll——"

"Oh, I will, I will like, Andy!" she interrupted, her eyes smiling through spilling tears. "I'll like it so much! To be hidden up there in the country, nobody knowing where I am, nobody telling me what to do——"

"I'll be telling you!" They couldn't talk fast enough to satisfy the long-pent rush of words. Quite suddenly she was strained against him and his mouth was hard and hot on hers.

"How—how about making love to another man's wife?" Dina presently asked breathlessly. Then they were laughing, and the happy murmuring was going on again.

"You won't forget, Dina?"

"I can't forget a thing that's in my mind every instant, Andy."

"He'll give you the baby? I know you'll never leave Margaret."

"He? Oh, Rogers. Oh, Rogers, yes, he'll—of course he will."

"He seems to adore you."

"He does. But—but she's mine. Rogers would never—he's so generous—beside," Dina stumbled on, "Aline says—he says she said that she hoped there'd be other children here someday—she told him that."

"Aline did?" Andy asked levelly.

"Rogers told me so. It touched him to the heart, he said."

"Then he really intends to divorce you and marry her? You know, I feel a little sorry for that guy; he's so damn simple," Andy observed thoughtfully. "She hopes there'll be other little children here someday, does she? He'd better be damn glad he's got *one* child!"

"I feel horribly sorry for him."

"He evidently believes everything Aline—well, I was a fool about her a year ago, so I can't say much," the man said. "And now you know what I came to say, Dina," he added, getting to his feet, "and I've got to telephone for a taxi."

"No, I'll have Hinz get Hall. You've plenty of time; that was quarter past that just struck. Oh, Andy, if I could only have a little more of you, talk to you!" Dina said. "But wait; don't you want to come in and say hello to Rogers? He'd like to see you."

"Listen," he said when Hall had had his instructions and departed. His arms were tight about her, and his big lean fingers were tipping up her chin. "The only person I want to talk to is you!"

"You'll write me?"

"I'll write you on the plane tonight if you want it in writing!"

"I want *everything* in writing," she said greedily. And then, with a sudden change of color, "Andy, did Aline ever tell you anything about me—about me and Rogers—and Margaret?"

He stood looking down at her steadily. His own expression sobered a little.

"I think I know what you mean. Aline, when she was angry once, said something—— I told her I wasn't interested. As a matter of fact, I think I told her to shut up."

"Was it that Rogers married me because I *had* to be married to someone?"

"Oh, don't repeat such damn gossip! She and Caroline Holland say things about their closest friends that—forget it! I never would have thought of it again if you hadn't mentioned it. She scared herself to death by mentioning it," Andy added with a smile. "She asked me three times not to quote her, because Rogers —I think she said Rogers—had said he'd sue her for libel if she talked too much. Which gives you a good idea of how much foundation they had for it!"

Dina gripped the lapel of his coat. In the soft diffused light of the great hall she looked small and frightened.

"Suppose—suppose I said that it was true, Andy?"

"I wouldn't have to believe you, would I?" he asked gently, his eyes serious.

"I've known all along that I had to tell you about it. I have to tell you now. That's what I want you to write me from the plane tonight," Dina said bravely. "That it doesn't matter. That someday we'll have the Connecticut farm and you'll paint Margaret and the apple blossoms."

"You mean that it *is* true, Dina?" Andy said after a moment of silence. He was holding her by the shoulders, drawn away so that he could see her face. His voice was grave.

"Yes, it's true."

"And what are you crying about?" he asked, for her face was washed with tears.

"Because—because you believed in me and now you don't. Nobody could," Dina finished in a miserable little undertone.

"I believe you to be a complete little fool," Andy said.

She looked up, her face shining, and now both arms were on his

shoulders and his locked about her and she was laughing with
wet, incredulous eyes.

"You'll always be to me what you've been from the beginning,"
he said, "the sweetest, truest, and best woman God ever made. So
suppose you shut up on the topic once and for all?"

"Oh, but——" she began, her voice trembling between tears and
laughter. He put his hand over her mouth.

"That explains, of course, why he'll let you go," he said.

"I've—I've never been his wife, you see."

"And Margaret—Margaret's ours?"

"Ours!" Dina echoed, her face all the more radiant for the tears
that stained it.

Andy took out a big handkerchief and dried her eyes as if she
had been a small child; then he cupped his hands about her loose
waves of hair and pushed them gently up, and Dina laughed
shakily and caught at one of the hands and kissed it.

"That's that," he said. "It explains everything that's puzzled me.
There's no use talking, he's a good old guy!"

"He's wonderfully kind!" Dina said fervently.

"Now, look here, darling," Andy began, "I've got to go. You've
told me all I want to know about this, and the only thing for you
to do is forget it. I've already forgotten it!"

"There's one more thing," Dina said courageously. "When I
first came here to talk to Rogers he didn't know me, he'd never
heard of me. That night when you and Aline came to dinner was
only the second time I'd seen him. I didn't know you then or
Aline either, but I knew that he wanted to make her think he was
interested in me, that he wasn't sitting at home pining for her.
If I'd known you——"

"You don't think I'm resenting anything that winds up this
way?" Andrew demanded. Dina laughed.

"No. But someday I'd like to tell you—I want you to understand——"

"You'll never tell me. Six months of happiness and you'll forget
it ever happened."

"What is it?"

This last was from Dina and addressed to Hinz, who had
approached.

"Sorry, Mrs. Holland, but Mr. Holland had asked for the car to
take Mr. Vere Holland home. Hall is here now——"

"Oh, that's all right."

Dina led the way to the library. Rogers and Vere had just
finished their game.

"Here's Andy, Rogers," she said, "catching the seven o'clock
plane. Could Hall take him to it first and then take Vere home?"

"Hello, Andy; glad to see you," Vere spoke up. "Say, lissen, I'm
not going home; I'm heading for San Francisco, and the airport is
right on the way."

"Can't stay for dinner—no, you're flying," Rogers put in. "Well,
let's see. It's half-past. Better be on your way. Come on, Dina, I'll
take you on for as devastating a game of Russian bank as ever
was played in this or any man's club."

"Not Russian bank!" Dina smiled a farewell to the men who
were leaving, groped in the table drawer for the dominoes.

Andy went first. Dina did not know why, but she had an odd
pang of premonitory fear, of uneasiness, as she saw Vere follow
him from the room. Vere and Andy! But she'd told Andy everything! Vere couldn't hurt her now! Vere wouldn't want to!

But as she sat down and scrambled the dominoes with both
hands she was conscious of a little chill. Deliberately she shook it
from her and brought her attention to the game.

"Five, one, eh? I can beat five, one. Mix 'em for me, Rogers. I
feel full of arrogant confidence tonight!"

Three days later Dina's letter came. It had not been written on
the plane after all, but it came by air mail.

Dina had expected it on the morning after Andy's departure.
She had thought that he would mail it from some way station and
that the next westward-flying plane would bring it to her. As hour
after hour had gone by, and night had given way to morning and
morning to night, a faint echo of the old sickness of a year earlier
had come back to her, the misery of waiting, waiting, the strong

hold she must keep on herself not to go mad with the need t
have this waiting end. Her eyes ached for the sight of the envelop
on Rogers' table, at her place at breakfast, in Lily's hand as Lil
came upstairs.

It was there at last, and for a few minutes she could not ope
it; she carried it away to solitude and quiet, to drink in the fir
ecstasy of its words in peace.

But the instant her eyes met the opening phrase she knew it w
not to be peace. Dina followed the few lines, stunned, crushe
the letter spasmodically in her hand. She pressed her free han
to her heart as if it were in physical pain. Presently, swallowin
with a dry throat, she said aloud, "Oh no, no!".

After a time in which she walked vaguely about her room an
out onto the high balustraded balcony and back again amon
the curtains and rugs and chairs, she uncrumpled the letter an
read it again.

"Dear Dina," it began. "I did not understand what you we
trying to tell me, but I know now what it was. You asked if
would 'make a difference,' my dear. Of course it does. I'm sorr
but it does! I can't help it; it *does!* It means that for a long tim
we may not see each other again and the little farmhouse in Co
necticut gets a key turned in its door forever. Forgive me fo
hoping it might have been different; I know now that it coul
not be. For if you were unhappy about it, I would be too. I'm goin
to Spain next month with Barry de Rivas; not to paint, just t
help him with his cameras and his articles. I'll send you th
prettiest shawl I can find to remind you of Andy."

The last word was set by itself as a signature; there was n
other message.

Dina felt as if her room was a box, a square, warm, suffocatin
box picked out of the world and set on top of stairs and wal
like a prison cage. When she stood at the window, breathing har
swallowing the salt water that gathered in her mouth, the oute
spaces looked like a prison too; stuffy trees, stuffy garden walk
with tulips and primulas being moved from flats to their place
in the rich wet loam.

"That was it," she said aloud. "You see, I didn't tell him. I thought I told him; I thought he understood. But he didn't! I said did Aline tell him that 'I had to marry someone?' And that might have meant anything; it might have meant that I was poor and Rogers was rich and I just 'had to marry' someone!"

She had on her old brown coat now; she was walking fast through the bare orchards where the plows had left shining surfaces on the deep-cut clods. Sun was shining everywhere on the frosted roads, and steam was rising here and there from the farms and the barns. The air was fresh and wet. Underfoot the ground was heavy, and Dina's shoes were immediately thick with mud.

"No, but I told him about Margaret!" she said. A jay perched on a fence gave a hoarse cry and mounted in a flash of blue to a young redwood. "But even that," Dina's swift thoughts ran, "even that needn't have meant what it did. It might have meant that Rogers knew I hadn't loved him, that Rogers didn't feel she really belonged to him. I thought I was telling him! It was so hard for me to tell him! And all the while he thought I was just saying that I hadn't known Rogers very well and had married him just because I was poor and wanted to get a rich husband!

"Oh, Andy, it wouldn't have made any difference to you if you really loved me! Nothing you'd ever done would have changed me —not if you'd forged checks or been in jail. You needn't have written me that. You needn't have said, 'Of course it makes a difference!' Oh, if I could only walk so fast that I could walk away from it!" Dina said loudly, in the woods now, climbing over fallen logs and scrambling through wet ferns. "If I could get lost, if I could die up here!"

She sat down on a stump to catch her breath, took the letter from her pocket and read it again.

"I hate you," she said. "I won't keep you."

She tore it into tiny pieces, pushed them under a great rock. Then she began to cry. She kept her head down on her arms a long time.

"Bad as all that?" a woman's voice asked her lifelessly.

Dina looked up and saw the speaker; a woman perhaps twice her age, in an old blue dress and heavy sweater. They looked somberly at each other for a full minute. The woman had a rake and was leaning on it, studying Dina.

"Lord, lord, I wish I could cry like that!" she said.

"I don't especially enjoy it." Dina gulped. She got to her feet. "You—aren't you a long way from home?" she asked.

"Twenty feet," the other said laconically. "I've a week-end place here below the Skyline Boulevard. I was clearing my path."

Dina walked along beside her toward a shingled brown cabin, a small garage, a length of rustic fence with "Getaway" burned upon the gateposts.

" 'Getaway,' " Dina said. "That's what I've been trying to do!"

"And that's what I've been trying to do. My name's Martha Morse," the woman told her.

"Mine's Dina Holland."

"Come in," said the woman, opening the door.

Dina followed her into a cabin exactly like a thousand, ten thousand others strewn along California beaches and hidden among California hills and yet so individually precious and unique to its owner that the cost of every plank and brick, kitchen hook and striped cotton curtaining had been an investment in content.

This particular cabin consisted of a fair-sized room with a blackened fireplace, into which dust and rubbish and redwood sprays had been recently swept and where they were smoldering in mid-morning leisure, and two adjoining strips of rooms, a kitchen and a bathroom. The main room held four bunks with screening burlap curtains, a brown bare table, mismated comfortable chairs, a cheap worn rug whose colors melted into the general scheme, and a high tide of books and papers, magazines, pamphlets, manuscripts.

"What I'm trying to forget," said Martha, "is a boy. Fourteen days after tomorrow; New Year's Eve was his birthday. I was to pick him up after football practice, but I telephoned him to come home with another boy. It happened on the way home. Only one of thirty thousand last year in this one country," she added in a irm, hard voice as Dina did not speak, "but it happened to be my own. We built this house together; we gathered the stones for this fireplace; he burned the name on the gate. This was our Shangri-la."

"You are his mother." Dina stated it rather than asked it.

"I am his mother. And I have to come here and face it just so often," Martha Morse said, and Dina knew that she was talking to herself, that she was thinking aloud. "I have to sit here, without any clods of mud on the floor or any guns left lying around in the bunks or any books face up on the kitchen table, and face it."

"I can't face it," Dina said simply.

"I've had two months."

"You were alone here Christmas?"

"I couldn't be anywhere else. Yours—your trouble—what you were crying about—wasn't a child?"

"Oh no. My little girl's fine. But I've made a horrible, silly mess of my life," Dina said, "and I just can't bear it."

"It is hard to have to bear what you can't bear," Martha observed dispassionately. "I can't bear life without Tad and sometimes I have to."

"You're all alone?"

"No, I'm not all alone." Tad's mother spoke with sudden definiteness. "I gave up my job in November and moved out to a district I knew on the fringes of the city. You see, I was at the City Hall for seven years," she said, "since Tad's father and I were divorced, and I knew where our local crop of gangsters is coming from. So I moved out there, took three rooms, furnished them, and began to make friends with the neighborhood's little boys. This year I'm going to get them a play field. Someday we'll have a branch of the scouts out there."

"That's brave," Dina said simply, her eyes shining.

"It's not a cure, but I have times of being happy, and I'm always tired, always busy, glad to get to bed at night," Martha said without enthusiasm. "I had a sick baby to care for right up to Christmas Day; then they took her to the hospital and I came down here."

"I loved a boy; we were on a week-end party," Dina began, as unexpectedly to herself as to the other woman, "and afterward I found I was going to have a baby. Another man, much older but very kind and generous, wanted to marry me, and for the baby's sake I said yes. My own people were poor, migrant labor and on relief, and I couldn't see any other way out. Now he wants to divorce me and marry another woman, and the baby's father—the man I loved so much a year ago—wants to marry me."

"Hm! And you're in love with the man you married?"

"No, I love him, but not that way. No, I love someone else," Dina explained. They were both seated now on a shabbily upholstered window seat. The boy had sprawled here, Dina thought, chewing apples and reading pulp magazines.

"But they think you ought to marry the first man? Your mother thinks that would be wisest?"

"No, my mother doesn't know, nor my father. No. But you see," the girl went on with a little difficulty, "the man I care for didn't know either. So I told him. And—and it makes a difference to him. He says it does. He says I would think of it and he would think of it."

"Hm!" Martha Morse said again. "Well, that's hard on you." And there was a silence.

"And do you think you will keep all these boys from becoming gangsters?" Dina's tragic young eyes were very earnest when she spoke again.

"No. But I may keep one. If I'd had a family that I could have done something for, I'd have done that," Martha said, always in the same unemotional tone. "But I didn't. I didn't have anyone. If I can give some boy a push in the right direction, that'll be my monument to Tad. I won't have any fun doing it; I don't expect to. But it's something."

Dina stood up.

"Thank you very much," she said simply.

"For not much," the other said with a brief shred of laughter. "I thank you for stopping in. It's done me good to talk a little. You said your name was Howard?"

"Holland."

"Well, Mrs. Holland, just remember that we women have got to bear things sometimes that there's no bearing."

"I know." Dina came out under the redwood again and took the wet trail down the hill. A heavy blanket of fog had blotted out the sunshine now; the morning had turned dark and the leaves dripped.

But though she felt no lighter of heart, it was with a braver spirit and a more unselfish courage that she made her way home through the bare orchards and over the rutted roads, and Rogers at luncheon noted nothing amiss.

Chapter 21

Dina and Rogers had taken Margaret and Margaret's nurse to
Stockton on Christmas Day in a car laden with presents, but the
visit had not been a success, and Dina never thought of it without
a conscious reddening of her cheeks and a sensation of shame in
her heart.

They had found Donny and El'ner just recovering from chicken
pox and Dina's special little favorite, Lou, wretched with fever
and a cold. Margaret therefore had been sent away at once with
Hall and Ida and had spent her Christmas Day in a smiling circle
of friendly black faces. Dina's father had been discovered unshaven
and haggard; he had at once disappeared, to return after an hour
clean and dressed and with a bottle of bourbon from which he
continually offered Rogers a drink. Upon Rogers good-naturedly
saying that he would have his with plain water, Art had exclaimed
that that was all he would get. The joking remark had somehow
missed fire; it had sounded rude and cheap in Art, and although
Dina had known that her brother was only trying to help them
carry off a difficult situation she could not apologize for him. Art's
laugh had said, "Ha! These rich people think we have carbonated
waters in the house as a matter of course!" and took the attitude
of all attitudes that Dina hated to find at home.

Then her presents had been much too handsome. She had no
thought that they would have presents for her, too, and that the
small girls' new coats, with bags and hats to match and something

242

n the way of a paper bill lining the bags, must stand in contrast
with the family's feeble little offerings of handkerchiefs and five-
and-ten perfume. El'ner and Lou had not felt any self-
consciousness; with the divine aristocracy of childhood they had
presented their gifts. But Dina's mother had cut her to the very
heart with love and loyalty and shame by apologizing, and Myrna
had dashed away and returned with red spots in her cheeks and
defiant eyes to say that she had not finished her presents for Dina
and Rogers but would send them before New Year's.

"Why, Myrn', you have too!" El'ner had said, round-eyed. "You
tied them in silver paper!" To which Myrna's only answer had
been an angry, "Mama, make her shut up!"

Dooley, now thirteen years old, a bold, handsome gypsy of a
child who was incapable of the finer sensitivities, had saved the
situation for the moment by saying boldly, "Well, I made you and
all the girls candy, Dina, but it didn't harden. It always hardens,
but this time it didn't. So I'm not going to put it in the boxes
because it'll smear them all up, and I can use 'em some other
time!"

There had been a general laugh in which Dooley had joined
with no sign of embarrassment. On the whole the day had not had
much happiness in it nor much mirth. There had been no effect
of a happy, spirited big family living a comfortable, harum-scarum
life; Dina had written her mother that she and Rogers would
come up for dinner and was accordingly disappointed that at
half-past twelve o'clock no table had been set, no meal was ready,
and the beds had not even been made.

Her mother had explained that she had thought, of course,
"dinner" to Rogers and Dina meant seven at night; Myrna had
been sure they would expect an evening meal.

"But, Mama, our dinner was always at noon!"

"I know, Dina, but Myrna said you always had it at night."

Dina had been cheerful and resourceful about it. Art had taken
her in the car to find the nearest open delicatessen store and they
had returned with enough cheese and rye bread and doughnuts
and candy for three meals. Rogers had eaten with great gusto;

indeed, both he and Dina had been ravenous after the long col
ride, but the feast had been spoiled by her mother's apologies, by
the constant running back and forth of Dooley and Art, and b
Myrna's proud, hurt excuses that she had an engagement and im
mediate disappearance.

Dina's mother had cordially urged them to stay for the turke
dinner. The turkey had not even been dressed yet; he was a
magnificent sight, bronze-feathered, with his head done up in red
paper, but Dina had known that an hour's steady work would
be needed before he could be made ready for the oven and tha
if onions were to be peeled, cranberry sauce strained, the table
set, Rogers would be in for a long dull afternoon.

Beside that, there had been the consideration of the baby. The
long drive home would be cold and late for her. Dina and Rogers
had been to a dinner the night before, too, and were expected at
their own home for a very quiet Christmas party tonight; just
three bachelor friends of Rogers, with bridge to follow, no dressing
or fuss. So they must go home.

Now had come the most trying time of all, for Lou, feverish
and headachy, was quite small enough to turn baby when the
time came to part. She wanted her Dina to stay with her—oh
please, please, just for this one night—and chop her up ice the way
Dina had done when Lou had been sick before.

"Don't you 'member, Deen?" the dry little voice had pleaded
"Don't you 'member you kept putting it in my mouth?"

"I'll certainly chop you the biggest bowl of ice you ever saw
darling, and leave it here. But don't you see, there's my poor baby
who's been at Ida's house all day, and maybe she's been crying
and I have to get her home."

It was no use. Lou had gone from whimpering to screaming and
tossing herself about, and Dina had had to delay matters for half
an hour while the little girl's wails rang through the house.

Then Lou had fallen quiet, soothed perhaps by the ice as well
as by Dina's voice and drowsy from the little white pill the doctor
had said she might have every four hours.

But Dina had felt the grip of the hot, thin little hand all the way home, and in her ears had echoed Myrna's scornful farewell. Myrna had reappeared just as the Hollands' big car had been ready to leave and had commented upon Dina's distressed, "I hate to leave Lou!" with a sneering "Why do you, then? I think you're a beast!"

"I'll not go back there again for six months; I do them more harm than good!" Dina had told herself bitterly on the drive home. And to Rogers' amiable, "We caught the family unawares, sure enough," she had responded darkly, "My family is *always* caught unawares!"

After a while, when Rogers had fallen asleep in the car, when Ida had entered into spirited conversation with Hall on the front seat and little Margaret had drowsed off, Dina had felt a softer mood come over her and had quietly cried for an hour, uncomforted and unobserved.

She loved them all so! She wanted so to be proud of them, to have them handsome, happy, and funny when Rogers was there! It had all been so horrible!

She had felt it infinitely soothing to reach home, to have a hot bath, quiet great rooms, a trailing evening frock, and the company of four appreciative men. The turkey had been preceded by canapés and a thin soup and a lobster dish bubbling in a casserole and so did not seem like turkey at all; a sliver of white meat, a dab of dressing, not turkey in the Cashman fashion of loaded plates and seas of gravy washing about mountains of mashed potato, not turkey watched by every separate member of the family as it roasted, and basted by all the women, and finally planted on the table with nothing whatsoever to precede it and only mince pie to follow. But dignity and ceremony and beautiful service had their merits; she could appreciate them the more because nothing in the memory of the Christmas visit to her family had been satisfying. Even the gift of a new radio, which she had thought, when Rogers had suggested it, a veritable inspiration, had somehow missed fire. It had appeared that the Cashmans had recently paid ten dollars

down on a somewhat inferior instrument, and they had show
some little disappointment in finding Dina's present only a repe
tition.

So Dina sank back into the stately, old-fashioned comfort c
the Holland house gratefully. But even here there was no sense c
permanency. All this was not to be hers for long. Aline woul
supplant her here, and she must make other plans.

Aline did not let her forget this, and as in Rogers' infatuate
eyes Aline could do no wrong Dina could make no protest an
could only try to keep Hinz and Mrs. Bucket, who bitterly re
sented the usurper, from open mutiny.

No day passed without a reminder from Aline that she expecte
soon to be mistress of the old house. She brought Caroline t
lunch, and they completely ignored Dina as they walked abou
appraising the old Chinese cabinets and discussing the history c
the rugs. Aline asked Mrs. Bucket how many of the old crysta
goblets were left, who was Mr. Holland's butcher? One day Din
found her and Caroline at the linen closet, Mrs. Bucket standin
in sulphurous silence near them while they admired the heav
old sheets and old-fashioned banquet cloths.

"I think we will see how we get along without our dear ol
housekeeper," Aline murmured airily to Caroline when Mr
Bucket had gone. But with Rogers she was always gentle an
hesitant. "Let's not change anything, Toppy. I love the darlin
old place just as it is! We used to have some of our happiest tim
here, and I want everything to be just the way it was," Aline woul
say.

On a certain day when Rogers was away, however, Aline cam
to the house with a keen, handsome young architect she intro
duced as Sanford Smith, who she explained was going to do som
old-fashioned rooms for a museum and would love to see th
Holland place.

"Rogers is not here, you know," Dina reminded her.

"I forgot! But I spoke to him about it and he said Mr. Smit
could go anywhere he liked," Aline said quickly.

"Oh, that's all right then." While Aline took the newcome

through the downstairs rooms Dina went up to explain to Mrs. Bucket.

"So that's the way it's going to be, is it?" the housekeeper said. "She'll not leave one thing the way it is, and when she's got it all torn up then she'll decide she can't stand it anyway, and they'll take a place in town. Well, I thought this was coming a year ago, and perhaps I'm lucky that it's been put off so long. There doesn't seem to be any end to the way that men can mess up the lives of women!" she went on, getting up to fuss with the litter of souvenirs and treasures that covered her old-fashioned bureau. "I'll miss you and I'll miss the baby. We'll never see you again. She'll see to that!"

She moved picture frames, vases, trays, glass and silver jars, and Dina knew it was to conceal and control the tears she could not hold back.

"I'll miss you—and the house—and Mr. Holland," Dina said hesitantly, "but I knew from the beginning that this might happen and that this is what he wanted to have happen."

"Men are crazy!" Mrs. Bucket muttered, going to her big wardrobe, opening one of the heavy doors, fumbling among dresses and coats, and, with her head well concealed, vigorously blowing her nose. "I looked at the two of you, you and her, the other night at dinner," she said, returning to her chair and her needlework, "and I said to Hinz, 'It must be God made men so blind for some purpose!'"

There was a knock at the door. Aline and her architect stood outside.

"There are some doors locked out here," Aline complained. Dina went hastily to join them, and they crossed the upper hall.

"Ida sometimes locks the nursery door when Margaret is asleep," she explained, "but all these doors are open."

"Could be turned into one?" Aline murmured to Sanford Smith.

He walked to the fireplace in Rogers' room, hammered lightly with a beautifully groomed long, clean hand on the wall, stepped out to the upper balcony.

"Could be," he admitted. "But, my dear Mrs. Havens," he presently said, "I doubt if it's worth it. The place is hopeless, really.

These clumsy old houses were built like forts; tear off the cupolas and porches and you've not made even an impression. You can't lower ceilings and narrow doors!"

"I know, I know," Aline agreed. "Mr. Smith has a very similar house he has to remodel, and he wanted to get some ideas from this one," she said to Dina.

Dina felt the subterfuge somewhat obvious, but there was nothing she could say. She opened the door of her room; Aline walked about it rapidly, clucked in despair over the bathroom.

"How many people does he keep in the house?" she demanded.

"People?"

"Servants."

"Oh? Oh yes, servants. Well, there's Chong and his boy and Lily and Hinz and the outside ones, Hall and Mr. McPherson and Porty Joe."

"And Bucket."

"But she," Dina protested, a little shocked, "isn't a servant."

"Oh, isn't she?" Aline asked, raising her eyebrows. "What I'm trying to work out is where I'll put my maid," she added, turning an indifferent shoulder to Dina and speaking now to the architect. "I had to let the woman I had go, but she's not got another position and she wants to come back."

"You must have a dozen unused rooms up here." They went about, peering and murmuring, and Dina perceived not only that Aline was planning the complete reconstruction of the cumbersome old mansion but that she was carrying on a brisk flirtation with the personable Sanford Smith.

Anger rose in her heart. But why be angry? There was nothing she could do. If she were uncharitable enough to describe the whole scene to Rogers, he would only laugh.

"That hellcat!" he would say with relish. "She told me she wanted this place to be our home forever and forever, and she evidently meant it! Didn't give you any trouble, put you out, did it?"

To which Dina would have to reply only an amiable "No."

Aline and her escort finally went downstairs. Dina remained in her own room, unable any longer to act the part of agreeable guide. She went to the window and stood there, looking down at the gardens and the drive, the ache of parting already strong in her heart. Evidently women like Aline could do pretty much as they pleased; for some inscrutable reason the laws of morality and decorum never closed down upon them. In a few weeks Dina would have to leave all this dignity and comfort and security and Aline would be mistress here.

While she watched, Aline and Sanford Smith came out to the man's cream-colored, one-seated open car, parked down by the entrance. He went around it to open the door for his companion, who got in with some little flourish of settling and getting comfortable. When he was in his seat they put their arms about each other for a long kiss, and his arm was still encircling her as they drove away.

Dina stood immovable for a long time. No use to tell Rogers this either; it would merely sound catty and feminine. But it deepened the cloud that hung so darkly over her in these days.

It had been upon this mood of doubt and uneasiness that Andy's letter had fallen with shattering force. Her friend, the stronghold of all her thoughts in these last weeks, was gone now, and she and Margaret would have to face the world alone.

What made it harder was that Rogers was sure that she shared his new mood of happiness and confidence. He was seeing Aline constantly; he would come back from a luncheon engagement as absorbed as a boy in his own felicity, willing to give Dina occasional glimpses of it, occasional fond quotations from Aline, but almost entirely oblivious to Dina's gathering problem. She knew, from hints that he had dropped almost unconsciously, that he felt sure that she and Vere would presently straighten out the whole affair by a quiet marriage.

"That boy's tremendously improved," he said more than once. When one morning he and Dina and his lawyer had a short session, and Dina signed various papers and was handed a formidable brown envelope that contained all the documents necessary to the transference of the Stockton property from Rogers to herself, he quite innocently betrayed his attitude by saying to Dina after Callaghan had gone: "Of course that doesn't mean that I won't keep an eye on you and Vere."

Vere was constantly at the house. Usually his calls were short, and he was always much quieter than he had been. Sometimes, if Margaret was out on the lawn in the sunshine, he and Dina and the nurse were together for an hour, but on these occasions Dina never sent Ida away, and she received any comment Vere made about the little girl without response.

Vere had a job. He was working as a clerk in the office of a San Francisco attorney who was a friend of his father and at the same time was being coached for the bar examinations which he would attempt again to pass later that spring. But on Saturdays and Sundays he was free, and on other days he might drop in late for a drink and a game with his uncle before dinner or stay for dinner and make a fourth at bridge afterward.

Only once or twice in the first weeks of the new year did he remind Dina in words that he was longing for complete forgiveness, but in many little ways the evidences of it were inescapable, and she knew that Rogers thought it would be the natural and most advantageous solution of her problem.

It was late in January. She was with Rogers in the library just before dinner when he suddenly said to her:

"Look here, I want to talk to you, and I don't know that I'll ever find a better time! Sit down over there," he added, taking his own fireside chair. "A lot's been going on, and I don't know how much you know about it. You know, I suppose, that Aline has gone to Reno? She gets her divorce about the first of March, and she wants me to go up to Reno about the first of May."

May! A respite! But wasn't it the plan that Dina was to be the one to go?

"She didn't want me to be there when she was there," Rogers explained with the indulgent air he always used when mentioning Aline's vagaries. "Now she doesn't want me to go too soon, so that everyone will draw the inevitable conclusion."

"But everyone *will!*" Dina exclaimed scornfully.

"Personally, I don't care what anyone thinks," Rogers observed mildly. "But there's more to it than that. Aline wants to go East in March, get some clothes, see some people, sort of break her friends in to the idea of marrying again so soon. I'll be back in mid-June, and then I suppose"—he tried for an indifferent, a casual tone, but ripples of pleasure broke through the expression of his face and pride sang in his voice—"I suppose the big hawk will light," he finished.

"Now, what about the rest of it?" he presently resumed as Dina made no comment, merely watching him with wide-open, serious eyes. "This is what I want to say, and then you can speak up if you like. If you prefer to go to Reno in—say March or April, that's all right with me. It's only a matter of six weeks, and it's a fascinating little city. But if you don't, *I* go. The reason I've taken it for granted that I'll be the one to go is that I know the town and I know the ropes. Then again, I thought it would be tougher on you; you'd have to get settled, find a place for yourself, the baby, and Ida; I thought you'd be more comfortable here with Bucket. However, suit yourself.

"The thing I'm going to ask you straight out is this: what are the chances of your patching things up with Vere? I know he is more in love with you than ever. I've seen that ever since he's been dropping in here so often the last few weeks. In every way it seems a sensible arrangement. And I can tell him that he's getting one of the sweetest companions any man ever had!"

He added the last phrase with his big-brotherly smile. Dina did not move her eyes nor speak.

"You know he's very anxious for it, Geraldine? The boy seems to have steadied and seems to be really in earnest. There's no question he loves you very deeply."

She cleared her throat.

"Yes, I know," she said faintly.

"He told you so?"

"Well, yes. Yes, he said so."

"Wouldn't it be the natural arrangement? For the baby's sake and everyone's sake? Oh," Rogers added, smiling into the fire as he stuffed his pipe, "I know Vere's young. All boys his age are fools; it's a callow time. But he's a nice kid, as boys go, and he's had his lesson. He got poisoned by Caroline's ideas for a while and acted like more or less of a fool, imagining that there wasn't anything to marrying the Worthington girl except wanting to, but he's sobered down now. He told me the other night that he'd never really cared the snap of his finger for Kit Worthington. Now he's talked his mother over to this idea of marrying you. At first Caroline raised particular hell, but I had a talk with her too, and she saw how the boy felt. We've all spoiled him, Geraldine, but he's a decent enough fellow at bottom!

"Aline was all against it too," he went on, thinking aloud now, his half-smiling eyes on the fire. "She's not—never has been—a particular admirer of yours. She resented my marrying you. Well, you can't blame Aline! Now I suppose she doesn't like the idea of your becoming 'Mrs. Vere,' as you'd still be in the family. However, I've convinced her it's all for the best.

"How about it?" he added, surprised at Dina's silence and glancing at her curiously. "Anything to prevent?"

"If—if he had stood by me last year, there wouldn't have been anything to prevent it," Dina said in a not quite steady voice.

"Well, too late for that," Rogers murmured, frowning in faint disapproval.

"Yes, too late to make that right," she agreed, looking thoughtfully down at the red embers in the grate.

Rogers continued to eye her, puzzled and not quite pleased.

"Wouldn't it be something to make it right?"

"I don't know," she said drearily.

"Why, what's the matter with you, Geraldine?" he said in the affectionate tone of one reproving a child. "After all, Margaret is as close to him as to you——"

"Oh, not as close!" she interrupted him warmly as he hesitated, trying to meet her mood. "Not as close! Not close at all. The Vere I knew a year ago," Dina pursued, not looking at her companion, "doesn't seem to have anything to do with this Vere."

"But you like him?" Rogers argued. "Come now, you like him. Why punish him longer than you have to? It would mean so much to me, Geraldine, to have you still a member of the family and to have little Flyaway upstairs coming to visit me sometimes. Isn't it exactly what you were thinking about a year ago?"

"Thinking!" she echoed, still not moving her eyes to his. "Praying, lying awake nights, crying for! Wishing every time the telephone rang that it might be him, waking up every morning wondering if there might be a letter!"

"Yes, I know, I know," Rogers murmured soothingly, for there was a rising storm in her voice. "But that's past, Geraldine. Here you are, the same boy and girl, with no reason in the world why you can't be happy together."

"There *are* reasons, Rogers." She was trying to hold her emotions in check; she had laid one hand on her breast as if to keep down the feeling that shook in her voice and smoldered in her eyes. "I am not the same girl," she began quietly. "Never the same girl again! I killed that girl who danced and worked in Meyer's and cooked dinners and thought that if ever she married it would be someone who thought she was the most wonderful person in the world! I killed her," Dina repeated feverishly, getting up to stand with her back to the fire now and looking down at him with blazing eyes. "She died in those nights when I lay awake, tossing and wondering, looking at my little sisters and thinking how ashamed they would be of me! She died when I waited and waited, and everything that had been young—young in my love for Vere——"

She was crying now and stammering, and Rogers, his face all concern and sympathy, put out a hand toward her.

"My dear, my dear, don't feel so badly! There isn't any need to remember all that!"

"I don't have to remember it!" Dina went on, uninterrupted. Her face was wet with tears, but sheer anger kept her voice steady. "I don't have to remember it because it was *me*," she said. "It is me, burned into me, burning what used to be me away. Nausea and cold mornings and thinking, 'Oh, why doesn't he send me some word? Why doesn't he say he loves me?' Weeks of it, and no money, and having to come here to you begging, whining, one more girl who couldn't say 'No!'

"And I'm not that sort of girl," she began again vehemently, silencing her companion with a quick movement of her hand. "I never have been that sort of girl, to have Caroline and Aline discuss, for you to talk to Vere about! 'It would square her, Vere, and after all it's your child, and she's a dear little friendly thing——' "

"Oh, shut up!" Rogers interposed, almost as roused as she was. "Nobody ever said anything like that!"

"No, I'm not that sort of girl," Dina repeated feverishly, her nostrils dilating and her breast moving quickly. "I never was. I was poor and I lived in a dirty house and I never had much training, but I always knew better than that! I always looked at the girls who ran with boys and stayed away nights as being different from me! Even Fran, who'd been married and who didn't care much what she did—I never felt she was like Nellie O'Connor and me——"

"I *ask* you not to talk that way!" Rogers put in grimly.

"I *will* talk this way, because I don't think it's fair," Dina went on breathlessly. "Aline and Caroline can discuss me, can say, 'Oh, why not let him marry the poor girl; it'll steady him!' Vere's father can write from New York, 'Go ahead, you're the best judge!' You can sit there and decide what I shall do. Who thinks about me? Who realizes what it is for a woman to be frightened and lonely and sick—frightened and lonely and sick—for weeks and weeks—with no one to turn to! Or how she feels when she has to marry a man she's seen only twice, just to protect the child"— her voice broke—"the child she loves more than anything in life! The child she doesn't want anything ugly or shameful ever to touch! A lot of men, a lot of divorced women deciding what she shall do, men taking care of her when her whole body is torn in two having a baby, men coming to tell her that she can't walk for months, everyone pitying her and trying to help the poor little fool who's gotten herself into this mess!"

"Geraldine," Rogers said quietly. He had given up his attempts to silence or calm her; he was lying back in his chair, fingers locked on his stomach, bulging gray eyes regarding her from behind the strong glasses.

"No," she said at white heat, "I'll not stop! I want to say that I'm not the same girl all this happened to. I've studied; I've read books; I've thought! And I'm not going to marry anyone, not for *years*. I'm going back to my mother, and if anyone follows me there, I'll go further! I'll get away! I've got to think it all out! I've got to be by myself with Margaret! I'm *done!*"

"I see now how you feel," Rogers said mildly after the long moment of silence that followed. "I'll not try to stop you, my dear."

She broke suddenly. She was on her knees beside him, one arm locked tight about his neck; he felt her cheek wet against his own.

"I'm—I'm a woman, don't you see, Rogers?" she sobbed. "And I've got to know—about myself and my baby and what's right for us, without anyone else telling me anything again! You helped me so once; won't you help me now?"

Little Lou Cashman, feverish and weak, opened her eyes at twilight to find a dream come true. Here was Dina back again, with an apron over her cotton dress and a tray in her hands. The room was dim with sweet, dying spring light; there were violets in a glass cup on the table, and here was Dina, without her hat or furs or any of the beautiful clothes that made Lou feel she was a stranger, but just her old self.

"Hello, mosquito, how do you feel?" Dina said, sitting down beside the bed.

"Oh, Deen, Deen, did you come?" Lou faltered, wide awake.

"I did, and I brought Margaret, and Mama's giving Margaret her supper in the kitchen, and you've got to eat yours!" Dina answered.

"And are you going to stay all night, Deen?"

"I am. And for lots of nights. Now, sweetheart," Dina said in a suddenly urgent and lowered tone, "if you cry I'll go right out and wait until you stop! Mama tells me you've not been to school since Christmas."

"I'd be well one day and then all wabbly and coughing the next," Lou confessed, one small thin hand locked tight in her sister's. "I won't cry if you'll just stay," she pleaded.

"She's going to stay," Myrna said from the doorway. "Her husband's going on a trip, and she's going to stay weeks, aren't you, Dina?"

"I certainly am," Dina agreed. She was spooning chicken soup carefully into Lou's obediently opened little mouth. "Dooley's being a darling, and she's going to sleep on the couch in the back parlor with Margaret's crib next to her, and Ida goes home to her own family at night, and I sleep right here where I can keep an eye on you!"

"Oh, Dina, I can't help crying a little, but I'll eat, truly I will— milk and everything," Lou faltered gallantly, "and I'll stop coughing if you rub me with that giggly stuff; I'll stop tonight!"

"You needn't be ashamed of crying," Dooley, who had come in for a sight of Dina, reminded her little sister generously, "becuz we all cried when she got here, didn't we, Dina? Mama began to cry, and Donny grabbed hold of Dina's skirts and began to cry, and then little Marg'rit cried, and I did too. Becuz Dina's going to stay with us and we'll have fun—and games at the table, like we used to have, won't we, Dina?"

"We'll have everything," Dina said. "But now all of you clear out of here and let Lou finish this. Chong made that for you, Lou, because Mama'd written me you loved the soup I brought up last time. But tomorrow I'm going to get three big chickens and make you some better than that!"

The door closed on the others. She was alone with Lou. She sat steadily feeding the invalid, and Lou looked at her with eyes that could never drink their fill of the adored face. And deep in Dina's heart there was at last a certitude, a something like content.

Chapter 22

AFTER INFINITE DISCUSSION it had been arranged that the Cashman family should go to the lake for a six weeks' holiday. John Cashman, rejoicing in the prospect of fifteen free days, would drive the car, his wife and small son by his side. In the back seat, in a rampart of luggage, would be Myrna, Dooley, Lou, and El'ner.

Dina and the baby would remain behind to keep house for Art and, after his vacation, for her father; but after four weeks her mother would return, and then Dina and Art would drive up to join the younger girls at the lake for two weeks more. This plan being infinitely satisfactory to everyone, and Mrs. Cotton having brought over the key of the cottage at the lake, great struggles in the matter of packing and wardrobe and luggage questions had arisen, but these had all been settled by the first of July, and the plan had included a six o'clock start so that some of the long two-hundred-mile trip would be made before the heat of the day.

Dina had never had much faith in this six o'clock start and was not surprised, four hours later on the appointed morning, to find the house still cheerfully filled with her swarming family and the dilapidated car still standing at the gate. She rather hoped at this point that they would get off sometime during the day, for the last forty-eight hours had been anything but restful, and she was looking forward to a few weeks of quiet and solitude.

Her father, whose attitude toward recipients of relief and migratory labor had recently become one of pitying scorn, was impressive as he directed the children's activities. With his black, Mun-chausenlike mustache, his intellectual forehead bared by receding thick gray hair, his lean, active form clad in well-worn slacks and a thin old blue shirt, he was typical of a million other house-holders everywhere, a man eager for holiday and already enjoying every phase of it.

His daughters circled about him excitedly. The day was burning hot; their young faces were wet and their soft hair clinging to their temples as they dashed to and fro. Dina and her mother had filled a cardboard box with sandwiches; a small bucket, packed with ice, held milk bottles; fruit they could buy on the way. But sweaters—they must all have sweaters ready for the mountains!

"If you can believe it's ever going to be cold anywhere!" Dina said, wiping her face with a sweep of her arm.

"Dina, d'you know why I love this?" Myrna, eating a dripping peach, her body bent into a right angle to avoid the juice, asked contentedly. "It's because we're doing what other people do."

The emphasis on the last five words was so solemnly impressive that Dina laughed.

"I mean," said Myrna, unabashed, "that other people go to the mountains in summer. I don't care if it's all mosquitoes and poison oak and prickly heat. We're doing what other people do! After vacation I can say to people, 'Oh, we took the Cottons' cabin up at the lake.'"

"I know just what you mean, Myrna." Dina wondered if they would ever really get started. It would be so blissful to darken the rooms, clean up the kitchen, have a bath, and while Margaret slept after lunch lie restfully with a book on the bed beside her. "I wonder if we hadn't better whip up a salad or something for lunch, Mama," she asked. "It's after eleven."

"Why, my goodness, these sandwiches are supposed to be lunch, and we were going to eat them on the way!" Ethel said, discouraged. "What possessed Donny to have a nosebleed this morning of all mornings I don't know!" she added.

"He was awake 'most all night, asking if it was time to start for the lake," Dooley, busy with her own peach now, put in.

"Well, thank the Lord, he's asleep now!"

"But, Mama, we can't start until I go over to Beverly June's and get her bathing suit!" El'ner protested tearfully.

"Well, trot right over there now and be quick about it!" Dina directed her impatiently. "Run, now!"

"You come with me, Lou!" El'ner pleaded.

"And don't let those peaches drip all over you, so's you'll have to change before we start!" their mother called after them.

"At this rate, Mama, you'll have to have the sandwiches for supper, somewhere on the road."

"I wish you'd put that box of animal crackers in, Dina, for Donny and El'ner."

"And for heaven's sake, let's put in some books for when they get rampaging," Myrna suggested.

"Mama, I'm closing this bag!" the man of the house shouted from the front hall.

"I s'pose there'll be towels in the house, Dina?"

"She said everything. And do make them take care of things, Mama."

"I gave 'em a real good talking to. I said Mrs. Cotton might lend us the cabin next year if we took good care of it this time. But she said there wasn't nothing really to hurt. And they'll be out of doors most of the time. Whew, it's hot!"

"It's awful. I believe I'll hard-boil some eggs for a salad—we've loads of tomatoes." Dina began preparations for an informal lunch, and the meal was welcome when at twelve o'clock the whistles blew and Art came home and the expedition was not yet on its way.

However, everything really was in order now, and lunch was absolutely the last delay. Donny, one cheek very red and his whole small person damp and hot and fretful, was at last awake; Margaret had been picked from her pen on the side lawn and fed and put to bed, and no amount of cogitating could suggest to any member of the family a forgotten item or a possible improvement in arrangement.

"With that hall door wide open, Dina, you'll have an awful time getting rid of the flies."

"Ida and I'll go at 'em as soon as you're gone."

"We don't want anything; we're just going away for the summer," Myrna said to the tall stranger who had walked in through the open front door and now stood smiling at the entrance to the dining room. They all looked up. Dina's heart leaped.

"I'm not selling anything at the moment, except myself," Andrew Havens said. He came over to Dina, and she held his hand while she introduced him, stammering and laughing. The bigness, the dearness of him overwhelmed her; just the sound of his voice and the look of that crooked smile were enough to set all the bells in the world to ringing. Andy was back in her life again!

"This disgusting table!" she apologized, laughing. As if anything mattered now! Her mother had already made a place for him; Myrna had dashed for a fresh napkin; Art gathered the remains of the salad upon a plate. "The family is just off for the lake," Dina explained, "and they were so late starting that we got some sort of lunch together. Dooley, will you go out like a darling and get some ice for Mr. Havens' tea? Andy, what brings you this way?"

"The most important deal I ever tried to put over in my life," Andy answered significantly. Dina stooped to the floor suddenly to retrieve a napkin that was not there.

"Staying tonight? Dina and I'll take you up to Pietro's, where it's several degrees cooler, for dinner," Art said cordially. Dina's eyes danced as she looked at her brother. Art liked Andy!

"Yes. I checked in at the Stockton about an hour ago," Andy said. Dina went to the kitchen with a pile of used plates, hid her face for a second in the roller towel, came back with a great wooden chopping bowl of fruit.

"Royalty," Andy said as hands on all sides stretched for the peaches, the pears and figs, plums and apricots and cherries that heaped the bowl.

"California royalty," Dina agreed. Her father, with a great air of executive impatience, now stated that they must get started. Myrna came out with a wet towel and, as if these sisterly attentions were an everyday matter, wiped the surprised faces and hands of the two youngest members of the group. She then said dutifully: "I have their sweaters, Mama, and the animal crackers."

"I surely do hate to leave you this mess!" Mrs. Cashman said plaintively.

"It's nothing, Mama." Dina's voice sang. "Kenota is coming over after lunch, and I'll have him tackle the worst of it, and Ida and I can whip through the rest in half an hour. Art, before you go," she said, delaying her brother with a hand on his shoulder, "if we should want to take Andy up to Pietro's this evening, how could we go?"

"I'll get Burke's car."

"I have my car," Andy put in.

"Oh, that's all right, then."

"For the last time . . ." John Cashman said warningly from the doorway. Everybody scrambled in a rush to the sidewalk, and the family packed itself rapidly into the car.

"Poor Dina, having you come up this day of all days!" fifteen-year-old Myrna said to Andy conversationally. Andy laughed.

"Well, it means I'll have a little visit with her by myself," he said with his kindly grin. Myrna was thrilled to the soul; she reflected that if she couldn't tell this to Bee'triz she would at least write Bee'triz a full account of it from the lake.

The burning sun beat down; the four doors slammed in quick succession. Lou endangered the entire expedition by dragging Dina suddenly toward her for a last sticky kiss. The engine started; gears jerked. They were off.

"Well, that's that!" Dina panted then, turning to Andy with a smile. She wore faded cotton Chinese coolie clothes, a long high-collared jacket, wide trousers; her hair was tumbled, her face pale from the heat. But Andy's first remark, made under his breath, was: "My God, you are lovely!"

"Sit down a minute," she said, sitting down herself on the shady top step. "If you could know what's been going on in this house since five this morning!" Dina added, laughing. Her hand was again safe where she had so often hungered to have it, in the grip of his own big hand. "No butter," she went on, "no gas in the car, man at the gas station discovering a connecting rod loose, Mama getting a toothache and going to the dentist at ten, Art going off to work with the key of the Cotton shack in his pocket, Donny getting a nosebleed and having to be put to bed with an ice pack on his nose, Miss Taylor calling here from the Community Center to say that the Giddings children's spots weren't chicken pox, so our children didn't have to go into quarantine—we knew that anyway, but it made a long interruption! Oh-h, and they're off at last! Oh, peace, rest, quiet, solitude!"

"I like them all," Andy said.

"Tell me about yourself! You can see how it is with me. What brings you here?"

"You."

"Nothing else?"

"There isn't anything else."

"Why, Andy!" she said. And as he looked at her without speaking but with a world of love and hunger in his eyes, she went on in a little confusion: "You'll have to give me a little time to get Ida and Kenota started and get a bath and change, and then why don't you and I and Margaret—I was thinking of this while this madhouse was getting off—why don't we go off in the car to some place where it's cool, where we can talk?"

"I don't want you to do any of that until I say something to you," Andy said. "I came back here because I can't live without you, Dina."

"It—it is hard going," she admitted in a trembling voice, with a shaky little laugh.

"But you're happy here? You're *radiant*," he said.

"Since you arrived, perhaps," Dina amended it. "No," she added in a more serious voice, "I *am* happy here. They need me, and my being here has made a difference to them all. They all cried when I came back the end of January, and I cried too. I've had a baby since I lived at home; I know now what it means. I look at my mother and think that she gave seven of us a start—oh, I know she and my father didn't think it all out and plan it all out, or they'd have stopped with Art and me!" Dina interrupted herself to concede with another little laugh. "But the fact remains, here we all are, eager to live and loving our meals together and our jokes and our helping each other, and she and my father did do that much for us if they didn't do much else!"

"You've been here since January, haven't you?"

"Right after you left."

"And you're divorced?"

"Well," Dina said frankly, "I don't know whether I am or not. I don't understand it at all. Aline was to get her divorce in March."

"She did," he put in.

"She did? Well, then it seems that she had some scruples about Rogers being in Reno too soon after she was, so she was to go to New York and get clothes and then come back. Rogers wasn't to go to Reno until early in May, but that would mean that we were divorced at least two weeks ago, and I've not heard from him or from his attorney."

"You never agreed to a divorce, Dina."

"I didn't have to. I didn't contest it; that was all. No opposition, no questions."

"Rogers never went to Reno," Andrew said. Her eyes widened as she brought her glance about to him surprisedly.

"Rogers didn't! Who said so?"

"Vere."

"Vere? When'd you see Vere?" Dina asked, reddening.

"Yesterday. Rogers has gone away. When did you last hear from Rogers?"

"Why, I—it was March, I think. Maybe earlier. No, March. I wrote him that I was happy here, and busy, and Margaret simply fine, and everything all right. He answered and said he would let me know how things were going and if he had to see me about his plans. That was the last! Then we're not—not divorced!" Dina ended, flushing again.

"He went to Honolulu."

"Aline join him there?"

"No. Vere says he left Honolulu before she returned from New York—and from Honolulu he went to China."

"Rogers did! What for?"

"Nobody seems to know. I came out here because I couldn't do anything else," Andy said. "First, of course, I tried to get in touch with Rogers. Aline had written me, quite affectionately and pleasantly, telling me that she had obtained her decree and that she and Rogers were going to be married in June. When I telephoned her yesterday at Caroline's she was quite short with me, said that Rogers had gone off to Honolulu and from there had sailed on a freighter for the Orient and that she felt some explanation was coming to her."

"But that doesn't sound like Rogers at all!"

"Well, then I telephoned Vere, and we had dinner together last night. Of course he told me how he feels. He said you'd run away from all of them and that his uncle had told him that to follow you here would be suicidal to any hope of winning you."

"And it would, too," Dina said definitely.

"He said maybe you had gone to Reno and gotten the divorce yourself, but he was sure it would have been in the papers. He thinks now that you're waiting for a California divorce, after an interlocutory year."

"I'm completely bewildered," Dina said. "I don't understand any of it. Why shouldn't Rogers get a divorce? That was what he'd been working for for months! Why shouldn't he let me know if he wasn't going to? I've been thinking"—her face was very red and her tone distressed—"I was free, free to live on here in the little hole I've crawled into," she said, "and now I don't know what I am!"

"That's your side of it," Andy said. "I want to get started on mine. Remember the way we parted last Christmas and what I wrote you?"

"Is it likely," Dina answered, looking away, "that I should forget?"

"Do you know what I thought when I wrote you that?"

Her eyes came around to him.

"Of course I know."

"That you wanted to marry Vere."

"That I wanted to marry Vere!" Dina echoed sharply. "What on earth could make you think that?"

"Because he told me so. Do you remember that Hall, your driver, took me to the airport that night and Vere went along?"

"Perfectly. He certainly couldn't have told you that I—I——"

"But he did," Andrew said simply as she stopped, stammering.

"That wasn't what I was trying to tell you at all!" Dina exclaimed. "I was trying to tell you about Vere and me."

"What you were trying to tell me I perfectly well understood," Andy told her. "I said to you that I had told Aline to shut up when she mentioned it, but that didn't mean I didn't believe it. I knew right away that it was true. It explained everything. Rogers' attitude toward you and yours toward him, and the way he spoke of the baby. So when we talked that day in the hall I knew. But what I hadn't done," Andy went on, "was connect Vere with it! So that night, when we were going to the airport and he told me that he and you were going to be married, it was a thunderbolt. I told him that I imagined you didn't have any definite plans after a divorce, and he said very seriously that there was a reason why you and he should be married—it was a matter of honor.

"Well, Dina, it all broke on me then. 'Vere is the man over whom she's been breaking her heart,' I thought, 'and all I've been is a sort of spare-tire comforter, somebody to amuse her with his devotion if she can't get the man she wants to marry. Vere is the father of Margaret, of course, and Dina'll not feel things are right unless she marries him!'

"I wrote you fifteen letters on the plane," he went on, "but not one of them would do. I was almost out of my senses, I guess, knowing you'd expect a letter to show I understood and being so sure that at last I did! What I sent wasn't what I wanted to say, and it occurred to me afterward that you might take it to mean something entirely different, but I sent it anyway. And I've not thought of anything else since."

"But *I* thought," she explained in her turn, her eyes shining, "that what I'd been trying to tell you about Margaret and me might have meant something else to you at the time. I mean about just 'having to be married.' A girl might say that if she was discontented at home, and especially if she had married a man twenty years older. And about not loving Rogers—I mean not being in love with him. I thought that you had listened to all that, thinking it meant just that I'd married for money, which, it seems, any girl can do without losing her self-respect," Dina finished simply.

"Oh yes, any nice girl can do *that*," he said.

"So that what I *was* trying to say," she recommenced, "about myself, would have fitted both ways. I thought—I've thought all this time that after you left me the truth occurred to you and you understood, and it—it made a difference. You said that in your letter, you know, 'It does make a difference.'"

"And I came out here now expecting to find you married to Vere," Andy said.

"No, never that," she told him, smiling into his eyes. He put his arm about her, and in the silence of the hot, still, deserted hour they kissed each other.

Chapter 23

"Art," said Dina when they were twenty miles away from the hot city, having their supper on a wide porch over a stream, "Andy and I want to tell you something."

"Shoot," said Art. But he looked surprised. He had been wholly absorbed in an extraordinary coincidence. A girl that he knew had come into Pietro's for dinner with her family, and after a bow that crimsoned his handsome young face Art had remained in a haze of felicity, paying no attention to his companions. "Gee, she is pretty," he murmured.

"Listen, Art. Mama doesn't know this. But Andy and I are going to be married. Rogers and I are going to be divorced. So if you'd like to go over and talk to your friend——"

The opening statements did catch Art's attention, and he grinned from one to the other amazedly.

"What do you know," he said simply. "Rogers sore about something?"

"No, not at all. It's all mixed up," said Dina, "and someday I'll tell Mama the whole thing. Art," she added as his fatuous gaze wandered again, "why don't you go over there and join that girl?"

"Oh lorsy, that's pro'bly her father and mother," objected Art, shivering at the thought.

"Well, if it is, they'd probably be delighted. You can see they're bored to death. They've hardly spoken to each other in the last five minutes. Go over and try it anyway; you don't have to stay."

Nerved to the ordeal, Art rose from his seat and hesitantly approached the group a few tables away. Dina watched concernedly as the girl looked up, smiling, as father and mother smiled over introductions, as Art inserted himself into the chair next to his charmer. The two young brothers goggled at him amiably; the older folk were obviously well pleased with the arrangement, and when Art and the girl rose to dance Dina knew that the evening was going to be a success for her brother.

She and Andy were free to talk now. They were hearing each other's voices; they were together again. The moments went by and were hours; the summer moon passed slowly over the world, and still they talked on as if they never could be satisfied.

"About Vere, Dina. You won't marry him?"

Her candid eyes were full upon him. She shook her head.

"Never. That was one of the things I had to think out. Whether I should. Whether there was any—any moral question there. But I've thought it all over, and there isn't."

"He loves you, you know."

"Perhaps he does, the way Vere loves anyone. But I've seen his name among the guests at Del Monte and at week-end parties. He's not heartbroken," Dina said sensibly.

"Then let's drop him and never mention him again. So it's only about us, Dina. You will get a divorce from Rogers?"

"Why, that's what we'd planned. I can't think why he didn't go through with it. As soon as he gets home I'll see him and find out what his idea is. It won't," Dina said, flushing a little and looking up under the wide brim of her summer hat, "be a divorce in the regular sense, you know, though people may think it is. I've never been Rogers' wife."

"Then why——" he began and stopped.

"Because he wanted to annoy Aline. She'd hurt him so terribly running off with you, Andy."

"I don't see that marrying you had anything to do with us."

"It did, though. She was worried that first evening when you came to dinner, remember? Oh, Andy," said Dina on a long sigh, "let's not have any more misunderstandings and separations!"

"Never," he said. "You're mine now, and I'm going to hold on to you."

"Could Rogers have gone to Reno, gotten his divorce, and then gone away?"

"Not according to Vere. Aline, you can bet, would know! She was furious! Anyway, my dear, you'd've been notified."

"Imagine! You telephoning your former wife to see if the man she's going to marry has gotten his divorce!" Dina mused on a smile. "What a mix-up! And I having to write to Rogers, or his lawyer, to find out if I'm divorced!"

"So we go to the Connecticut farm after all."

"Did you see it?"

"Did I see it! I saw it in April, just after the snow had melted, when the little peepers were piping away in the marshes and the willows were out. But you don't know Connecticut winters, do you?"

"I've never seen snow, except that once in the mountains."

"Well, you ought to see what a little farmhouse looks like in the snow. Low windows with the white coming up to the sills, and attic rooms with dormers, and a long string of barns, all powdered with white."

"It sounds so lovely! Like a Christmas card."

"And we have neighbors, Dina. All sorts of artists and actors and writers tucked away in that valley, and a community house where they all meet to sing and dance and have dinner."

"Andy, after I talk with Rogers shall I go up to Reno?"

"I would, if he hasn't. Have it over. Then you and I quietly get married, and off in the car to see the October leaves along the Housatonic!"

"A river?"

"A river. And we'll drive all through the New England towns, Dina, and see the maples and the old wide streets lined with trees and the churches. And we'll go to places like Gloucester and Barnstable and Concord."

"And you'll paint!"

"Lord, won't I paint!" said Andy. "We'll go everywhere and stay in queer little inns, and we'll drag Margaret along, in little slacks, you know, bossing the other kids. And thirty years from now we'll look back—we'll be settled down then on the farm—and the kids will all be marrying off, and we'll say, 'Wasn't it glorious! The ships and the hotels and the strange streets and the meals on terraces and decks and sidewalks!'"

"But we'll never have just this again," she said. "I mean this night, so hot and with the moon so white on the oaks, and us here, talking, and thinking, 'We're together again!' and being so much in love and yet hardly knowing each other at all."

"No, we'll never have this again." Their hands were locked on the table; they were silent for a few minutes, looking at each other.

Art presently came back. Amanda had had to go home with her folks, but gee, she was a cute girl all right, all right. And she had an aunt in Stockton that she was going to come and visit.

Pietro's was closing now; it was midnight. Waiters were stacking the tables; the orchestra was gone; the guests were gone. Yesterday had been a scorching day and tomorrow would be hotter, but in the dead center of the night, here in the mountains, a chill had crept over the world; Dina shuddered a little as they got into the car and was half drowsy against Andy's shoulder as they made the trip home.

He came into the hot, odorous hallway of the Cashman house with her and they had a moment together. Dina, laughing and sleepy, leaned against him and he kept his arm about her. Both were dusty and tumbled; she had taken off her hat, and her hair hung in curls about her face.

"It's settled now, Dina," Andy whispered. "Just as soon as we can we're going to be married?"

"Forever and forever."

"And you do love me?"

"And I love——" she murmured, half asleep. "You're asking me if I do!"

"And I may come in tomorrow morning? I'm starting back in the afternoon."

"You may come to breakfast." She was being kissed again; she
tightened her arm about his neck.

Later, when he was gone and she was reading, Art came ambling
into her room in his pajamas and seated himself sociably on her
bed.

"Oh, he is going to ask me all about it," Dina thought, her whole
body one ache for sleep. Instead Art intended to tell her every
detail of his extraordinary meeting with Amanda Hale and everything he had said to Amanda and Amanda's enchanting replies.
Dina found herself actually swooning off to sleep between confidences.

"Come on now, Art; it's after one," she presently roused herself
to say maternally. "Even if tomorrow's Sunday, this is silly! Go
to *bed*."

"Well." Art reluctantly removed himself, pausing in the doorway to say fondly: "Gee, that was a hunch of yours about my
going over there, Deen. I was scared to death, but Amanda said she
never would have forgiven me if I hadn't come. She said she never
would have asked me, that she would have died first. But her
mother said Amanda was always talking about me after that time
we met at the Johnsons' party——"

"Oh, go to bed, I'm dying!" moaned Dina, snapping off her light.

"Gee, she is a peach!" she heard Art murmur as he departed.

Andrew appeared at about ten o'clock on the following morning,
a burning Sunday morning, and he and Dina had the day together,
planning and talking and sometimes silent, only to begin the
happy planning and talking again.

Margaret was in her pen in the shady side garden when Andy
got there. There was a Sunday stillness and emptiness in the quiet
streets, and Art was still asleep. In the garden were a few col-
lapsed wicker chairs. Andy drew one near to Dina's, stooping
occasionally to toss back into the pen some toy that Margaret had
discarded, lying back comfortably to drink in fully the peace of the
shabby old garden that was scented with peppers and border pinks

and to stare up through apple-tree leaves at the white, cloudles
sky.

"I hope they're all swimming today," Dina said of the absent
family.

"It made a difference to them, your coming back, didn't it?"

"It made a great difference to me, I know. You see, when I lef
home first, Andy," Dina said, replacing buttons on Donny's well-
washed, faded coveralls, "there really wasn't much use in trying to
get things right or clean or comfortable. We lived in a shack on a
railway siding that all through the wet weather was one pool of
water and mud; we had four rooms, packed with useless dirty
junk, no closets, no plumbing. One of my mother's children was
born there and one died there; it was all poverty and grease and
darkness and crowding.

"When they came here at first they were all dazed. They didn't
know how to act in a house with double parlors, bathroom, piano,
hot water. It changed everybody. My sisters especially waked up
to the fact that we were people—not migrants and relief cases—
and that it is really easier to pay bills, keep your house clean, and
live decently. They were all struggling about to express that—that
promotion, in their different ways, when I came back last January
I'd been living under such different circumstances; I'd learned so
much from Mrs. Bucket and from Rogers' home that I could help.
And now, somehow I think now," Dina finished thoughtfully,
"things will never go back to where they were. I wish there was a
yellow cottage with a piano and a refrigerator in it for every family
in the country!"

"What'll they do if you go away again, Dina?"

"It won't matter so much now. You saw Art last night. They're
all following individual lines; they're established."

"I've been thinking that what I'd do," he said, "is see Rogers'
lawyer. Who is his lawyer?"

"Callaghan, Frank Callaghan, in the Russ Building. He'd know,"
Dina agreed.

"He'll know where Rogers is and why that divorce didn't go

hrough. Then I'll get in touch with Rogers; cable if necessary.
hen we can plan your going to Reno."

"I'll hate Reno."

"Not necessarily. You can be quiet and obscure there, I believe.
t isn't all dude ranches, gambling, and bingo games. Only six
veeks anyway. Say mid-September. Then we get married, climb
nto my car, and drive away into the Rockies. Now, about
Margaret?"

"I've thought that out too. If we go to the Connecticut place—
ut it's not in order, is it?"

"No, but we can rent a little place in—oh, say Salisbury, and keep
n eye on the changes."

"Then I'd fly back here and pick up Margaret and Ida. They'll
e perfectly happy with my mother in the meanwhile. In fact, I
on't know what my mother'll do without Margaret; they all adore
er."

"We'll board in Salisbury or we'll find a place to keep house
here. Every afternoon, when I've finished work, we'll drive out
o the farm and see about whitewashing and getting a heating
lant in."

"What bliss," Dina said in a low tone.

"Bliss! You wait until the willows and the lilacs begin to bloom
n April and the creeks begin to run. You can hear them rushing in
he night; I don't know a sound like it. Then some June day we'll
nove in and have our first supper on our grapevine terrace——"

"It's too much." Dina picked up the baby and carried her into
he house for bath and lunch, and Andy followed her. When Mar-
aret had been disposed of Ida set the table, Art was awakened,
nd Dina baked finger rolls and garnished a small mold of chicken
spic with iced tomatoes and crisp lettuce. Her brother made their
uncheon a late breakfast when he appeared shaven and dressed
nd still obviously wrapped in dreams of last night's ecstasies.

The three of them lingered long at the table, for the dining room
vas the coolest room in the house, its windows shuttered against
he hot lances of the day. Andy was painting murals for the lobby

of an Oakland hotel and had to go away at five o'clock, but it was understood that he would return on Saturday—and every Saturday—and Dina was content.

Content! Her heart could hardly hold its richness of joy. Even when he was gone his presence seemed to fill the house; she saw the tall lean figure everywhere; she heard his voice. Sometimes she would stand still in some particular spot, reliving the moment when he had said a special thing, when he had put his arm about her and kissed her.

It was all happiness ahead. Hot weather was happiness, and going to the clothesline in the back yard to gather in Margaret's stiff, sweet white wash was happiness, getting to bed at night with the book she could not read because of dreams was happiness. When her mother and father came back from the lake Andy was there and they all had a particularly luxurious Saturday supper together, and the next day Andy went with Art, Margaret, Ida and Dina up into the cool blue mountains and to the shore of the lake.

They found Donny and El'ner, Lou and Dooley and Myrn hilarious and sunburned and welcoming; the brown cabin under the great pines and junipers smelled healthily of wood smoke and bacon; wet bathing gear hung on the little spruces near the door. Dina took charge thankfully; it was good to be cool, to be actually chilled by the clear lake water, to fish for trout and eat them with bacon and corn bread for breakfast, to lie idle under the trees and watch Margaret sifting and piling the slippery needles and the rough cones.

When the holiday was over she had a long talk with her mother and although Ethel Cashman was sorry about the divorce she was not surprised.

"I knew all along that something was queer there," she said. "Women don't come home for six months if everything's all right."

"Everything's always been all right between Rogers and me. But he wants to marry someone else now and so do I."

"He's going to give up his baby?"

"Yes, Margaret's mine."

"Well, I hope to goodness he don't take back his house!"

"This house? But this is mine, Mama, with the deeds all deposited in a locked box at the bank."

"I know. But you can't ever tell." Ethel liked Andy, and his suggestion that he and Dina drive West every winter for a six weeks' visit did much to reconcile the family to the new plan.

"And the girls'll be coming East to see us on the farm."

"You won't get me East, thanks," said Dina's mother feelingly. That last year there just about fixed me. Tornadoes and cyclones and blizzards and slush and furnaces getting out of order and me expecting Donny!"

"Well, there are other things," Andy argued mildly.

He had ascertained that Rogers was returning in mid-August; he was coming up on a freighter, and the exact day of arrival was not certain, but Callaghan had a cable from Manila and knew he was on his way. After that there must be another delay of some weeks before Dina and Andy would be free to marry, but they were willing to wait, with happiness drawing closer every day. Andy had arranged with the lawyer for an immediate interview with Rogers, and Dina planned to go down and see him herself.

In the end she saw him before either Andy or the lawyer did. She was standing in the garden one August afternoon, watering the thirsty flowers in a hot, lingering sunset and holding with her free hand a letter from Andy, when Rogers walked around the corner of the house and saw her.

Dooley was guiding the tottering Margaret in one of her first walks on the grass; Myrna was sprawled on the lawn reading; Lou and El'ner—whose heads Dina had recently washed—were busy with combs and towels. Dina had on her favorite coolie clothes, much washed and faded to palest green blue; brimmed white straw hat, untrimmed and lined with green oilcloth, was pulled down over her bright hair.

Andy, the letter said, wanted her to come down to the city to see his murals. She could stay at the Hotel Oakland. Ida would help Mama with Margaret, and if Dina started a ham boiling tomorrow—and baked it on Tuesday—it would carry them over . . .

She looked up and saw Rogers.

The sight of him, homely and fat and goggle-eyed, yet always friendly and reassuring presence to her at least, gave her suc surprise and pleasure that she had put her arm about his neck an kissed him before she had time for thought.

"Rogers! You're back! You know all these people, of cours and look at Margaret Holland, walking. But when did you get i and what a *trip!*"

"Hello, my dear." He was glad to see her too; his glasses wer frosted, and he took them off and wiped them. "Well, here you ar in the middle of them all!" he said, sitting down and wiping hi forehead. "It seems to me this is the hottest weather I ever knew.

"We've had a broiling summer. But we all got up into th mountains for a while. You look so comfortable in all that whit Rogers; are those what you wear in the Orient?"

She sat down near him; the others gradually faded away; Id took the baby in for her supper.

"It's good to see you," Dina said. "Was it a wonderful trip It sounded so from what Mr. Callaghan said."

"Then you've seen Callaghan?"

"No, I didn't. But Andy did. Andy Havens. Did *you* see Ca laghan?"

"I've not seen anyone. I got home this morning about ten an took a look at my mail. Then I knew I had to see you."

"I wrote you to know if the divorce had gone through," Din said simply; her eyes widened childishly on a smile.

"Well, of course you should have been told," he said, blinkin his bulging eyes. "No, there's been no divorce."

"No divorce!"

"No. That's what I came to see you about. I don't want divorce."

"Why, Rogers! I don't understand. Guess I must be dreaming

"No, I was the one that was dreaming. I dreamed about on woman for twenty years," he said. "I'm awake."

"You quarreled?"

"No, we didn't quarrel. I went away before she got back fror

"Not Aline! You sound more and more like a lawyer." He linked at her, smiling. "Geraldine, those were happy months for 1e when you were in my home," he said. "You're—I suppose you now you are the sort of person who makes people fond of you?"

"I'm awfully grateful if it's so. I know that no girl ever had a .inder friend than you've been."

"I oughtn't ever to have married anyone; I'm not the sort that ught to marry!" he said fretfully. "I like living there alone, with >erhaps a sweet girl and a baby visiting me now and then. For ears I thought Aline had robbed me of something I wanted. Now know I never wanted it. Bucket takes care of me; I have every-hing I need. Why in the name of all that's sane should I go out of ny way to tangle up my life with Aline?"

"Could she sue you, Rogers?"

"For what?"

"Breach of promise—or something like that?"

"Nonsense, but she'll try to talk me round; she's always been ble to talk anyone into almost anything."

"I suppose you'll have to see her," Dina said slowly.

"That's where you help me out. I've no right to ask you any avor, but that's where you can save me," Rogers said.

"You've every right to ask me anything! But I don't see how I an help."

"By saying you refuse to divorce me, Geraldine—by saying you'll ontest it."

Dina was a little pale.

"You mean in court, with a lawyer?"

"I don't mean anything except a letter saying that never, under 10 circumstances whatsoever, will you consent to a divorce."

"Oh, I thought I was done with all that fuss," Dina said under ler breath.

"Don't misunderstand me, Geraldine. I'm not asking you to ome back. I love you as I've loved very few women in my life, >ut always as if you were my daughter—my good, square, amusing ittle friend. A man can love a woman that way, especially when he's younger, no matter what they say. All I want is delay. I want

Aline to know that there is a deadlock and let her go stalkin
someone else."

Dina remembered a somber February day in the old Hollan
mansion, a day when Aline had gone airily through the house su
gesting improvements, suggesting the changes she must have fo
her own tenancy. She remembered standing at the window of he
bedroom, looking down on the drive, and seeing Aline come ou
with the young architect and seeing them kiss. Stalking someon
else? Why, Aline had been flirting desperately then with the ver
man who was to rebuild her new home as Rogers' bride!

She crushed Andy's letter in her hand, crushed back all the jo
all the hope that had been irradiating life for the last enchante
weeks.

"I'll write you what you want, of course, Rogers," she said.

"It may not be for long, my dear."

"It won't matter how long it is if it keeps her from wrecking you
life. Now come in and say hello to Mama," Dina said, suddenl
feeling very tired.

"I knew you'd do whatever I asked!" His tone was deep in grat
tude and relief.

"It wouldn't be anything to what you did for me," said Din
She put her hand in his as they walked toward the house.

Chapter 24

"Now, let's you and I have an understanding, you bad boy," Aline said, freeing herself from Rogers' arms after his friendly welcoming kiss with more ease than she liked or had anticipated. "Sit down here—no, where I can hold your hand—and let's talk! What's all this about and what's the matter and what have I done?"

She had come to his house, self-invited, on this second night after his return from his long trip, dressed for dinner. She had said Caroline would be with her, but Caroline had not come. And, as always, Aline was beautiful beyond the lot of ninety-nine out of every hundred women in the world—beautiful with that challenging completeness that was Aline's alone. Her slender body was swathed in burgundy-colored velvet; her bare ivory arms were ringed with heavy, strange, oriental jewelry; her head looked oriental too, the black hair shining like enamel, the flawless skin as smooth as tinted magnolia petals; her mouth was colored a deep burgundy too, and her mysterious fathomless eyes were filled with their own peculiar light. Set against the tapestry of a high-backed chair, and with the subdued light of one garden lamp filtering over her and mingling with the early moonlight on the terrace, she was like a Velasquez portrait of medieval aristocracy and grace.

The night was warm, the garden below scented with sharp autumn scents, cosmos and chrysanthemums, and with the faint odor of burning brush. Rogers did not take the place suggested but sprawled in his own favorite basket chair some feet away and took his pipe from the pocket of his worn coat.

"To begin with," said Aline, "I want to say this; I've said it to Caroline and I mean it. You did just exactly what I would have done. I mean you just wanted to wash your hands of the whole damn business; you wanted to think; you wanted to get it all straight; and you took to the road! Why not? I knew just what you were going through and I respected you for it. Well," she added after an imperceptible pause, during which Rogers did not make the expected protest or offer the expected explanation, "that's that."

Aline stretched a beautiful hand for a cigarette, bent forward as she lighted it. Rogers made no gesture of helping her, but then it would not have been like him to do so. That would have meant that he was treating her formally, and Aline did not mean this meeting to be formal. But she wished he would relieve her of the entire burden of the conversation.

"I mean," she began again, using the favorite formula that peppered all her talk, "I mean that like a fool I told one or two of my friends that you were getting your divorce and that we were going to be married immediately. Katty von Behrens even offered their place for a honeymoon. Our honeymoon at last, Toppy, after all these years!

"I mean I actually was that close to it!" Aline added in a silence.

Rogers took his pipe out of his mouth.

"I know. That was the plan," he said briefly and put it back again.

"Well, exactly, that was the plan!" Aline echoed eagerly. "So, I mean what happened to the plan?" she demanded winningly. "I mean, here I was having to say to people, 'But he's not divorced!' When I got back from New York you can imagine how I felt when they told me you were gone! I mean I'd shown Katty and Zoe and Louise some of my trousseau, and of course it made me feel like a fool. Maybe I am a fool about you, anyway."

She smiled her slow oriental smile, spread her hands appealingly.

"Not a line or a note——"

"I sent you a note, following up that talk we had before you ever went to Reno. Remember the night I told you it was all off? But I wrote it, too, and sent it by Hall."

"I never got it!" Aline said quickly.

"I don't know what happened to it, then. He came back and said he had left it. But we'd talked it all out anyway. We'd settled it."

"I don't remember settling anything at all. Except that you hadn't gotten a divorce, as you promised to, and that you ran away. But I knew that you'd be home someday, Toppy, and that we'd talk it over and straighten it all out. I mean I haven't changed in the least. I mean I did go to Reno and get my divorce, and so where am I?"

"Look here, Aline," said Rogers, "I've been married twice, and you've been married three times. We're sensible people; we're not kids jumping into experiments. It seems to me that if one or the other of us comes to the conclusion that it would be a mistake, that ought to be enough."

"It wouldn't take me very long," Aline answered him patiently, "to convince you that it wasn't a mistake. That it was the happiest thing that ever happened to either of us. I mean that you've never been spoiled, Rogers, and I want a chance to spoil you. With all the dinners you've given in this house, dinners when poor Anna was alive, bridge dinners, men's dinners, you've never known what real hospitality is."

She looked so lovely, so entirely the alluring woman, as she said this that to Rogers himself it was strange that he could answer with outward calm:

"You never can tell, can you? It might work out."

But he was more shaken than he knew. He felt the curious power she had always held over him since as a boy he had seen a sixteen-year-old girl dancing in black lace with poppies in her hair.

"I think we could tell!" Aline said quickly. "You're the oldest friend I have."

"Light a fire in there, will you, Hinz?" Rogers said to the butler, hearing him busy with the fastenings of the tall french windows.

"It's lighted, sir."

"Good. And bring in this chair, will you? I brought it out here for Mrs. Havens.

"Aline," Rogers said when they were settled with drinks and canapés by the fire, "has it ever occurred to you that it might be Dina?"

"Dina!" she echoed quickly. "You mean she's fallen in love with you? That's nonsense, no matter what she says. Caroline tells me that Vere is mad to marry her now."

"I don't know that she's fallen in love with me. I know that she refuses me a divorce."

A silence, while Aline looked at him steadily.

"What are you talking about?" she said then.

"Hasn't it ever occurred to you that might be it?"

"But—good gracious, it was all arranged!"

"We may have thought it was. But perhaps," Rogers said mildly, "she changed her mind too."

"Well, I can inform her," Aline said, swallowing, "that people can't change their minds like that! If I ever made anyone a promise in this world, I meant it. I mean I'm so made constitutionally that it would be impossible for me to break it."

"Sometimes even a marriage vow is broken," Rogers observed impersonally. An exquisite color flooded her face.

"That's different," she said shortly. And returning to the attack, she added, "Do you mean to tell me that that girl has had the nerve to face you down on that?"

"I'm not saying I tried very hard to dissuade her," Rogers admitted musingly, his eyes on the fire, a half-smile that his companion found infuriating on his face. "But that's the fact. She won't give me a divorce."

"Well, you certainly can make her."

"I don't believe I can. The last thing she said to me was, 'If we are ever divorced, it will be because I ask for it, not you.'"

"You're just back; you haven't seen her since January; she's living up the country somewhere"—Aline summarized it rapidly, speaking half to herself—"and I can tell you that she's changed her mind. I mean that Vere is really in earnest this time; Caroline knows about it and Van approves, and if you talk it over with her again, you'll find her in a very different position. Why, Toppy," she argued, leaning forward so that the beautiful cleft bosom, the velvet-sheathed body, the flawless face under its shining ebony waves and loops of hair were close to him, "you and I know that girl's history. She was a slum girl, working in a bakery or something, a girl Vere met at a dance hall and got into trouble. We know that! You married her out of sheer sympathy for Vere and Caroline and Van, to save them all a cheap breach-of-promise suit! What earthly claim has she on you? I mean don't be utterly ridiculous!"

"The claim she has on me is legal after all, Aline," he said coldly.

"Legal! Well, legal or not, you could tell the world a story about that woman that would mark her and her child, too, for life. What more does she want than that Vere will marry her; what better way could there be of straightening that whole wretched business out? To let her bully you, to let her be the one to decide," Aline rushed on with angry emphasis on the pronouns, "is just weak. It's weak, Toppy. Go and see her now or have Callaghan write to her and tell her exactly and precisely what she's *got* to do, not what she wants to do. I mean just where she gets off."

"I expected a letter from her today. It didn't come, but it will probably be here tomorrow," Rogers began.

"It very probably says that *she's* gotten the divorce or is going to."

"Caroline would know that, I think," Rogers offered.

"Caroline certainly thinks she is going to marry Vere," Aline said. "If he was *my* son he wouldn't marry her!" she added in an undertone. "But that's neither here nor there!"

"Hinz says dinner's ready, Rogers," said a voice from the doorway. The man and the woman at the fireside turned as if electrified, but if Rogers gave a perceptible start it was lost in the still deeper amazement of his companion. Dina had come into the

room, a demure and well-brushed Dina in a dark-blue lace dress
that Rogers had seen many times before, with two melon-pink
waxy japonicas from the garden for its only ornament.

"Hello, Aline," she said, coming forward. "No Caroline? I
thought she was coming too."

She slipped easily into her big chair, completing the semicircle
by the fire, smiled at the other two.

"No, nothing for me, Hinz," she said to the butler. "We'll be
coming right out. I wasn't sure I could make it today, Rogers,"
Dina went on, "so I didn't write. I left the baby with Mother. But
I've had a talk with Mrs. Bucket and a hot bath, and it seems good
to be here again!"

"I was just telling Aline . . ." Rogers began.

"Of your reconciliation," Aline put in as he paused. She was
breathing a little hard, and her carved ivory nostrils were flaring
and narrowing like those of a restive horse, but she gave no other
sign of whatever she might be feeling.

"It could hardly be a reconciliation when there wasn't ever a
quarrel," Dina said innocently. "I don't think we ever quarreled,
did we, Rogers?"

"I don't believe we ever did." She knew he was all but speechless
with surprise and satisfaction. "Unless it was about Russian bank,"
he added.

"Oh well, I won't play Russian bank," Dina declared firmly.

"Because you have never mastered its intricacies, my dear."
Rogers' tone held just the pleasantly teasing note of the husband
and householder.

"I didn't bring Margaret, Rogers, because I wasn't sure just how
things were here. But I might have known," Dina said, all house-
wife, "that Mrs. Bucket would have everything in perfect order.
Crib all ready, canned vegetables and fruits on the upstairs pantry
shelf."

"You're very devoted to your little girl, aren't you?" Aline asked.
Dina smiled dreamily, brought her eyes from the fire to meet
those of the other woman.

"She's very cunning just now," she said, "walking and talking.

But, Rogers," Dina interrupted herself to say apologetically, "here you are back from real adventures and we've not asked you anything about them! Tell us about the ship you went off in—a freight ship, wasn't it? Wasn't it horribly uncomfortable? And let's go out to dinner before we get started, for Chong has probably half killed himself getting up something extraordinary!"

A friend's car was to come for Aline when she telephoned for it. Pleading a headache, she had Rogers telephone immediately after dinner. Neither Rogers nor Dina attempted to persuade her to change her mind, but both knew that no powers of pleading could influence her to do so. While Rogers telephoned, Dina and Aline were alone for five minutes. Of that short interval Aline took immediate advantage, wasting no moment upon pleasantries.

"You think you are very clever," said Aline, looking at the younger woman through narrowed lids. "You think that by this kind of play-acting you'll hold Rogers and incidentally hold Rogers' money. I'd like the low-down on it. Why didn't he get a divorce?"

"I really don't know," Dina answered candidly. "I had gone up to Stockton to be with my mother. The first thing I heard was that Rogers had gone to China."

"I want to tell you something and I want to say it quickly," Aline said. "I can make it very well worth your while to drop this silly nonsense and get your divorce as you promised to last winter. Vere's mother is my oldest friend, and if you happen to want to marry Vere——"

"Vere asked me to marry him," Dina said simply as Aline, seeing that she had made no impression, paused with her shrewd cold glance as fixed as a snake's upon Dina's face, "when he thought we were going to be divorced. But this way," she finished, "seemed wiser."

"It won't be wise for Rogers, I warn you," Aline began again quickly, "to have his wife discussed as you may be discussed."

"I think people have said everything of me that they can say," Dina answered, unruffled.

"And you propose to live along here with Rogers?"

"Well, that's what most wives do, isn't it?"

"That has nothing to do with it!" Aline said sharply.

"I couldn't rouse the Harrison garage at all," Rogers said, returning, "but it occurs to me that Hall's here; I don't know why I didn't think of it before. Where are you staying, Aline?"

"With Caroline. Did you tell Hall?"

"Yep, and he's waiting. But why rush? That aspirin may ease up your head any minute." But even as he spoke Rogers was walking with her toward the hall, and when he came back five minutes later he was alone, and Dina had heard the front door slam and the movement of a car on the drive. "Geraldine," he said, "what inspired you?"

"I only thought of it after you left Stockton yesterday," she explained. "I'd promised to write you a letter, you know, but when I thought it over it seemed silly not to come myself. It seemed so much more convincing to be right here instead of your handing her a letter from me. In the first place," she went on, back in her seat now, with Rogers opposite her in the old way, "I knew you'd never hand it to her. I was afraid she'd talk you over."

"She would have, she would have," said Rogers, pulling on his pipe, stretched luxuriously in his low leather chair, smiling at space. "I'm weak, Geraldine. I was beginning to think, 'Damn it, it is Aline, after all, and lord, but she's beautiful, and what of it? If she wants to try it here for a while and then get a divorce——'

"No, no, no," he interrupted himself, "it wasn't really getting me! But when you walked in, Geraldine, calm and affectionate and just the lady of the house welcoming a guest——"

He was silent again, and Dina was silent too, her hands clamped on the arms of her chair as they had been in many a talk beside this fire, her eyes fixed on his.

"Well, you're a remarkable girl," Rogers finished. "Someday the lad'll come along who'll be good enough for you. But meanwhile you'll pull me out of the tightest hole I ever got into. Whew! Never again. Now what do you plan to do?"

"I thought—I was thinking, driving down——" Dina began.

"How'd you get here, by the way?"

"You had the big car in town, and Mrs. Bucket sent Porty Joe with the green car. I telephoned her last night and had a long talk."

"You're deep, that's what you are. Well, go on. How'll we manage this?"

"I was thinking this, Rogers. Suppose I go home every Monday and stay until Friday or Saturday. Then come down here so that at the club on Saturday or Sunday we'll be seen together."

"You don't have to do that every week end. Just until Caroline and Aline accept the idea."

"Well, nearly every week end."

"She'll have a grand powwow with Caroline as soon as she gets there!"

"I suppose so."

"Lord, Geraldine, this is one house with you in it and another without you!" Rogers said.

They sat in silent contentment until Hinz respectfully interrupted.

"Would you and Mrs. Holland like the cribbage board, sir?"

"By all means!" Rogers answered. "I was eleven up."

"Nine. Don't you remember I won two games and I said you were a baseball team ahead?" Dina asked.

"Nine it is. This is fun!" They were both laughing as they drew up their chairs.

But Dina did not laugh in the long watches of the night, and she was not laughing when she met Andy in San Francisco the next day. Her wire had said, "Under the clock at the Saint Francis at one," and it was in one of the high-backed red velvet chairs in the hotel foyer that he found her, sitting erect, lovely in her autumnal costume of browns and blacks, strangely pale.

"You did come down after all!"

"I came down yesterday."

"But you look tired; you've no color at all," Andy said solicitously as they reached the street. "Don't you want lunch?"

"Yes, somewhere," she said nervously. "But not here. Everyone will know us in here. Where could we go to walk?"

"To *walk!* I thought you said you were hungry?"

"I am. But I was thinking of the beach, maybe—the cliffs somewhere, or some place in the park. Let's go out to the Cliff House—I want to go somewhere we won't be seen."

"I know. We'll go to Julius' Castle." He helped her into a taxi, took her hands and held them tight. "What's the matter, darling?" he asked.

"Just—I'll tell you. But first let's get seated."

"You drove yourself down yesterday and got tired?"

"No; I telephoned Mrs. Bucket and she sent Porty Joe for me."

"I don't seem to place Mrs. Bucket."

"Rogers' housekeeper."

"Oh. Oh yes. And she sent up for you. But why didn't you telephone me? I'd have come like a shot. And why didn't you let me know you were down here?"

"Well, because——" She waited while he paid the driver and while they entered the little hillside restaurant and found a table in an ingle close to a great window overlooking the city and the bay. "Andy," Dina said then, "Rogers is back."

"I saw that in the paper yesterday."

"Yes, and he came to Stockton to see me on Monday. That's—that's why I came down. He wants me to go back to him. I have gone back to him."

"What—darling! This doesn't make sense!" Andy said.

"He doesn't want a divorce."

A long silence. Andy looked at her steadily; Dina looked away.

"I see," Andy said then, clearing his throat.

"No, of course you don't see," she said in a low voice, "but I do. I see what I have to do."

"You mean he wants you to go back to him." Andy said it patiently, not making it a question. "Why? I thought it was all a plan—I thought you never had been his wife——"

He stopped. Dina looked at him honestly, her cheeks suddenly red.

"Yes, that's true. But he wants me back."

"You mean—I don't get this," Andy muttered. "Anything, anything," he said to the waiter. "Bring us lunch; you select it. But, Dina," he resumed, "you can't do that."

"I have to," Dina said.

"You mean that now, after his throwing you out, after his saying he wanted to marry Aline—all that's wiped out, and now he wants you back!"

"Apparently," Dina said faintly.

"But you don't *want* to!"

"I want . . ." she began. Her voice thickened and her eyes filled, and she went on in a low tone that she tried to hold steady. "I want to marry you, of course, Andy," she said.

Instantly his hand came out and covered hers.

"But that's what you're going to do, darling," he said, "and he can marry Aline."

"He doesn't want to now."

"Doesn't want to!"

"No. That's it. She does."

"And you're to be the buffer?"

"As long as I'm his wife, and won't give him a divorce, she can't."

"But everyone knows what the plot was!"

"I know. Aline came down to see Rogers last night. She was to bring Caroline, but Caroline didn't come. Aline was dressed as if it was a party. She was going to fix it all with Rogers."

"Well?"

"Well, I was there," Dina said simply.

"So she couldn't. I see."

"She went home very early—she said she had a headache—and Rogers and I played cribbage."

Andy's handsome hard face was grim.

"Why should you do that for him, Dina?"

"Because I must. Oh, you know," Dina burst out, suddenly abandoning the quiet repressed manner she had forced upon herself during the beginning of the talk, "you know what a goggle-eyed *simpleton* Rogers can be! Mrs. Bucket tells me that his first wife was a hypochondriac, always imagining something was wrong with her, but that he took it all with the utmost seriousness, had nurses,

sent her away for cures, believed everything. All his life he's believed everything Aline ever said about wanting to be a country
lady, gardening and having a houseful of children! Until this year,
that is; now he knows. I don't know what he discovered or saw or
suspected, but last night just before I went upstairs he said to me,
'She couldn't play fair with me even while we were engaged!' And
I know she hasn't, from something I saw. She doesn't love him.
And he was good to me," Dina went on, her lips suddenly trembling, "and I'll stand by him. She shan't have him!"

"But great Allah! Can't he tell her so? Hasn't he any spunk at
all?" Andrew said loudly.

"No, Rogers hasn't. Or not where she's concerned. He's loved
her too long, or thought he did. Anyway, she has some hold on
him."

"And he feels that keeping you there, young and lovely and—
and dear as you are—will keep her out? So you don't matter, and
nothing matters except that that fat—that toad," Andy said
angrily, "is to be protected by the ruination of your life!"

"Well, after all, you took her away from him, Andy," Dina said
timidly, "and that started all this."

"I'd never heard of him! She never told me about being engaged to him!"

"He stood by me," Dina persisted.

"Not because he felt any obligation to you!"

"No, but he was always kind—when I was so ill, when the house
was full of nurses and Margaret was squalling."

"How long, presumably, will this delightful arrangement go
on?" Andy finished a ramekin of mushrooms and crab meat and
truffles with three savage bites.

"I'm finished too. We'll have the salad," Dina said to the waiter.
To Andy she answered simply, "I don't know."

"Can you see," Andy argued, "what the reverse situation would
be? Can you think how you'd feel if I was going back to live in
the house with some attractive woman, dine with her every night,
stand before the world as her husband? How'd that seem to you?
Would you believe—would it make sense to you that I never was

going to touch her, to put my arm around her, to remember that after all she was my wife?"

"As to that," she said, her face hot, "you needn't worry. It would never occur to him to make love to me, to feel that I was anything but what I've been from the beginning—the daughter in his house, who keeps away complications."

Andrew looked at her a long time. When he spoke his voice was gentle.

"You are a wonderful woman, Dina. I wonder who else would do that?" he said. He saw her bite her lip, saw her face wrinkle, but when she spoke it was with complete self-control.

"There's something I want to say to you, Andy, and now may be my last chance. You'll be going East, and my plans are nowhere. I may get a divorce in five months; it might be five years."

"It won't be five years," he said steadily.

"No, it won't be five years. When you're kind to me," Dina said, blinking and gulping and attempting a smile, "you break—you break me all up. But we're going to part for a while anyway; we'll have to forget our little Connecticut farm for a while, and I want you to know something before you go. It's this——"

She looked down at the table in silence for a full two minutes. The waiter took away the plates, put cheese and coffee before them, withdrew.

"It's this," Dina began again. "I am your wife. Forever and forever, until we're both old, I'm your wife. When you've gone I'm going to live ahead all the years, years when I'll pour your breakfast coffee, with the snow outside or the hot summer morning; years when we'll take Margaret and the other children off for beach picnics, pin up their clothes, dry off their sandy little feet; years when you'll take me to galleries and everyone will know that that's Andrew Havens, the artist, and his wife; years of evenings together, Andy, when the fire's burning, and you look up from your book and I look up from mine, and we smile at each other; all the years there are—your *wife*.

"And one thing more," she went on as he did not speak, and they looked at each other with brimming eyes, "I'll never love any other man. You can marry someone else; you might die; it wouldn't make any difference; I'll never belong to anyone but you.

"I'll live on thinking that, Andy. I'll not change. And I'll write you and tell you all about things at Mother's and things down in Rogers' too. I'll send you pictures of Margaret, and no matter how long it is, I'll be living for the day when we two get into your old car and start off into heaven together!"

She was so stirred that she had to put her elbows on the table when she had finished and cover her eyes with her hands. For a long time Andy did not speak. Then he said:

"Dina, will you give me tomorrow?"

"Tomorrow?" she echoed, swallowing, smiling, wiping her eyes.

"Yes. I think I'll go tomorrow. Jim Robinson, the curator, is here; he's lecturing at Town Hall at two o'clock. I'll drive East with him. But I'll have all tomorrow until—well, until five. Will you come to town again and lunch with me, and we'll go up into Chinatown and buy each other presents as we did that first day?"

"Oh yes, I'll do that!" she said eagerly and gratefully. And then in a whisper, "Oh, Andy, I love you so!"

"Love! You don't know anything about love," he said gently, his lean, sunburned face wearing its pleasantest smile. "But someday I'll show you what it is. So we have today and tomorrow, Dina."

"I'm meeting Rogers tomorrow afternoon. There's a wedding at four, but I can skip that and meet him at the reception. He wants people to see us together. But we have until then! Andy, you are so kind not to make this too hard for me," Dina said, her wet eyes trying to smile at him.

"I'm dazed. The bullet has gone clear through me," Andrew said. "Now I'll tell you what we'll do. We'll walk to the garage—that's quite a walk—and get my car and go out and sit on the cliffs. Or go over the bridge into Marin, if you like, and walk there. And tomorrow we'll see the mural and do Chinatown and then maybe, if you're tired, go sit in some dark movie where there are comfortable chairs and I can have my arm around you. Then we'll say good-by, and I'll pick up Robinson and we'll be on our way. We're starting late because of his lecture."

"You'll go through Stockton?"

"Not if I can help it! Dina, will you do one thing for me?"

Her eyes, bright and dark with tears and happiness and relief, answered him.

"Tomorrow, you know, when we're shopping in Chinatown, I wish you'd do something for me. Are you a Catholic?"

"No. Mama was when she was a little girl, but she didn't bring us up to any religion. Why?"

"Neither am I a Catholic. But you know that old red brick church right on the edge of Chinatown; that's one of the oldest Catholic churches in San Francisco. That's the old cathedral—Saint Mary's. Will you go in there with me tomorrow and go up to the altar and say that you'll be my wife forever and ever, in sickness and in health, for richer or poorer, until death do us part?"

Their hands were locked together. Dina's eyes were shining, her lips parted like those of an awe-struck child.

"Oh, you know I will; you know how I will love to do that, Andy! However did you think of it?"

"I thought of it just now. When you said how you would think ahead across the years and think of yourself as always my wife. All right then," Andy said, signaling for the check, "we'll get the car. We have until five o'clock today and we have tomorrow!"

"Tomorrow will be the hardest!" she half whispered, keeping very close to him as they went into the street. And she counted the hours jealously. "Until five—that's only two and a half hours, Andy; and then tomorrow, ten to four—that's only six more."

"We'll pack 'em!" he said. But for both of them the present ecstasy and the thought of the coming parting were almost too much, and when she and Hall left Andrew at his hotel the following afternoon Dina looked white and wan.

"I think I'll not get out, Andy. Good-by, dear."

"Good-by," he said. And for Hall's benefit he added, "And a million thanks for everything!"

But he had kissed her in the darkness of the almost empty movie house, had kept his big arm about her, and she could remember that. She could remember the marvelous moment in the old church when they two had knelt in a dark back pew and stared at the altar that was blazing with candles for Exposition and had whispered their vows.

"I'll always be your wife, Andy, forever. In sickness and in health. For richer, for poorer. Until death do us part."

They had come out of the church solemn and with eyes strangely alight. There had been no flowers, no kisses, no joyous congratulatory group, but Dina had known that many a bride had felt less married than she did as she and Andy, with their flimsy Chinatown packages, walked to a little French restaurant in Bush Street for lunch.

It had been bewildering, unreal, to go from him to meet Rogers, to be caught into a tide of a.real wedding party, to move in a dream among chattering groups in a city mansion. A score of friendly voices had greeted Dina as the reception went upon its milling, laughing, crowded way.

"He got back Monday. Yes, I was with my mother while he was on his travels," Dina had said over and over again. "My baby's quite small, you know."

"And you'll both be home now for a while?"

"For a while."

Rogers had been in great spirits as they drove home.

"See Vere there?"

"No, I didn't. I didn't get out of the dining room once I'd gotten in there. Things were so congested that I helped to pass coffee."

"Vere spoke to me for a moment; he asked for you, and I said very casually that you were there somewhere, that we'd gotten separated somehow in the crush. He said, 'Oh, she's here, then?' and asked how he could telephone you, and I said, 'At the house any time,' and that was all."

"Aline wasn't there?"

"No, but Caroline was, and Aline will get a full account of it."

Dina had rested against the comfortable cushions of the big

car. He had promised her a letter tomorrow. She would look no further than that.

But as the days and weeks went by a great blankness seemed to come over her, a languor of soul and body; the voice of Andy was continually in her ears and the touch of his hand on hers. Dina would lie flat in the long wakeful nights, remembering, remembering. She thought of the streets through which they had walked, of the little restaurant tables where they had lunched; she thought most often of the old cathedral and of Andy and herself kneeling and whispering in one of the shadowy pews, and her heart shook within her, and she felt that she could not live with the knowledge that he was going further and further away from her.

Chapter 25

CHRISTMAS CAME, and this time Dina's family came down to spend a day with their married daughter and to marvel at the big house and impressive state in which Dina lived. Rogers—himself the suggester of the plan—had said that he probably would not be able to be present at the one o'clock feast but, loitering on from moment to moment, he had remained to the end, which had come with surprising abruptness.

For the Cashmans were not experienced in social niceties. They arrived at noon, cold and car-tired; they admired the house; they left Dina's present, tied nicely in ribbons and silver paper, and accepted their own presents quietly, stowing them in the cars for examination later. They did full justice to the hearty dinner, Myrna trying her young conversational arts upon Rogers, Donny solemn, with a napkin tied about his neck, Margaret kept up after naptime to occupy the high chair.

But when the meal was over there were unmanageable silences, and Dina's father said restlessly that they had better begin to think of starting for home. It was a long run and a pretty cold day. At half-past two, to Dina's secret relief, with thanks that were expressed in their awed faces and subdued manners rather than by anything they said, they left in two cars, everybody well muffled and Art grinning in great if secret pride over his first pair of fur-lined gloves.

Five minutes later Margaret was asleep and Dina was off for a rapid walk through the hills and roads.

"I'm glad we did it," she said to Rogers that evening when they were going in the big car to a quiet Christmas dinner at Woodside. "They'll talk of it forever! But it's a funny thing—I feel more at home—I mean here, than I do even at home. But I told them Margaret and I would be up tomorrow, to stay three or four days, and it'll be then that I get the whole reaction, all about every chair and table and maid and dish!"

"I could see they were taking it all in," Rogers said. And then, in a businesslike tone: "Now listen, I may go on to play cards at Ned's tonight. All right if Hall takes you home around ten?"

"Fine. But I'm glad we had them," Dina repeated. "It was a happy Christmas Day!"

"Perhaps the happiest that the old place ever knew," Rogers said thoughtfully. And when she heard one of his rare, half-involuntary admissions that he was satisfied Dina was satisfied too.

In the cold spring weather and over roads against which flood waters were brimming she drove to and fro between her husband's home and her mother's every week. Dina came to know all the turns and the gas stations; she and Margaret and Ida welcomed the first waves of rich green grass in February and the first white and pink of the orchards. Acacia was powdered gold in the dooryards of the villages through which they drove; there were days in which Dina arrived in driving rains; there were hot days when her forehead was wet beneath the brim of her hat.

Art had had a raise; Myrna had a job with the telephone company; Dooley spent all her spare moments at the hospital and was going to start training as a nurse when she was eighteen; Art had Amanda and bored his sister into actual sleep with confidences about her; Dina's mother was having all her teeth replaced; her father had been put on a strict diet by the company doctor and discussed fats and calories at all meals; little Lou still clung in silent passionate devotion to her oldest sister, cried regularly when Dina went away, welcomed her back as one returning from the dead. Dina brought all the girls down in turn for week ends at the Holland mansion, but although the novelty entertained Myrna and Dooley, it was only Lou who really enjoyed them.

So the weeks went by, and it was summer, and this year the Cashmans rose to the dignity of having a cabin of their own at the lake; one hundred dollars' rent for two months, but Dina paid it, and Dina was sure it was worth it. Again they loaded the car and again the family packed itself into it, but this time it was Dina and Art who took up the first delegation; their mother, self-consciously clicking the new teeth, would remain at home to take care of the man of the house, following the children only when his vacation began.

It was hot July weather as they drove up past the flat river country and into the mountains; this was sheer delight and adventure, and Dina's mood of excitement and joy affected all the rest. The woods were green, pressing against the winding white road; long before they came to the lake itself they could see other lakes, still and cool and sapphire blue between the great shoulders of the hills.

A stop at the grocery; the usual moving-day order of butter and eggs and bread and coffee. The smaller girls roamed about with baskets; their purchases filled two high, heavy paper bags.

"Oh, I wish everybody in the world could have as much fun as we do!" Dina said when they had found the brown cottage perched on a great waterside outbreak of boulders and had investigated its three bunk-lined rooms and started their first fire in the great black-mouthed chimney. The sun was sinking now; long lances of light touched the golden shafts of the pines; every high tuft of green stood apart in the crystal clearness as if seen through water; bees were going home; spears of tobacco-brown yarrow and clouds of blue Michaelmas daisies lined the rocky path that led down from the cabin porch to the water.

The Cashmans were into the water like fish restored to their natural element; other groups of bathers were enjoying a dip at the end of the hot day; two young swimmers went by with the speed of dolphins curving through the lake and shouted a welcoming, "Hello, girls, you got back, did you?"

Myrna, as she swam gallantly beside Art and Dina, told them that the swimmers were Berkeley boys, Stuart Wilson and Mart Pepper.

It was only fifty feet to the great flat-topped rock still baking in sunlight, but the Cashmans were not experienced swimmers and were glad to get there. They lay like three seals, panting and occasionally shouting a warning to the three small sisters who were busily splashing, digging, and shouting with a few other children on the narrow strip of beach.

Two other swimmers came up to their rock, hung there breathless for a moment, swam away again. When a third stranger was suddenly there, dragging his dripping form up to a level several feet away from them, sitting with his back toward them, they paid him no attention.

But after a moment he said, "Hello, Dina," and Dina turned with a sudden stop at her heart and looked at him. In that dazzling second the beautiful summer world about her, the satin lake and the ripples against the rock, the green-tufted, golden-shafted pines rising high above the brown cabins into the sunset sky were heaven itself.

"Andy!" she said. Art and Myrna were gone, swimming back to the shore, and the world was all themselves, man and woman, their dripping hands together, their eyes seeing nothing but each other.

"I arrived here today," he said. "I'm over at the hotel. I thought you people wouldn't be here until late tonight. But when I saw you drive by I got my bathing suit out."

"But who told you we'd be here at all?"

"Rogers."

"You've seen him?"

"I telephoned him, night before last, from New York. And then I flew, and we had a talk today."

"From New York? But, Andy—you can stay how long?"

"I don't know. Until Sunday anyway."

"Only until Sunday!"

"That's three days."

"Yes, that's richness." Dina took off her cap, shook her mop free.

Her slender long body was stretched on its side; she rested one elbow on the smooth, weatherworn boulder, supported her cheek on her hand. "Oh, we're talking together again!" she said under her breath.

"I'll ask you all to dinner tonight over at the hotel."

"Oh no, not tonight. Give Myrna a chance to get her organdy out and press it. Andy, how goes it?"

"It goes well, darling. And with you?"

"I reported to you every week that it goes well too. It's done what I wanted it to do, Andy. Aline doesn't ever see Rogers now; she's stopped telephoning and trying to see him. He's happy, really happy, and sometimes you wouldn't know him for the man he used to be. I mean with Margaret, for instance—but of course," Dina broke off to say, smiling, "Margaret is the irresistible baby of all time, saying everything and running everywhere."

"I took a look at her on the beach with Ida. With a mosquito's bathing suit on and a straw hat."

"That's a sun suit. But Margaret doesn't discriminate; she is probably swimming by this time. But tell me—tell me what brings you and whether you're half as glad to see me as I am you!"

"I'm awfully glad, Dina," Andy answered seriously. "Well, what brought me was, of course, telephoning to Rogers," he added.

"Rogers doesn't know we love each other," she said quickly. "Oh, of course he knows we're good friends," Dina amended it, "but he doesn't know about those few minutes in old Saint Mary's."

"Rogers may not know that detail, but he's known all along how things were with us."

"You think so?"

"Leave it to that old fox. Oh yes, he wrote me about six weeks ago and asked me to come out this summer," Andy said, "but what brought it to a head yesterday was an item in the paper."

"An item in the paper?"

"Yep. To the effect that my late bride," the man went on, "was married to J. Beardsley Mackinnon last Tuesday night."

"Aline married! And to Beardy Mackinnon! But he isn't—he

isn't that dull, rich, old, talkative Mr. Mackinnon who goes tarpon fishing!"

"I don't know him. But that seems to tally with what Rogers said."

"But he's—he's sixty! And he's so dull!"

"Aline felt it would be wise to marry, apparently," Andrew said noncommittally.

"But why *him*?"

"It was marry somebody or face a suit for alienation of affection," Andy answered. "A Mrs. Sanford Smith, so I am informed, threatened to sue. She threatened, as a matter of fact, last fall, but Aline went away and the thing died down. However, it started up again about two months ago when they were on the same steamer going to Hawaii, and I gather that the way Aline behaved down there was enough to start fifteen suits. Smith was to be there a week, studying the site for a house, and he stayed five. Mrs. Smith was at home in California with the children. Aline got back last week, and on Tuesday she married Mackinnon."

"I suppose he's been following her around for years, perhaps," Dina said, still amazed, "but nobody ever takes Beardy very seriously."

"Rogers is pretty well set up about it," Andy said. "He says that Mackinnon was divorced fifteen years ago and flashed on the divorce lawyer a statement he had made his wife sign agreeing to an alimony of a hundred a month and no authority over possible children. Well, there weren't any children, but Rogers is pretty sure that he's made some such conditions now."

"But then why should she *do* it? Oh yes, I see," Dina added on second thought. "She couldn't face a lawsuit. But what a—what a mess of a life!" she added.

"And have you thought what it means to us?" the man asked.

"But of course." Her eyes were wide. "Rogers will agree to a divorce now?"

"Agree to it! I telephoned him, asked if I could see him if I flew out. Of course he suspected it was about you. Anyway, he said,

'Come ahead,' and we talked it out last night. There were tears in his eyes when he talked of you, Dina. He said, 'She's earned all the love and all the happiness any woman ever had. You see that she gets it!'"

"But, Andy——" It was her anxious, little-girl look. "You see, I've just got the youngsters up here for the summer. Mama won't be up for a month yet. Donny had pneumonia and he's got to be built up, and Myrna and Art have to go back to their jobs in three weeks; they can't change their vacations now and I can't let them down. Do you think we could wait until almost September?"

"Listen, birdbrains," he said, "where do you think you are?"

"Why, I'm at Piny Cove at Lake Tahoe."

"You're in Nevada now, innocence."

"I'm—— Oh heavens, this *is* Nevada! Oh, I always think only of Reno. But of course I'm in Nevada!"

"You're just across the state line. I've checked it. So all you have to do is to drive over to Reno—won't take you an hour—and see Rogers' lawyer and establish your legal residence. He's George Hammersmith, and Rogers phoned him last night when we got through talking. Then six weeks from now, my darling, you and Rogers and I will drive to Reno, and all the family can come along later for the wedding."

"Oh, Andy," said Dina, "is it coming right this time?"

"It would seem so. If you could see Elmover you'd think so. All I've done is have a few fallen trees cut up for my wife's firewood next winter and removed two dead rats from the parlor. The rest is up to you. But I've been living in the barn chamber since June."

"Will you stay for tomatoes and corn and weenies for supper?"

"Try to get rid of me. I'll wash the dishes and sweep up, and then you and I'll take a walk. There's a moon ordered."

"Can you imagine a sultana or a begum with ropes of emerald and pearls from here to that inlet?" Dina said, standing now, her young sleek figure silhouetted against the last of the warm light in the west.

"Why should I?"

"Because I want you to know that I wouldn't change places with

er! Ah, you can dive," Dina said enviously as he poised himself
beside her, "but I have to slide in like a baby."

"I'll teach you to dive tomorrow. We have all the tomorrows
from now on," Andy reminded her.

She did not answer in words. But with a quick movement she
was close to him, his arms about her, her beautiful mane of hair
fallen back, her lips against his. For a long moment they strained
together hungrily, as if the kiss never would be done. Then they
were swimming together toward the shore. The swimmers were all
gone from the beach now; the tall pines and the rocks and the
lipping waters had the warm summer evening to themselves.

Dina swam close to Andy. Presently she put a hand on his
shoulder. It was good, even so near to the safe shallow water, to feel
him strong and steady beside her.